Neither detective took a sea. as ~~~~~ way nd down the hall to Trevor's room. She knocked and pened the door. The room was cluttered with clothes, ooks, CDs, and sports equipment.

Trevor was sitting on the bed, talking on his cell hone. He seemed clearly agitated when he looked up t Jordan. "Detectives are here to see you," she told im as innocuously as possible. Even then, Jordan's eart was beating like a drum.

Trevor made a face, told the person on the line that e would call back, and hung up.

"What the hell do they want now?" grumbled revor.

"I have no idea. Just come out and talk to them." rdan realized that she had inadvertently gripped the orknob so tightly that her knuckles hurt.

As soon as Trevor entered the living room, Jordan w the detectives surround him in a menacing way, d a sinking feeling came to her stomach.

"Trevor La Fontaine," one detective said in a formal ne of voice, "you are under arrest for the murder of elson Neilson and Gail Marshall...."

PERSUASIVE EVIDENCE

R. BARRI FLOWERS

LEISURE BOOKS NEW YORK CITY

For H. Loraine, Mom, and Dad.
Thanks for always being there
and believing in me from the very start.

LEISURE BOOKS ®

October 2004

Published by

Dorchester Publishing Co., Inc.
200 Madison Avenue
New York, NY 10016

ISBN 0-8439-5469-8

Visit us on the web at www.dorchesterpub.com.

ACKNOWLEDGMENTS

I would like to thank all those who have contributed in some way to the publication of this legal novel, including those great minds who educated me in the world of criminology and law at Michigan State University's School of Criminal Justice; as well as those associated with my many criminology and legal nonfiction books, which prepared me for taking on legal fiction.

Many thanks as well to my agent, Michelle Grajkowski, who believed in my work right away and stuck with it till accepted. I'd also like to thank my editor, Don D'Auria, for recognizing what a great legal thriller he had in his hands, and making me a part of the great Dorchester family of terrific authors.

PERSUASIVE
EVIDENCE

CHAPTER ONE

The jurors listened intently as the female prosecutor delivered her dramatic closing arguments. She was stunningly attractive without fully appreciating it. Her caramel complexion sharply contrasted the long, groomed raven locks with brunette highlights framing a face that was as taut as it was determined. At five-nine, she was the picture of lean perfection in a wrinkle-free Ann Taylor solid gray suit, pink silk blouse, and low-heeled gray pumps. Her voice was clear and precise, and she pulled no punches in assaulting the defendant with well-chosen words designed as much for their sting as their shock value.

"Ladies and gentlemen," she said, "we are *not* talking about a Sunday school teacher here, but a ruthless killer who stalked his victims, raped them, and then bludgeoned them to death. The last victim was on the floor literally begging for her life doing everything humanly possible to prevent him from hurting her anymore.

"But you know what? He just didn't give a damn. In

5

fact, this plea for mercy gave him even more pleasure as he raped her again, then beat her to death."

Springing back to her feet effortlessly, she hung on that last note while refusing to look at the defendant. Not yet, anyhow. She wanted to maximize the moment. She looked squarely at every member of the jury one by one, seeking to detect any signs of leniency for the monster on trial. There were five women and seven men in the box. Six of the jurors were white, four African-American, and two Hispanic.

They would decide the fate of Raymond Allen Wilson, a thirty-eight-year-old black man charged with killing seven prostitutes in Portland over a three-year period. The trial had lasted almost four months, and had now come down to the nitty gritty. In spite of the overwhelming evidence against the defendant, the prosecutor knew full well that a conviction was no sure thing. Much less the death penalty. The defense attorney had done a masterful job in using the currently in vogue child-abuse excuse in combination with a history of mental illness, to paint a picture of a sick and pitiful victim rather than a cold-blooded sexual serial killer.

Would the jury buy it? she wondered with dread. Or would they see through the subterfuge?

The prosecutor glared at the twelve jurors as though they were the enemy, then left them hanging with a flawless flip of her head, causing the long locks dancing on her slender shoulders to change direction in midair. In what had become a well-practiced move, she took three measured steps with the grace of a ballerina and stood before the defense table. She met the chilling coal-black eyes of the smug defendant with the fierce hazel of her own gaze, as she said to the jury: "This man—if you can call him that—deserves about as much sympathy from you as he gave to his victims. If you allow what he has done to go unpunished, you'll be sending a message to every sexual serial murderer who comes along that it's perfectly okay to handpick your victims, rape them, and do whatever the hell else you want to them, and then cry, 'But it ain't my fault. It's everybody else's.'"

She snarled at the accused, then risked a furtive peep at his attorney, whose fierce competitiveness matched her own. Once again the prosecutor, always in control, smoothly turned back to her main audience. Planting her hands firmly on the wooden railing of the jury box, she leaned forward, swallowed a quiet sigh, and said: "There can be only *one* justice in this trial. You must find the defendant guilty as charged, and sentence him to death. Anything else would be a travesty and a victory for the defense—and defendant. Thank you."

Only then did she allow herself to offer a sanguine smile to the five women and seven men. It was not a real smile but a *thank-you-for-all-your-trouble smile, now do your job right and let's get on with our lives.*

It took the jury exactly thirty-five minutes to deliberate before returning a verdict of guilty on all counts.

A week later, during the penalty phase, Raymond Allen Wilson was sentenced to life in prison without the possibility of parole.

Feeling somewhat less than victorious with the killer's life spared, Assistant District Attorney Jordan La Fontaine left the courtroom, briefcase in hand. Alongside her was co-counsel in the trial, A.D.A. Andrew Lombard. Standing six feet tall and naturally trim, the thirty-year-old looked dapper in a Brooks Brothers navy suit. Dark curly hair lapped on his forehead in bangs, and his close-set blue eyes seemed to sparkle whenever you looked at them. Which was what Jordan found herself doing at the moment, even if she thought he was a bit too young and too white for her tastes. Her mind turned back to the trial.

A couple of minutes earlier, Raymond Allen Wilson's attorney, Simon McNeil, had stormed out of the courtroom without comment. Jordan could almost read his thoughts, knowing how he hated to lose almost as much as she did. But then, she mused, he would at least be able to go to sleep tonight knowing that his client did not have a date with death—unlike those whose lives the killer had taken.

"If you ask me," said Andrew in a deep voice with a Brooklyn accent, "I'd say we got the best we could expect from that jury. I mean, hell, that bastard's off the streets for good."

"Try telling that to the families of the victims," Jordan said. "We promised them true justice would be served— meaning an eye for an eye. Make that two eyes for the fourteen he shut permanently. You know as well as I do that Wilson could live at least another fifty years in prison. That's not exactly the Christmas gift the families were hoping for."

"Maybe not, but I'll guarantee it won't be a picnic for Wilson in his new home." Andrew narrowed his eyes at her. "Do you know what they do to baby-faced, slightly built people like him on the inside? I'm sure you've got a pretty good idea without going into the gory details. The asshole may wish the State had given him a lethal dose of poison when all is said and done."

Jordan had her doubts about that. In her thirteen years with the Multnomah County D.A.'s office, she had found it ironic that killers seemed to fear dying more than anything else. It was odd under the circumstances.

They rounded the corner in the wide corridors of the Criminal Justice Center. The marble floor shone as if it had been polished, in spite of the nonstop traffic in and out of the building. There were several trials in various stages, as judges and lawyers scurried to wrap up their cases before the year came to an end.

Andrew eyed Jordan and noted: "There's a rumor floating around that you and Jerrod Wresler are right at the top of the list for the Homicide Division Bureau Chief opening."

I've heard it too, thought Jordan, tightening her slender fingers around the handle of her black leather briefcase. But then she had heard it all before. Only to see herself passed over for someone else—usually a man—less experienced or qualified. Although she and Wresler were roughly equals in terms of time served, being a woman of color would likely work against her, Jordan believed. Even if she had proven herself time and time again. She had learned not to get her hopes up too high.

"If I were you, Andrew," she said, downplaying it and batting her lashes outrageously at him, "I wouldn't pay much attention to rumors."

He laughed uneasily. "That means it's probably true. And, lady, like it or not, you're the hottest thing the D.A.'s office has going for it right now. They need this more than you do. I'd say you're a cinch for the job."

Wishing she could be as optimistic, Jordan put on her best face, and said hopefully: "Only time will tell."

Speaking of which . . . Jordan glanced at her watch. Damn! she thought. It was almost five-thirty. In less than seven hours it would be Christmas morning and she *still* had not bought gifts for her kids.

"I have to go," she said abruptly, stopping in her tracks. She wasn't ever sure where to get started in her search for the right presents.

Andrew frowned. "A few of us are heading over to The Ranch for a little Christmas Eve celebrating. You're coming, aren't you? Please say yes!"

Jordan gave him a well-meaning smile. "I'll try," she told him, though she doubted she'd be missed too much. "I promise. But first I have some unfinished business." She gave him a friendly peck on the cheek. "If I don't see you before then, have a merry Christmas, Andrew. And tell everyone else the same!"

She left him flat-footed as she darted off, while thinking in a daze: What the hell does one buy for a precocious fourteen-year-old and mature nineteen-year-old these days?

For Jordan, buying gifts was especially important this year. It was a way of bringing the family together when they needed it most. This was the first Christmas her late husband, Eric, would not be sharing with them.

CHAPTER TWO

He watched and patiently waited to make his move.

The townhouse was almost pitch dark. Only the soft, muted light filtering through the partially closed blinds from the lamp in the courtyard penetrated the darkness. Like a cat, he moved stealthily from room to room, using his instincts more than sight to make his way around, learning all he needed to.

In the bedroom, he opened a dresser drawer and removed some panties. He put them up to his nostrils and breathed in. Though they were lightly scented with detergent, he could still smell *her*. It was an undeniable turn on, and he felt aroused.

He drank in the smell for another moment or two, then forced himself to put the panties back in the drawer. He had planned this too carefully. There was no room for slip-ups.

Moving without sound, he retraced his steps and peeked out the window overlooking the courtyard. Christmas lights blinked on and off outside various townhouses. Light snowflakes had begun to fall and melt upon contact with the grass.

He heard—or thought he heard—a noise and practically jumped out of his skin, but just as quickly regained his composure. Now was not the time to panic, he told himself. If anyone had reason to be frightened, it was *her!*

He took his place and waited patiently even as he heard the key in the front door.

The woman held her wrapped packages between her and the door while fumbling with the key in the lock. Oh, no, don't you do this to me—not tonight, she thought, knowing the lock had a tendency to freeze up when it was really cold outside. It didn't help to be trying to hold on to several boxes at the same time. Finally, with a bit of elbow grease and determination, she managed to turn the lock and open the door.

She put the gifts on the floor—actually they put themselves there—turned on the foyer light, and kicked the door shut. The warmth inside instantly hit her skin through the layers of clothing she wore, making her tingle with satisfaction. She removed her coat and hung it on the coatrack.

It had been a long day and even longer night. What she needed right now was a nice hot bath and a glass of wine. Not necessarily in that order.

In the kitchen, she grabbed a green apple from the fridge, took a big bite out of it, and poured herself a generous glass of Chardonnay. At first she thought she heard a noise and looked around, unnerved. Nothing. It was probably just the wind, she decided. Or maybe her next door neighbors making love. The thought amused her.

With apple and wine in hand, she went to the living

room, kicking her high heels off along the way. She reached behind the end table and plugged in the tree lights. It was one of those small artificial trees, more for effect than anything. But at least it helped keep her in the holiday spirit. She admired the tree and its flashing lights in the corner of the room.

She sipped her wine en route to the bathroom, where she turned on the water to the tub full blast.

In the bedroom, she stripped of her dress, stockings, bra, and panties. Then off came the clips that held her long, blond hair in place, followed by a choker and earrings. She strode naked to the closet for her robe, which was hanging on a hook behind the door. She caught a slight movement in her periphery. At first she thought it had come from the closet. Perhaps a reflection of some sort. Then she realized it actually came from the room.

There was someone else in the room.

Before she could react, someone had grabbed her from behind.

She struggled as the robe fell to the floor, determined to fight her attacker whom she identified by his smell. She tried to wrest herself free from his hold.

But he was too strong. He had his hand clasped tightly over her mouth, muffling her scream almost to the point of silence. Her legs flailed at thin air as he lifted her off the floor, holding her tightly against his body. She could feel his erection rubbing against her buttocks through his clothing.

The terror she felt was unimaginable. I don't want my life to end like this, she cried inside.

Not by him.

Yet there was no escape. Every part of her felt paralyzed. She was at *his* mercy.

And he had none, she knew.

The blade seemed to come from nowhere, shining in the low light as if to further terrorize her. It was at least twelve inches long. And sharp enough to cut into flesh and bone with the simplicity and viciousness of a man possessed.

She said a silent prayer and hoped there was a God to have mercy on her soul, squeezing her eyes shut.

With lightning quickness, he sliced evenly and deeply across her throat. Blood gushed out thickly. She began to choke on her own vomit. And that was just for starters, she knew. When he got through with her, she would be a sorry sight for the person unlucky enough to find what he left behind.

It overlooked the Columbia River in Portland, Oregon, where the moonlight floated on the surface like crystals, and colorful Christmas lights decorated nearby houses up and down the river. Beyond that was the Columbia River Gorge and its magnificent forests and waterfalls—including the 620-foot Multnomah Falls. The Devil's Edge, as it was known because of the almost sinfully exquisite vantage point it offered, was a place where young lovers nestled in cars and made out away from inquiring eyes.

This was likely what the young black couple had in mind as they steamed the windows of the '99 Chevy and lustfully closed themselves off from the rest of the world. It had been the lone car in the parking lot when they arrived this night.

Only now were they joined by another vehicle that had moved in so quietly it did nothing to disturb the young couple's preoccupation with one another. Its single occupant studied the Chevy parked several spots over, while deeply inhaling a cigarette's nicotine into his lungs, then exhaling plumes of smoke from his nostrils. Finally, as though bored or perhaps eager to get it over with, he reached into the glove compartment and took out a .25-caliber automatic weapon.

One final drag of the cigarette, before he squashed it in the ashtray and left the vehicle quietly with the gun held firmly by his side.

Disregarding the rare sight of snow mixed with rain in the Portland area, he approached the Chevy slowly and deliberately. His boots picked up moisture with each step. He came up on the passenger side of the Chevy, and for a moment watched the goings-on inside with interest.

The female was on top of the male in the backseat, her skirt spread across his lap like a blanket as she moved up and down on him. Their mouths were locked like two love-starved mammals in heat. The trance was broken when she heard something outside. Abruptly, she withdrew her lips against her lover's protestation and looked toward the passenger window. She saw what appeared to be a man, with a maniacal look in his face. Only then did she notice the gun pointed directly at her.

An almost suffocating scream left her mouth as the window was shattered by gunfire. She was struck in the face, killing her instantly.

Her young lover, still caught up in the throes of passion, barely had time to size up the situation. But he needed no time to know that danger lurked and he was the next target. Gripped with a thirst for survival, he pushed his lover's corpse off him in one fluid motion, and made for the back door on the driver's side. In his panic and desperation, he had failed to notice that the assailant had anticipated his move and was waiting for him. He found himself staring into the barrel of a gun and instinctively tried in vain to lunge for it.

The first bullet only grazed his left cheek, but the force of it violently propelled him onto his girlfriend's waiting corpse. The second bullet struck him in the back, severing his spine. A third bullet lodged somewhere between his brain and cranium. But by then he was already dead.

The killer regarded the motionless bodies amid the shattered glass with a sense of self-satisfaction, then briskly walked away. Back in his vehicle, he calmly lit another cigarette, drew deeply on it, and drove off, while singing a few lines of "I Saw Mommy Kissing Santa Claus."

CHAPTER THREE

The end had come without warning. Eric La Fontaine had no family or personal history of heart disease. But that didn't stop him from dropping dead while playing golf. The coroner's report said that he died of a massive heart attack. He was only forty-three. It had happened last spring, leaving Jordan a widow at age forty-one, with an eighteen-year-old son named Trevor, and a thirteen-year-old daughter named Kendre.

They each dealt with the grief in their own way. Jordan had pushed herself into her work as a prosecutor for the district attorney's office more than ever, allowing herself virtually no social life. And what had it gotten her? she thought. Nothing but little respect and always the promise of big things in her career. She was still waiting for that ship to come in, so to speak, but wasn't holding her breath.

What her new life without Eric had afforded Jordan was plenty of loneliness. It was something she wouldn't wish on her worst enemy. Eric had been her life for more than twenty years. It would take time before she was ready to embark on a new relationship. But even with that realization, she still found it difficult to come home every day to an empty bed. And wake up alone.

Then there were her kids. Jordan sensed them drifting away from her like leaves on a windy day as they got older, and she had to be the mother and father. Trevor was in his second year of college at Portland State University. After living on his own for a year, he had moved back home last fall, unable to support himself and be a student at the same time. This, in spite of having a scholarship that paid most of his tuition. When Jordan saw him at all, they rarely seemed to be able to have a civilized conversation. It was as if they had become strangers since Eric's death. Or perhaps because of it.

Kendre had been struck the hardest perhaps by her father's death. She had been an honor student, but now her grades were steadily dropping. She had reached that age when rebellion seemed almost inevitable, and it was compounded by her reluctance to talk about her father. It was as if she somehow blamed him for leaving them.

This was their first Christmas without Eric, and maybe the time had come for them to put the past behind them and become a real family again with a future to look forward to rather than dread.

Jordan clung to that thought with optimism as she drove her green Subaru Legacy into the throngs of cars crowding into Jefferson Center, one of Portland's most popular malls. She hated this last-minute shopping that seemed to have become a bad habit of late. But there was never enough time in her day to do the things she really wanted to.

Maybe next year, she mused, thinking: I'll believe it when I see it.

*　*　*

"Merry Christmas to you too." Jordan smiled at the chubby-faced cashier, and grabbed her bag. She had just purchased two dresses for Kendre that she hoped her daughter would like, knowing how fashion-conscious teenage girls were these days. One was a peach faux-wrap dress with ruffled edges and a decorative tie at the side; the other a China blue gathered-strap dress with a flowered embroidery around the bottom.

Jordan squeezed past other antsy shoppers and went into a music store looking for CDs. Admittedly, she wasn't sure what was in and what was out for today's teens, still living in a time warp herself with Billie Holiday and Sarah Vaughan. When a clerk who looked like she wasn't much older than Kendre asked if she needed help, Jordan seized the opportunity, saying: "I'd like to purchase two or three CDs for a fourteen-year-old girl going on twenty. Any recommendations?"

The young woman put on a big smile and declared: "I think I can help you out—"

By the time Jordan left the store, equipped with CDs, she felt that half her task had been accomplished.

The other half could prove to be more difficult. Eric had always bought Trevor's gifts and always seemed to know exactly what he wanted. Jordan roamed the mall, growing increasingly tense, until she spotted some hiking boots in a store. She recalled how Trevor had offhandedly remarked to her last summer that he wanted to spend some time hiking in the Cascades. Maybe the time had come to give it a go, Jordan decided. At least now he would be prepared. Along with hiking boots and a backpack, she got Trevor some accessories for the Ford Explorer he had inherited from his father.

Satisfied, Jordan decided there was still time to have a drink with her colleagues before going home.

* * *

The Ranch was located a block from the Criminal Justice Center in downtown Portland. It was a popular hangout for young prosecutors and old ones trying to recapture their youth.

Jordan spotted Andrew at the table along with fellow A.D.A.s Fred Edmond, Amanda Clinksdale, and Jerrod Wresler. They were loud, laughing, and boozing it up. Everyone was urging Andrew on to empty his mug in five seconds flat. He did it in four to hoots and cheers.

Andrew wiped his mouth with the back of his hand. He stood and smiled when he saw Jordan, waving her over. "Hey, glad you could make it, Ms. Dream Prosecutor."

Not for long, she thought, glancing at her watch and noting it was nearly ten o'clock.

"Barely," Jordan said with a sigh. "Traffic out there's a bitch, as I'm sure you can imagine."

"Why do you think we're in here?" Andrew wrinkled his nose. "Better to stay out of the way of the crowds and get smashed instead." He chuckled at the absurdity of his words.

A chair was grabbed from another table, and Jordan sandwiched between Fred Edmond and Jerrod Wresler. "What're you drinking?" asked Edmond.

"I'll have a martini," Jordan told him.

"Well, all right then—martini it is, Ms. La Fontaine."

She smiled as he flagged down a waitress and ordered, along with another scotch for himself. Edmond was a veteran prosecutor and the only other African-American at the table. At a rotund fifty-four, he reminded Jordan of a black Jackie Gleason, but with a much gentler disposition, like Santa Claus.

"This wasn't much of a party without the A.D.A. *sistah* on hand," Wresler slurred in Jordan's direction.

"I doubt that," Jordan responded. "Looks like you've more than held your own without me, Wresler."

He downed his drink, showed straight white teeth, and croaked: "Hey, what can I tell you: Sometimes you have to simply make the best of a bad situation."

"Yeah, right." Jordan rolled her eyes, amused, as others laughed.

Jerrod Wresler was to Jordan probably the best-looking man in the D.A.'s office. A youthful thirty-seven, he was tall at six-two, and with a tightly defined body, always looked as if he had just come from a workout—even when wearing three-piece tailored suits. The dark of his eyes matched thick, jet-black hair, aside from a peculiar streak of gray that ran from the center of his brow to midway across the top of his hair like a skunk. A square-jawed face often sported a crooked smile that somehow seemed to enhance his good looks.

Jordan maintained a healthy respect for him as a talented trial lawyer, though she knew Wresler was vying with her for a promotion and had a reputation for being ruthless and, at times, heartless.

"So I hear congratulations are in order, La Fontaine," Wresler remarked tonelessly.

"I just did my job," Jordan said, sipping her drink.

"But *not* quite good enough," he spat. "If I'd gotten to try that case instead of you, the bastard would be asking for his last meal instead of enjoying an extended vacation."

Jordan took a deep breath, resenting the insinuation. "If you call spending the rest of your life in prison a vacation, then maybe you should plan your next trip there, Wresler. I hear that there's some bargain package deals these days for pretty white boys like you."

Edmond let out a boisterous laugh. "Let's see you top that, J.W.!"

"If I were you, Wresler," joked Andrew, "I'd quit while I was ahead. Jordan's got the answer for everything you can dish out."

"If you were me, Lombard," Wresler barked, "you sure as hell wouldn't be *you!*"

Andrew's jaws tightened. "Now what the hell is that supposed to mean?"

Amanda Clinksdale wrapped her rail thin arm around Andrew's and sought to defuse the situation. "It means if you were Jerrod, you'd be just another asshole." She flashed an effervescent smile around the table, her short, crimson hair forming a wreath around a narrow face. "C'mon you guys, we're a team here—remember. And it's Christmas Eve. Don't be the Grinch."

"She's right," seconded Edmond, hoisting his glass. "Why don't we drink up and be merry." He downed his scotch on the rocks as if by example. "Even very merry!"

Jordan welcomed the reprieve from being in the hot seat. She didn't feel like tussling with Wresler in a battle of egos, or basking in the glory of her victory in court. After all, nothing could bring back those poor women Raymond Wilson had set his deadly sights on.

Her attention was diverted to a table across the room, where Simon McNeil was seated and looking directly at Jordan, as though on a mission. He acknowledged her with a raised drink in toast. Jordan's throat suddenly felt dry and she avoided his gaze.

Eric and Simon had been partners in Portland's best-known African-American–owned law firm. They had specialized in criminal defense cases—until Eric's death, which had left Simon to run it alone. Then Simon had reluctantly agreed to represent Raymond Allen Wilson, pitting Jordan and Simon directly against one another for the first time. They had each won a few battles along the way, but she had won the war. Their friendship had been put on hold during the course of the trial, punctuated by his display of poor sportsmanship afterward. Jordan had feared that the damage done to their friendship might be irreparable.

"Damn, you're good, lady," Simon said with conviction in a baritone voice as he stood before Jordan like an African warrior. Her mind wandering, she had not even seen him walk over. He stood close to six-four, was fit as a fiddle at forty-two, and was wearing one of his trademark Italian blue suits along with Bruno Magli shoes. His bald head shimmered, and intense gray-brown eyes surveyed her against the backdrop of an even pecan complexion.

"Eric would have been proud of your performance, Jordan," he said admiringly.

Jordan suddenly felt lightheaded. "Will you excuse me?" She got up and ran to the bathroom, grateful to find it was empty. She wasn't sure what had come over her. Was it Simon mentioning Eric's name? Or was it simply Simon?

She couldn't deny that the brother was drop-dead *handsome*. Or further, that a physical—even sexual—attraction had existed between them for years. But neither had let it go beyond that for both practical and personal reasons. Jordan was happily married and so was Simon. Even after Eric's death, Jordan had managed to keep Simon at arm's length, though he made no secret that he wanted her.

And you want him, Jordan told herself, maybe more than she cared to admit. But not at the expense of his marriage, and definitely not in spite of it. She would never do to another sister what she wouldn't want done to herself.

As it was, she thought: I am all alone and available. But only for the right man and right circumstances.

Simon McNeil didn't seem to figure into that equation.

Through the mirror Jordan watched Amanda Clinksdale enter the bathroom. Her normally pale white complexion was cherry with mild concern. She walked up to Jordan wearing a magenta Liz Claiborne dress,

23

which somehow made her petite frame look slightly less thin than it really was.

"Hey, what happened to you out there?" Amanda asked.

"I just felt a little warm," Jordan said, and thought: *Actually hot!* "Once you hit forty, it comes with the territory, when you least expect it."

Amanda's brow furrowed above apple-green eyes. "Then I guess I'd better try to make the most out of the next eight years, before 'it' strikes me."

Jordan managed a smile. "Don't worry, it's not that bad. Doesn't really happen overnight, and usually not without some precipitating factor."

"You mean like Simon McNeil . . . ?"

Jordan bit her lip, but tried to remain unaffected. "Simon and I go way back," she said. "Not easy beating a friend in court, but I'll get over it."

"Question is, will he?" Amanda eyed her warily.

Jordan turned to look at Amanda's mirrored reflection, while thinking about Simon. "We're both professionals. I'm sure we can get past this." It was the in-between-the-lines of their friendship that really unnerved Jordan.

Amanda clutched her handbag a bit tighter, seemingly satisfied for now. "Well, shall we go back out there and see if they've made complete asses of themselves in our absence?"

"Good idea," Jordan said, knowing she couldn't duck Simon forever, nor did she want to.

Facing herself in the mirror, Jordan decided that her face looked drawn. She countered this by applying a small amount of blush on her high cheeks. Seemingly not wanting to be outdone, Amanda brushed her hair and recoated her lips in bright red.

The two women left the bathroom together.

* * *

The phone rang twice before the voice answered with a lazy: "Hello."

"It's me, Kendre," said Jordan, talking on her cell phone. "I'm at The Ranch with some people from work. I shouldn't be too long."

"Chill, Mom," Kendre said. "It's Christmas Eve. Enjoy yourself. Trevor ain't here. And even if he was, I'm sure we can get along just fine without you. We always do."

Jordan felt the sting of her words as surely as if she'd been bitten by a bee. And the guilt, too. She also picked up the attitude and disrespect her daughter seemed to be rapidly developing, as though a contagious disease among teenage girls. Is that what single motherhood was all about when trying to raise teenagers who seemed to think only about themselves?

Jordan could hear some muffled giggles coming from the line, as if Kendre had company. "What's going on there, Kendre?"

"Uh, Lenora's here," she answered tentatively. "I invited her to spend the night."

Jordan pursed her lips. "You might have asked me if it was all right." *Or doesn't it matter what I think as your mother, who never gave you permission to invite anyone for a sleepover on Christmas Eve of all nights?*

"I didn't think you'd mind," said Kendre sweetly. "Her mom and boyfriend went to Seattle for Christmas. Lenora decided not to go. I didn't want her to spend Christmas alone."

"Oh you didn't, did you?" Jordan retorted, knowing her clever little daughter had boxed her into a corner. What could she possibly say: *I'd hoped we could be together this one Christmas as a family—and only our immediate family, which didn't include friends?*

As it was, Jordan knew that at the end of the day, she

25

didn't have the heart to tell Kendre her friend had to go. Not on the night before Christmas. After all, this was, as they say, the season of goodwill toward men. Or in this case a seemingly lost fifteen-year-old girl.

"Lenora can stay," Jordan gave in. Instead of thanks, there was only silence on the line, as if staying was a given as far as Kendre was concerned. Jordan threw her arms up in defeat and asked: "Do you know where Trevor is?"

"Do I ever?" Kendre responded coldly, and Jordan could almost see her long eyelashes batting.

Jordan knew that as a young and active man, Trevor could be almost anywhere tonight. But she also knew him to be responsible. And, since it was Christmas Eve, she expected him to show up soon to help out on anything that needed to be done. Especially since Eric was no longer around.

Jordan could hear muffled whispering away from the phone. "Anything else?" Kendre said with a yawn.

Jordan was determined to keep her cool with little Ms. Ungrateful Brat. "No, nothing," she said tersely. "I'll see you in a bit."

"Take your time," offered Kendre in a parting shot, and hung up.

Jordan snapped shut her phone, feeling as if her kids no longer needed her. They were too busy with their own lives to give a damn what she wanted or needed. Was she just as much to blame with her own busy life— sometimes at their expense?

"Didn't mean to scare you off." The smooth voice startled Jordan.

She turned around to find Simon standing so close that she could smell him. He was wearing Quorum cologne and a wide grin.

"You didn't," she told him in a steady voice. "I needed

to call home." Which was partially true. The other part was that she needed a bit more time to get herself together before rejoining the others at the table—along with Simon, who had apparently made himself comfortable with his sometimes adversaries from the D.A.'s office.

Jordan had to admit she loved the smell of Quorum on a man. This man.

"How are Trevor and Kendre doing?" he asked with almost fatherly interest.

"They're doing fine," Jordan said, thinking about the phone chat with Kendre, Trevor's absence, and Eric's death. "It's going to take some time . . . for all of us."

"I know." Simon took her hand in a comforting way. "Look, I've said it before and I'll say it again. If there's anything I can do, Jordan—"

Despite the tension between them recently, Jordan truly believed he was sincerely concerned about the kids, knowing how much they had meant to Eric, as his best friend and law partner. Though she considered that Simon's interest was also clearly in her. She felt relieved to know that he didn't seem to show any ill effects from her whipping his ass in court.

She smiled at him genially. "I'll let you know, Simon."

He looked pleased. "Buy you a drink?"

Jordan hesitated, absorbing the heat of his gray-brown eyes. He was still holding her hand.

Having a drink with him was probably not a good idea, Jordan decided.

"Call it a victory drink," Simon insisted, practically tugging on her arm. "I owe you that much."

It was hard to say no to Simon McNeil, Jordan thought, even when she wanted to say: *You don't owe me anything. I won, remember?* Especially when he stood so close and smelled so damned good.

27

"All right, Simon," Jordan said. "Only we'll make it a Christmas drink."

He smiled. "Why not? The holiday is upon us. Merry Christmas, baby—"

Jordan followed Simon to his table, and studied him the way men studied her—shamelessly and admiringly. There was no harm in being attracted to the good-looking brother attorney, she told herself. What sister wouldn't be? He was the complete package. Including, unfortunately, she thought, already spoken for.

As they made their way through twists and turns between other tables, Jordan was aware that her own contingent had spotted them in the crowd and seemingly could not take their eyes off them. She could almost hear the rumor mill floating up all types of speculation. It was more amusing than anything else. In her mind, it was perfectly normal for adversaries to have a drink together. Especially since they were friends first, and remained such.

"I've missed you," Simon said to Jordan at the table, as if one of them had been on a long sabbatical.

I've missed you too, Jordan admitted to herself, that was, she thought: the Simon McNeil *outside* the courtroom. Instead, she asked, "So how's Frances?"

Simon's eyes lowered thoughtfully, and he put the glass of Pinot Noir to his mouth. "She left me."

Jordan's gaze widened in shock. "What? When?"

"Last month." He looked depressed. "She met someone else and they plan to have a life together. One that doesn't include me."

Jordan was still reeling over the news. *Last month.* "Why didn't you tell me?"

Simon shrugged his broad shoulders. "Wasn't exactly the type of thing I wanted to talk about. Besides, we both had more than enough on our minds without complicating things further—"

Meaning the trial, Jordan thought, suddenly feeling

as though it paled in comparison to their personal struggles.

Instinctively, she reached across the table and patted his hand. It had suddenly turned cold and clammy.

"I'm so sorry, Simon," Jordan whispered, and wondered if she truly meant it. She took back her hand guiltily.

Simon sipped his drink. "Don't be," he muttered. "It hasn't been working for a long time between us. It was only a matter of time before one of us got up the nerve to leave." He took another drink. "It just pisses me off that she beat me to the punch."

Jordan was speechless. All this time she had assumed that Simon and Frances had a happy marriage. But then, few marriages were ever what they seemed from the outside looking in. Even her marriage had seen its share of strain in recent years. Financial pressures, professional differences, and problems in the bedroom had nearly ended their marriage on more than one occasion. But she had stayed, committed to making it work no matter what.

"I moved out of the house," Simon was saying. "Too many damned painful memories and way too big for just me. I'm renting an apartment here in town."

Simon gave Jordan a look that told her he was trying to say something with his eyes that his tongue was withholding. Finally, he said it: "You know I'm crazy about you, Jordan—"

She felt the bile rise in her throat, but managed to maintain her equilibrium. "You have a funny way of showing it," she said with a short, nervous laugh. "Over the last four months you've treated me like your worst enemy."

He wet his lips with wine. "Let's get one thing straight—you were *never* my enemy," he insisted. "Don't you realize it was sheer hell trying to keep up that façade? I only did what I felt was necessary to maintain professional integrity during the trial. As long as I was representing Wilson, I owed it to his defense to go to bat for him one hundred percent—even if that meant giving the performance of my life, if you could call it that."

And what a performance it was, thought Jordan, admittedly impressed. He would never know just how much she had feared he would turn the jury in his client's favor and allow the serial killer to go free. To some degree Simon had won one over her, she mused. He had convinced the jury to spare Raymond Allen Wilson his life. Could she blame Simon for that? He did what he had to do. What any lawyer worth his expensive suit would have done. Even if it meant sacrificing—or putting on hold—whatever it was *they* had until the case was behind them. Or the next one began.

Jordan regarded Simon over the rim of her glass. "I'm glad the trial is over and we can go back to being friends again," she told him honestly, even while wondering exactly what the term "friends" meant as it related to them.

Simon leaned forward and gazed steadily into Jordan's eyes. "Maybe it's time we were more than friends." He placed his hand atop hers. "Come home with me, Jordan."

His hand had warmed up, noted Jordan. So had her entire body.

The man was propositioning her right here and now.

And she was falling for it, hook, line, and sinker.

Once she got past the disbelief and her own weakening as a result of what was clearly a sexual request, Jordan responded unevenly: "I can't, Simon. It's late . . . it's Christmas Eve. There are gifts to be wrapped . . . food to cook—"

"Just for a while," he pleaded, squeezing her hand. "I need you, Jordan. Tonight. We need each other."

Jordan bit down on her lip and fought back the

twinge of desire that swept through her like a wind-blown blaze. It had been so long. There had been no one since Eric. She had not allowed it, despite the fact that men continually came on to her, both on and off the job. It was as if she felt that to succumb to her own needs would somehow be trampling on Eric's memory.

For the first time since his death eight months ago, Jordan rejected that thinking. Denying her own wants, needs, and desires would not bring Eric back. Whatever they had was gone forever, she thought, whether she wanted that or not. She deserved to still feel wanted, especially by the one man she did want.

Simon McNeil.

Jordan turned her hand into his, both moist with heat, and said: "I just need five minutes to say good-bye to the gang."

CHAPTER FOUR

Officers James Kirkland and Gretchen Fitzgerald were the first to respond to an anonymous call that a woman was in distress at 7054 Mountain Drive. When they arrived, they saw a dark Ford sedan parked in front of the townhouse. They recognized the car as one of their own, or at least the department-issued type driven by those at the detective rank. To the uniformed patrol officers, the car was almost like a slap in the face for officers like them who did the gritty work on the force.

Had a detective been the first to arrive at the scene?

Neither officer gave the familiar car much further consideration, or bothered to run a make on the license plate. Not yet anyway. Right now their chief concern was that a woman inside was hurt or maybe even dead. Every second counted.

They entered through the front door, which was unlocked. Their guns were drawn, but they did not sense imminent danger. The house was eerily silent. No creatures were stirring, not even a mouse.

The little silver Christmas tree glowed weakly in the

corner of the living room as if it was getting ready to burn out for good.

"Hello?" called Officer Fitzgerald. No response. "This is the police. Is anyone here?" There was still no response. Nervously the petite, auburn-haired officer looked at her hulking, black, bald partner. "What do you think?"

"You don't want to know," he said with a bad feeling in his gut. "Just watch yourself."

They proceeded cautiously, stepping into the kitchen and then the bathroom, where the water running in the bathtub was overflowing and was now making its way into the hall. Both feared there would be a body in the tub, and were relieved to see this wasn't the case.

Officer Fitzgerald was the first to enter the bedroom. What she saw made her want to puke. A naked woman was lying spread-eagle on the bed. It was a woman, wasn't it? In the near darkness it was hard to tell because there was so much blood. And guts. Everywhere. The body, or what was left of it, had been badly mutilated.

Officer Kirkland's shifting coal eyes were drawn first to what appeared to be movement on the floor at the side of the bed. He quickly pointed his gun in that direction and, recognizing that it was a man, said: "Don't move, asshole!"

The man did move, if only to show his face. And only then in the dim light did Officer Kirkland recognize him.

Simon was waiting by the hood of a silver Mercedes when Jordan walked up to him.

"I've been freezing my ass off," he complained, hands pocketed in a gray topcoat. "I was beginning to think you'd chickened out."

She nearly had, feeling she might be getting into something she'd regret. But it was Christmas Eve and her kids seemed too preoccupied to care if she came home a little later than planned.

And she was lonely.

"I'll follow you," Jordan told him self-consciously. If this was going to happen, there was no sense drawing undue attention to it.

She trailed Simon to a downtown luxury high-rise apartment building, where they took the elevator up to the fifteenth floor. A small part of Jordan wanted to turn around at the door and run like hell. A greater part could not get inside fast enough.

The young couple had driven to Devil's Edge expecting fireworks . . . Christmas bells ringing . . . some passion to heat up a rather chilly night.

All this changed when they came upon the Chevy that looked like it had been in a war zone. Fragments of glass were strewn all over the place. There appeared to be two people in the backseat. They were not moving.

The young couple bravely left their vehicle for a closer look. Neither had to be a physician or medical examiner to know that the occupants of the car were no longer among the living. Worse, the young couple was sure they recognized the victims.

Even more unsettling to one of them was recognizing the driver of the vehicle that had just sped past them from the scene of the crime, as if to get as far away as possible.

CHAPTER FIVE

She had barely gotten to marvel at the panoramic, colorful view of the city from the living room windows on this night before Christmas, when the first kiss came.

"I want to taste you," Simon whispered greedily.

"Then taste me," Jordan responded just as anxiously, if not a bit edgy.

From that moment on, it was all they could do to get to the bedroom. It was a large room with peach walls and deep blue carpeting. Contemporary furnishings were perfectly situated, with a painting of Mount Hood at dusk occupying one wall, and a spider plant hanging in the corner.

Their mouths locked in passion, Simon carried Jordan to the king-size bed, surprising and exciting her at the same time. She hadn't been carried to bed since the first year of her marriage . . . make that the first night. Jordan savored the romantic overture as if she were a newlywed all over again.

"I want to taste more of you," Simon insisted. He trailed kisses down her blouse and halfway down her skirt, before burying his head beneath it. He kissed Jordan through her pantyhose, and then used his tongue on her, driving her mad with delight.

"Ohhh, Simon," she said, biting her lip. "That feels so good."

The suddenness of this intimate act gripped Jordan so that she had little time to think about the embarrassment of such personal and private fulfillment.

"I've wanted you for a long time, Jordan," Simon muttered. "Now I intend to have you . . . in every way—"

He continued to kiss between her legs, and Jordan could barely think about his words. *How long exactly had he wanted her?* She wondered if on some level that want had been mutual, in spite of the self-imposed restraints.

The raw sensations and long absence from such feeling in her most sensitive area caused Jordan to lose all self-control. She let out a hoarse cry, selfishly grabbed hold of Simon's head, and held it in place between her legs while she reveled in the intense pleasure he gave her.

She could have gone on like this forever. Simon had a real knack for oral gratification. Yet she knew fair was fair. So she pushed him away, flat on his back. When Simon tried to object, she put a finger to his lips, wanting him to experience this.

Unzipping his pants, Jordan took out Simon's full erection and slid her mouth over it. She played with him and watched his face contort with delight. Then she quickened the pace and intensity, bringing him all the way to the base of her throat.

"Uh-hh, damn," he moaned, trembling. "No more, baby! Let's do this right."

Simon lifted Jordan as though she was weightless, and began ripping off her clothes while she tore off his.

Laying each other down, they wasted little time, kissing and touching fervently. They had sex as if there were no tomorrow. Or perhaps like old lovers reacquainting themselves.

Like a man possessed, Simon drove hard into Jordan in rapid motions. As a woman equally possessed, she wrapped her legs around his back and met him halfway, and then some.

Within moments the two had mercifully satisfied their immediate needs.

Now they could make love.

Jordan took the top position this time, cradling Simon and watching with feeling as he buried his face in her full breasts, fondling her nipples with his tongue and sending spasms through her. She gasped to the scintillating delight he gave her up and down, all over, making her wonder how she had been able to go so long without a man. She realized it was because she hadn't allowed herself to get over Eric. But now the time seemed right to let him go.

And to discover the passion of the man whose rock-hard body sat rigidly beneath her. She bent down and kissed his face, then his lips ravenously, her long locks brushing against his bald head.

Soon Simon had rolled Jordan onto her stomach. She contracted around him with each stroke, luxuriating in the feel of him inside her.

Finally they ended up in the missionary position again, and huffed and puffed and clawed their way to the finish line, each arriving at the same time in one incredible orgasmic explosion.

Jordan had nearly forgotten what it was like to be touched, held, caressed, and made love to. Now she suddenly had an experience she would not soon forget. Simon McNeil had proven to be everything she possibly could have imagined, and so much more.

I wish I could just go to sleep in his arms right now, thought Jordan dreamily. But reality was beckoning her.

Simon's warm breath tickled Jordan's cheek. "I like you much better in the bedroom than the courtroom," he murmured, giving her a peck on the neck.

"Ditto," she said.

He looked at her with eyes that were wary. "This isn't going to be a onetime thing, is it?"

She hoped not. "I hadn't really thought about it," she said, knowing it was dangerous to look too far ahead, no matter her own selfish desires. He was, after all, still married.

"Maybe you should," Simon said, propping on an elbow. "You mean a hell of a lot more to me, Jordan, than a one-night stand. I hope you feel the same way?"

"I do, Simon," Jordan assured him, and sat up, covering herself with her arms, as if he hadn't already seen all there was to see. "It's just best that for now neither of us makes any promises we may not be able to keep. Let's take it one day at a time—okay?"

Simon put on a crooked, confident smile. "Fair enough. As long as the days become nights *and* more days and weeks and . . ."

Jordan stopped him with a kiss on the lips. While she appreciated his optimism, she knew that men were usually overly optimistic after sex. But she had to be realistic. They each had other obligations that were not simply going to disappear because it worked out better for them.

Besides, Jordan was unsure if he *really* wanted more than a sexual relationship or, for that matter, if she did.

"I have to go," she said abruptly, having shamelessly lost complete track of the time.

"I know," Simon said.

Jordan got to her feet and began gathering her

clothes. Next to her skirt and his pants, she noticed a book of matches that said "Club Diamonds" on the cover. They must have fallen from his pocket during the heat of the moment.

Had he gone there before The Ranch? Jordan wondered, almost embarrassed that she was already thinking like a jealous girlfriend. Or an insecure wife. Both, of course, were ridiculous and way too premature, she thought. He owed her no explanations about what he did before her and who with, though she assumed the one he was sleeping with before her had been his wife, Frances.

Standing up, Simon seemed too preoccupied to even be aware of the matches or Jordan's misgivings. She left them there for him to discover in his own good time.

She silently admired him—his perfectly sculpted body—until he'd put on his pants, before asking as she buttoned her blouse: "Mind showing me where the bathroom is?"

"Not at all." Simon took Jordan's hand and led her to a huge bathroom just beyond his bedroom. He chuckled. "Guess I should have given you the grand tour first but, to be honest with you, at the time that was the last thing on my mind."

"You're forgiven." Jordan smiled at him, feeling a little flushed, even knowing full well that she was at least as guilty.

In the aquamarine-tiled bathroom, which had matching olive hand and face towels on two racks, Jordan noted several long strands of blond hair in the sink, which certainly didn't belong to Simon. And not to Frances either, she thought knowingly. *Not unless she had turned white on her.* There was the faint but distinct smell of a woman's perfume in the air.

Just how the hell many women had he brought here?

Jordan asked herself, a twinge of resentment sweeping over her. Was she little more than another notch on Simon's belt? A roll in the hay as his sort of damned Christmas present to a lonely *and* vulnerable widow?

Reality quickly stepped into Jordan's thoughts. She had no special claim to him, whether or not some part of her wanted to make such a claim. Who he spent his time with was his business. Wasn't it?

Leave it alone, girl, Jordan told herself. *Don't make waves. Simon's going to do what Simon wants to do. Just don't expect more out of him than what already happened.*

Jordan made herself presentable and cut the light out when she left the bathroom.

"Let me walk you down," Simon told her at the door, looking as if she'd discovered his secret life.

"I'll be fine," Jordan insisted, forcing herself to give him a reassuring smile, adding, but not sure it was such a good idea: "Call me." She gave him a nice kiss, and was gone.

Nat King Cole's soulful rendition of "The Christmas Song" serenaded Jordan from the radio as she drove home. She admired the Christmas decorations displayed on homes and businesses, while thinking: Too bad all this beauty will have to come down in a week. Snowflakes were actually sticking to the ground just in time for Christmas, as if through divine intervention for those who believed that a white Christmas brought the spirit alive.

All of a sudden Jordan felt as if anything was possible. She and the kids could bury their differences and start fresh. The New Year was coming fast. What better time to be optimistic?

Even romance, which had eluded her since Eric's untimely death, suddenly seemed alive and well.

The possibilities were endless.

Simon McNeil—mysterious, complex, and all—just might be someone she could have a future with. Only time would tell.

Yes, optimism lives on, Jordan mused happily.

Jordan sang along with Nat, pretending to be his daughter, Natalie Cole, laughing at the sound of her own voice next to his.

When the song ended, a news brief said solemnly: "A woman was found stabbed to death tonight in her home on Mountain Drive. Arrested and charged with the murder was her ex-husband, Graham Turner, a homicide detective for the Portland Police Bureau. . . ."

The news brought Jordan off her high. She didn't know Turner personally, but had heard of him. Without being privy to the facts, Jordan found herself thinking like a prosecutor. Police were generally only arrested and charged with such a heinous crime when there was hard evidence. Which made her wonder what in the hell had possessed Turner to do it—on Christmas Eve of all nights, for heaven's sake?

"More tragic news on this Christmas Eve . . ." the voice continued as if in apology. "The bodies of a young man and woman were found in a car on Devil's Edge within the last hour. Both had apparently been shot to death in what may have been a gang- or drug-related hit. Their names are being withheld pending notification of next of kin. The police have not made any arrests at this time."

CHAPTER SIX

It was supposed to be their dream house. Jordan and Eric La Fontaine had purchased the seventy-five-year-old, two-story, four-bedroom brick home six years ago. It was located in the Portland suburb of Ashland Heights, which boasted a 425-acre lake and all the fishing one could handle. The living room's double-hung windows offered breathtaking views of Mount Hood and Mount St. Helens. For the La Fontaines, the city's low crime rate, good schools, and clean living, along with affordability made the house too much to pass up. The proximity to the shops and entertainment in Portland was equally appealing. They had completely renovated the house and had just begun to call it a home when Eric had died suddenly.

Jordan was not thinking of that on this Christmas morning, even if on some mental wavelength Eric was always there. Instead her thoughts were on preparing dinner, opening gifts, and being a family again. She knew Eric would have wanted for all of them to carry on with their lives as best as possible.

Also weighing on Jordan's mind were those awful crimes that had marred the spirit of Christmas in the Rose City, as Portland was known, the night before.

The young couple slain had been identified as Portland State University students, Nelson Neilson, twenty-one, and Gail Marshall, twenty. Both were African-American and had planned to marry on New Year's Day. The police had yet to release any details as far as a motive, dismissing earlier reports that it was drug or gang-related. The killer was still at large.

After being formally charged with the murder of his thirty-four-year-old ex-wife, Victoria, Graham Turner, thirty-eight, was being held without bail on Christmas day. The black veteran police detective was apprehended at the scene of the crime without incident.

Jordan fully expected all hell to break loose in the D.A.'s office over these two cases. But at least for this day she planned to put them on the backburner and enjoy Christmas with her family; along with stealing some lingering pleasant thoughts of last night with Simon McNeil.

"This is so cool, Mom," gushed Kendre after opening the gift-wrapped box and lifting out the peach faux-wrap dress. She held it up to her body, just as with the other dress moments before, then declared excitedly: "I can't wait to wear it to school!"

Jordan couldn't have been more pleased. She had been afraid that she'd lost her touch in buying Kendre clothes appropriate for a fourteen-year-old. "I'm glad you like the dresses, honey." She smiled gratefully at her daughter.

Kendre beamed, her jet-black micro braids straddling straight shoulders. She had her mother's big hazel eyes and high cheekbones, and her father's full mouth and almond coloring. Already five-seven, Kendre's ever-changing body was all her very own—thin and shapely, and maturing a bit too fast for Jordan's comfort.

"And the CDs are *right on*," Kendre said, clearly impressed. "I never realized that you had such an ear for today's sound, Mom!"

"There are probably a lot of things you don't realize about just how hip I am, kiddo." Jordan was enjoying this rare rapport between mother and daughter, even if she knew part of it was under false pretenses. Her true taste was far removed from what kids today called music.

They were in the cozy family room in front of a large Christmas tree that had been decorated only a week ago. To Jordan it was the most beautiful tree they'd ever had, as well as the most difficult to appreciate as Eric was not there to see it.

"This is for you, Lenora." Jordan handed her a gift, surprising Kendre's best friend, who was about twenty-five pounds heavier while three inches shorter and a couple of shades darker. It was something Jordan had planned to save until Kendre's fifteenth birthday. But since Lenora was a guest—Kendre's guest, no less—it made more sense to make her feel right at home for Christmas.

"For me?" Lenora cooed, batting fake long lashes wildly. "How sweet." Wearing a curly shag, she pushed back some strands of burgundy hair that hung over her brow, and tore open the wrapping paper containing a small box. Inside was a silver bracelet.

Lenora, seemingly overcome with gratitude, surprised Jordan with an almost choking hug. "Thanks a lot, Mrs. La Fontaine!"

Once she caught her breath, Jordan said, "You're welcome, Lenora. Merry Christmas."

Jordan saw a twinkle in Kendre's eyes that suggested

she knew the gift had been earmarked for her, but she appreciated this even more.

"Sorry I didn't get you anything," Lenora said weakly.

"Don't be silly," Jordan told her. "I'm sure it wasn't your plan to spend Christmas day with us. Besides, my gift is having you girls enjoy being with one another for the holiday." Inside she thought: Now why in the hell would Lenora's mother "abandon" this child while gallivanting off to Seattle with her boyfriend?

"Well look who's *finally* decided to put in an appearance before Christmas was over," Kendre said wryly.

They all turned to see Trevor lazily entering the room, barefoot and wearing a black robe around oversized gray sweats. Six-two, he was the spitting image of his father—trim, with a muscular upper body, long lean legs, and intense black eyes. Trevor sported short sideburns, and a goatee on a full face.

"Merry Christmas, everybody," he said with a yawn, and played with his russet-colored dreadlocks.

"Merry Christmas," they all responded.

Trevor walked up to Jordan and pulled a gift out from behind him. "This is for you, Momma."

Jordan lit up, while thinking that Trevor had continued to call her "Momma" since he could first talk; whereas Kendre had abruptly shortened her name to "Mom" upon turning thirteen, as if too grown up now for her own good.

Jordan took the unwrapped novel by Tananarive Due and smiled warmly at her son. She gave him a big hug and kissed him on the cheek. "I'll enjoy reading this, Trevor. Thank you."

He shrugged it off with a half grin. "Hey, I have to do right by my girls." He then produced two other unwrapped gifts, as if by magic, and favored Kendre and Lenora.

45

Jordan watched the girls comparing their gifts, then Trevor as he moved to the tree and picked up one of his own. He had come in last night after Jordan, going straight to his downstairs room, seemingly in no mood to see or be seen by anyone. When she knocked on the door out of concern, Trevor simply said he'd had too much to drink at a party and was going to bed. Though she sometimes worried—as single mothers tended to do—that he was drinking too much and had some questionable friends, Jordan had left it at that, happy Trevor was home safe and in one piece, considering the misfortune that had struck some others on Christmas Eve. She thought about the sad and violent ending to the college couple's young lives, in particular, and then the police detective's slain ex-wife.

That notwithstanding, Jordan mused, gazing at Trevor as he opened another gift while wearing an amused smile, he seemed fine now and ready to share in the holiday with his loved ones.

"I think it's time we started being a *real* family again," Jordan announced at the dinner table. She had gone the extra mile in fixing turkey and dressing, mashed potatoes and gravy, greens, cornbread, and sweet potato pie for dessert—staying up half the night in the process. She wanted to make the holiday dinner as special as possible, as though Eric were still with them. Or, more realistically, as a celebration of their ability to carry on without him, as she knew he would have insisted.

To Jordan's surprise, Lenora had gone home upon learning that her mother had come back, apparently alone, after getting into a fight with her boyfriend and leaving him stranded in Seattle. *That poor child*, Jordan had thought sadly. With her mother carrying on like that, was it any wonder Lenora and so many other kids these days were left confused?

46

"Who says we aren't a *real* family?" Trevor looked across the table, his thick brows touching. "This is about as real as it gets." He glanced dispiritedly at Kendre. "Ain't that right, String Bean?" Trevor had periodically referred to his sister that way since she was five years old and, as he put it, "skinny as a string bean." Didn't matter that since then she had begun to fill out nicely in all the right places.

Kendre shrugged as though she wasn't quite sure what constituted a real family anymore, now that one member was gone.

"It can get better," Jordan insisted. *Much better.* Following a sigh, she noted: "This is the first Christmas without your father. We can't live in the past anymore. He wouldn't want that."

With a typical sneer, Kendre snorted: "So what are you saying—that we're just supposed to *forget* Daddy ever existed?"

Jordan could feel the perspiration forming under her arms. This was going to be harder than she thought. Not that she expected it to be that easy. Was it ever?

"Of course not." Jordan gazed warmly at her daughter. "But your father is gone, Kendre, and he's not coming back, no matter how much any of us may want that. *We* are all we have, honey. I just don't want to lose you, too." To Trevor, she said, to make it clear: "Or you—"

They all seemed suspended in a time warp for several seconds of silent reflection, broken only when the doorbell rang.

"I'll get it!" Kendre sounded grateful for the interruption. She sprang from the table like a jackrabbit.

Jordan waited for Trevor to say something. Anything. But he might as well have been off on a distant world. He had been that way all day to one degree or another, even when trying to seem cheerful. She wondered what was on his mind, but decided to let him talk about it when he was good and ready.

Kendre returned with a nervous look on her face. "It's the police, Momma. They want to see Trevor."

CHAPTER SEVEN

Homicide Detectives Mike O'Donnell and Carl Paris were conducting the investigation into the deaths of Nelson Neilson and Gail Marshall. After apologizing for the intrusion on a day that was supposed to bring good tidings, the detectives went about the task they were paid to do—question all potential witnesses and suspects. Even if this one happened to be the son of a prominent local criminal prosecutor.

As if they were welcome guests, Jordan offered the detectives a seat in the living room, which was small by some standards but comfortable and evenly proportioned in a shade of beige with maple hardwood flooring. O'Donnell, the larger of the two and about forty, had a short carrot top. He pounced onto a burgundy loveseat. Paris, who was thinner, bald, African-American, and maybe ten years younger, sat lazily in a forest green twill accent chair near the fireplace, where the fire had almost gone out.

Jordan sat on the burgundy sofa beside Trevor, a thousand thoughts running through her head. She could see Trevor trembling, but attributed it more to the shock of hearing that his friends had been murdered than being questioned by police.

For her part, Jordan saw this as nothing more than routine legwork required when investigating a homicide. This notwithstanding, she couldn't deny that being put on the hot seat in her own home by people she was used to working with, left her just a bit unnerved.

"We understand that you knew the victims?" O'Donnell spoke with a thick voice, favoring Trevor with sharp blue eyes.

Trevor nodded. "Yeah," he said tersely. "We went to the same school."

"That being Portland State?" O'Donnell pretended to glance at a notepad.

Another nod from Trevor. "Right."

O'Donnell rubbed his long, red nose. "Would you say you knew them well, Mr. La Fontaine?"

Trevor hesitated, shifting his eyes to Jordan and back, then shrugged. "Not real well. I mean, I saw them around, but we didn't hang out together or anything."

O'Donnell gave an eye signal to Paris to take over. "Do you have any idea why anyone would want to kill them?" he asked directly. Paris took his own notepad out and a pen, almost as if expecting a long list of suspects to be revealed. Or maybe just one.

Trevor thought about it, and said tonelessly: "No, man, I don't have any idea."

Paris gave him a long look with bulging black eyes. He peered at Jordan and she half expected him to ask her what she knew about the crime or victims, but Paris refrained.

Paris turned back to Trevor, flipped shut the notepad, and said as if he didn't mean it: "Well, thanks for your time. If we need to speak to you again, I assume you'll be around . . . ?"

"Yeah, sure." Trevor hunched his broad shoulders. "I'll be right here or at school."

Paris seemed satisfied for the moment.

Both detectives stood. At the door, O'Donnell said lamely to Jordan: "Merry Christmas, Counselor."

The autopsy report read like something from a horror novel. Sometime between 7:30 P.M. and 8:30 P.M., the victim—a blonde green-eyed, thirty-four-year-old female Caucasian—died of multiple stab wounds. Her throat had been cut almost from ear to ear. The windpipe and gullet had been completely severed, the wound sliced all the way to the spinal cord. There were deep bruises along the jaw line, caused by perhaps the strong pressure of fingers squeezing it.

The victim had been sliced open from the breastbone to the rectum. The right breast was completely severed; the left breast had the nipple sliced off. There was a deep, jagged incision along the lower part of the abdomen and several incisions on the left side of the body. She was also stabbed repeatedly in the vagina.

The angle of the wounds, left to right, suggested that the mutilations were committed by a left-handed person using a sharp blade, measuring twelve to fifteen inches long.

Jordan closed her eyes for a moment as she felt herself become sick at the thought of what she'd just read. This, combined with the graphic crime-scene photos she'd viewed, left her with rage, grief, and disbelief.

"I want *you* to handle this case, Jordan." District Attorney Wilson Bombeck peered at her from across his large metal desk in an ill-fitted Franco Uomo dark blue suit. The fifty-eight-year-old Bombeck was short and stocky, with a deeply receding hairline and grayish-white hair. Gold-rimmed glasses made his beryl blue eyes appear larger than they really were.

Jordan sat motionless, wearing a teal blue suit and matching pumps. She twisted in her seat and waited for him to convince her that this was a case she really needed. A white female victim and a black male perpetrator always spelled trouble for any prosecutor—but especially for an African-American woman who tried to avoid racially charged cases like the plague.

I don't need that type of headache, she thought, but knew that it wasn't really her call.

"We have all the evidence we need to convict Graham Turner of first-degree murder for killing his ex-wife," Bombeck said confidently. "But the fact remains that he's a fourteen-year veteran of the Portland Police Bureau who's done a damned good job by most accounts. Not everyone wants to see him go down—no matter what he did . . . or, er, was alleged to have done." Bombeck knitted his thick brows pensively. "We have to draw the line in the sand, Jordan. We *have* to be on the side of the victim, plain and simple."

I thought that was always supposed to be the case, Jordan mused dryly. She knew though that politics often played as much a role in the cases they prosecuted as the chance for a conviction. This was even truer when it involved an interracial killing.

"What's Turner saying about this, if anything?" Jordan asked. It had all been pretty tightlipped up to now, as though it were the world's best-kept secret. Had he confessed? Semi-confessed? An accused person's mind-set shortly after the crime often said a lot about his or her feelings at the time of the incident. Not that anything could justify what had been done to Victoria Turner.

"What the hell can he say that every two-bit killer hasn't already said to try and dig himself out of a very deep hole?" Bombeck threw his arms up dismissively. "The bastard murdered his ex and was caught red-handed!"

52

Jordan recalled that Turner's hands were stained with blood at the time of his arrest, almost awash in it.

Bombeck leaned forward, and said earnestly: "I'm not going to pretend that this is just an everyday murder case. You know and I know that because Turner's black and his dead ex-wife was white, it's O.J. and Nicole all over again—only this time we need a conviction."

Jordan's jaw tightened. "And you want a black woman to be the one to convict this black man of killing his white ex-wife?" She knew how this would play in the press. Not to mention the D.A.'s office.

Bombeck looked at her unblinkingly. "That's right. We have to put ourselves above the fray in prosecuting this case. The fact is, like it or not, you're the best person for the job, race aside. It's damned important for this office that we not run away from any controversy this may generate."

How about I walk away quietly? thought Jordan, already beginning to feel the heat.

"It's also important to *you*, Jordan," Bombeck stressed, "that you go out and get this son of a bitch just as you would anyone—white, black, Hispanic, or Asian—accused of a crime of this magnitude." He gave a deliberate sigh, and Jordan could almost read what was coming next.

"Let me be frank, Jordan—I've been seriously considering you for the vacancy as the head of this office's Homicide Division. Maybe it's time you took that big step in your career." He sat back in his chair smugly, while she put a surprised look on her face for his benefit. "Get the job done in this case—and that means *no deals*—and you can call yourself Bureau Chief."

So that's it, Jordan thought, reading between the lines. *Either I get a conviction against Turner, or the job I've worked my ass off for goes to Jerrod Wresler.*

She would be damned if she let that happen—not without a hell of a fight.

She wasn't about to make it easy for Bombeck to tell her: *Can't say you didn't have your chance to move up the ladder, Jordan. You just weren't good enough.*

"I'll begin working on it right away, Wilson," Jordan promised him. And she promised herself a conviction.

He smiled warily. "I'm counting on it, Jordan."

"I'd like to have Andrew assist me."

"No problem. He's yours for as long as you need him."

Jordan was already beginning to strategize, aware that every advantage she had in this trial could go a long way toward achieving victory. She wondered who she would be up against, hoping that there would be no butting heads again with Simon. At least not in the courtroom.

Glancing at the file folder on her lap, Jordan noted that there were traces of semen and hair found in and outside the victim's vagina. There was no indication that she had been raped. More importantly, preliminary DNA tests showed that neither the hair nor semen came from Graham Turner.

Jordan looked at Bombeck and asked what he made of this. "She had sex with somebody else other than her ex," he said wryly. "In this case, the victim's sex life is immaterial. She could have been with someone at any time that day." He seemed to think about the implications of his words, and said: "Even if we find the guy Victoria Turner slept with, there's nothing in that file to point to anyone but Graham Turner as the killer."

Jordan was inclined to concur. But it was still a piece of the puzzle that may have inadvertently led to Victoria Turner's death. Jealousy was the obvious motive, even if the victim and suspect were no longer married.

Jordan noted in the file that the anonymous call to

54

the Police Bureau had come twenty minutes before police arrived at the scene. The caller was believed to be a
female.

But what if it was really a male who didn't want to be
identified as a witness to the crime? Maybe even the
victim's lover.

Bombeck looked impatiently at his gold-tone Seiko
watch. "Well . . . unless there's something else on your
mind, Jordan, I've got work to do. And I'm sure you do
as well."

In fact, there *was* something else on Jordan's mind.
And it had nothing to do with the matter at hand, other
than the timing and also being of a criminal nature. She
asked offhandedly: "What's the latest word on those two
college kids killed on Christmas Eve?"

Bombeck shifted uncomfortably in his chair. "We're
still investigating. We've only just started."

"Any suspects?"

He paused. "One or two."

To Jordan this suggested an arrest was imminent.
This pleased her, considering her son was acquainted
with the victims.

For some reason she said to Bombeck, "Trevor knew
the two students."

Bombeck glanced at her sideways. "The two that
were killed?"

Jordan's breath quickened and she responded defensively, "Yes . . . he recognized them . . . from the university." That was not a crime in and of itself, she reminded
herself. "The police questioned him to that effect." She
saw nothing wrong with this in a routine yet thorough
investigation.

"Did he know anything?" Bombeck put a fat hand to
his glasses.

"Nothing that they couldn't have gotten from any

55

other students familiar with the victims as far as being cordial on campus. Trevor didn't know them well." This fact alone made Jordan feel much better under the circumstances. The last she'd heard, they were still suggesting that the crime may have been gang violence or a drug deal gone sour. She and Eric had worked hard to keep Trevor and Kendre out of gangs and away from drugs. There was no indication that they had failed in this regard.

"Well, that's good to hear," Bombeck said in a wavering voice. "You've got enough on your plate to contend with. I'm sure the police and this office will get to the bottom of this."

Jordan took some solace in that, only imagining what those students' parents must be going through. It was always most painful when the victims were young people who had their whole lives ahead of them. Snuffed out like spent candles on Christmas Eve.

CHAPTER EIGHT

An accident had slowed traffic on Interstate 5 for miles.

Cursing under his breath, Detective Harry Coleman finally got out of what used to be the fast lane and weaved his way to the next exit, nearly hitting another car. The driver, a middle-aged woman who could barely see over the steering wheel, gave him the finger. He responded in kind.

Stupid bitch.

He wasn't really surprised by all the road rage these days. Between gridlock and all the other crap people had to put up with, it was a wonder they all didn't go berserk sooner or later.

He came up to Ninth Street and hung a sharp right. It was a shortcut to the Criminal Justice Center he'd learned after nearly twenty years on the job as one of the city's finest. The last ten years he had been on the Portland Police Bureau's homicide detail. The last six years he had been partnered with Graham Turner.

Coleman was almost forty-five, though he sometimes felt more like sixty. Other times he felt like a man half his age. He attributed that to his daily workouts at the police gym, allowing him to maintain a trim physique on his six-one frame, and the two high-potency multi-vitamins he popped each day. Admittedly the jury was still out on the vitamins, but hell, what did he have to lose. His still-black-as-the-dead-of-night hair had thinned considerably on top in just the past year, but his eyesight was still 20/20, and those baby blues as pretty as ever.

He had put in at the beginning of the year to have Christmas Eve and Christmas day off so he could spend it with his wife and three kids. Coleman owed them at least that much since he was hardly there for them any other time of the year. They had gone down to San Diego to visit his mother-in-law for the holiday, only getting back this afternoon. It was then Coleman had learned his partner had been arrested for murdering his ex-wife.

Coleman pulled into the parking lot of the Criminal Justice Center in his department-issued vehicle. For some reason he couldn't fathom, the lot was practically filled to capacity. He squeezed his midsize car between a Honda and a station wagon, shut off the engine, and thought about the trouble Graham Turner was in.

His mind was spinning. He could almost see the headlines now: INTERRACIAL LOVE TURNS TO MURDER, COP ARRESTED. Coleman bit his lip. He really liked Turner—on and off the job—and didn't give a damn that he was African-American. Or that he preferred white women. Why not? It wasn't like there weren't plenty to go around. Besides, it took two to tango. Women had the same choices as men. And that one made her choice. Now he had to wonder if she'd made the wrong one.

He had known Victoria Turner even before Graham became his partner. They had been introduced at a police picnic the year before. Coleman had taken a liking to her right away. She had those California-girl good looks—yellow hair, big breasts, sweet curves. He recalled thinking that Turner was one hell of a lucky bastard.

But Turner's luck had run out when Victoria filed for divorce three years ago, citing everything from wife battering to sexual incompatibility, to the standard irreconcilable differences. Turner had taken it pretty hard. Who wouldn't? The man loved that woman almost to the point of obsession, and he had done everything in his power to win her back.

And it had nearly worked. There had been a brief reconciliation—twice. In Coleman's mind, the two seemed meant to tough it out and spend the rest of their lives together. But in the end it was not to be. The divorce was finalized a year ago, and Turner took full blame for what had happened.

Coleman knew Graham Turner never got over Victoria. Even though there had been plenty of other women to share his bed before and after, Turner always compared them with Victoria and it was never favorably.

Now she was dead. And the people they both worked with believed Graham Turner did it.

Could he really have murdered Victoria a year after they had already gone their separate ways? The thought was very unsettling to Coleman as he headed toward the jail.

"You look worse than hell itself," Coleman remarked without prelude. And that was being kind.

The man before him looked as if he had already been condemned to die—or worse. His bald head lacked the shine Coleman had been accustomed to seeing. Sable eyes were puffy and reddened like a man too long without sleep. His face, with a milk-chocolate complexion, looked puffy and bruised. Black and gray stubble formed a shadow across his chin and neck. Turner wore the jail's bright orange uniform. It fit tightly around his muscular, six-five body.

All in all, thought Coleman sadly, it was a pitiful sight to see a man who had spent the better part of his life upholding the law now locked up like a common criminal.

A criminal accused of cold-blooded murder.

They were in a six-by-nine cell. A guard stood outside listening as if his very life depended on it. Though Turner was not being allowed any visitors other than family, Coleman had pulled some strings to get in to see him.

"Just tell me one thing," Coleman said. Man to man, eyeball to eyeball with Turner he asked, "Did you kill her?"

"No, man, I didn't." Turner's voice was so quiet, Coleman had to replay the words again in his mind. "I loved her too much to want to see her dead. I'd sooner have killed myself."

As Coleman understood it, the evidence against his partner was compelling—though largely circumstantial. But as experience had taught him, that was hardly the same as guilt. Further, in all the years they had known each other, Turner had *never* lied to him. Why start now?

In his mind, Coleman answered his own question: Maybe I'd lie too if it meant saving my ass from a possible date with death row.

After studying the face of what looked to be a broken man for a moment or two, Coleman said, "Why don't you tell me how you ended up in this mess—from the beginning?"

CHAPTER NINE

Simon had left a message for her to call him. Jordan had done so right away, finding that she needed to hear his voice.

"I've missed you," he said in a husky tone.

"Haven't I heard that before?" Jordan teased, sitting at her U-shaped desk in her corner office.

"Yes. It was true then, and it's even more true now."

Her heart did a little leap. Whether she wanted to admit it or not, Jordan had found that not seeing Simon in two days had left her wanting him in the worst way. Not to mention the best way.

"So what do you want to do about it?" she asked coquettishly.

"I want to see you," Simon replied.

"When?"

She heard some sounds as if Simon was riffling through his day planner. "Can you drop by the office at, say, three?"

Jordan had to consider her own appointments. Mainly

she didn't want to appear too eager. "If you can make it four, you've got yourself a date."

"If that's what it takes to get you over here, four it is, darling," he said. "If I have to wait any longer, though, I just might go nuts."

Exactly what did he have in mind during this office visit? Jordan wondered, smiling and tingling at the thought, remembering their last encounter all too vividly. In a controlled voice, she said: "I'll try not to be a minute late."

Jordan hung up, but was still transfixed for a moment or two. Simon had called her "darling." Was it a term of endearment? Or of untamed lust? She wasn't sure it made any difference at this point. She wanted him as much as she knew he wanted her. The rest was something they'd have to talk about when the time was right.

Andrew Lombard showed up in Jordan's office five minutes later to go over the case against Graham Turner.

He had studied the file just as Jordan had, and had come to basically the same conclusion. "Looks like it's pretty much open and shut," Andrew said. "We've got the murder weapon with Turner's prints and the victim's blood all over it. We got the man himself caught at the scene of the crime, the knife in his hands—or should I say *left* hand. We got ourselves an apparent stalker who beat the hell out of his wife when they were married, then decided he couldn't—or wouldn't—let her live without him." Andrew ran a hand through his curly hair. "Somewhere along the line, Turner must have snapped and went for the jugular."

"He went for a lot more than that," Jordan said. "The killer not only slit her throat, but saw to it that even in death she would be horribly mutilated. We're not talking about love here—but hate."

"Kind of scary, isn't it?" Andrew turned those amazing blue eyes on her. "This is a *cop* we're talking about. Makes you wonder how many other cops are out there—carrying guns, knives, and even powerful fists—who are just loose cannons waiting to explode at any time against anyone, especially someone they're intimately acquainted with."

Jordan frowned in anger. "Probably more than either of us cares to admit, Andrew. Right now, our job is to concentrate on one cop, and everything that can help us win a conviction of murder in the first degree."

"Agreed." Andrew sat up, paused. "So you're okay with the interracial thing here?"

Jordan's eyes widened in surprise. "Why wouldn't I be?" she asked defensively. "I'm a professional. Being African-American doesn't mean I think it's okay for black men to kill white women, any more than for black men to kill black women; or, for that matter, for whites to kill outside their race or within it. My job is simply to stick to the facts of a particular case and convince a jury that we know what the hell we're talking about in representing the D.A.'s office. Do we understand each other?"

Andrew turned red in the face. "Perfectly, Jordan. Sorry I asked. Never meant to offend you."

Jordan forced a smile. "You didn't." Maybe just a little, she thought. "So let's get to work. . . ."

She arrived at Simon's office at four o'clock on the dot. It occupied half the tenth floor of the building located in Portland's prestigious waterfront district. This was Jordan's first visit to what used to be Eric's co-office since she had cleared out his things six months ago. It had been painful to box up his law books, degrees, family photos—everything that had made Eric La Fontaine a successful attorney and good husband. Now she had returned to the place where he started under very different circumstances.

What would Eric think about her and Simon as lovers? A thrust of fresh guilt stabbed at Jordan. She knew that Eric and Simon had always been competitive in driving each other to be the best they could be. But that was in business and sports. She was not a part of the equation. She could only hope that Simon's interest in her was *not* because she was Eric's widow, but rather a beautiful woman and human being.

"Your timing couldn't be more precise," Simon said, startling Jordan. He greeted her in the reception area with a friendly kiss on the cheek, then stepped back, looking debonair in a tailored tan suit. "Glad you could drop by, Jordan," he said formally.

"I said I would if could find the time," she said equally formal as the receptionist—a new, younger, prettier one since Jordan had last been there—looked on with keen interest.

After a quick introduction of Jordan as his late partner's wife and very good friend, Simon eyed the receptionist and told her: "Naomi, hold all my calls during our meeting."

Jordan suppressed a smile as she followed him into his office. He closed the door and locked it.

Then he attacked her with an open-mouthed kiss, trapping her against the door. He put a hand inside her blouse on her bra, cupping a breast. His fingers ran across her nipple. Jordan sucked in a deep breath and his scent, and began to quiver from head to toe.

With some effort, she managed to pull herself away from the onslaught. "I hope this isn't the way you conduct *all* your business meetings, Counselor," Jordan gasped.

Simon flashed her a wicked grin. "Who said anything about business?" He closed the distance between them. "Believe me, this is strictly personal."

His hands went around her small waist, pulling Jordan up to him. She could feel the erection in his pants brushing against her skirt. "See what you do to me, Jordan?"

The same thing you do to me, a voice within her said.

He kissed her again. Their bodies rubbed together. Jordan felt her resistance—what little there was—breaking down. She was giving way to the same almost animalistic craving that had fueled her—and Simon—the other night.

She clung to him, wrapping her legs around his waist. He cupped her buttocks and carried her to the desk, where papers parted like the Red Sea, and down Jordan went with Simon on top of her. She helped him unzip his pants, even as he struggled to remove her stockings and panties.

Jordan watched as Simon drove into her, grunting. She felt him inside her and urged him in even deeper, while suppressing her own moans for fear that Naomi or others in the office might hear them. It was torture keeping perfectly silent.

They went at it for five minutes—although it seemed much longer—before stars went off, as each reached an orgasm, one right after the other, then tried to catch their breath.

"We should have been together years ago," Simon declared after a final, wet kiss.

Jordan pulled her skirt down and twisted it around. "You know that wasn't possible, Simon," she said uneasily, and the ghost of Eric suddenly seemed to be haunting the office.

Simon zipped his pants. "Maybe it was, but neither of us was willing to face up to it."

Was he suggesting that they should have had an affair—while they were both married? Jordan was shocked.

"I never could have left Eric," she stated flatly, looking up at Simon with her head angled. "Whatever problems we had, they weren't bad enough to give up on my marriage."

"What the hell did *he* ever do to deserve you?" Simon's brow creased. He put the weight of his eyes on Jordan, and said before she could respond: "Give me a chance to make you happy, Jordan. As soon as my divorce comes through, I want us to be together—forever!"

Jordan was stunned by his words. Was he talking about marriage? Love?

Do you really know what you're saying, Simon? Jordan thought with some misgiving.

From her own position, Jordan wasn't sure just how far she was prepared to go with this relationship. *Were they even in a relationship?* Did she really need to complicate her life any more than it already was?

Yes, Jordan thought positively, looking at Simon as he stared back at her. *I very much want for you to be a part of my life. But only to a point—for now.*

She kissed him lightly on the lips. "I think we've already come a pretty long way in just a few days, Simon, don't you?" She used her finger to wipe lipstick from his mouth. "Why rock the boat until we can be sure it won't tip over at the first sign of trouble. Besides, I have two kids I'm still trying to keep up with and, as of this moment, you still have a wife."

Simon stood speechless, which was probably best at this point for all concerned, thought Jordan.

"I can see myself out," she told him, and left.

CHAPTER TEN

Harry Coleman lay on his side of the bed, facing away from his wife of eighteen years, Jobeth. In each of those years he had seen their sex life diminish a little bit more so that now they hardly had sex at all. Maybe once a month, if one or the other really pressed the point. He blamed himself. It had been great in the beginning. At least it was for him. But then the babies started coming, and she started to balloon out and was never able to regain the form that had once made Jobeth Ms. Multnomah County.

It affected him more than he had ever told her. But Coleman still saw Jobeth as a good wife, mother, and friend. He loved her for all those things and wouldn't trade her for a dozen Christie Brinkleys.

Coleman's thoughts turned to his visit with Graham Turner. He still couldn't get over the pathetic sight of his partner. Turner was a shell of his former self, once the envy of every man on the force for his workout ethic and quick wit. The man was now running for his life and scared to death. Who the hell wouldn't be in his shoes? He'd gone from good guy to bad guy overnight, and suddenly faced the prospect of spending the rest of his life behind bars—or worse, death by lethal injection. And all for a crime he didn't commit.

Coleman lay there as his wife rolled around to face him. He could feel her violet eyes staring at his back. Her breathing quickened and her mouth seemed poised to say something. As if he couldn't guess what was on her mind.

"You want to talk about it?" she finally asked, tentative.

"Not really," he said, knowing damned well she wouldn't leave it alone. It wasn't her style. Jobeth fancied herself an amateur psychologist who had all the answers. Or thought she did.

"We have to talk about it, Harry." She brushed up against him.

"Maybe tomorrow," he lied, wishing he could somehow miraculously fall asleep.

Jobeth persisted. "Keeping your feelings bottled up inside isn't the answer. I'm your wife, in case you've forgotten. When you're hurting, I'm hurting."

Her feet caressed his. He had to admit it felt soothing, and he caressed her feet back. He also knew she was right. It was better to get it off his chest. And who better with than the only person he could ever count on when all was said and done?

"I went to see him today," Coleman said lowly.

"I know." She wrapped an arm around his waist. "How could you not?" Jobeth's voice rang with compassion, which was just the opposite of her initial reaction when she had heard about Graham Turner's troubles. In fact, Coleman remembered, when they first listened to the news story together, the first words to come from Jobeth's mouth were: "That *poor* woman. Why did he have to kill her?"

She quickly retracted the statement, but the words stuck like a chicken bone caught in his throat. Or worse, thought Coleman, like a judge asking a jury to disregard damning words they just heard. His own wife had forgotten the words they were supposed to live by—innocent until proven guilty—and had already made up her mind that Turner was guilty. Just as many of his colleagues had, Coleman knew. At least privately.

And the prosecutor assigned to the case—Jordan La Fontaine. He had seen her in action. African-American, good-looking, impartial, and tough as nails in the courtroom. The D.A.'s office had picked the right person for the job in counteracting the race card in this case of alleged interracial homicide. La Fontaine would not stop until Turner was sitting on death row.

"How's Graham doing?" Jobeth's words invaded his thoughts.

Coleman faced her with a scowl. "How would you be doing if you were sitting in some stinking rat hole with nothin' to do but watch your whole damned life pass before your eyes?"

Jobeth brushed platinum blond bangs from her face and gave him a confused, hesitant look, but remained mute.

"They're trying to railroad him, Jobeth," Coleman spat. "Graham Turner is one tough son of a bitch who was probably too obsessed with his ex-wife and obviously heartbroken when she walked out on him—but he's no killer. Especially of Victoria. He'd never want to see her end up like she did—butchered worse than an animal." Jobeth could read Coleman like a book. So it was no use in pretending otherwise. "The way this thing is stacked against Turner, I may be the only chance he's got to prove his innocence."

And that was easier said than done, Coleman thought. Especially since he was ordered to stay on the sidelines on this one. Problem was, he always had trouble obeying orders. Especially when they stank all to hell.

CHAPTER ELEVEN

Jordan sat in the passenger seat as Trevor drove her to the Criminal Justice Center. Her car was in the shop for repairs on her brakes.

Looking at her son's profile behind the wheel of the Explorer, Jordan was reminded so much of his father, with his well-defined, handsome features, so long as she ignored the gold stud earring in Trevor's right earlobe. Next week he would be starting classes again at Portland State, majoring in Sociology or Criminal Justice. He still didn't seem to know exactly what he wanted to do with his life, and she wasn't going to put any additional pressure on him to make up his mind. He had time to sort things out. Meanwhile, why not take full advantage of the college experience?

Of course it was never quite as simple as it sounded, Jordan realized. In a way, she felt sorry for kids today. So much was expected of them, as if the entire future of the world rested on their shoulders. And if they failed, heaven help them.

Jordan could only hope that Trevor and Kendre were

adequately equipped to deal with life's challenges; and that *she* was, as their mother and only parent.

"Heard anything about the investigation into Gail and Nelson's deaths?" Trevor glanced at Jordan, breaking her musing. Jordan thought she detected a nervous twitch in his face, similar to when he was young and something troubled him.

"The police are still working on the case," she told him. "As far as I know, they don't have anyone in custody."

"Oh," he said nonchalantly, and turned the corner, staying just within the speed limit.

Jordan had sensed that something was wrong ever since the detectives had visited the other day. She had been waiting for Trevor to tell her what was on his mind. But he had kept it to himself. *Did he know something pertinent to this case?*

"What is it, Trevor?" Jordan asked, feeling a bit nervous.

"Nothing," he said, refusing to make eye contact.

Jordan narrowed her eyes. "There's obviously something weighing on your mind—so don't tell me nothing." She sighed. "If you know who might have killed those kids you have a duty to come forward, Trevor. We're talking about a double homicide here!"

Trevor pressed on the accelerator and increased his speed by ten miles an hour. "I said I don't know who killed them," he said, raising his voice sharply. "Why would I?"

Jordan asked herself the same question and didn't like the answer. "Maybe you're trying to protect someone out of a misguided sense of friendship?" she suggested.

Trevor's speed increased even more. "I ain't protecting nobody, okay!" he insisted. "Get off my case!" He took a ragged breath.

"Okay," Jordan said, surprised by his outburst and not sure what set it off. Instinctively she placed a hand on his arm, muscled beneath a black leather jacket.

"Trevor, if you want to talk to me about anything . . . remember, I'm here."

Trevor understood that, and faced her. "Yeah, Momma, I'll remember," he said.

"Good." There was some relief in Jordan's voice that the lines of communication were still open between them, whenever he was ready to talk. She decided that she had let her imagination run wild for the wrong reasons. Hadn't she?

Noting Trevor's speed, Jordan snapped at him: "Will you slow this damned car down! What are you trying to do, kill us?"

Trevor immediately let up on the accelerator. "Sorry," he muttered. "Guess I didn't realize how fast I was going."

Jordan accepted this absentmindedness, but warned him, "Well, please watch that speed limit when you're driving. I can't fix tickets, even if I wanted to." Not to mention, she thought, accidents that could be prevented.

They pulled up to the Criminal Justice Center. Jordan opened the door and said, "I'll catch a ride back with someone from the office. Don't forget to pick up Kendre and Lenora from the mall. They're supposed to be waiting for you in front of Barnes and Noble at four."

He nodded, though still seeming miles away. "No problem. I'll be there."

Jordan closed the door and watched briefly as he drove away, wondering if, in fact, there was a problem.

The arraignment was held before Judge Roy Appleton, a fifty-something rotund man with bulging, fierce brown eyes, a gray goatee, and reddish sagging face. Jordan La Fontaine and Andrew Lombard were representing the State. Representing the accused was a black attorney named Lester Eldridge. In his mid-forties, he was slight in build and just under six feet, with closely cropped curly gray hair, and a deep cleft in his chin. He wore black horn-rimmed glasses and a crumpled brown suit, which to Jordan made him look more like a history professor or mild-mannered reporter than a criminal defense attorney. But she was smart enough not to judge a book by its cover. The brother would nail her ass to the wall in this case if given half a chance, she thought. She didn't intend to let that happen.

Standing beside Eldridge was his client, Graham Turner. Jordan had seen him on television—and imagined that they may have crossed paths in the course of law enforcement—but only now got a good look at the man she hoped to convict of murder. He was quite tall, and she wondered briefly if he'd played basketball in high school. The thought quickly left her when she realized it merely conformed to stereotypes of tall black men.

Graham Turner was bald and his chiseled face was freshly shaven. He looked slightly uncomfortable in a tight blue suit. All in all, Jordan thought he was a nice-looking man and one who probably had little trouble attracting women—except perhaps the one who had left him. That one rejection had apparently thrown him over the edge.

Men like Graham Turner lived on power and control, Jordan told herself. Being a cop was not enough of a high for this man. He wanted his chosen woman also to be subject to this power trip. When she rejected it, he killed her, saying, in effect, that no one else could have her.

Graham Turner seemed to have it all going for him in looks, charm, and reputation as a good cop. But then, Jordan knew few defendants actually fit the fictional depictions of an unattractive, down-and-out killer. It was on the inside where most murderers were truly ugly.

Only then did Jordan become aware that Detective Turner was staring at her, almost through her. His dark eyes were sharp and menacing. Was he trying to intimidate her?

"Are you ready for this?" Andrew whispered to her.

Jordan squared her shoulders. "Ready as I'll ever be." She forced herself to turn to Andrew. "At least for this stage of the battle." It figured to get tougher with each step toward the trial, she mused, even if the case against Graham Turner seemed like a lock.

"Ever go up against Eldridge?" Andrew asked.

"No, but I hear that beneath that unassuming façade he fights like hell for his clients—most of whom happen to be crooked police, lawyers, and other government or public figures."

Andrew stiffened. "If it's a fight the man wants, why don't we give it to him?"

"Oh, we will," Jordan said strongly. She looked at the defense attorney, who said something to his client, and then both gave her a nasty look.

After Judge Appleton went through the obligatory preliminary comments, he read the charge of murder in the first degree to Graham Turner, and said, "Do you understand what you're being charged with, sir?"

Following a long pause, Turner replied: "I do, Your Honor."

When it came time to argue for or against bail, Jordan told the judge, "Your Honor, due to the *very* serious charge against the defendant and the brutal nature in which the victim was slain, the State asks that bail be denied."

Appleton took note of this and nodded at the defense attorney, indicating his turn.

Eldridge stepped forward, cleared his throat, and said in a strong baritone voice that belied his appearance, "Your Honor, my client is a fourteen-year veteran of the Portland Police Bureau. He has given his life to this city and has many times put his life on the line in the performance of his duties. He is completely—one hundred percent—innocent of this crime for which he's being charged, and wishes only to have his day in court." Eldridge glanced at Turner, and back to the judge. "Due to my client's high-profile visibility in the community and lack of *any* previous convictions—not even a parking ticket, Your Honor—I ask that Mr. Turner be released on his own recognizance."

Jordan had to suppress a laugh at this ridiculous attempt to paint Graham Turner as a pillar of society who was harmless and somehow deserved his freedom. She doubted that Eldridge seriously believed the judge would fall for his no-bail plea, but would gladly have settled for a reasonably low bail.

He didn't even get that.

Bail was denied and the shocked accused was escorted back to jail.

CHAPTER TWELVE

Detective O'Donnell sat in his office with Detective Paris, going over the facts of their case. So far what they knew for certain was that Gail Marshall and Nelson Neilson were shot to death with a .25-caliber handgun. The bullets were fired through a gun barrel that had six lands and grooves and a right-hand twist. The ejection and firing pin marks on the three shell casings found at the scene were a perfect match. All of which indicated to O'Donnell that they were looking for a single assailant who was seen leaving the scene of the crime in a white Ford Explorer.

The motive was something they were still working on, though they had some definite theories, and at least one serious suspect. But they needed more evidence . . . perhaps a witness who saw the actual shooting.

O'Donnell looked at the crime-scene photograph of Gail Marshall and winced. Her face had been blown off. It had once been very pretty. He had seen her high school graduation picture. But someone had ruined that pretty face all to hell. An open casket was out of the question.

Despite being on the job for almost nineteen years, it never got any easier looking at these photos, thought O'Donnell. "These kids never even had a chance," he grumbled, wishing he could meet the killer in an alley somewhere. Just the two of them. Nobody ever had to know what he'd do to the bastard. "Hell, this could have been my kid." He slid the photo across the desk to his partner.

It was not lost on O'Donnell how similar Gail Marshall was to his daughter. She was white and Gail was black, but both were around the same age, and trying to make something of themselves.

Paris grimaced as he looked at the ghastly photo, putting it alongside one of the other victim, Nelson Neilson, who had also taken a real hit. "Damned shame," Paris moaned, hating that they had to be African-American. It was just the type of thing that a brother didn't want to see happen—not when they already had more than their fair share of problems with crime in this community. Now this. "To think, in two days these two would have been married. One hell of a wedding gift someone gave them."

The detectives eyed each other miserably before O'Donnell said, "What about the fingerprints lifted from the car?"

"Just the victims' prints and some others we haven't identified." Paris riffled through the case file. "Whoever killed them doesn't have any prints on file that we've located." He lifted a sheet. "But we do have one good shoe print—a size eleven—found near the car that the snow and some mud left behind. It didn't come from either of the victims or the kids who discovered the bodies."

O'Donnell thought about that for a long moment before the trance was snapped when an officer entered the doorway. Behind him was a couple in their late thirties. Behind them was a young woman, maybe eighteen or nineteen. At first, O'Donnell didn't recognize her. The long brown hair was different, curlier than before. She looked younger too, not like the first time he saw her—when she was obviously made up to look more mature for the boy she was with.

"This is Mr. and Mrs. Stan Venus," noted the officer. "And their daughter, Tracy. She has something to say that I thought you'd wanna hear."

O'Donnell and Paris exchanged curious glances.

At the gentle urging of her parents, Tracy shyly stepped forward. With tears in her eyes, she stammered, "I-I recognized the person who was in the Explorer."

CHAPTER THIRTEEN

Jordan was putting dishes in the dishwasher when she heard the doorbell ring. She expected either Kendre or Trevor to see who it was, but when neither seemed in any hurry to do so, she left the dishwasher door open and went herself, gritting her teeth, thinking, Why do I have to do everything around here when I have one grown kid and one who thinks she's grown, living in the house?

Jordan was casually dressed in jeans and a sweatshirt, and her hair was a mess, but she wasn't expecting visitors. Whoever it was would just have to deal with it.

Jordan thought it might be Lenora. She wondered what the child's mother was up to now. Or maybe it was Trevor's on-again, off-again girlfriend, Rhonda.

Jordan opened the door to find Detectives O'Donnell and Paris standing there, sullen looks on their faces.

She didn't hide her surprise any better than the last time.

"Detectives," Jordan said in a controlled voice. "What can I do for you?"

"Is your son here, Mrs. La Fontaine?" asked O'Donnell tersely.

Jordan felt suddenly nervous. She said, "Yes, I think so."

"We need to see him, ma'am," Paris said swiftly, failing to meet Jordan's eyes.

In spite of resenting their presence, Jordan still hadn't realized the significance of this visit. They want to pump Trevor for more information on anything he might have known about the murdered coeds, she thought. After all, he was at least loosely acquainted with the victims. Strictly procedure. Nothing more. So she allowed them into the living room and said succinctly, "Wait here."

Neither detective took a seat as Jordan walked away and down the hall to Trevor's room. She knocked and opened the door. The room was cluttered with clothes, books, CDs, and sports equipment. Jordan had decided when Trevor moved back home that she would no longer clean up after him as though he were a child. If he wanted to live in a pigpen, so be it.

Trevor was sitting on the bed, talking on his cell phone. He seemed clearly agitated when he looked up at Jordan. "Detectives are here to see you," she told him as innocuously as possible. Even then, Jordan's heart was beating like a drum.

Trevor made a face, told the person on the line that he would call back, and hung up.

"What the hell do they want now?" grumbled Trevor.

"I have no idea. Just come out and talk to them." Jordan realized that she had inadvertently gripped the doorknob so tightly that her knuckles hurt.

She watched Trevor stand, looking tense in a black

81

fleece pullover and khaki gabardine trousers, and waited for him to lead the way.

As soon as Trevor entered the living room, Jordan saw the detectives surround him in a menacing way, and a sinking feeling came to her stomach.

"Trevor La Fontaine," Paris said in a formal tone of voice, "you're under arrest for the murder of Nelson Neilson and Gail Marshall—"

"What—!" The word screeched from Jordan's mouth.

Trevor's face contorted with dismay. "Is this some kind of joke?"

"Do you see me laughing?" Paris shot him a cold look.

"I didn't kill anyone, man!" spat Trevor, his lips trembling. He looked to Jordan to intervene.

"Wait just a minute here," Jordan demanded, panicked.

O'Donnell ignored her as he roughly twisted Trevor's arm behind him and slapped a handcuff around first one wrist, then the other. "You have the right to remain silent. . . ." O'Donnell began.

By now, Kendre, hearing the ruckus, had stormed down the stairs. "What are they doing to him, Mom?" Terror was written all over her face.

"Anything you say can and will be used against you. . . ." continued O'Donnell.

Jordan felt trapped and helpless in her own home, with both her children caught in the crossfire. "Stop it!" she insisted to the detectives, who were unnecessarily rough with Trevor, who was *not* resisting them. She felt she had to do something.

"I'm an assistant district attorney for the Multnomah County D.A.'s office," Jordan said. "There's obviously been a big mistake here—"

"We know who you are," O'Donnell cut her off snidely. "And there is no mistake." He glared at Jordan disrespectfully. "My advice to you is to stay out of it—unless you want to be charged with obstruction of justice,

Counselor." He gave Kendre a hard look as if to reiterate the point. "Same goes for you."

Jordan put an arm around Kendre to prevent her from attacking the detectives to protect her brother.

Trevor was shepherded out of the house and into a police car in spite of his protestations, while Jordan was forced to stand by powerlessly, stunned by the entire thing.

"Can't you do something, Mom?" Kendre cried, her body trembling. "Trevor didn't do anything."

Jordan, who hadn't had a chance yet to think clearly, knew she had to keep from falling apart. Trevor needed her now more than ever.

"Yes, I know, honey." Jordan hugged Kendre. "It's going to be all right." She could only hope.

Jordan ran to the phone to call the only attorney she could imagine calling in this situation.

"Simon, it's me," she said on an erratic breath. "I need your help."

Jordan had been served a search warrant and was once again forced to watch while police went through the house, yard, and garbage looking for any evidence that could be used against her son. She knew the routine well, having spearheaded the very same thing against countless others. Now the shoe was on the other foot, and Jordan had a whole new appreciation for the frustration and resentment others must have felt when facing the same humiliation and utter helplessness.

Among other things, the police seized clothing from Trevor's room, a .25-caliber gun Jordan kept in her closet for protection, and Trevor's Explorer.

After changing into a sweater and some designer jeans, Jordan agreed to meet Simon at the police station where Trevor was being booked. There she dodged questions from an overzealous press who had already gotten wind that an assistant district attorney's son was being arrested for murder.

"I got here as fast as I could," Simon said, looking a bit disheveled but still handsome in a Barberini blue suit.

"This is crazy," Jordan said. "Trevor didn't do what they say he did—" She could not even bring herself to say the word murder. He was her son. She had not given birth to and raised a cold-blooded murderer.

"Don't worry." Simon looked at her in a way that made Jordan take comfort in his words; then he took her hand. "We'll get through this together."

At that point, Jordan only wanted to get through it period.

When they were allowed to see Trevor, he had been put in the standard bright orange jail attire. He looked scared to death and embarrassed to be in such a position—but still like an innocent man, Jordan told herself. The three of them were sitting at a table in a small conference room where attorneys and their clients often conferred.

"I'm going to do the best I can to get you out of this predicament, Trevor," Simon said in a fatherly tone. "But you've got to help me. I need to know everything you know about what happened to Gail Marshall and Nelson Neilson. And I mean everything."

Trevor lowered his head, almost in shame, then lifted it to look desperately into Jordan's eyes. She made herself smile at him the way she had when he'd gotten into trouble when he was a little boy. Only she knew the stakes were far higher now.

Something had told her all along that Trevor had been holding back. But why? And for whom?

"You were there?" It suddenly dawned on Jordan. "Where the killings took place?"

Trevor nodded slowly. "Yeah. I needed to be by myself

84

for a while," he said, his hands pressed together on the table as if in prayer. "I drove to Devil's Edge just to chill, to think about things. . . ." He looked across the table at Simon, then Jordan. "That's when I saw the car and the shattered window. I parked next to it and took a look." He sighed, closing his eyes and then opening them. "They were there in the backseat. I didn't know if they were dead or alive. I just wanted to help them, you know?"

Jordan saw the sincerity, desperation, and regret in his eyes.

"What happened next?" Simon asked patiently.

"I opened the door and felt both of them." Trevor frowned. "I got blood on my clothes. I knew they were dead and—I guess I just freaked, man." He nervously ran a hand across his dreadlocks.

"What did you do then, Trevor?" Simon asked.

Trevor licked his lips. "I got in my car and left."

Simon furrowed his brow. "Why didn't you call the police?"

"And tell them what?" Trevor's eyes widened skeptically. "That I just found two people I know dead—and I just happened to have their blood all over me? I'm not crazy, man. What do you think they would have thought?"

"I know what they're thinking now," Simon responded cynically. "That you're guilty as hell of carrying out two murders."

"Why didn't you come to me, Trevor?" Jordan asked with an angry and hurt expression. She'd always tried to make herself accessible to her kids no matter what they were going through, but she'd obviously failed Trevor when he needed her guidance and support most.

"I didn't want to get you involved," he responded. "I figured someone else would come and find them sooner or later." He turned away. "But a car came just as I was leaving. They saw me."

"That was one hell of a stupid thing you did, Trevor." Simon raised his voice. "Didn't your parents teach you that you don't run away from the scene of a damned crime if you're innocent?" He narrowed his eyes at Trevor. "You *are* innocent, aren't you?"

"Simon!" Jordan glared at him. "Can't you see he's telling the truth? Trevor is not a killer!"

"I'm sorry, Jordan," Simon said without regret, "but I have to hear him say it." He turned to Trevor. "Well . . . let's hear it. Are you innocent?"

After taking a deep breath, Trevor said, "Yes, I'm innocent. I didn't kill them!"

Jordan breathed a sigh of relief in hearing the words, even if she knew in her heart that Trevor would not have committed such an act. She and Eric did not raise kids who didn't know right from wrong or value human life.

"Then there must be something else going on here," insisted Simon, leaning forward. "What is it, Trevor? What aren't you telling us?"

Trevor stood up and turned his back to them, walking away from the table, ruminating, as Jordan tensed.

When he turned around, Trevor said weakly, "We were all at a party that night. I got into a scuffle with Nelson. After it was broken up, I said something to him like, 'You're dead, man.'" Trevor came up to where Jordan was sitting and said shakily, as if she was the one he needed to convince, "I didn't mean it literally, Momma."

You're dead, man! The chilling words rang in Jordan's head, causing it to pound. Others had no doubt heard the not so veiled threat that turned out to be prophetic—and could now use the words against Trevor in a court of law.

Admittedly Jordan the prosecutor would have had a hard time buying Trevor's story. After all, it was her job to trip up suspects and take everything they gave her in trying to convict. But for Jordan the mother, it was an entirely different matter. She had no doubt Trevor was telling the truth, and even understood why he had held back in coming forward. But she feared that unless the real killer was found, her son had dug a hole so deep for himself that even Simon might not be able to get him out of it.

CHAPTER FOURTEEN

On the final day of the year, the tavern in West Sacramento, California, stayed open until the wee hours of the morning. Bartender and co-owner Veronica Sanchez waited until the last customer left before closing. As usual she counted up the proceeds for the night, locked them in the safe, and called the security company to tell them she was leaving.

Veronica, a Hispanic single mother of three small children, was pushing forty, but took good care of herself and could have easily passed for thirty. Her long, silky black hair added to her appeal, and she prided herself in the ability to wear it in different but equally captivating ways. This late night she had it in a loose chignon high atop her head.

Veronica took her job seriously. Yes, she flirted a bit with the men who frequented the tavern, but she always knew where to draw the line. And most of them knew when they were too close to stepping over it.

Of course, you always got the newcomers who thought they could get into your pants by buying you one drink or telling you how pretty you were. Just like the young man who had been there tonight. He had said he was from Oregon, just passing through. He didn't say if he was coming from Oregon or running from Oregon. She didn't ask. Ask them few questions, they tell you few lies.

He was cute, Veronica thought, but not that cute.

Her only real passion in life was her kids. Their dad turned out to be a real jerk, but at least he'd provided her with two beautiful daughters and one handsome son. As soon as she put away a bit more money, Veronica planned to sell her interest in the business and go back to the Midwest, where she was raised.

After locking up, Veronica headed for the brightly lit parking lot, where there was only one other vehicle beside her white Toyota. A dark green or blue van was several spots away from her car. The lights were off and no noise was coming from it. Her best guess was that its occupant was probably sleeping it off inside after one drink too many. Probably a wise move, she thought, even if it was way too cold to be sleeping in a van with no heat on. That was their problem, she thought, eager to get home to her little ones.

Veronica got in her car and locked the door. After putting on her seatbelt, she put the key in the ignition and started the engine. She was suddenly startled by a knock on the driver's side window.

It was the cute young man from the tavern. A cigarette dangled from his mouth, smoke filtering into the air. He gave Veronica an easy smile and indicated for her to roll the window down. Her first thought was: no way. But there was something about him that made her feel he was harmless. Maybe it was the honesty in his gray eyes. Or the sexiness of his half grin. That was probably his van over there, she speculated. Maybe he ran out of gas.

Veronica rolled the window down a quarter of the way, just to be on the safe side, smiled at him, and said cheerfully: "Haven't you had enough New Year's celebrating for one night?"

"Not quite," he responded. "Only need one more thing to really ring in the New Year in grand style."

Veronica batted her big, brown eyes uneasily. "And what, I'm almost afraid to ask, might that be?"

He gave a coarse laugh and his features took on an ominous look. "In this case, action definitely speaks louder than words." He pointed a gun in her face.

At first Veronica thought it was some kind of cruel joke. Surely he wouldn't actually shoot her. On the first day of the New Year. What for? If it was money he wanted, it certainly wasn't worth dying for. She wondered briefly if he planned to rape her, sending waves of fear throughout her body.

"Look, just tell me what you want—" Veronica's voice faltered and she suddenly could barely think straight.

He flashed her a crooked smile. "Yeah, I'll tell you what I want. I want your life, bitch!"

Veronica thought about her children. Her biggest regret was that she would not even have the chance to say good-bye.

Then it was too late. The man pulled the trigger. The bullet hit her right between the eyes. She went into darkness—but not death—instantly. Death did not come until the second shot exploded into her chest.

Both shots rang into the night like firecrackers. Much like the gunshots that had been fired into the air by New Year's Eve revelers. No doubt anyone who heard the two shots going into Veronica Sanchez's body assumed they were merely part of the celebration.

Which was precisely what the killer had banked on.

He took one more drag on the cigarette and flung it into some nearby bushes.

Time to head back home, he thought. He had a long drive ahead of him.

By the time Veronica Sanchez's remains were discovered later that morning, her killer would be long gone.

Without knowing it, Sacramento and Portland had a common and deadly enemy.

CHAPTER FIFTEEN

Jordan allowed Simon to talk her into having a drink at The Ranch after leaving Trevor in custody. His arraignment wouldn't come until tomorrow and, given the serious nature of the charges he faced, there was little chance he would get bail.

Jordan doubted that her reputation as an honest A.D.A. or influence in the D.A.'s office would make any difference. Not in a case involving a double homicide. Nor was she sure she would want it to. If Trevor was to have his name cleared, there could not be even a hint of collusion or compromise on her part.

She looked across the table at Simon, who was holding a glass of merlot close to his lips, apparently absorbed in thought. He had made no attempt to turn what was supposed to be a strategy session into a sexual encounter. Instead, he had handled this in a strictly professional manner, as though his own life was on the line. Which was more than Jordan could say for herself. Her emotions had swung between needing Simon to represent her son and needing him for herself.

"I shouldn't have gotten you involved in this, Simon," Jordan said with a rush of guilt.

Simon rolled his eyes dismissively. "Nonsense," he insisted smoothly. "You did the right thing calling me. With any luck, we can get this whole mess straightened out without losing more than a few nights of sleep."

"What if we can't?" she asked, and sipped her wine. "What if Trevor is bound over for trial?"

Simon's brow creased then smoothed. "Should it come to that," he said thoughtfully, "then I'll give him the best damned defense money can't buy—the defense of someone whose mother I care a great deal for."

Jordan felt the intensity of Simon's soulful brown-gray eyes and the sincerity of his deep voice. It was hard to believe this was the same man who would not get within two feet of her during the Raymond Allen Wilson trial, as if she had a disease.

Of course, he had gotten a lot closer than that since then.

She turned her thoughts back to the subject at hand. "I don't want any special favors, Simon," she began deliberately. "I have some money saved up." About twenty thousand that was supposed to go towards Kendre's college. "I can pay you your going rate—"

Simon tossed aside the suggestion with the flick of his bald head. "I don't need or want your money," he asserted. "I want to help Trevor." His gaze lowered, then lifted, meeting Jordan's eyes solidly. "Remember, Eric was my partner *and* friend. I owe it to him to look after the family he left behind. That includes Trevor."

Jordan felt grateful for his support more than she could say. Still, she wondered if what happened between them had been a mistake. Had Simon slept with her because he somehow felt responsible for her—including her physical needs?

Or was it because he truly wanted her?

Simon seemed to be reading her thoughts like a book. He reached out and took hold of Jordan's hands. "But I also want to be there for you—the gorgeous woman I hope to have a future with. . . ."

Right now that future was the last thing on Jordan's mind. She would do well just to survive the latest crisis to hit her life like a Mack truck.

"You mean a lot to me too, Simon," she told him sincerely, wrapping her hands around his long fingers. It frightened her just how many emotions he had managed to stir in her. "But now is certainly not the time to talk about *our* future." She took a long, thoughtful breath and slowly slid her hand from his. "Under the circumstances, I don't think it would be fair to either of us."

Simon seemed to blink back his displeasure. He responded in a strained voice, "Yeah, I guess you're right." He finished his wine and put on a professional face. "So why don't we talk strategy on Trevor's predicament? Then you can tell me about the case you're working on."

When Jordan got home, Kendre came running down the stairs—or stomping down was more like it. Her eyes were red from crying.

"Where have you been?" she demanded, a hand against her hip. "I've been going crazy wondering what's happening with Trevor. I hope they realized it was a mistake to arrest him for something he didn't do. . . ."

Jordan looked at her daughter with woeful eyes, realizing that Kendre really didn't understand anything about the law. At least when it applied to a member of her own family.

She approached Kendre, feeling a slight buzz from the wine. "I'm sorry, honey. I should have called. I was with Simon." Saying this, she realized how it must have sounded and quickly added, "He's trying to arrange to have Trevor released until—"

Kendre's brief look of hope turned dour when the word *until* registered in her mind. "Why are they saying Trevor's a killer?" she sobbed. "Why didn't you tell them they had the wrong man, Mom?"

"It's not that simple," Jordan said, but knew it was falling on deaf ears.

"*Dad* would have done something," Kendre spat. "*He* wouldn't have let them just take Trevor away like that for the whole world to see!"

Jordan tried not to let the hurt show. Kendre had always had an exaggerated sense of her father's abilities. Jordan had gone along with it because it was what Eric wanted—to be all the world, all the universe— someone who could do no wrong in the eyes of his little girl.

Now Jordan questioned the wisdom of creating this flawless image of a man that she could not hope to compete with in the land of the living.

"Maybe you're right," she said. "Maybe your father would have known how to handle this situation. I can only do what I'm capable of. And right now I think I could use all the support I can get." She looked at Kendre pleadingly. "We both could."

Kendre sniffled, held her ground, and then, without warning, ran and hugged Jordan for dear life. Jordan pushed some of her daughter's braids from her face, kissed her smooth brow, and murmured weakly, "We'll get through this, sweetheart—somehow."

Jordan prayed that the truth would come out and Trevor would be exonerated before the damage done to her family became more than any of them could handle.

CHAPTER SIXTEEN

He waited for her on the steps of the Criminal Justice Center. At eight-thirty A.M., she showed up. Jordan La Fontaine was as striking up close, he thought, as she was ferocious in the courtroom. She was wearing a dark blue suit that seemed tailor-made for her streamlined figure, along with a gray blouse and navy pumps. And although he wasn't usually impressed with these braided hairstyles that were in vogue today, the long braids did look nice on the assistant district attorney. He couldn't help but think that if they ever made a movie about *this* prosecutor, she could definitely play herself.

Those thoughts were quickly cast aside as Jordan moved up to the step where Harry Coleman stood on one foot, the other firmly planted on the step above.

"Ms. La Fontaine?" he said. She looked at him the way one might an obstacle that was standing in her way. "Detective Harry Coleman."

She seemed to be in a hurry, but said politely, "What can I do for you, Detective?"

"I need to talk to you about Graham Turner." Coleman placed both feet on the same step. "He's my partner."

Jordan regarded the detective with a strange mixture of curiosity and caution. "Look, Detective Coleman, if you have something pertaining to the case—"

"Nothing but my gut feelings," Coleman said shrewdly. "Turner didn't kill his ex-wife. Someone set him up."

Jordan flapped her eyes in annoyance. "I know how you must feel, Detective," she said as if she actually expected him to believe that, "but this case was given to us by *your* department. If you have a beef regarding it, I suggest you take it up with them."

He stepped into her path before she could move, and said not too kindly, "I'd rather take it up with you."

Jordan's head snapped back. "I beg your pardon?"

"Ms. La Fontaine, things aren't always what they seem, no matter how strong the evidence. You should know that as well as anyone."

She gave him a wary look. "What's that supposed to mean?"

"Well, it's like this . . . It means I know your son is being investigated for the murder of those two college kids," he said. "But something tells me you don't think he's guilty . . . the hell with whatever kind of *solid* case they've got against him. Am I right?"

Jordan's nostrils flared and she squared her shoulders. "The two cases are entirely different."

"Are they?" Coleman scratched his chin, aware that he was skating on thin ice in practically holding an A.D.A. prisoner. But it was a chance he was willing to take, under the circumstances. "The way I see it, Counselor, these cases are joined at the hip. And you're caught right in the middle."

He stepped aside. She gave him a rude look and was fast on her way.

Coleman watched as Jordan La Fontaine entered the building, certain that he had gotten to her.

But right now, Coleman mused, Turner was still a long ways from becoming a free and innocent man.

Coleman had the feeling that there was not much time to swing the tide in his favor, before Turner had the book thrown at him with no way out.

"Use your head, Turner," Coleman urged his partner. "Your life may depend on it. Can you think of anyone who might've wanted to frame you for Victoria's murder?"

They were in an interrogation room that both had been in many times before. Only this time it was Turner in the hot seat rather than some lowlife. And it was getting hotter by the moment.

"You tell me," said Turner cynically, rubbing his wrists where the handcuffs had been. "We're partners, remember? If someone *we* busted wanted to set me up by killing Victoria, why wouldn't they also do Jobeth and try and make *you* the fall guy?"

Point well taken, thought Coleman. A worse thought was if some asshole had murdered Jobeth *and* the kids. Could he have lived with that? Would he have even cared what happened to him?

He wondered if this was basically the way Turner felt, having lost Victoria forever, ending any chance they had to get back together—even if that chance had been slim to none.

"Maybe it wasn't someone from the job," Coleman suggested. "Maybe it was personal?"

Turner leaned back in his chair, his face showing the strain. "Man, I loved her," he muttered. "Maybe I didn't deserve her. But she sure as hell didn't deserve *this*— you know what I'm saying?"

"Someone thought she did," Coleman said. "The only

question is was it someone who hated *you*, or someone who hated *her?*"

"Maybe it was someone who hated both of us." Turner slumped in his seat. "But I don't know who, though I've been wracking my brain. Victoria and I didn't exactly hang out in the same circles—not anymore." He sucked in a deep breath, frowning. "It just doesn't make any damned sense why someone would want to do that to her. . . ."

"Tell me about the phone call again." Coleman leaned on the table, hating to see his buddy going through this hell.

Turner rubbed his head. "Like I said, I got a call telling me Victoria needed to see me." His eyes shifted reflectively. "So I went over there—"

"You didn't recognize the voice?"

"No. Almost sounded like it was coming from a tunnel."

"Hmm," mused Coleman. "But definitely a male?"

Turner considered this, and said, "I don't know, man. Could have been a female. Too damned hard to tell. At the time I just wanted to get over there, thinking Victoria might be in trouble."

"Did you have reason to believe that?" Coleman looked at him through narrow eyes.

"Not really. Just a gut feeling. The call was eerie. On top of that, Victoria wasn't very interested in seeing me much since the divorce."

Coleman took this in. "And you think Victoria was already dead when you got there?"

Turner paused. "Yeah, man. She was definitely dead."

"And that's when you were hit from behind?"

He nodded. "When I came to, the cops were all over my black ass like ants on a piece of rotten meat."

Coleman watched him closely, for but a moment thinking more like someone who was questioning a suspect rather than his partner. Still, he knew he had to press on. "And that's when they found the knife in your hands—*your* knife . . . ?"

There was a slow, reluctant movement of Turner's head in acknowledgment. "I told you, man, the knife was lost—or stolen—a few months ago. I don't know where the hell it came from, but it *didn't* come from me."

Then it could only have come from the person who found it or the one who stole it, Coleman decided. But he knew proving that would be a whole different matter.

CHAPTER SEVENTEEN

After leaving Detective Coleman on the steps of the Criminal Justice Center, Jordan had gone in, shaken from his callousness and boldness. Did he really expect to pressure her into believing Graham Turner was not guilty based on his gut feelings and, worse, relating it to the case against Trevor? Who the hell did Coleman think he was? Did he know something that she didn't?

The conflicting thoughts were still on Jordan's mind as she showed up at the D.A.'s office. He was on the phone, but waved her in as though she were a long-lost friend.

"Tell him we'll reduce the charges to second-degree murder," barked Bombeck. "Take it or leave it."

He slammed the phone down and Jordan thought his face showed the stress and strain of being the district attorney, whose decisions could affect so many lives. But right now there were only two lives Jordan was most concerned about—her own and her son's.

She walked up to the side of the desk, almost as if she were about to attack Bombeck, and demanded, "How long have you known that my son was under investigation for murder?"

Bombeck's face took on a crimson glow and he removed his glasses, shifting his eyes downward. "Not until they were ready to arrest him," he said tonelessly. He made himself look up. "I'm sorry, Jordan, really I am. But there was nothing I could do."

What did she expect him to do? Jordan asked herself. Warn her? Would she have wanted that had it been anyone but a member of her own family?

But it *was* a member of my own family! she thought. Bombeck at least could have been upfront with her once he knew her son was about to be arrested. He owed her that courtesy. She hardly would have aided and abetted in Trevor's flight from justice. Especially when he was innocent.

"He didn't do it, Wilson!" Jordan said with conviction and, realizing how that must have sounded, thought, Isn't that what every mother says whose child is accused of murder? In her role as a prosecutor she'd heard it all. Now the shoe was on the other foot, so to speak, and Jordan had to deal with the fact that it was Trevor being targeted as a killer.

Bombeck stared at her. "Why don't you have a seat, Jordan," he said. "Please."

Jordan became aware that she was standing over the D.A. in what could be interpreted as a threatening posture, and backed off. She sank into one of the leather chairs in front of his desk. She wanted to speak, but her tongue seemed stuck to the roof of her mouth.

Bombeck, his hands clasped, drew a breath, and said, "I'm sure you believe in your son, and I'm sure it's with good reason. But I have to tell you, Jordan, there's enough circumstantial evidence against him to put it before a grand jury."

Jordan suddenly felt sick to her stomach. She knew

that it only took a minimal amount of evidence for a grand jury to indict. The evidence would have to be much stronger to get a conviction, but an indictment would be akin to guilty in the press and difficult to live down, even if Trevor was eventually exonerated.

"I've assigned Jerrod Wresler to the case," Bombeck said flatly, "assuming the grand jury returns an indictment."

What a damned surprise, Jordan thought sarcastically, even if it did give her a bit of a start. She was barely able to restrain her emotions, feeling as if the people she worked with were ganging up on her. Hell, she wouldn't be at all surprised if Wresler had jumped at the opportunity to prosecute her son—considering the stakes for both himself and her. And those stakes were getting greater by the day.

Bombeck's brows twitched as he said, "This isn't going to be easy for any of us, Jordan. I hope to hell your son—Trevor—is exonerated." He took a long pause. "Until then, we have to play this by the book."

He waited for her to respond. Finally, Jordan opened her mouth and said what she knew in her heart was right: "I wouldn't expect it to be any other way." Her eyes widened when she added purposefully, "In the meantime, there's a killer running loose out there somewhere."

Bombeck considered this for a moment. Then he asked, "Are you going to be all right?"

Do you really care? Jordan eyed him with suspicion. "I'll be fine," she said. As long as Trevor was accused of a double homicide, she was never going to be all right.

Putting on his glasses, Bombeck surveyed Jordan with some misgiving. "I'd understand if you want to give the Turner case to someone else, Jordan. I mean, just until this thing with Trevor is resolved one way or the other."

"I said I was okay." Jordan's voice rose. She was not about to lose her case to another ambitious A.D.A. That would be playing right into Jerrod Wresler's hands, and it would give Bombeck a perfect excuse for passing her over *again* for a long overdue promotion. "My work is very important to me, Wilson. You know that," she told him evenly. "Especially now that Eric is gone." She sighed. "I can handle the case *and* my personal life, as I always have."

And what choice did she have? Jordan couldn't throw away everything she had worked for. Not now. Nor could she let her son be thrown to the wolves—or one wolf in particular. At least not without letting the prosecutor know he could expect one hell of a fight from the defense. And all-out support from Trevor's mother.

CHAPTER EIGHTEEN

Jerrod Anthony Wresler had always gone after things that were just out of his reach. Like the time when he was five years old and his mother told him to stay out of the cookie jar. Then, as if to torture him, she would put it on the shelf just beyond where his skinny outstretched arm was capable of reaching. Eventually he figured out what he needed to do to get what he wanted. In this case, it was using a chair.

Ever since that time, Jerrod Wresler had found ways—some more creative than others—to get exactly what he wanted. That included all four of the women in his Yale Law School class. It had been easier than he thought it would be. His natural good looks and charm had been sufficient enough for him to win even the most stubborn girl over.

When that failed, there was always blackmail. He wasn't above using what information he had to manipulate someone into seeing things his way, or at least going along for the ride until he decided it was time to end.

Wresler's latest challenges were in the district attorney's office. First, there was the matter of getting the promotion that was rightfully his. He would be damned if he'd just stand by and watch Wilson Bombeck give the Bureau Chief job to Jordan La Fontaine. The fact that she had been on the job one year longer than Wresler didn't matter to him. Nor did it matter that she was probably every bit as good as he was in the courtroom, and had her own reasons for wanting to get ahead.

What did matter to Wresler was that he had worked his ass off and kissed too many asses, positioning himself for the rise from law clerk to A.D.A. to Homicide Division Bureau Chief to Superior Court judge. Hell, maybe he'd even try for the Governorship of Oregon someday—if not the President of this whole damned country.

And nothing was going to stand in his way. Not if Wresler could help it. And he could help it, now that he'd been given one plum of a case if he ever saw one.

As soon as he'd heard that Jordan La Fontaine's son of all people was the chief suspect in a double murder, Wresler had kept his eyes on the case. Could this be the one big break he needed to distance himself from her?

When it became evident that an arrest was imminent, Wresler had volunteered to take on the case, aware that most of the prosecutors in the office had too much respect for La Fontaine to want to go after her kid. Not to mention they were uneasy when it came to sensitive race issues in this politically correct atmosphere. A lifelong bachelor with no kids, and feeling no particular reason to give minorities preferential treatment, Jerrod Wresler had no such weakness or loyalties. He fully intended to nail Trevor La Fontaine's ass to the proverbial wall, and his mother as well.

When I'm through, there will be no one standing in my way for the grand prize, mused Wresler, a big smile on his face.

* * *

No sooner had Jordan left Wilson and taken the elevator down one floor to her own office than she spotted Jerrod Wresler in the hall. He was talking to Amanda Clinksdale, who seemed to be hanging on his every word. They stopped talking when they saw her, as if they were keeping some dirty secret.

Amanda seemed to be searching for the right words when she said, frowning, "I'm sorry about your son, Jordan—"

"Don't be," Jordan said proudly, and sneered at Wresler. "Trevor was just at the wrong place at the wrong time. He didn't kill anyone."

Amanda looked obliquely at Wresler, who peered at Jordan. He said confidently, "I wouldn't be too sure of that, Jordan, with all due respect. We've got a pretty strong case against your son . . . and I'm sorry to have to say that—"

"Like hell you are!" Jordan's spine stiffened. She came back to his words "*we've* got a pretty strong case." Did that mean Amanda was assisting him? Then she looked at Amanda, whose wavering eyes gave her away.

"Oh for heaven's sake, don't look at me that way, Jordan," Amanda said guiltily. "I'm only doing what I'm paid to do."

"Aren't we all?" Jordan glared at her, then glared at Wresler. "I don't care what type of case you think you've got, Jerrod," she told him. "You—both of you—are going after the wrong man!"

Wresler stood his ground, regarding Jordan icily. "I don't think you're in any position to be objective on this one, Jordan."

"And you are?"

He twisted his lips. "This isn't anything personal."

"Yeah, right." Jordan's blood pressure rose to the boiling point, even though she knew that this was just as much about the way the system worked as the parties involved. "Of course it's personal. You know it. I know it." She sucked in a breath and slowly exhaled. "Just don't expect me to roll over and play dead," she warned. "It's not going to happen."

CHAPTER NINETEEN

Accompanied by two officers, Jordan and Andrew went over the murder scene, hoping to uncover anything that might have been missed earlier relative to the case against Graham Turner. Victoria Turner lived in a modest but comfortable single-story townhouse in Northeast Portland. Each room had a combination of French and contemporary furnishings, plants that were fading fast, and framed Impressionist art prints.

Jordan found herself admiring this woman whom she only knew posthumously. Victoria Turner seemed to have a true gift for decor. In fact, Victoria had been supporting herself largely from her work as an interior designer. Court records she'd filed against her husband showed that alimony had been infrequent, if not nonexistent. When it came at all, it usually fell short of the court mandate.

Jordan believed this was yet another means by which Turner was able to exercise control over his ex-wife. Did Victoria have any clue when she came home that night that he would be waiting for her? Had she even had time to react before he slit her throat? At least the poor woman had died well before Turner really went to work on her face and body, if the medical examiner was to be believed. Jordan shivered at the thought.

"This is where it happened," Andrew said, wrinkling his nose. They were in the master bedroom. The brass bed was still outlined where the mutilated body had been soaked in its own blood. "My guess is that Turner was waiting for her in the closet."

Jordan slid open the door and looked in at the variety of colorful dresses, suits, blouses, and pants lining the closet—appearing as lifeless as the one who had owned them. She tried to imagine what it must have been like to be brutally assaulted and murdered by a person you once loved.

The thought caused Jordan to shudder, and she slammed the door shut as if that alone would shut out the demons.

"Turner was hiding over here when the police arrived." Andrew stood on the side of the bed that was obscured from view from almost anywhere in the room except when you were right upon it. "Of course, he's claiming he was hit from behind and left here to be found." Andrew groaned sardonically and shook his head. "Gimme a break. The man showed no signs of a concussion or even a bump on the head. I'd say he concocted that tale as a way to save his ass when caught in the act."

"I agree," said Jordan, not believing one word of Graham Turner's so-called defense. She could not begin to compare his case with that of Trevor's. Guilt was written all over Turner's face and the evidence backed it up, as well as the motive; whereas Trevor used poor

111

judgment and choice of words, and was now paying the price. But this did not make him guilty of murder, she thought.

Jordan peeked out the mini blinds. She saw the courtyard and some children at play, probably unaware of how close the aura and smell of death were. By chance, Jordan looked up at a window directly across the courtyard. She could see an elderly African-American woman standing there, seemingly staring right at her. Then she disappeared from view, as if it had been Jordan's imagination. Or because she had something better to do.

Could the woman have seen something that night? Jordan wondered. As far as she knew, the woman wasn't on their list of witnesses. The blinds had been drawn when the police arrived, meaning they probably were when the killing took place—preventing potential witnesses from seeing inside.

"Anything interesting out there?" Andrew asked.

Jordan broke away from the window. "Has anyone talked to the old woman who lives in the townhouse right across the courtyard?"

Andrew glanced out the window and said, "You mean Mrs. Sanderson?" Jordan half nodded. "I'm afraid she can't help us," he said glumly. "Suffers from Alzheimer's and doesn't have a clue about what goes on in her own house, let alone her neighbors'. Her husband takes care of her. Looks like he didn't see anything either."

"Too bad," muttered Jordan regretfully. "Their unit probably has the best view of this room, if only the blinds had been open that night."

"Forget it," Andrew advised. "Turner may be a psychopathic murderer, but he's not stupid. Don't forget, he's a cop. And cops know how important eyewitnesses can be to a crime, especially ones they commit."

Jordan looked at herself in the mirror over the dresser. Her face looked drawn and her eyes were a bit bloodshot from lack of sleep, a recurring problem in her life of late. When sleep did come, it was often accompanied by nightmares.

"Someone reported the crime," Jordan noted to Andrew, watching his reflection in the mirror. "Maybe it was someone who had firsthand knowledge of the murder . . . like a witness."

Andrew knocked on the wall. It made a hollow sound. "These walls are like papier-mâché," he said. "Any commotion could probably wake up the dead or the living anywhere on this block. And it still wouldn't mean they saw a damned thing or even know what they thought they heard. I'm not sure if the caller was just a crank or really knows something—"

Jordan put any further debate on hold as she realized it was almost three o'clock. Kendre had a dental appointment at 3:45.

She pulled alongside the curb and watched as kids streamed from Beaumont Middle School and spread out in different directions in an almost mechanical fashion—seemingly oblivious to the chilly January temperatures. Some got on school buses, others in cars, and others walked home. Jordan noticed one group of girls leaving the school. Kendre and Lenora were among them. When the group reached the sidewalk, Kendre spotted the car and said something to Lenora. Lenora responded, and Kendre separated from the girls. She was wearing a black denim jacket and a pair of embroidered blue jeans. The latter fit a bit too snugly, Jordan decided, while wondering if Kendre had gained weight recently. Her daughter had been blessed with a naturally good metabolism, which translated into a slender physique. Still, there was a window where a few pounds could come or go.

"Hey, Mom," Kendre mumbled dispiritedly as she hopped in the front seat, throwing her books in the back.

Jordan smiled at her, but Kendre had turned to wave to her friends.

"How was school?" Jordan asked as she pulled away from the curb.

Kendre hunched her shoulders but said nothing.

"Does that mean good or bad?" Jordan looked at her.

"It means neither, okay?" Kendre tossed her braids across her left shoulder and stared moodily out the window.

It had been like this ever since Trevor was arrested, Jordan thought. Kendre had been depressed, sullen, and somehow she blamed Jordan for not being able to do more to help him. Or was it for just being a lousy mom? She hadn't been able to figure that one out yet.

The more Jordan tried to reach out to her, the more Kendre withdrew. Jordan hid her own pain in this inability to connect with her daughter. They needed each other now more than ever, yet seemed as far apart as the earth and moon. But they would overcome this latest strain in their relationship and become mother, daughter, and friends again. Having Trevor out of jail and getting his life back to normal would go a long way in the healing process for all three of them, Jordan told herself hopefully.

"I hate going to the dentist," Kendre complained, folding her arms for effect.

"You and everyone else." Jordan glanced at her daughter. Not even her trademark sneer could take away from the beautiful teeth she had. The dentist made sure they stayed that way.

114

They drove in silence for a few minutes when Kendre dropped a bombshell of sorts on Jordan.

"I'm having my period," she said without looking at Jordan.

That explained the extra weight and the *extra* lousy attitude, thought Jordan. "For how long?"

"Six months," Kendre answered nonchalantly.

This caused Jordan to raise a brow. "Why didn't you tell me?" She would have liked to know that her only daughter was having her menstrual cycle.

"It was no big deal," moaned Kendre on a sigh. "Lenora got hers when she was twelve."

"No cramps?" Jordan asked.

Kendre shook her head.

Count your blessings, Jordan thought, pleased. One month at a time.

Jordan pulled into the dentist's parking lot thinking that she had been expecting the news Kendre finally decided to share with her sooner or later. She had even discussed with her daughter tampons and instructions on how to use them.

Now that Kendre had been introduced to womanhood, Jordan wondered how long it would be before she began to experiment with sex, assuming she hadn't already. The thought concerned Jordan. The last thing she wanted or needed was for Kendre to become sexually active at this stage of her young life. She'd seen too many girls' lives ruined as a result.

I won't let that happen to her, Jordan thought resolutely. Kendre may think she knows it all, but that won't stop me from doing whatever I need to do in her best interests.

While waiting in the dentist's reception room, Kendre said quietly, "Everybody thinks he's guilty."

"What?" Jordan's voice cracked, causing an elderly couple and a young woman to look. She decided to ignore them. In a hushed voice she asked Kendre, "Who?"

"All the kids at school." Kendre's face dropped and she said dismally, "They think Trevor murdered those two . . ."

CHAPTER TWENTY

The crime scene tape was still there, sealing off the property from the curious, crazy, and crooks. Since Coleman felt he didn't fit into any of those categories, he disregarded the yellow tape, deciding that a little breaking and entering was just part of the job—or at least part of his unofficial investigation.

He easily circumvented the obstacles to enter Victoria Turner's townhouse. At the back door, he used a credit card and some good old-fashioned manipulation to open the lock.

Inside he looked around, careful not to touch anything he didn't need to. The real killer must have done the same thing, he decided—checked the place out, mapped his strategy, then moved in for the kill.

Room to room Coleman went, taking mental notes, trying to think like Victoria's killer. It had to be someone she knew. A boyfriend or a wannabe boyfriend, he decided.

According to the official investigation, there was no boyfriend—at least not a steady one. In fact, thought

Coleman, they practically had Victoria being celibate, in spite of the semen and pubic hair found on and in her body. Whatever she was, he mused, the woman was definitely not without male companionship. Perhaps more than one person.

Coleman walked into the bedroom. It was fair-sized, but still too small for his standards. Nothing seemed particularly out of place, aside from what the investigators and technicians left behind. But then, this was no burglary, he thought. Not by a long shot.

Coleman could see on the still bloodied bed and body impression that it was Victoria Turner's final resting place before she breathed her last breath. He replayed in his mind Turner's account of what happened when he came in that night.

The killer had planned this right down to the last detail, Coleman thought. He had lured Turner to the house and into the bedroom. Then he knocked him out, put the knife in his left hand, phoned the police, and waited somewhere for Turner to be charged with the murder and mutilation of his ex-wife.

At least that sounded plausible to Coleman. He still hadn't quite figured out why yet, much less who did it.

Wearing plastic gloves, he began sifting through drawers, hoping his colleagues may have overlooked or dismissed something that could exonerate Turner and point toward someone else. There was jewelry—some of it expensive. Too damned expensive to come from alimony and a part-time job as an interior decorator, Coleman told himself.

He looked at her lingerie. Much of it was colorful and sexy. And X-rated. He wondered who she wore these for, if not Turner. . . .

Coleman always prided himself on being quick with his instincts and even faster with his .38 Smith and Wesson revolver if he sensed danger. But this time he was a step too slow on both counts. Before he could even turn around, he knew he was in trouble.

"Put your hands up!" a voice boomed. "You heard him, asshole," said another, equally hostile.

Coleman raised his arms reluctantly, almost embarrassed that he had been caught like a common thief. Even worse, his hands were still clutching a pair of satin crotchless pink panties. "This isn't what it looks like—" he tried to say, red-faced, to two stone-faced cops, guns aimed squarely at his chest.

A half hour later he tried to tell the same thing to his boss. Captain Arthur Fisher, a paunchy, balding man of fifty-two with bushy black eyebrows and a long red nose, was not amused. Two officers had been dispatched to the scene after a neighbor reported a possible break-in at 7054 Mountain Drive. The burglar turned out to be Detective Harry Coleman.

"Just what the hell did you think you were doing messing around at a crime scene while the investigation is still in progress?" Fisher glared at him impatiently, the two standing face to face.

The cat had caught Coleman's tongue. Big time. There was no way out, he knew, except to be up front about it. "I was looking for evidence," he said.

"What evidence?" demanded Fisher gruffly. "You were warned to stay away from this damned case. Do you want me to suspend your ass or fire you?"

"Neither, sir." Coleman swallowed in deference, hoping to dodge this bullet.

"Then do us both a favor and stay the hell away from that house and anything that has to do with this case and Graham Turner!" Fisher's narrowed eyes locked with Coleman's. "Am I making myself absolutely clear, *De-tective?*"

Coleman was about to give the pat "yes, sir" line, while thinking: Go to hell. Instead, he decided it was worth tugging the line a bit.

"I think Turner is being railroaded, sir." He gave an exasperated sigh. "I know how it looks—the evidence and all—but looks can sometimes be deceiving."

"They can also be *very* accurate," said Fisher, unimpressed. "Especially in the face of overwhelming evidence. Turner's been a walking time bomb for some time now. The man finally decided to explode and he's gotta answer for it, simple as that. This department's credibility is riding on it!"

"What about *Turner's* credibility?" Coleman cocked a brow, realizing he was stepping over the line here, but determined to go to bat for his partner. "Don't we owe him the benefit of the doubt?"

"He has that benefit by being given the opportunity to prove himself innocent of murder," said Fisher coldly. "That's the best Turner can expect, given the fact that he was found at the scene, murder weapon in hand, and the victim dead in her own blood just feet away. Now this discussion is over—and so is your meddling, Coleman." To further emphasize his seriousness, Fisher added: "And that's an order!"

He dismissed the detective with a wicked stare.

Coleman's mouth was a crooked line. He thought what he didn't dare say: Up yours, Captain.

CHAPTER TWENTY-ONE

The murder weapon was still missing.

The gun seized from Jordan La Fontaine's home was a .25-caliber pistol with a barrel that had five lands and grooves and a left-hand twist. Nelson Neilson and Gail Marshall were killed with a .25-caliber weapon that had a barrel with six lands and grooves and a right-hand twist.

This potential sticking point was not lost on Jerrod Wresler as he sat at his desk across from Detectives O'Donnell and Paris. Amanda Clinksdale was standing in the corner as if to hold it up.

Wresler knew that if he were the defense attorney in the case, he would argue all to hell: no weapon, no conviction. Of course, that wasn't the way he saw it. Not in this case.

So La Fontaine had used a gun other than the one found at the suspect's residence, Wresler convinced himself. The circumstantial evidence still put him at the scene right around the time the medical examiner estimated that the victims were killed. Not to mention they had the witness who heard Trevor La Fontaine threaten to kill Nelson Neilson. Gail Marshall was simply caught in the crossfire . . . or maybe she was even part of a deadly love triangle. As far as Wresler was concerned, Jordan La Fontaine's son was guilty of two cold-blooded killings. He was convinced that the grand jury would back him up on this.

Now what the hell would Trevor La Fontaine have done with the gun after he shot two people? Wresler asked himself. He'd get rid of the damned thing as soon as he could. And since the Columbia River was at the backdoor of Devil's Edge waiting to gobble up some cold steel like a grizzly bear eating salmon, what they needed to seal up this case could be at the bottom of the river.

Damn that bastard! And his mother!

Wresler sucked in a deep breath and put on a more relaxed face as he told his audience, "We'll hang the bastard by his balls with or without the murder weapon."

"It may still show up," Paris suggested. "Sometimes evidence turns up in the strangest places. The La Fontaine kid might've even pawned the gun."

"Maybe he gave it to his momma to put away for safe keeping," O'Donnell offered with a humorless chuckle, chomping on gum so hard saliva foamed at the corners of his mouth.

Wresler was neither amused nor persuaded. Not that he would put anything past Jordan La Fontaine if it meant saving her son's ass, along with her own career. But that would be too easy and too dumb. Whatever else he may have thought about her, La Fontaine was not a woman apt to making foolish mistakes that would likely catch up with her. No, Trevor La Fontaine committed the murders and disposed of the murder weapon all by himself, and probably put it where no one would find it. But that wouldn't stop them from trying.

"There were no powder burns found on any of Trevor

La Fontaine's clothes," noted Amanda, glancing at the case file. She looked around at the others as if for explanation, settling her green eyes on Wresler.

He, in turn, studied her from head to toe. He liked what he saw. She was, as always, impeccably dressed in a black suit with a three-button jacket, straight skirt, and a red silk V-necked sweater. Her outfit was completed with leather pumps on two-inch heels; all complementing her petite body and red hair. He looked now at her alabaster taut, attractive face, focusing in on the gaze directed at him. Only when she broke their eye contact did he respond.

"He got rid of the gun," Wresler reasoned. "La Fontaine probably got rid of the clothes, too." He disregarded the fact that no powder burns were found on the suspect's hands or body either, choosing to focus more on what they did have. Once he got the grand jury's go ahead to proceed, Wresler planned to introduce into evidence, among other things, clothes found in Trevor La Fontaine's bedroom that had traces of blood that matched the victims' blood types. DNA tests would likely make it conclusive.

"Has anyone checked to see if similar killings have occurred in the area recently?" Amanda asked with a hint of doubt.

"Of course," said O'Donnell, cracking his gum loudly. "This is definitely an isolated case. Those two kids were targeted. And we got the man who pulled the trigger."

On a rainy January afternoon, nearly three weeks after the deaths of Gail Marshall and Nelson Neilson, a grand jury indicted Trevor Zachary La Fontaine on two counts of first-degree murder. His arraignment was held three days later.

The defendant, looking distant, stood beside his attorney. Both wore black suits, as though attending a wake.

The prosecutor, wearing a gray suit, along with a look of intimidation and utter confidence, was standing a few feet away. On the bench was Judge John Benson, a slender, African-American man of forty with a short salt-and-pepper Afro, who looked as if everyone was his enemy.

Jordan observed this from behind the defendant's table where she sat in support of her son. Being on the other side of the fence, she knew what to expect from this proceeding, but made herself hope for the best.

"Your Honor," Wresler was saying determinedly, "we have two young people dead just a week before they were to be married, for crying out loud. Killed execution-style by someone who knew them both." He gave Trevor the benefit of his frosty eyes. "In light of the two counts of murder in the first degree that Mr. La Fontaine is being charged with, we ask that he continue to be held without bail."

Wresler smugly deferred the floor to his counterpart, Simon McNeil. Jordan bit her lip as she watched Simon try to pull off a miracle. Trevor turned to look at her, and she offered him a supportive smile while crying inside. How could her son end up in this predicament? she asked herself, unbelieving. Was there no end in sight?

Simon said a word or two to the judge to try and soften him up, then said, "The State's case is purely circumstantial, Your Honor. Trevor La Fontaine has never been arrested before. He grew up in a home where both parents were well-respected lawyers and decent, law-abiding people." Simon turned his gaze to Jordan, smiling with his eyes. "I'm sure you know Jordan La Fontaine, Your Honor."

"I'm sure I do." Judge Benson nodded at Jordan civilly. "Mrs. La Fontaine."

Jordan nodded back politely and felt a little better in the exchange.

"No one more than the assistant district attorney," emphasized Simon, "with the exception of the defendant, wants to see this case put before a jury. In the meantime, Trevor La Fontaine is a bright college student at Portland State. He's already missed more than a week of school this semester, jeopardizing his education and graduation. It makes no sense to have him stay in jail another night for a crime he did not commit."

"Maybe he didn't," Benson said with a catch to his heavy voice, "and maybe he did. Doesn't really matter at this point. The defendant is being charged with a double homicide, Counselor. Not even his mother's distinguished career with the D.A.'s office can diminish that." He blinked at Jordan almost in apology, then tensed while saying, "Bail is denied."

The prisoner was remanded back into custody.

Jordan had to choke back tears as she watched her son taken away like a dangerous animal. All the color seemed to have drained from his face.

She was left to wonder if Simon was capable of saving Trevor. Or was Jerrod Wresler holding all the cards in deciding Trevor's fate?

CHAPTER TWENTY-TWO

Two days later Jordan took Simon up on his offer to make her dinner. Kendre was spending the night with Lenora, and Jordan had decided what she needed most was a good friend. Simon had been that and much more. How much more was yet to be seen.

They had promised beforehand not to dwell on Trevor's troubles or Jordan's impending prosecution of Graham Turner for this one evening.

"It won't make the system go any faster," Simon had said. "Besides, we've both been working our asses off and the stress level is flying off the Richter scale. We deserve a little quality time."

Jordan bought herself a new dress for the occasion. It was gold, silk chiffon with a low neckline that showed a hint of cleavage. She wore strappy black heels. She put her hair up, and wore a pearl necklace and matching earrings.

Had she gotten carried away with this? *Maybe he'll think I'm throwing myself at him.*

"You look great," Simon said enthusiastically, after removing her coat.

"So do you," she responded. He was wearing a blue striped shirt, dark pleated slacks, and a three-button light cream sportcoat. He smelled good too, Jordan thought, breathing in his Kouros cologne.

The food smelled good, too.

She couldn't remember the last time someone had actually made a real dinner for her. Kendre had mastered microwave dinners and fast food while Trevor, like his father, shied away from cooking like it was a disease that afflicted only women.

"Can I get you something to drink?" Simon was still admiring the view beneath her neckline.

"Wine, if you have it."

"I have it," he said. "Let's see . . . there's pinot grigio and cabernet franc. What's your pleasure?"

"The pinot grigio sounds good." She was already beginning to feel more relaxed.

"Pinot grigio it is." Simon smiled. "Make yourself at home. Be right with you."

When he left, Jordan observed that Simon had added some things to the apartment since her last visit. Little knickknacks here and there. She saw an oil painting of the sea on one wall that wasn't there before. The place was suddenly beginning to seem more like a home than a temporary residence.

Did that mean he was planning to stay here on a more permanent basis? That was a good thing, wasn't it? Jordan could imagine this being their perfect little hideaway for romantic get-togethers. It was anything beyond that in the real world that Jordan was still unsure about.

Simon found her at the window in the living room admiring the view of the city at night. "It's easy to fall in love with, isn't it?" he said, handing her the glass of wine.

Jordan tasted it, the liquid going slowly down her throat. "Yes," she acknowledged, feeling a slight chill. "Especially from up here."

"My thoughts exactly." He stood close to her, their bodies touching. "Sort of like the way I feel about you, baby."

"Don't, Simon . . ." She flashed him an admonishing look. "Remember, we agreed not to get carried away too soon."

Or maybe it was just me, Jordan thought.

"I can't help it," Simon said. "Dammit, Jordan, every time I'm near you, every time I touch you"—he ran the back of his hand down her soft cheek—"I know what I feel is real . . . for both of us. You know what I'm saying?"

Jordan looked at him and could see the sincerity in his eyes. It scared and exhilarated her at the same time. This was all still so new between them, yet it felt as though they were old lovers with a long history of romancing. Did they really have a future together? Or would the ghosts of the past and the tensions of the present always cast a shadow over them?

"I feel the same way, Simon," she told him honestly, if not uneasily. "But . . ."

"But you don't know if Eric would approve—is that it?" When she didn't respond, Simon said, "Or does our relationship hinge on whether I can get Trevor off?"

Jordan regarded him severely. "I think you know me better than that."

He appeared skeptical. "Do I?"

She felt anger in her veins. "If you don't, then maybe I shouldn't be here right now."

After a moment, Simon's hard face softened, and he said, "I'm sorry. Of course you should be here. This really isn't about you at all." He paused. "It's about Frances. . . ."

Jordan cocked a brow and her curiosity shifted gears. "What about her?" She was almost afraid to ask, but she knew it was time to learn more about Simon and Frances's breakup.

Simon put his glass to his lips in thought and glowered. "She wants everything: the house, the Mercedes, even the cabin." He drank more. "Damn her. She left me, not the other way around. Why the hell should I have to give in to her demands?"

Jordan could feel the frustration and bitterness oozing from his pores like sweat. Guilt overcame her. In the constant battle she was having with her personal and professional struggles, she had failed to notice that he was also hurting, confused, and battling his own demons. Or was it one demon in particular that he was fighting?

Jordan held Simon's hand reassuringly. "Things will work themselves out. I'm sure that in the end, Frances will be reasonable in working out a settlement."

Did Jordan really believe that? Or was it more wishful thinking that Frances wouldn't try to take Simon to the cleaners? I shouldn't get involved, she thought, but she knew, I am involved—with Simon. Frances gave him up and now she will just have to deal with it.

"I wish I could be as sure," Simon groaned. "The truth is that Frances is a greedy, selfish bitch, and I wouldn't put anything past her to try and make my life more miserable."

Jordan regarded him with wide-eyed shock. She hadn't realized that the animosity between them ran so deep. How could she have not seen it whenever the four of them got together? Had Eric known?

She reached out for Simon again. "I could talk to her

if you'd like." She had no idea what she'd say. What could one say in such a situation?

Simon considered the notion. "I'm not sure that would be such a good idea," he said. "Frances doesn't listen to anyone but Frances . . . not even old, well-meaning friends."

You mean, a friend who becomes your estranged husband's lover, thought Jordan.

"It was just a suggestion," she said, wishing she hadn't made it.

"And I thank you for that." Simon smiled. "Believe me when I tell you that your presence in my life has helped more than I could say."

"Me too."

Jordan felt the tenderness of Simon's mouth upon hers, lingering for a few moments before he pulled away. "Nice to know we're there for each other. A good foundation to build any worthwhile relationship on."

Before Jordan could respond, Simon said, "I don't know about you, but my stomach's growling. Why don't we go check out what's on the menu for tonight."

Jordan smiled at him. "That sounds like a splendid idea."

"Graham Turner has been out to get his ex-wife one way or another for some time," remarked Simon as they sat on the couch with wine after dinner. It had been a delicious meal of mustard greens, fried chicken, rice and brown gravy, with lemon cake for dessert.

Jordan had been surprised to learn that Simon knew Graham socially, having gotten together with him and some other cops every now and then to shoot hoops.

"You knew this?" Jordan raised a brow, setting her wineglass on a coaster on the coffee table.

Simon twisted his lips. "Not in so many words. But you know, there was talk. Not to mention a history of domestic violence. The brother apparently had a major-league chip on his shoulder before and after his divorce. He apparently turned that into homicidal rage."

Jordan sneered. "And I'm supposed to feel sorry for Graham Turner that he sliced up his ex and now is being held accountable?"

"Not at all, baby," insisted Simon. "Turner has no one to blame for where he is but himself. I have to tell you that it really pisses the hell out of me when the criminal justice system allows assholes to beat up on their wives and girlfriends, gives them a damned slap on the wrist as punishment, then wonders how it could have happened when the bastards finally lose it and kill these women."

"The system isn't perfect." Jordan was surprised to find herself defending it, if not Graham Turner. "Even if we wanted to, we couldn't lock up every man who threatens his wife or ex-wife. Or for that matter," she reluctantly admitted, "every man who abuses a woman. There's barely enough room to hold the people already behind bars." Jordan brushed up against Simon and said without realizing the irony, "Then there are always people like you just waiting to use every trick in the book to get the Graham Turners of the world to walk free."

Jordan quickly realized what she'd said and regretted it. "I'm sorry, Simon . . . I didn't mean . . ."

"It's okay, Jordan," Simon told her smoothly. "You're right, it's attorneys just like me—and Eric—who know how to play the system to fight for our clients. That's the way it works in America. Sometimes we actually get the good guys off the hook for crimes they're accused of."

Jordan sipped her drink, knowing in her heart just how valuable defense attorneys like Simon were. They defended people who otherwise might unjustly be swallowed up by a system that was supposed to presume innocence until proven guilty. Simon would *need* to use every trick in the book to let Trevor walk free, Jordan told herself.

If Simon was thinking the same thing, he wasn't saying. Instead, he kept the subject on Graham Turner. "I personally wouldn't touch that case with a ten-foot pole. Don't need the headache or hassle or politics of defending a black man charged with killing his former white wife. Not only would I rather not go head to head with you in the courtroom again, but a killer cop, or an accused one, is bad news all the way around. Especially for the victim."

Both quickly soured of the conversation and turned their attention to each other. Jordan welcomed it when Simon undid her hair and began to play with it. Then without warning he tilted his face and kissed her lips, long and hard. It was as if every moment of the evening had been slowly but surely leading up to this. He put his tongue in her mouth and she tasted the wine, the food, and him.

Jordan's body ached for his. She lifted up Simon's shirt and ran kisses down his flat chest. Then she unfastened his pants and kissed him where his erection threatened to rip through his underwear.

"You feel really good to me, baby," moaned Simon, allowing Jordan to continue for a moment before pulling up and resting his face on her chest. He pulled her dress off her shoulders and down her body, exposing her breasts. When his tongue began to brush lightly, teasingly across her nipples, Jordan felt like screaming with delight.

Instead she climbed atop him, straddled Simon's body, and began to make love to him, determined to give him everything she had this night, and more.

Later he made love to her with the same desire, overpowering physical attraction and lust.

Finally, they made love to each other and held nothing back.

Though she clung to the afterglow of sexual fulfillment, Jordan knew what she was feeling went well beyond an orgasm, potent as it was. She was starting to fall in love with Simon McNeil.

CHAPTER TWENTY-THREE

Vancouver, Washington, was right across the Columbia River from Portland. With crime and the cost of living on the rise in the Rose City, many Oregonians were flocking across the Glen Jackson Bridge to Vancouver. It offered affordable housing, a myriad of shops and stores and, among other advantages, a good school system. The latter was precisely what drew Constance Larchman there after teaching in Oregon's public schools for fourteen of her thirty-eight-and-a-half years. She wanted only what was best for the children and her. Vancouver's school administrators really seemed to give a damn about the kids and what it took not only to graduate, but to make a real life for themselves beyond school. At least that was the case at Clairemont High, where Constance Larchman taught English.

On this night, Constance had stayed in her class-room well after the students had gone home for the day. Grading papers had always been a pain in the ass, but finding the ones that really stood out made it seem worthwhile. Besides, it wasn't as if she had anything to rush home for—unless you counted her cat, Daffy.

Constance had been on her own for ten years now, ever since her live-in lover had decided she was not thin, pretty, or blond enough for his liking. She never gave another man a chance to break her heart or humiliate her. She had decided she was better off on her own, choosing to devote herself to her students, who appreciated her.

It was quarter to seven when she left the building and headed for her dark blue Honda. The wintertime rain the Northwest was famous for had been coming down all day and showed little sign of letting up. Under a flimsy umbrella, Constance still managed to get drenched by the time she got behind the wheel. All she could think of at the moment was getting into some dry clothes, feeding Daffy, and watching the tape of her favorite soap opera, *The Young and the Restless.*

Although her apartment was only three miles away from the school, Constance Larchman would never make it home alive.

When she heard the loud bang, Constance knew immediately what it was. "Oh, hell!" she cursed under her breath. What else could go wrong in her life? Her right front tire had blown out. She pulled the car to a stop on the shoulder in what looked like the middle of nowhere. Actually it was formerly a farmer's field on both sides of the road that had fallen into disrepair with a sea of weeds, some as tall as Constance's five-four height. The city had purchased the property and was in the process of converting it into a park.

Her mind returned to the matter at hand and, along with it, renewed frustration. She had never changed a tire in her life. Never even had a flat. *I'm sure not prepared to stand out there in high heels in the pouring rain and pretend I know what I'm doing.*

Walking the rest of the way home was an equally unappealing option. What would really be nice is if a Good Samaritan happened to come along and volunteered to change the tire, she thought. Then she would be happily on her way.

As luck would have it, or so she thought, a van did come. And it stopped.

There is a heaven after all, or at least an angel, Constance thought, clasping her hands in prayer.

She watched through the rearview mirror as a tall, slender young man emerged from his vehicle. He was wearing a hat much like the one her father used to wear when going fishing up at Bass Lake. The lights from his van were still on as he approached her. Constance licked her chapped lips and considered whether to play the dumb woman in distress role or pretend she was just about to show her mechanical aptitude when he showed up. She let the window down halfway, and was immediately hit in the face by raindrops.

"Having a problem, lady?" the man asked politely, the brim of his hat shielding his eyes.

For that matter, thought Constance, the rain and glare of his headlights made it equally difficult to make out his face. All she could really see clearly was a cigarette dangling from one side of his mouth, as if merely a prop.

"I think I have a flat tire," she said tersely, straining her eyes to focus on him.

He seemed to be studying her as well. "That's too bad," he said. "Especially in this weather. Maybe I can help. Do you have a spare?"

"I'm sure I do."

He flashed her a half smile. "Good. Why don't you pop the trunk and I'll have you on your way in no time flat, if you'll pardon the pun."

Constance gave a little chuckle, while thinking, I wonder if I should give him a tip or something? Did peo-

ple actually tip young men who happened along to assist a damsel in definite distress? Or just tell them gratefully, I can't thank you enough?

She pushed the button and watched through the
rearview mirror as the trunk sprung open. Only then, as
the trunk lid blocked the van's lights, was Constance
able to see her rescuer more clearly. But it was not him
that her eyes fixed upon. Nor did she focus on the
steady stream of smoke filtering from his mouth and
nostrils like a chimney. It was what was in his hand that
Constance locked on.

He was holding what looked like a gun.

Yes, it was a gun—and it was pointed at her.

Constance Larchman gasped and actually found herself paralyzed with fear.

He watched the horror in her face, just as he had in
the faces of the others, and found himself just as turned
on by it.

It fueled his rage, his urge, and his desire to do what
he had to do.

He pulled the trigger. The glass shattered. Her face
exploded, and she slumped onto the steering wheel.

He admired his handiwork briefly, then walked away
from the new corpse.

All in a night's work, he thought, drawing deeply on
the cigarette one final time before flicking it to the wet
street.

He drove past the car with the flat and wondered if
anyone else would bother to offer its occupant assis-
tance in this nasty weather.

CHAPTER TWENTY-FOUR

Jordan spent the entire day with Andrew, going over the evidence, testimony of witnesses, and other preparations for the trial, which was just over a week away. It had been a grueling two months since Graham Turner's preliminary hearing. Both sides had filed motions to suppress evidence, admit evidence, locate evidence, and dismiss or maintain witnesses. The prosecution had scored a major victory when key DNA evidence was ruled admissible. Blood found on the murder weapon and the defendant's clothes and person belonged to the victim, Victoria Turner, and would be used to bolster the State's case. As far as Jordan was concerned, they were ready to get a conviction against Detective Graham Turner. Which also meant that he could be sentenced to death now that the D.A.'s office had decided he deserved nothing less.

"I think Officer Fitzgerald's testimony could still use some work," Andrew was saying as he sat across from Jordan in the conference room. "Fitzgerald knows what she saw when she went into the victim's bedroom, but she's having a tough time articulating it in a way the jury can relate to. Believe me, Lester Eldridge will jump all over her if he thinks Fitzgerald is a weak link in the chain."

"Get her in," commanded Jordan. "We'll iron out the rough spots of her testimony till she gets it right." She glanced at her notes. "What about Officer Kirkland?"

"He's solid," Andrew responded confidently. "He recognized Turner right away—still holding the murder weapon, like it was glued to his fingers."

"But not actually using it?" Jordan knew the defense's best shot was to maintain that someone else had placed the knife in Turner's hand—the person who had, in fact, used it to kill and mutilate Victoria Turner.

"The man had enough sense to stop stabbing when he heard someone coming." Andrew leaned back in his chair, running a hand through his curly hair. "But with the circumstantial evidence we have, Turner might just as well have had the knife still lodged in his ex when the officers came in."

Jordan drifted off for a moment as she thought about another important trial coming up. Trevor's was slated to begin less than two weeks after Turner's. Jordan felt her blood race with apprehension and anger. Her son's life was on the line now that Jerrod Wresler had decided to ask for the death penalty—almost as if to punctuate his arrogance and desire to come out on top in the race for the Bureau Chief of the Homicide Division in the D.A.'s office. What scared Jordan most was that the police had all but given up on looking for any other suspects—the real killer—no doubt encouraged by Wresler's seemingly ruthless pursuit of Trevor.

She refocused on Andrew, who was writing something down, and saying, "The 911 operator who took Victoria Turner's call six months before her death, complaining that Graham Turner was stalking her, is expecting a baby in two weeks. So we may want to get her on the stand early . . . and hope for the best."

"The best for her would be to have her baby in the hospital," said Jordan, "not in the courtroom. We'll see how she's doing when the trial starts."

Andrew drew a breath and eyed the clock on the wall. "It's getting late. You hungry?"

"Starved," she said. "But I think I'll eat at home. Kendre looks for any excuse she can to gobble up junk food— or not eat at all, depending on the day of the week." Jordan dragged herself up. "We've covered pretty much all we need to for now."

Andrew remained seated, staring at her. "Look, I know how hard this has been for you, with Trevor and all . . . If you ever need to get away to be with him, don't worry about it. I can cover things here—and in the courtroom."

If it were anyone else, Jordan would have doubted his sincerity as well as his ability to get the job done. With Andrew, she knew he meant what he said from the heart and was capable of delivering if called upon to do so.

"Thanks," she told him, laying a hand on his shoulder. "I appreciate that." She smiled. Noting that he was recently divorced, but good looking and definitely in the market, Jordan said, "If you're not careful, Andrew, some lucky woman is going to snatch you up one of these days."

He flashed her a wide grin. "I don't have any problem with referrals," he hinted.

"I'll keep that in mind."

* * *

As she did every day, Jordan visited Trevor in jail, often bringing him anything that was allowed. It was a hell of a way for them to rediscover one another, but to Jordan this was an opportunity to mend fences and show her son all the love and support he would surely need during these trying times.

"You look nice," Trevor said sweetly, kissing Jordan on the cheek, as they exchanged a long hug.

He was looking better than the last time she had seen him. She and Simon had finally talked Trevor into cutting his dreadlocks after his stubborn streak had resisted any change of, as he had put it, "who I am." She thought he looked more self-assured and less intimidating, noting that he'd lost weight, giving him a more svelte appearance.

Jordan touched Trevor's hair, smiling at him. "You look great too, honey."

They sat down. For a while neither said anything. They were content to ponder their thoughts silently.

"How's String Bean?" Trevor finally asked.

"Busy with school," Jordan said. "Kendre is taking drama classes this semester."

"Good for her. I always thought my sometimes overly dramatic little sister was a natural-born actress."

"Well I wouldn't give her an Academy Award just yet." Jordan saw the pain of rejection or loss in Trevor's eyes. "She's not ready to come see you yet, Trevor," she apologized for Kendre. Though Kendre was generally too young for jail visits, Jordan had arranged for her to visit Trevor, had she wanted to. "It hurts her too much knowing you're in here. Just give her some time—"

"Why not?" Trevor shrugged indifferently. "I seem to have plenty of it to give."

It was hardest for Jordan to see him like this. *My baby boy isn't a baby anymore. He doesn't deserve to be here. What could I have done to keep him from being in this mess?*

"Don't blame yourself for any of this, Momma," Trevor said. "I know if it were up to you I'd be back in school right now and this would be nothing but a bad nightmare. Somebody else's. But it's real and I've gotta deal with it just like everyone else in here."

Jordan wiped tears from her eyes. "You're going to beat this, Trevor," she promised. "Simon is working night and day to build your defense. He'll create enough reasonable doubt that the jury will have no choice but to acquit."

Trevor rolled his eyes. "How are you paying for his services anyway?" He cocked a curious brow. "I'm smart enough to realize people like Simon don't come cheap—even if he was once Dad's partner."

"I had some money put away," Jordan replied nervously, not sure she was ready to go down that road.

"That *much* money?" He narrowed his eyes. "Come on, Momma, give me some credit. Even with your salary, you can only put so much in the bank. What'd you do, promise to join his firm if he got me off?"

Jordan didn't know if he was serious or just being respectful. She had not told either of her children that she was seeing Simon intimately. And she wasn't sure why. Maybe she was afraid they would think less of her. Or believe that it was for all the wrong reasons.

"Simon's a good friend," she said. "He was also a close friend of your father's—whose name is still part of the firm. The money isn't important to Simon. He only wants to help you any way he can."

Trevor seemed content to leave it at that. "Let's just hope he can. Being stuck in here for a couple of months sure makes you appreciate things you used to take for granted—like real food." His head lowered and lifted. "It gets worse when you think that you could end up being executed for something you didn't do."

Jordan sucked in a deep breath. "That will *never* happen," she said. "Not while I have a leg to stand on." Even listening to her own voice, Jordan knew it sounded flat and unconvincing. How could she guarantee something for which there were no guarantees? Not when Jerrod Wresler was on a witch hunt—determined to put the screws to Trevor as a way to get to her.

"You're standing on *two* legs when you're prosecuting the cop for offing his ex—ain't that right?" Trevor pursed his lips.

Jordan reacted, not sure where he was coming from. "His case is not the same as yours."

"I think it is," Trevor said brusquely. "Isn't he claiming he's innocent?"

Jordan widened her eyes. "Do you think Graham Turner is innocent?"

He shrugged. "How would I know? Maybe your case against him is bogus, just like theirs is against me. When brothers are accused of murder in this country, the tendency is to believe they're guilty, no matter what."

Jordan could not believe what she was hearing. Her mouth tightened and she said, "Listen to me, Trevor. It isn't about rounding up black men and finding them guilty of murder. It's about doing the right thing when the evidence suggests a person is guilty, no matter what race they are. I believe Graham Turner butchered his ex-wife and the facts of the case support it. If a jury agrees with me, he has to pay the price for what he did. But that doesn't mean that you have to go down with him as an African-American man who's being wrongly accused. Your father and I always taught you that justice can sometimes be blind, but far more often than not, the truth will eventually right the wrongs."

Trevor nodded. "Yeah, I know, Momma. I'm just spouting off at the mouth for no good reason. You're doing what you have to do, and I respect that."

Jordan breathed a little easier now that they'd gotten over that hump and cleared the air. She decided to take this opportunity he'd given her to delve a little. "Tell me about the fight you had that night with Nelson Neilson."

Trevor stared into space. "Not much to tell really."

"What was it about?" Jordan shifted her body. It occurred to her that Trevor had not been really specific concerning the fight.

Following a pause, Trevor muttered, "He said some things to Rhonda that I didn't like."

"What things?"

Another pause. "Things he wanted to do with her."

"Sexual things?"

"Yeah."

And the press portrayed this man as part of the All-American Couple, thought Jordan, irritated. She wondered if his fiancée had any idea what type of jerk she was about to marry.

"Then what?" asked Jordan.

"Then I kicked his ass," Trevor said flatly. Then he gazed squarely at Jordan and stated softly, yet emphatically, "But I didn't kill him, Momma. I swear it!"

Jordan looped her fingers through his. "I know you didn't, baby," she told him. "And when this is all over everyone else will know, too."

The phone rang, jarring Jordan from what had been a restless sleep. She rolled over and grabbed the receiver from the phone on the nightstand, noting on the radio clock that it was nearly eleven P.M.

144

"Hello," she said in a sleepy voice, hoping it might be Simon, wanting to be comforted through his smooth as silk words and sexy voice.

"Hi, Jordan. This is Frances—hope I didn't wake you . . ."

"Oh, hello, Frances," Jordan managed meekly. "And no," she lied, "you didn't wake me. I was just lying here waiting for the news to come on."

Jordan felt a shiver in hearing from Simon's wife. In her mind she knew they would have to talk sooner or later. I wish it had been later, she told herself. She felt as if it was she who had come between Frances and Simon, rather than Frances who chose to leave her husband for another man. Then there was the fact that Simon seemed in no hurry to have them talk, as if they'd be at each other's throat, fighting over him like alley cats.

"I wanted to call sooner," Frances said, "but I really didn't know quite what to say." She paused and Jordan waited, not sure what to say herself. "I read about Trevor. I know how hard this must be on you."

Oh, no you don't, thought Jordan. How could you?

"It has been hard," she admitted, "but we'll get through it . . . somehow. Trevor did not kill those students!" Jordan found herself shaking.

"Oh, I know that, girl," Frances said reassuringly. "I know the police have the wrong man in custody." She breathed into the phone. "I see that Simon is representing Trevor."

"He wanted to do it," Jordan responded self-consciously. And she wanted him to, she knew.

"I'm sure Simon will work his magic in this case," remarked Frances. "He usually does if he has anything at all to work with."

Jordan couldn't help wondering if Frances believed there was so little to work with that Simon needed to be a damned magician to pull this one off.

145

R. Barri Flowers

"Guess you heard that we split up?" Frances asked hoarsely.

Jordan swallowed. "Yes, he told me. I'm sorry, Frances." Inside, she asked herself: Why should I be? After all, you left him, not the other way around. Right?

Frances made a guttural sound as if sipping a hard drink, and said, "We've been having our troubles. I guess things just finally reached a breaking point."

Not to mention your involvement with another man, Jordan thought, but suggested: "Maybe you should have tried to work things out with Simon."

I can't believe I just said that, Jordan thought. She realized that if they had stayed together she wouldn't have allowed herself to become involved with and fall in love with Simon. But another part of her really believed that every marriage was worth saving—even Simon's.

"It's too late for that," Frances said bleakly. "There's another man." She sighed. "He treats me right. I want to give us a chance."

Jordan recalled Simon saying, "She wants everything: the house, the Mercedes, even the cabin." To share with her new love, Jordan thought.

After sitting up, Jordan sucked in a long breath and said what was on her mind: "I'm happy for you, Frances, if this is what you really want. I just hope you'll do the right thing by Simon and ask for a fair settlement in ending the marriage. He deserves the chance to move on with his life without being taken to the cleaners."

Frances moaned and demanded: "What's he been saying to you?"

"Nothing that you haven't, Frances. I just don't want there to be any misunderstandings or lasting regrets between you two. I had my own with Eric . . . and now he's no longer here to—"

Jordan tried hard to maintain her composure, while hoping she hadn't said too much. In the end, the tears came and she knew they were not only for what she'd had and lost with Eric, but what Simon represented for her and her kids in the future.

CHAPTER TWENTY-FIVE

He rang the doorbell.

It was five-thirty on a chilly Wednesday, and Coleman waited impatiently outside the condo. He had been trying to talk to Desiree Bryar for weeks now. She was said to be the best friend of Victoria Turner, according to Victoria's mother. Desiree, a fashion model, had gone to Europe shortly after Victoria's death, before anyone could question her about what she knew or didn't know.

Coleman had found himself frustrated as he attempted to clear his partner of the murder of his ex-wife. Stonewalled at practically every turn, Coleman was looking for something—anything—that could give him a lead. And since Graham Turner's trial was only days away, he knew that every day from here on out counted. Unless he could gather some hard evidence soon to give to Assistant D.A. La Fontaine—whom Coleman had found himself unable to compromise—Turner could probably kiss his freedom good-bye.

Possibly for the rest of his life, thought Coleman, which could be very short if Jordan La Fontaine had her way.

The door opened and Coleman saw a tall, attractive, light-skinned African-American woman in her late twenties. She was razor thin and, by the looks of it had a nice pair of boobs, real or not. Her blond-brown hair was in long corn rows, and her bold green eyes gazed unenthusiastically back at him. She was wearing a purplish silk suit that clung to her like a second skin.

"Ms. Bryar, my name's Coleman," he said in his tough cop's voice. He removed his I.D. "I'm a homicide detective with the Portland Police Bureau. I need to ask you a few questions."

She batted fake long lashes involuntarily. "About what?"

"Victoria Turner's murder."

A shadow of despair fell across Desiree's face. "Come in."

They sat at the small oak country dining room table in a place that was otherwise short on furnishings, save for four wicker dining chairs, a sofa, rustic loveseat, and a pine armoire. Guess she doesn't spend much time here, Coleman mused.

When Desiree offered Coleman a glass of sherry, he took it thinking, What the hell? This isn't exactly official business.

He listened as she talked, with her legs crossed, about what a wonderful friend and nice person Victoria Turner had been.

"She didn't deserve to have it all taken away from her," Desiree lamented. "Not like that . . ."

Coleman sipped the sherry and gazed at this woman who looked as if she hadn't eaten for days. Is that what modeling is all about—starving yourself to death? he wondered.

"After it happened, I had to get away." Desiree drank the wine as if by habit. "I just couldn't deal with knowing my best friend had been brutally murdered . . . by Graham, of all people."

Coleman's head jerked back and he thought cynically, Maybe that's because he didn't murder her, of all people.

"Yes, he kept trying to get back into her life," Desiree pointed out. "And yes, he was an asshole most of the time—even to the point of scaring Victoria . . . and me sometimes. But I never believed Graham would *ever* go that far. He loved Victoria. And in her own way, she never stopped loving him."

This Coleman could believe, in spite of everything else. He asked himself if Turner would kill a woman who still loved him and maybe left open the door just a crack for them to get back together.

Coleman finished his drink, resisting the temptation to ask for another. "I'm going to be straight with you, Ms. Bryar . . . Desiree. I believe the wrong man is about to go on trial for Victoria Turner's murder."

Desiree's eyes popped wide. "What do you mean?"

"Isn't it obvious? I think Graham Turner is innocent." Coleman fixed his gaze on her. "And I think *you* can help me prove it."

Color stole into Desiree's face. "I don't know how I could . . ."

"Was Victoria dating anyone that you knew of when she died?"

Desiree downed more sherry, and crossed her long and slender legs the opposite way. "Victoria dated lots of men," she said. "And sometimes women . . ." Her voice faltered. "It was her way of feeling independent and free after her divorce. She loved to try different people . . . new things . . ."

"Like drugs?"

She reacted as if he'd spoken a dirty word.

"I'm not a vice cop," Coleman promised. "Besides, you can't arrest a dead woman." Nor did he have any desire to arrest the living one in front of him for what she may have done in her spare time.

"Sure, she experimented some with marijuana and cocaine," Desiree admitted. "Who doesn't every now and then—except maybe cops . . . ?" She met his eyes mockingly.

There weren't any drugs in her body at the time of death, according to the autopsy, Coleman remembered. That didn't mean Victoria wasn't a user, though. It only took a day or two to flush out the system or make it look like she was clean.

"Was she involved with anyone in particular who used drugs?" Coleman leaned toward her.

Desiree gave a nervous twitch. "I don't know," she replied a little too quickly. "Victoria didn't tell me about everyone she knew or dated."

"But she told you about *someone* . . . ?" He watched her like a hawk, his instincts kicking in like crazy. Maybe this was the break he'd been looking for.

Desiree's eyes avoided his. "There was someone—a man—she saw off and on. But she never told me his name."

How damned convenient, thought Coleman, bristling. Desiree could be lying for whatever reason. But rather than try and force something out of her, he decided to take another approach. Right now she was his only source of potentially useful information. He couldn't afford to alienate her.

"Where did Victoria meet this man?" Coleman asked coolly.

Desiree seemed to search her memory. "I think it was

at a place called Club Diamonds. We hung out there sometimes."

At least it was something to go on. Maybe in this case, diamonds turned out to be a gal's worst enemy, Coleman thought humorlessly.

Favoring Desiree with a friendly smile, Coleman got to his feet and said, "Thanks a lot. You've been a big help."

How big, he told himself, remained to be seen.

CHAPTER TWENTY-SIX

He planted his face squarely between her legs and let his tongue taste her, then envelope her clitoris like it belonged to him. Her body tensed at first, then loosened in a steady quavering. She began a long cry of ecstasy, and it turned him on. He continued to move in closer, enjoying her sweet juices, dense curly hairs . . . even the erotic naturalness of her scent was driving him crazy with desire. But he maintained his control. She suddenly let out a piercing scream, grabbed wildly at his hair, and pushed her body into his face.

"Mmm. Yes. Yes! Ahh. Uh huh—" Amanda moaned breathlessly. "I can't stand it! Oh . . . !"

Jerrod Wresler kept flicking his tongue expertly as he listened to and felt her orgasm, holding firmly on to her slender hips. He liked getting women off, especially the first time. Each woman was different. Some resisted their own feelings. Others offered little self-restraint, releasing themselves to him fully and unconditionally.

Amanda was definitely type number two. Getting her into bed had been far too easy. The moment he kissed her, that cool, reserved facade had disappeared completely and she succumbed to his charms just like those before her—reverting to animalistic longing.

He intended to take full advantage of her for as long as he needed to.

And she was ripe and ready as ever to be taken.

His erection was now full and demanding attention.

Wresler lifted his face, detecting a tiny note of embarrassment in Amanda's expression, but she pleaded desperately, "For heaven's sake, Jerrod, put it in—please . . ."

Without a word, he was more than happy to oblige her, not to mention relieve his own almost uncontrollable need. He spread her thighs even wider, moved between them, cupped her tight ass, and slid right in without missing a beat.

Amanda wrapped her legs high around his back as he pounded against her. His face crushed into her breasts. He bit into one nipple, then the other, causing her to wince and whine. Her nails clawed at his back and buttocks. He yelped from the pain and hummed from the pleasure.

"Oh, Jerrod—" Amanda's voice cracked when he slowed down. "Don't stop! Not yet . . . or I'll *kill* you—"

Don't worry, bitch, he told her in his mind, I won't stop. Not yet! Not till I get what I want from you.

He took her like Samson must have taken Delilah: aggressively, decisively, and victoriously.

"Now I see where you get all your energy in the courtroom," quipped Amanda afterward, beads of perspiration dotting her forehead. She kissed his penis, still erect.

"All in a day's work," Wresler said, smoking a cigarette. He had been a smoker since he was thirteen, quitting off and on but always coming back to it. Ever since they'd banned smoking in the Criminal Justice Center a couple of years ago, he had been reduced to sneaking a quick smoke in the public bathrooms in the building or forced to go outside. Neither sat well with him, but it wasn't the first time he had made sacrifices to get what he wanted. And it sure as hell wouldn't be the last.

"Hey, you got anything to eat here?" he asked, suddenly hungry for something other than her.

Amanda wet her mouth and showed teeth. "I think I can probably whip up something edible."

He chewed on steak and eggs while she sat barefoot with her legs folded, wearing only a bloodred silk charmeuse robe, and sipping orange juice.

He listened while she talked, mostly about herself. She had come from a wealthy family in New York, following her father's footsteps into prosecutorial law. Wresler learned that Amanda had been in a relationship for eight years that ended last year when he ran off with her best friend.

At thirty-two, Amanda Clinksdale believed she was at the crossroads of her life. She was either going to be married and settled down by the time she was thirty-five, or she would be a Bureau Chief by the time she was forty.

Wresler put his money on married and settled down—but not with him. Not that she had to know that. No reason to jump off the train just yet, he thought. Not while it's still running properly and full of steam.

"What about you?" Amanda asked, unfolding her legs. "Tell me something about yourself. Something I haven't already seen up close and personal . . ."

Wresler put another piece of steak in his mouth and considered the question. After a moment, he said, "I was born out of wedlock. My mother got involved with a sailor. He never knew about me."

Amanda's green eyes sparkled with fascination. "Have you ever wanted to try and find him?"

"Hell no." His throat burned at the thought. "I made it this far without him. No reason to change things." He downed some eggs with wine.

She wrinkled her nose. "Why haven't you ever married, Jerrod? Or is that too personal?"

He watched her nipples protrude from the thin fabric barely covering her breasts. It surprised him that he was becoming aroused again.

"Never found the right woman, I suppose," he muttered. "Or if I did, I didn't know it."

She was starting to look good to him again. Too good.

"More wine?" Amanda asked seductively.

"Why not?"

She refilled his glass and poured herself one. "Let's toast," she proposed.

"To what?"

"Convictions, promotions, and power." She ran a finger across his hairy chest. "Those are your greatest passions, am I right?"

Wresler smiled at her perceptiveness, and trailed his finger down her neckline, opening the robe and continuing down, down, down, until he reached between her legs. She moaned, licking her lips. Looking into her eyes, he responded to the question lasciviously: "Not at the moment . . ."

CHAPTER TWENTY-SEVEN

"Absolutely not!" Jordan's voice boomed.

"Why?" Kendre's mouth hung open rebelliously. They were standing toe to toe in her bedroom.

"Because you're way too young to be going on a hiking trip with an eighteen-year-old *man*."

"It won't be just him and me," pleaded Kendre. "Lenora, her boyfriend, and another couple are going, too."

Jordan refused to back down on this one, though she knew her daughter would probably hate her for it. In the short run. "No, Kendre," she said with finality, "I'm not going to let you go. Whether you're with others or not, he's too old for you, and it's too easy for him to want something from you that he can't have. Am I making myself clear?"

Kendre folded her arms petulantly. "Nkaki's not like that, Mom. He cares about me. Nothing's going to happen!"

"You're damned right nothing's going to happen. Nkaki can find someone his own age to hike with."

Jordan had heard Kendre's argument before: from herself. Before Eric, she had dated a boy in high school who was four years older than she had been. It was all supposed to be innocent, but one night one thing led to another, and she had lost her virginity. She was not about to let Kendre make the same mistake, and live to regret it later.

Before last night Jordan had not even known her daughter was seeing someone. Where the hell had she met this Nkaki? Why on earth would an eighteen-year-old be interested in a fourteen-year-old girl—even if she liked to think she was grown up? In Jordan's mind, there could only be one reason. And it wasn't to trek across the Cascade Mountains.

Looking at Kendre now and seeing the adolescent hurt in her face, Jordan softened her stance somewhat by suggesting, "We'll talk about it later." In her mind she thought intractably: Much later, like when you're eighteen. "Right now I have to meet with Simon. He wants to discuss Trevor's trial."

"Why does everything *always* have to be about Trevor?" Kendre complained. "Don't I count for anything?"

"Don't do this, Kendre." Jordan flashed her a look of disappointment. "Your brother is fighting for his life and all you can think about is yourself. It's about time you grew up, young lady."

Kendre stormed out of the room, her eyes flooded with tears and anger.

"You come back here!" Jordan demanded, but the words fell on deaf ears. She heard the bathroom door slam shut. Immediately Jordan regretted coming down on her like that. She wanted to run to Kendre and apologize, but resisted. She knew that, in spite of everything else, Kendre loved her brother dearly and was in just as much pain about Trevor being in jail as she was herself.

I'll let her cool off, Jordan thought.

* * *

The restaurant was located in the Columbia Square Mall. At noon it was packed, mostly with business people. Jordan sat across from Simon in a booth. They were each sipping a cafe latte while waiting for their lunch to be served.

"Every kid goes through it," Simon was saying understandingly. "No matter how much we try to guide them, they're still going to end up doing what they want to."

Jordan's eye brow shot up. "Are you saying I should let Kendre go hiking with this grown man?" she asked, flabbergasted. "She's never been hiking in her life. I doubt this is—"

"All I'm saying is to lighten up, baby. Your daughter's going through a rough time now. If you push her too hard, you just might push her away for good."

Jordan sulked as she tasted the coffee. What the hell did he know? He didn't have a fourteen- nearly fifteen-year-old daughter to protect from the vultures out there waiting to exploit her. It was far easier to dispense advice when talking about someone else's child. She wondered just how lenient he would be if he were Kendre's father. Or stepfather.

Though Jordan and Simon had been spending a lot of time together lately, there were still too many other things going on in their lives to be specific about precisely where their relationship was leading. Jordan wanted what was best for her and for her children at the end of the day. In her heart and soul she believed that to be Simon, who had the makings of being a great dad.

Jordan switched thoughts to something—or someone—else that had been on her mind. She looked at Simon and asked casually, "Have you spoken to Frances?"

"Not lately. Why?"

"She called me the other day."

Simon stared as if floored by the thought. "What did she want?" he asked, sounding nervous.

Jordan was still trying to figure that out, but said uneasily, "She doesn't know about us, if that's what you're worried about."

"I'm not worried," Simon said, clenching his jaw. "I just don't want her somehow to come between us by laying some sort of guilt trip on you. It's really over for Frances and me, Jordan."

"I know," she told him and sipped her latte. "Frances admitted she's involved with another man."

Simon eyed Jordan. "Glad she saw fit to share that information with you."

"We were friends, Simon," Jordan reminded him. "She knows you're representing Trevor. It only made sense that you would have mentioned the breakup."

Simon drank his latte. "Yeah, I guess you're right. The whole thing still turns my stomach. It'll take a while to get her totally out of my system . . . but I'm working on it."

Jordan gave him a skeptical look. "Are you sure you can work on that and us at the same time?"

Simon held her gaze. "I'm sure, Jordan. You're the best thing to happen to me in a long time. I don't want to lose you."

She felt a warmth spread through her and knew she didn't want to lose him either. "You won't," she promised with a reassuring smile. She watched his face relax into a smile.

The waiter brought their food. Jordan had chicken breast smothered in mushroom sauce; Simon had the broiled salmon. Jordan found herself admiring him as he ate.

"Wresler wants to meet with me," Simon said matter-of-factly between bites.

"Oh?"

"Yeah. I think he may be planning to offer us a deal."

She stopped eating. *A deal?* She didn't trust Wresler as far as she could throw him. And she certainly did not want to see her son agree to a prison sentence of any length for a crime he didn't commit.

"If Wresler wants to plea bargain, he must be under pressure to do so," Jordan argued knowingly. Wresler had a reputation for taking every case to trial, except those he feared losing.

"I'd say the man's definitely running scared," Simon agreed. "They don't have a murder weapon, and there are no actual witnesses to the crime." He scooped up some rice pilaf. His face creased into a frown. "But they do have witnesses who saw Trevor leaving the scene, and a DNA match of both victims' blood on and in Trevor's Explorer and on some of his clothing." The frown intensified. "And polls show the public believes Trevor is guilty, thanks in large part to the media attention on the case . . . and you as a prosecutor. If the jury buys into this sentiment, even mostly circumstantial evidence could result in a conviction."

Jordan's pulse quickened and her upper lip trembled. She knew that the lynch-mob mentality had gotten stronger in recent years as violent crimes increased and the public demanded action in dealing with violent offenders. It had become more or less guilty till proven innocent beyond a reasonable doubt. And no one wanted to believe that an assistant district attorney's son was receiving preferential treatment from the criminal justice system.

But my son is innocent of the charges, and he will not be the fall guy for this dual homicide. Jordan looked at Simon, remembering that he was Trevor's attorney and she wasn't, as much as she may have wanted to be.

"Are you saying you think Trevor *should* admit to something he didn't do for a reduced charge?" Jordan asked. She held her breath while she awaited his answer.

Simon regarded her levelly. "Not at all," he said tersely.

"I'm only saying I think it might be in Trevor's best interest to hear what Wresler's offering."

"How can it be?" Jordan asked. "Unless Wresler's offering to drop the charges altogether." Not on her life—or Trevor's—would she accept a plea bargain.

"I'm going to fight like hell for Trevor," Simon declared firmly, "no matter what the outcome. But let's face it, Jordan, there's always the chance—slim as it may be—that Trevor could be convicted of two counts of first-degree murder and sentenced to death. In the end, it has to be his call whether he's willing to take that chance."

Jordan stared at her plate dejectedly. She had talked many a lawyer into accepting a plea bargain for his or her client in the interest of justice and expediency. How many of those clients were truly innocent, but had been intimidated into pleading guilty for fear of the consequences in taking the case to trial?

In this instance, a trial could cost Trevor his life, Jordan realized. But a wrongful confession would cost him his freedom and scar him forever. As if he wasn't already scarred forever.

"Do what you feel is right as Trevor's attorney," Jordan told Simon through clenched teeth. "But I want to be there if and when you talk to Trevor about any deal."

Simon nodded.

As far as Jordan was concerned, Trevor would not settle for anything less than an acquittal on all charges. He was smart enough to realize that his future was on the line here. Not to mention his integrity and respect as a human being.

"What about other suspects?" Jordan thought out loud.

"There are no other suspects," muttered Simon sadly. "At least not officially."

"How about unofficially?"

He twisted his mouth. "Anybody who attended the party that night could have killed those two kids. Trouble is, the police have eliminated everyone who could be considered suspects. Of course, that leaves those unaccounted for. . . ." He poked a fork at his salmon. "There's no way of knowing exactly who was there and who wasn't or, for that matter, who may have been waiting outside. My investigator has been working overtime to try to come up with any solid leads on legitimate suspects. So far he's come up empty." A sour look appeared on Simon's face as he chewed slowly. "Whoever the murderer is, he or she seems to have vanished into thin air."

Or is very clever and deceptive, thought Jordan bleakly. Not to mention dangerous and deadly. Either way, she knew, it didn't bode well for Trevor.

CHAPTER TWENTY-EIGHT

Wresler had already downed two Bloody Marys when Simon McNeil walked into The Ranch. He looked as though he was lost until Wresler waved a hand as if hailing a cab, getting Simon's attention.

Wresler shook the defense attorney's large hand perfunctorily before the two sat at the table. "Glad you could make it, McNeil," he lied. The truth was, he didn't want to be there—not under the present circumstances anyhow—but had been pressured into arranging the meeting by Bombeck. The asshole D.A. was looking for a way out that would allow the La Fontaine case just to go away, while saving the career of Jordan La Fontaine.

"Your call piqued my interest," said Simon coolly. He flagged down a buxom cocktail waitress and ordered a beer.

Wresler studied his adversary. Simon McNeil kept himself in shape, just as he did. The man also knew his stuff as a defense lawyer, Wresler had to give him that much. They had bumped heads twice before and were dead-even on the scorecard. He intended to change that.

"I'm prepared to offer your client, Trevor La Fontaine, a take-it-or-leave-it deal," Wresler said, his mouth tight.

"I'm listening." Simon gazed keenly across the table.

A deep breath came from Wresler, and he said, "I'm willing to drop the charges from murder one to second-degree. La Fontaine does a minimum of ten years on each count, and avoids the death penalty."

Simon chuckled wryly. "Sounds like one hell of a deal, Wresler."

"It's a hell of a lot better than he deserves," Wresler snorted.

"If that's the case, why offer it?" Simon regarded him curiously.

"Why not?" Wresler glanced over his head at the approaching waitress. "It saves the taxpayers the cost of a trial and the family members the anguish of reliving what happened."

Simon paid for his beer, and put foam to his mouth. He glared at Wresler. "Since when did you give a damn about the taxpayers and family members? Sounds to me like you're just trying to save your own ass in a case you can't possibly win, man."

An amused smile crossed Wresler's lips, hiding the rage he felt inside. It was like a game of chess. McNeil was trying to bluff him without showing his own moves.

And vice versa.

"I think you know that's a load of crap," Wresler said with an edge to his voice. "I have all I need to get a conviction—and a death sentence. Are you willing to bet your client's life that I don't?"

Simon leaned back in his chair. "Come off the stage, Wresler. We *both* know you have no murder weapon and enough reasonable doubt to get a hung jury at the very least. If you want to deal, let's just drop a case that should never have been filed. If you don't want to insult me—and my client—then don't waste your time or mine."

That's good, McNeil, thought Wresler smugly. Damned good. But it's not good enough.

"The deal stands as it is, McNeil. I suggest you talk to your client about it before making any rash decisions. You have until tomorrow. I'll be at my office till six."

Simon finished off his drink. "Once a son of a bitch," he groused, "always one."

After McNeil left, Wresler ordered another Bloody Mary. Was it his imagination or was McNeil taking this far too personally? Wresler knew about his partnership with La Fontaine's late husband. With him out of the way, had McNeil taken his place in Jordan La Fontaine's bed as well as the firm?

The thought fascinated Wresler. He never had gone after La Fontaine himself, for practical reasons. Not that he hadn't found her to be attractive . . . and sexy as hell. Their career paths were too closely aligned for him to screw up by making a move on her and being slapped with a sexual harassment complaint. Or worse.

After he became Bureau Chief of the Homicide Division, Wresler would be powerful enough to take Jordan La Fontaine on in the bedroom. He imagined she'd be a sweet lay. But for the time being, Amanda Clinksdale would have to do.

Trevor was presented with the offer sheet, and the pros and cons. Jordan watched Simon closely, barely able to keep her thoughts to herself.

That bastard! She could imagine Wresler getting morbid delight over the anguish he was putting them— her—through. He had brought the cutthroat business of jurisprudence to a new level of nastiness.

"I had to present you with the deal, Trevor," said Simon professionally. "But I have to tell you, I think it sucks. As your lawyer, my advice to you is to tell Jerrod Wresler to shove it up his ass. You'll take your chances in the courtroom."

Trevor scratched his chin and looked at Jordan hesitantly. "What do you think, Momma?"

"No jury is going to convict you, Trevor," she said bravely. "Wresler knows his evidence is weak, and the burden of proof is on him—not you. I say we fight to the finish line."

The decision had been made.

CHAPTER TWENTY-NINE

"Why didn't you tell me?" Jobeth stood over him like a bad hangover, her blond bouffant in disarray.

"I couldn't," Coleman choked, sitting at the kitchen table.

"I'm your wife, Harry!" she yelled. "I had a right to know you'd been suspended. How do you think I felt calling the station and being told you hadn't been working there for more than three weeks?"

"I'm sorry," he said weakly, glad the children weren't home. "I was going to tell you, but I didn't know how. They blindsided me with this one." In nearly twenty years on the job, this was the first time he ever had been suspended. And if ever he got reinstated, Coleman intended for it to be the last.

Jobeth slumped down into a chair beside him, looking as though she'd lost her best friend. "It's because of *him*, isn't it? You just couldn't leave it alone, could you, Harry?"

Coleman stiffened. "No, dammit," he admitted sourly.

"I couldn't—can't. Graham Turner would do the same for me, I'm sure of it."

Jobeth leaned forward. "Do the same *what* for you— jeopardize his career for a man who's going on trial for murdering his ex-wife?" Her eyes were wide with fury. "Who the hell appointed you his savior, Harry? Why should you sacrifice what's best for your own family for a man who destroyed his?"

Coleman regarded his wife sympathetically, even if he resented her words somewhat. She had every right to be pissed. He knew it in his heart. He had put Graham Turner ahead of her and the kids. For what? To prove Turner's innocence in killing Victoria Turner when the deck was heavily stacked against him?

Maybe he had reached a dead end because there was nowhere else to go. Coleman suddenly lost his appetite. He conceded that he might have been the only person in the city of Portland who didn't believe Graham Turner was guilty. Maybe that was the problem.

But Harry Coleman had not survived being on the force for the better part of two decades without his instincts. Every fiber in him felt that Turner had been made a convenient scapegoat for someone else who decided that Victoria Turner was expendable.

Proving it had taken its toll on Coleman in more ways than one. He was not working out as much these days, making him less energetic and flabbier. He was popping vitamin pills like they were going out of style. He had borrowed money and spent what they were supposed to be saving, to compensate for the lost overtime. His marriage was falling apart . . . or so it seemed. And it was all starting to come back to haunt him like the Grim Reaper himself.

Coleman gazed at his wife. "I'll make it up to you, Jobeth," he promised, and meant it.

"How do you expect to do that?" Her arms were folded like she was his grade school teacher scolding him for being a bad boy. "Are you going to give up this . . . this crusade once and for all and start acting like a grown man with a family and responsibilities?"

She was definitely pushing it, but Coleman did not swallow the bait. "I always take care of my family," he argued vacantly. "You know that."

"I'm sure if you go talk to your supervisor and tell him you learned your lesson and will no longer step out of bounds, he'll lift the suspension and our lives can return to normal."

Normal.

What was so damned normal about their lives? Coleman asked himself. I'm a cop and cops don't have normal lives. He looked at her with irritated amusement. To be so smart in some ways, she was pretty naive in others.

"I'll see what I can do," he said to pacify her.

That night Coleman went to Club Diamonds. It was his third time there in a week. So far he had come up with no one who recognized Victoria Turner. He was beginning to think Desiree Bryar had invented the whole thing just to get rid of him.

Then Coleman showed the picture to an Asian waitress who was new to him. She was in her mid-twenties, tall, shapely, and wearing heavy makeup. Like the other waitresses there, she had on a sleek pink mini dress that was little more than a teddy. Holding the picture with long pink fingernails, she studied the face.

"Yeah, I think I seen her in here before."

Coleman became alert.

"Who is she?" the waitress asked, her long, black-blond hair hanging across one bare shoulder. "Your girlfriend?" She batted curled lashes at him coquettishly.

Coleman's mouth was a hard line. "What's your name?"

"Leona."

"Yeah, well, Leona, she was murdered on Christmas Eve."

Leona took an involuntary step backward. "You a cop?"

Coleman nodded. "I'm investigating her murder," he said truthfully, even if it was on his own time.

Her eyes widened with recognition. "She that cop's wife, the guy accused of killing her?"

"Make that ex-wife." He watched as Leona brought the picture closer to her face. "Have you ever seen her in here with a man?"

She thought about it. "Now that you mention it, I may have seen her in here the day she was killed . . . Christmas Eve." Leona put a hand to her mouth as if the enormity of the thought was terrifying. "I think she left with a man."

A glimmer of hope lit Coleman's face. "Can you describe this man?"

She shrugged. "Black, bald, maybe early forties. Didn't really get a good look at him, but I did see he was driving a fancy car. Saw him get out of it when I came on duty."

"What type of fancy car?"

"Mercedes," she said without hesitation. "Silverlike metal and very shiny."

Silver Mercedes. Coleman hummed to himself. The man was obviously into some money.

"You didn't by chance happen to notice his license plate number, did you?"

"Part of it," Leona said, to his surprise. "LEO was at the front. I remember, because I was thinking it reminded me of my name."

171

Coleman could barely contain his enthusiasm over this unlikely break. He stuck a ten spot in Leona's palm, and said, "Leona is a pretty name. Buy yourself a drink. On me."

The next morning Coleman showed up at records in the station he had until recently called his second home. Now he felt like a damned alien there, an alien been stabbed in the back by those who believed he'd stepped over the line in his pursuit of the truth in the Victoria Turner murder. He told Jobeth he was going to ask to have his suspension lifted. But that would have to wait until another day. As long as he was on paid leave, Coleman thought he might as well take full advantage of the time off—particularly now that he had a lead.

At the counter stood Stella Osborne. African-American, single, and in her late thirties. Short and shaped like a Christmas tree. Stella's ebony hair was in a Senegalese twist. Coleman flashed her a genuine smile, which she returned through her brown eyes. The two of them always had been friendly over the years, while avoiding becoming too friendly. She didn't believe in having affairs with married men, and he didn't believe in cheating on Jobeth.

"Well, hello there, stranger," Stella said in an almost girly voice.

"Hey, Stella." Coleman rubbed the bridge of his nose. "How are you?"

"Better than you," she said. "Heard you got suspended."

Word spreads fast when you're down, Coleman thought. "Yeah, a big misunderstanding. Maybe I'll do something about that."

Stella looked at him with regret. "I hope so." There was a moment of awkwardness before she said, "So don't tell me you came all the way down here just to see me?"

Coleman hesitated. "As a matter of fact, I did. I need a favor, Stella."

She regarded him warily. "Don't do this to me now, Harry. You know I can't—"

"Just a *small* favor," he implored, making himself smile his brightest smile. He removed a crumpled sheet of paper from his pocket and slid it across the counter. "I need to find out how many silver-colored Mercedes in town have a license number beginning with LEO." Coleman suspected there were only one or two at the most. "And while you're at it, run whatever names you come up with through DMV for the owners."

Stella gave a long sigh. "And how soon do you need this?"

Coleman made no bones about it. "Does yesterday sound soon enough? Or how about a month ago? Make that three months."

"Okay, okay," she said, "I get the picture." A furrow creased her forehead. "For your sake, Harry, I hope you don't get yourself into any *more* hot water. I'd hate to lose you around here for good."

He tossed her a crooked grin. "I plan to be around for a long time yet. Thanks, darlin'. Remind me to take you out for lunch when this is over."

Which he hoped would be sooner rather than later.

CHAPTER THIRTY

Jordan ran into Wilson Bombeck outside the Criminal Justice Center. He had been avoiding her like the plague for much of the time in preparing for the case against Graham Turner.

Color stained Bombeck's puffy cheeks, and he adjusted his glasses. "I've been meaning to check in on you, Jordan. How are you holding up?"

Or in other words, she thought resentfully, are you ready to get a conviction? And just maybe a big promotion—assuming your own son isn't convicted of murder too?

"We go to trial tomorrow," Jordan said. "We think we've got a solid case. You can expect our best effort in making sure Graham Turner never hurts anyone again."

"That's what I like to hear." Bombeck crinkled his blue eyes at her. "We're all counting on you and Andrew. Cops break the law, and they have to pay the piper just like anyone else."

Anyone else, pondered Jordan. Meaning Trevor?

"I haven't forgotten the presumption of innocence for

every suspect, Wilson." She glared. "I hope you haven't either."

His glasses needed readjusting again. "No, of course not." He gave an awkward sigh, then said unevenly, "I hear Trevor turned down a plea bargain."

Jordan decided to put him on the spot. "Wouldn't you, if it meant admitting to something you know you didn't do?"

Bombeck stared for a second before saying, "I hope everything works out for him—and you."

She flashed the D.A. a curt smile, and said wryly, "Be careful what you hope for, Wilson, it just might come true."

Jordan walked away without looking back and felt a some tiny satisfaction in imagining Bombeck watching her, jaw dropped, speechless.

The courtroom was buzzing, as the first day of the *People v. Graham Dylan Turner* trial commenced. Seven women and five men sat on the jury—a final compromise after the prosecution and defense each used all their peremptory challenges to dismiss potential jurors. Presiding over the trial was the Honorable Judge Sylvia Grayson, a fifty-six-year-old grandmother with frizzy blond hair. She had a reputation for being tough against criminals and tougher against attorneys in her courtroom.

Turner was seated at the defense table. He was wearing a dark navy suit and a mild-mannered look, no doubt intended to sway the jury as to his innocence. Next to Graham Turner was his attorney, Lester Eldridge, sporting a gray suit that looked too big for his lanky frame, and brown horn-rimmed glasses that seemed glued to his nose.

The prosecution team of Jordan La Fontaine and Andrew Lombard waited in readiness at their table.

"I guess it's now or never," remarked Andrew, straightening his colorful tie. His thick dark hair gleamed in the courtroom lights.

"Then I'll definitely take now," Jordan said, a soft smile tugging the corners of her lips.

"Should be a piece of cake."

"Don't bet on it. No trial is *ever* a piece of cake, no matter what you think you've got working for you. Always expect the unexpected, then be prepared to deal with it."

As usual during a high profile trial, Jordan felt butterflies in her stomach as she glanced across at the opposition. Eldridge was conferring with his client. When she had first entered the courtroom, Eldridge walked up to Jordan and they exchanged a few pleasantries that turned nasty. In spite of a less than bulked up exterior, he was intimidating in his own way, with a strong voice and an air of self-assurance that matched Jordan's own.

Eldridge put a hand to his glasses. "Just wanted you to know, La Fontaine, you're not gonna win this one—not if I have anything to say about it."

Jordan didn't flinch. "You're scaring me to death, Eldridge. If that's the best you can do, I'd say your client is in real trouble."

He buttoned one of three buttons on his Italian suit coat. "We'll see about that. No matter what the outcome, Turner did not kill his ex-wife."

"You'll forgive me if I choose to believe otherwise." She regarded him truculently. "And so will the jury, once they're presented with the evidence against your client."

Eldridge's dark eyes studied Jordan up and down. "I can see where your son inherited his viciousness, La Fontaine."

Jordan had expected such a comment from him as

an attempt to shake—or break—her. He had suc-
ceeded to a certain extent, but she did her best to keep
from showing it. Calmly she said, "Leave my son out of
this, Eldridge."

"Touched a nerve there, did I, Counselor?" He looked
pleased with himself. "I suppose, of course, you think
he's innocent? I wonder how it feels believing in someone that looks for all the world to be as guilty as hell?
Painful being on the other side of the track, isn't it? You
and I aren't so different after all, when you get right
down to it."

Eldridge gave a wicked chuckle on that note, and
walked away, leaving Jordan to feed on her own rage.

Jordan turned away from the defense table and her
unpleasant thoughts, looking squarely at Detective
Harry Coleman. He was sitting in the spectator section
and seemed to be acutely aware of her gaze, given that
his own was locked on her. She had heard that he had
been suspended for conducting his own investigation
into the case against his partner. Rumor had it that the
fiercely loyal Coleman was still doggedly determined to
somehow prove Graham Turner's innocence.

For an instant Jordan found herself wondering if
Turner could actually be innocent of murdering his ex-
wife, just as she believed with all her heart that Trevor
was innocent. Could the overwhelming physical evidence against Turner somehow be misleading . . . or
planted. And if he was innocent, who did murder her?

Jordan thought about the traces of semen and pubic
hair found inside the victim and around her genitalia.
These had yet to be accounted for, other than to rule
out Graham Turner having sexual relations with his ex
the day she was killed. From their investigation, it was
concluded that Victoria apparently had a string of
lovers and casual sex partners since divorcing Turner.

Any one of them could have been with her that day, but they had yet to find anyone with a positive match of the blood and hair type found on Victoria's body.

Could some secret lover have murdered Victoria and set up Graham Turner for some reason, perhaps as a payback for something he did as a cop? Maybe it was revenge by someone Turner had put away?

No! They had been over this a thousand times. There was no room for doubt now. Jordan was a prosecutor, and she had to go with the facts, not supposition. Or far-fetched theories. The evidence pointed toward Graham Turner as his ex-wife's killer, and it was Jordan's job to prove to the jury that he did it.

Just as it was Jerrod Wresler's job, Jordan thought with bitter irony, to prove Trevor was guilty of committing two murders.

She averted her eyes from the detective, focusing instead on the man she was about to try for the worst form of domestic violence.

Jordan had bought herself a new Belldini suit to wear on this day in court. It was lilac, with the skirt just below the knee. It went well with the off-white blouse she wore, along with low black pumps. She prided herself on wearing the latest fashions. Jordan dressed for the audience she was auditioning for—the members of the jury. It was especially important on this opening day of the trial that she leave an indelible impression on those who would be rendering a verdict in the case. She wanted them to see her as professional, competent, confident, and acceptably stylish.

Jordan carried these qualities to perfection as she sauntered toward the jury box. She measured her breathing and spoke without awkward breaks as she began her opening statement. "Ladies and gentlemen of the jury, you and I are here for one reason and one reason only—to seek *justice.*" She allowed the word "justice" to hang in the air for a moment like a cumulus cloud.

"Victoria Turner was only thirty-four when she died," Jordan continued. "Normally, she could have expected to live another forty-five to fifty years, if she was lucky. But her luck ran out on Christmas Eve. That was when she came home and found someone waiting for her. That someone was a man she was once married to— Graham Turner—a man she thought was out of her life for good." Jordan gave a dramatic pause and glared at the defendant. "But she was wrong. *Dead* wrong! Victoria Turner literally never saw him coming, but she sure as hell felt him after he reached her."

Jordan shifted her body while keeping her eyes trained on the jurors. "Using a fifteen-inch knife, the defendant first slit Victoria Turner's throat. Then, as if that wasn't good enough for the anger and contempt he felt toward her, he carved her up. Believe me, no one deserves to die the way Victoria Turner died."

Jordan stole a glance at Judge Grayson, who looked regal as she sat on her throne. The judge—her almost white-yellow hair curled in a way to make her look more down to earth—nodded as if to say she was in complete agreement. Up to this point anyway.

Jordan took a few practiced steps toward the defense table, where she could almost feel the heat of disdain. Turner gazed menacingly at her, while Eldridge refused to even meet her challenging hazel eyes.

"What is particularly tragic about this crime," she said, "is that Mr. Turner is a homicide detective—a man who normally investigates murders committed by others. Only, in this case, he decided to take the law into his own hands."

One more hard look at the defendant and Jordan moved smoothly back to the jury box. "The State intends to show that Graham Dylan Turner had a long history of physically and mentally abusing Victoria. And we will prove, beyond a reasonable doubt, that Mr. Turner continued this reign of terror even after the victim divorced him, right up until he planned and carried out the brutal murder of Victoria Turner. It will be up to you, the jury, to use that proof to make sure that her death was not in vain."

"I think you really shook them up, Jordan," Andrew said during recess.

Jordan was glad he felt that way, but she tempered her response. "Eldridge can shake the jury the other way when he gets his chance this afternoon."

Andrew rejected this with a shake of his head. "I doubt it. The man is good, but not *that* good. He can talk his ass off about Turner being a damned good cop who'd never hurt a fly. That's what he's paid for. But the proof of the pudding is in the tasting. Juries these days are way too sophisticated not to recognize a con job when they see it staring them right in the face."

Jordan wondered just how sophisticated juries really were these days. Could they truly distinguish between a defense con job and a prosecutor's con job? Would they believe Trevor was guilty—beyond a reasonable doubt—on the strength of Jerrod Wresler's opening statement, before the evidence was even presented?

"Heard the latest on the rumor mill?" Andrew broke through her thoughts.

"That depends on your definition of latest," Jordan responded, trying to recall some of the gossip that had crossed her path recently.

"Wresler and Clinksdale are supposed to be an item." Andrew tilted his head insinuatingly. "And I don't mean just in the courtroom . . ."

Jordan cocked a brow in surprise. "Really?"

"Word has it there's even talk of marriage somewhere down the line."

Amanda involved with Wresler? Jordan couldn't believe it. Marriage? No way. Had Amanda been that desperate and naive to think she could trap a man like Wresler into marriage?

Jordan knew enough about Wresler to know that he used women and spit them out like stale gum. Why should he change now? But it wasn't her place to give Amanda advice. Moreover, the two of them were not exactly on speaking terms these days, considering that Amanda was teamed with Wresler to try to give Trevor a lethal injection for a crime of which someone else was guilty.

CHAPTER THIRTY-ONE

"Are you sleeping with him?" Kendre asked, seemingly out of the blue.

"What?" Jordan looked innocuously at her from the other side of the dining room table.

"You heard me." Kendre gave her a point-blank stare. "Are you and Mr. McNeil having sex?"

Jordan barely knew how to respond, or if she should even have to discuss her sex life with her fourteen-year-old daughter. She decided to stall for time. "Why would you ask that, Kendre?"

"I'm not stupid, Mom!" She rolled her eyes. "Don't you think I know you've been seeing him?"

"He's a friend," Jordan said awkwardly. "And your brother's attorney."

"Why are you trying to keep it a secret? Don't I have a right to know if my mother's involved with a man other than my father?"

Jordan used a cloth napkin to wipe her mouth. "Your father is dead, Kendre," she told her, continuing to side-step the issue at hand.

"So you *are* sleeping with him! Admit it!"

Jordan bit her lip. There was no sense denying it. Kids were just too damned smart for their own good these days. This still didn't make it any easier discussing such intimate issues with her, Jordan thought nervously.

She sighed. "All right. Simon and I have been spending time together. I wasn't sure you could handle hearing this right now . . . with everything else. . . ."

Kendre curled a corner of her mouth. "In case you haven't realized it, I'm a big girl now, Mom," she said. "I never expected you to be by yourself forever with Daddy gone. He'd want you to have a life."

It surprised Jordan to hear her say that. She knew how close Kendre had been to her father, and feared she could never imagine Jordan being with another man. Obviously her daughter was more mature and understanding than she realized.

Suddenly Jordan found herself overcome with emotion. "I'm sorry, Kendre. I should have told you."

Kendre's eyes became watery. "Do you love him?"

A feeling of happiness swept through Jordan as she thought about it. "I think so."

After a moment or two Kendre stood and went to Jordan. She leaned over and wrapped her arms around her mother. "I want you to be happy, Mom. I really do. I love you."

Jordan held on to her daughter, grateful that when all was said and done they were there for one another. "I love you too, honey," she said tearfully.

For the first time in longer than she could remember, Jordan could see light at the end of the tunnel. But it was too soon to know if that light could be extinguished at any time.

The following evening, Jordan and Simon had dinner at Benny's Place, a soul food restaurant in Northeast Portland. They were seated near a window overlooking the Columbia River, sharing baby back ribs, sweet potatoes, and wine.

Simon's brow creased as he said tonelessly, "Frances wants to get back together."

The news hit Jordan like a bombshell. *Get back together? Why? And why now?*

She swallowed the lump in her throat, then asked him hesitantly, "What did you tell her?"

"I told her *hell no!* She made her damned bed and now she has to lie in it, but not with me!"

Jordan wondered if she should be elated or sad. After all, Simon was still married to Frances, which technically left Jordan on the outside looking in.

She took Simon's hand. It was cold and clammy. "Are you sure this is what you want . . . ?"

He squeezed her fingers. "I've never been more sure of anything in my life." Simon's eyes focused on hers. "What I want is you, baby."

Those were the words Jordan wanted to hear. "And you have me," she declared.

Simon beamed, leaned across the table, and kissed her. Jordan relished the taste of his lips for a few heart-pounding seconds, before pulling back.

"What?" Simon asked, sensing something was on her mind.

Jordan sipped her wine. "I told Kendre about us."

He sighed. "Oh, boy. How did she react?"

"She said she wants me—us—to be happy."

Simon grinned. "I always knew there was a reason why I liked Kendre so much. The girl obviously knows a good thing when she sees it." Concern suddenly dampened his enthusiasm. "What about Trevor? When this thing with him is all over, do you think he'll ever be able to accept us?"

Jordan had asked herself this very question more

than once. She knew that Trevor really looked up to his father, and would find it difficult to imagine her with anyone else. But she also believed that her son would respect her choice of Simon as a man she could be happy with.

"I'm sure Trevor will support our relationship," Jordan said confidently.

Simon smiled. "You know what—I think I've lost my appetite." He was playing footsies with her under the table. "For barbecued ribs, that is . . ."

Jordan's body tingled up and down as she watched the fire of desire dancing in Simon's eyes—a fire that was as hot as her own. "Let's go," she said.

•

CHAPTER THIRTY-TWO

LEO 472. Coleman studied the license number Stella had come up with. It was the only silver Mercedes in Portland that started with LEO. According to the Department of Motor Vehicles, the car was registered to Simon Leonard McNeil and Frances Jean McNeil of 6380 Denton Way in Portland.

So LEO 472 was Simon McNeil, the attorney, Coleman thought. He knew the man, or at least had heard of him—if it was the same Simon McNeil he thought it was.

In his car, Coleman called the precinct and asked to speak to Detective Mike O'Donnell. The two of them went way back. He was one of Coleman's few real friends on the force, aside from Turner.

In a moment, O'Donnell's boisterous voice came on the line. "O'Donnell."

"Hey, Mike, it's Coleman."

"Harry, you son of a bitch. Guess you don't have much to do with yourself these days besides calling us working stiffs, huh?"

"Yeah, not too much to do," Coleman admitted, "except try to get my ass out of the doghouse—with a little help from my friends . . ."

O'Donnell breathed loudly into the phone. "Hey, no problem. I've got your back, man. What can I do that won't get me fired?"

Coleman tensed. "That case you worked on where the two college kids were murdered at Devil's Edge," he began. "Isn't Simon McNeil defending the La Fontaine boy?"

"Yeah, that's right. Guess someone's gotta do it. Why do you ask?"

Coleman wasn't about to tip his hand at this point. Nor could he see any good reason to further strain his relations with the department—or ruin them with O'Donnell.

"Just checking," Coleman told him. "You never know when you might need a good lawyer. I figured if McNeil can get La Fontaine off, he could probably get anyone off."

"You got that right. As far as I'm concerned Trevor La Fontaine is our man. If McNeil can prove otherwise, he deserves an award as the best damned lawyer in the country."

"Yeah, I hear you." Coleman considered Simon McNeil, wondering just what type of skeletons he might be hiding in his closet. Maybe the man would soon need to defend himself in court.

"Say, Coleman, you aren't planning on committing any crimes, are you, buddy?"

"Only ones I can get away with." Coleman gave a loud chuckle for effect. "What can you tell me about McNeil?" he asked nonchalantly.

"Probably not much more than you can tell me," O'Donnell replied. "The man's probably making more money than you or I will ever see. McNeil's former partner in his law firm was his client's late father. Guess for

Trevor La Fontaine it pays to know people in high places. Not that it will do him much good in this case."

Coleman hung up. His mind was racing with possibilities. All of them revolved around Simon McNeil. Was he the man Leona saw leaving Club Diamonds with Victoria Turner? Could McNeil have been having an affair with Victoria Turner and killed her to keep his wife from finding out?

But why would he frame Turner? Was it just coincidental that McNeil happened to be defending the son of the very woman who was trying to put Turner away?

Or was Simon McNeil somehow trying to save his own ass while making himself out to be some kind of hero?

Coleman took his daily vitamins, downing them with a beer. Then he started the car and left before Jobeth and the kids got back from the mall.

The house at 6380 Denton Way had been put on the market. According to the next-door neighbor, the McNeils had separated. Simon McNeil was believed to have moved to an apartment downtown.

Coleman got on his cell phone and asked information for the number of Simon McNeil's law firm. When he called they said McNeil out of the office but could be reached at another number for emergency purposes. Instead he called Stella again.

"Stella, darling," Coleman said. "One more little bitty favor and I'm yours for life . . . if you'll have me."

Stella seemed to ponder the notion on the other end of the line. "Don't think I'm not keeping track of these markers, Harry. I intend to collect on every last one of them!"

Five minutes later Coleman listened on the phone as Stella told him, "Simon McNeil lives in the Waterfront

Tower at 18113 Alderwood Street. Fifteenth floor."

"If I could see you right now, Stella, I'd kiss you."

"I'd settle for just a hug, Harry," she grumbled. "Bye."

Coleman drove to the address and parked in the garage beneath the tower. Must be nice, he thought, to lose the wife and get this place as a consolation prize. *The monthly rent alone probably would pay half of my yearly mortgage.*

Just before he could get out of the car, Coleman saw a silver Mercedes with tinted windows drive by. The license plate was LEO 472.

Bingo!

The Mercedes pulled into a reserved parking spot. Coleman watched as Simon McNeil got out. Then a stunning, tall African-American woman with long hair got out. They kissed. And kissed again before walking arm in arm like newlyweds toward the building.

McNeil didn't waste any time getting over the wife, thought Coleman. Then he considered that perhaps he'd already been involved with this lady before splitting with the wife.

It was only when they walked right past his car, too busy noticing each other to notice him, that Coleman got a good look at the woman.

Well I'll be damned! It's Jordan La Fontaine, the prosecutor! If this don't beat all.

He watched them enter the elevator and head up before going over to check out the Mercedes.

Thanks to Leona and Stella, Coleman now had a chief suspect in the murder of Victoria Turner—Simon *LEO*nard McNeil.

189

CHAPTER THIRTY-THREE

Nevada State Trooper George Bentley sat in his patrol car just off Interstate 80, between Reno and Winnemucca. It had been a slow night, allowing him ample time to think about everything that was happening in his life. None of it was particularly satisfying. Jane, his wife of ten years, was threatening to divorce him because of his drinking problem. If he had a problem, it was her damned fault. She'd done nothing but bitch and moan around the house ever since they lost their only child to leukemia six years ago.

It was as if she'd given up on life and him. Bentley blamed himself for that. He'd tried everything to salvage what little they had left. When all else failed, and it usually did, he turned to the bottle. First beer, then bourbon. Sometimes he shared his alcohol with his girlfriend, Cynthia. She was the wife of another state trooper who was too busy with a girlfriend to notice how desirable his own wife was.

At least with Cynthia Bentley had a sex life. Sometimes it was even good. Whereas with Jane, sex had been absent for years—neither of them having much desire to be with the other. He'd thought of leaving her many times, but always backed down. Whether she knew it or not, she needed him. And in his own way, he needed her, Bentley convinced himself. They'd been through too much together. It would be difficult to be apart.

There was no future with Cynthia, he knew. She would never leave her husband, and Bentley would not let her. Whatever he felt for Cynthia, it was not love.

When he got right down to it, the only thing Trooper Bentley really loved was his job. Yes, it was stressful, at times boring as hell, with long hours and little respect from the people they were supposed to be serving. But it was his life and he was a damned good cop.

After nearly dozing off, Bentley was snapped to attention by the blur that whisked by him seemingly at the speed of light. Some asshole was in one hell of a hurry to get somewhere, he thought. *Well, I'm afraid they're gonna be late.*

He started the car and took off. Bentley could feel his adrenaline rising as he turned on the lights and siren in pursuit. The rush he got from going after the bad guys was probably the best part of his job. A fringe benefit was when the bad guy he stopped turned out to be a pretty lady. Almost always, she would act demure or like a lost puppy and try sweet-talking him into letting her off the hook. Sometimes he would, just for the hell of it. The intimidation alone was worth the effort.

He flashed his lights as he approached the vehicle. It was a green late-model van with Oregon plates. Long ways from home, he thought. *Must be missing the wife and kids mighty bad to break the law to see them.*

The van slowed down and pulled onto the shoulder. Bentley came to a stop a few feet behind it. His normal procedure was to run a check on the plates and see if the vehicle was stolen or if the owner was wanted. But this time he decided to forgo procedure, too tired to bother. Or maybe he was hoping it would be a pretty, sexy lady and it could all be handled informally.

He left the car with his flashlight and approached the driver's side of the van. It had a single occupant. The driver, a well-groomed, slender man, maybe in his early thirties, was smoking a cigarette nervously. He had already rolled the window a quarter of the way down by the time Bentley's six-five, muscular frame stood at it. He shone the light on the man's face, causing him to squint.

"What seems to be the problem, officer?" He drew on his cigarette, and exhaled a plume of smoke out the window.

"You're the problem." Bentley glared at him. "You were clocked going 88 in a 65-mile-an-hour speed zone."

The driver maintained a cool calm, and didn't look to Bentley as if he was intoxicated.

"There must be some mistake," the man insisted. "I definitely wasn't going *that* fast."

There was something about the driver that suddenly seemed disturbing, ominous, to Bentley. The way his eyes shifted—cold and calculating. The way he sucked on what almost amounted to a cigarette butt. Something definitely wasn't right about this one.

"Step out of the car," Bentley ordered. Even as he spoke, he took a defensive step backward and reached for his gun.

But he had underestimated the quickness of the driver, who had aimed a gun—it looked like a .22 or .25 caliber—through the opening in the window. It was pointed at Bentley's chest. He wasn't wearing a bulletproof vest, not usually needing one on the relatively harmless stretches of Nevada highway he covered.

Bentley heard the pop before realizing he was hit. Instinctively, he still tried to get his own gun out of the holster, but he was shot again, causing his hand to go numb. A third shot hit him right above the bridge of his nose and Bentley blacked out before his limp body crumpled to the ground.

The driver put one more bullet into the trooper's body, which was still moving involuntarily, bringing it to a deathly halt. He took a final drag on the cigarette and tossed it out the window, right next to the dead cop.

"Should have left well enough alone, man," he muttered. "Maybe in your next life."

The van sped off while the state trooper's blood began to stream onto the highway like a creek that had overrun its banks.

CHAPTER THIRTY-FOUR

On a cloudy Monday morning at the end of March, Trevor Zachary La Fontaine went on trial for his life, accused of the murders of Nelson Thomas Neilson and Gail Emily Marshall. The prosecutors, Jerrod Wresler and Amanda Clinksdale, huddled at their table going over their notes. At the defense table, Trevor was wearing a new navy blue suit. Next to him was his attorney, Simon McNeil, who chose a sleek dark gray suit for the occasion.

Jordan and Kendre sat in the first row behind them. It was important to Jordan that they show a united front as a family whenever possible, aware that the trial she was prosecuting was ongoing simultaneously two courtrooms down. She knew she walked a delicate balance in supporting her son and effectively handling her own case. It was her intention to get away from the Graham Turner trial only during recesses, off days, or times when the work was primarily procedural or formalities that Andrew could easily handle on his own.

Jordan looked at her daughter. Wearing a conserva-

tive cream dress with her micro braids in a loose ponytail, Kendre stared straight ahead emotionlessly. She
had surprised Jordan by insisting on being there every
day of the trial. Whatever deep-seated feelings stirred
within Kendre, she seemed to have come to terms with
what had happened to her brother and, more importantly, what could happen.

For her part, Jordan fully believed in Simon's ability
to sway a jury—despite having recently lost a case to
her. He was the consummate professional in the courtroom and not afraid to get his hands dirty if necessary
in order to prove his client innocent.

Jordan felt her knees go weak as she realized that she
had also just aptly described Simon's opponent, Jerrod
Wresler. Only for him, the defendant was always presumed guilty unless the defense could prove otherwise.

Wresler, immaculately dressed in a tailored soot-
black suit, was giving his opening statement.

"Why did Trevor La Fontaine do it?" he asked with a
theatrical shrug. "Revenge because Nelson Neilson embarrassed him in front of his girlfriend by roughing him
up? Anger because Gail Marshall laughed at his inability to fight back fairly against a man smaller than he? Or
maybe it was simply a case of jealousy because he
wanted Gail for himself but knew damned well that she
was out of his league. We might never know what drove
Trevor La Fontaine over the edge that day. . . ."

Wresler darted his eyes shrewdly at the defendant,
then—or so it seemed to Jordan—directly at her, as if
he got some particular delight in watching her squirm,
before narrowing in on the jury. "But what we do know,
irrefutably, is that on the night of December 24th—
sometime between nine and ten—Trevor La Fontaine
followed Nelson Neilson and Gail Marshall to the Devil's Edge parking area and *executed* them!"

Jordan's eyelids closed in pain as the words "executed them" cut through her like a dagger. Wresler had carefully painted a picture of Trevor as a ruthless, cold-blooded killer who didn't even deserve the benefit of the doubt. Would the jury play right into Wresler's hands?

"I had a clear conscience in going for the death penalty in this case," Wresler continued without flinching. "After all, the defendant showed absolutely no mercy in robbing the victims of their young lives. Why should his own life be spared, I ask you?"

Amanda Clinksdale used that moment to glance dolefully at Jordan, who met her eyes unkindly. To Jordan there could be no wavering. Amanda, once her friend, was now the enemy. To feel any different would be a mistake. A mistake that Jordan could live to regret. And one Trevor could die from.

Simon was smooth in delivering his opening statement. Unlike Wresler, he was short on the theatrics and long on the facts of the case, or lack thereof. Jordan released a slow breath in support as something told her Simon was making points with the members of the jury.

"This trial has very capable attorneys on both sides and a defendant on trial for his life," Simon said. "But what it doesn't have is a murder weapon or a plausible explanation for why a young college student with his whole life ahead of him would risk throwing it all away by viciously murdering two of his classmates."

He stepped back and turned toward Jordan. "Let's forget the fact that Trevor La Fontaine's mother is one of the high-ranking members of the very District Attorney's office that seeks to have her son convicted of murder and, if they have their way, eventually put to death . . . even as Mrs. La Fontaine is forced to put this case aside while performing her own duties as a prosecutor."

Jordan held his gaze in an instant of mutual respect

and admiration, glad that they were on the same team for this one.

Simon then glared at the prosecutors. "Let's even ignore the fact that the defendant's father was once my partner, and a damned good attorney in his own right, I might add."

A chuckle or two could be heard coming from the spectator section, though the jurors remained tight-lipped as they watched Simon intently.

He said, "What this all boils down to, ladies and gentlemen of the jury, is whether Trevor La Fontaine is truly the brutal and compassionless killer the prosecution would have you believe. Or is he an innocent victim—just like those he is purported to have killed. As a Good Samaritan, he went to their aid without regard for his own life and panicked when it dawned on him that they were already dead. How might that look to the authorities who seem hellbent on arresting young black men for any street crimes, with or without the facts to support it? Is it any wonder he left the scene—confused, afraid, and uncertain of how to proceed without making himself seem like a murderer?"

After a short breath, Simon concluded assuredly: "Trevor La Fontaine is certainly guilty of using bad judgment and fleeing the scene of a horrible crime. However, any one of you may have done the same had the circumstances been identical. But what he is definitely *not guilty* of is the murder of Gail Marshall and Nelson Neilson!" Simon narrowed his eyes. "It is your duty to judge Trevor La Fontaine strictly on the *facts*— not emotions, coincidences, or questionable circumstantial evidence. If you do that, then I am confident you will find him not guilty of the crimes for which he is charged."

Jordan fought back the tears while she gave her son a nod of approval, and squeezed her daughter's hand.

Kendre squeezed her hand back, and seemed as if she too had been reassured by Simon's opening statement.

It was only after they left the courtroom and were on their way home that Jordan learned Wresler had appeared to leave more of an impression on Kendre than Simon.

"Why did he have to say those awful things about Trevor?" she asked.

"He was just doing his job, honey." Jordan hated having to defend Wresler, but knew that in most basic respects it was the truth.

Kendre flatly rejected the notion. "Is it his job to crucify Trevor? I thought prosecutors only wanted justice, not a conviction by telling ugly lies?"

Jordan stiffened. "Some prosecutors want justice more than others," she admitted. She believed that Wresler was primarily interested in grandstanding at her expense so he could become the next Bureau Chief in the D.A. office's Homicide Division.

Kendre slumped wearily. "It's just not fair."

"That's where defense attorneys come in," Jordan pointed out. "Simon's job is to make it fair."

Kendre faced her mother. "Is that why Daddy became a defense attorney?"

"Yes." She smiled thoughtfully. "I think so. He wanted to make a difference for those who otherwise might have been at a great disadvantage in the system. Just like Simon."

"Why did you have to go to work for the D.A.?" Kendre pouted, and gave Jordan a look of disappointment. "Didn't you care about helping people like Trevor who were innocent?"

Jordan's heart skipped a beat. "Of course I did, and I do," she responded. "But I also wanted to help convict people who were not so innocent. Can you understand that, Kendre? Some people *are* guilty of committing crimes." At least one such person came to mind.

Kendre said nothing for a moment, gazing out the window. Abruptly, she turned to Jordan and said bleakly, "The jury's going to find Trevor guilty, aren't they? He's gonna die, isn't he?"

It was Jordan's turn to be silent, as her vocal cords seemed to go numb. With all her heart she wanted to tell Kendre: *Trevor will not be found guilty, sweetheart. He is not going to die.* But how could she guarantee that? In many ways, Trevor was no different than Graham Turner. His fate was tied to circumstances beyond the control of the prosecutor or defense. She could only hope that this was not a bad omen.

CHAPTER THIRTY-FIVE

Jordan called Doctor Albert Ravek to the stand. The medical examiner was fifty-five and walked with a noticeable limp, reportedly sustained from shrapnel when he served in Vietnam. His fine white hair contrasted sharply with deeply tanned skin. A dark blue suit fit loosely on his tall, thin frame.

Jordan waited a moment while the doctor adjusted his thick glasses before she began her questioning. "Doctor Ravek, you performed the autopsy on Victoria Turner, did you not?"

"That is correct," he said evenly.

"And what were the results of that autopsy?"

He shifted uneasily in the chair. "The victim died when her heart stopped due to loss of blood caused by her throat being cut."

Jordan could hear some murmurs as she faced the jury dramatically. You haven't heard the worst of it yet, she thought. But hear it they must, for only then could it really hit home what a brutal, despicable crime this was.

She moved to the other side of the witness box. "Doctor, can you be more specific about what the autopsy showed?"

Ravek sat up, pushed his glasses further back, and studied the notes on his lap. After a brief hesitation, he said, "Ms. Turner had a deep gash in her throat, stretching from one ear to the other. Her windpipe and gullet were completely severed."

Gasps could be heard in the courtroom.

Jordan used this moment to introduce photos that the defense had fought unsuccessfully to omit from evidence. They showed graphically just what damage had been inflicted to Victoria Turner's throat. State Exhibit 10-G was passed to the jurors so they could view it up close.

Jordan viewed the defendant with contempt as the jurors winced at what they saw. She walked back to the witness and asked, "Can you tell us what else you found?"

"The victim sustained bruises all over her face and body." Ravek spoke in a monotone consistent with that of a person who had probably seen it all from years of working on dead bodies.

"And, in your opinion, Doctor, what caused these bruises?"

"Pressure from a thumb or fingers."

Reasonable enough for the jury to accept, thought Jordan, as more photos were passed to them. Now for the hard part. "According to your report, Doctor Ravek," Jordan gazed at him, "Victoria Turner also suffered additional injuries."

"Yes," he said tersely. "Her right breast had been completely severed and the nipple from her left breast had been cut off." A reaction from the court caused him to pause before resuming his grim duty. "The victim was cut from the breastbone to the rectum. There were also several incisions across the abdomen and shoulders, as well as a number of stab wounds to the vagina."

The photographs of these mutilations were withheld from the jury's viewing, by mutual consent of the attorneys, though still admitted into evidence.

As soon as all was quiet again, Jordan asked Ravek, "In your opinion, Doctor, what type of instrument was used to inflict these wounds you've described—assuming there was only one type of weapon used?"

He took a deep breath and met her eyes. "I would say the murder weapon was a very sharp knife," he said confidently. "Based on the depth of many of the wounds, particularly to the throat and abdomen, the knife had to be at least twelve inches long."

Jordan walked to the evidence table and lifted what was believed to be the murder weapon—a stout backed hunting knife with a fifteen-inch blade—and brought it to the medical examiner. Holding it up for him to see, as well as the jury, Jordan asked, "Could this knife have caused the injuries Victoria Turner suffered?"

"Objection!" Eldridge rose to his feet. "Calls for speculation."

Judge Sylvia Grayson looked at Jordan with narrow blue-green eyes, heavily bagged underneath. "Rephrase the question please, Counselor," she snapped.

Jordan had expected the objection. Her point had been made. She said to the witness, "In your opinion, Doctor Ravek, could a knife similar to this one have been used to murder Victoria Turner?"

Ravek studied the weapon, but his mind had already been made up. "Yes," he said calmly. "A knife this size could have caused the wounds the victim sustained."

Jordan allowed this to sink in to the jury as she introduced the knife into evidence.

"Based on your findings, Doctor Ravek," she said, "does it seem likely that Victoria Turner's injuries were the result of a single assailant?"

"Objection, Your Honor," Eldridge protested.

"Overruled." Judge Grayson turned to the witness. "You may answer the question."

Ravek put a hand to his glasses nervously, then responded with composure, "It is my opinion that one person was responsible for Ms. Turner's murder."

"Is there anything in particular you can tell us about this person?" Jordan asked smoothly. "Such as what characteristics he or she may have?"

"Based on the angle of many of the wounds, which went from left to right, I'd say the killer was left-handed."

Which is exactly what Graham Turner was.

Eldridge wasted little time in trying to create reasonable doubt in Ravek's testimony.

"Doctor, can you say positively that Ms. Turner's killer was left-handed?"

Ravek flinched. "Of course not," he said. "But—"

Eldridge cut him off. "Isn't it possible that a right-handed killer could have used a knife backwards in cutting the victim from left to right, giving the impression he was left-handed?"

Ravek's jaw clenched. "Yes, it's possible, but from the—"

"Just yes or no, Doctor!" Eldridge demanded.

After a pause, Ravek admitted reluctantly, "Yes."

Jordan cringed in her chair. She thought she detected a slight smile on the lips of the defendant.

Eldridge was looking at her gleefully as he said to Ravek, "And isn't it also possible that more than one person could have inflicted the wounds to the victim?"

Ravek refused to buckle under without a fight. "I found nothing in my examination of the victim, sir, to make me believe there was more than one assailant."

Eldridge snorted. "Were all the stab wounds the same size?"

"No."

"Then isn't it possible, Doctor, that some of them were inflicted by a second person, using a different weapon?"

Ravek glanced at Jordan. She stood up in his defense. "Your Honor, the witness has already stated that he believes there was only one perpetrator in this crime."

Eldridge countered with, "He also testified that not all the wounds were the same size. In my book, that leaves plenty of room for doubt about the single assailant theory."

The judge looked into the air thoughtfully, then said, "Maybe you could help us clear up this discrepancy, Doctor Ravek."

The witness adjusted his glasses as Jordan sat down and pondered a redirect examination of him.

He explained: "The fact that some incisions were smaller than others does not mean that they were inflicted by more than one person. On the contrary, it would be impossible for one person to inflict knife injuries identical to one another. As a medical examiner, my job is to establish cause of death, and how it likely occurred. I stand by my belief that only one person was responsible for Ms. Turner's death."

Chalk up a small victory for the prosecution, thought Jordan. She watched Eldridge nearly lose his cool as he stomped back and forth in front of the witness stand.

Jordan turned to the spectator section, where she noted Turner's ex-partner, Detective Coleman. He had been seated there every day of the trial. But he seemed far more interested in her than anyone else. For the most part, she disregarded his unwanted attention. If the detective thought he could somehow bully her, he was dead wrong, thought Jordan. Whatever predicament Graham Turner had put himself in was his own doing. Nothing and no one could change that.

"In your autopsy report, Doctor," Eldridge was saying,

"you mention that traces of semen and pubic hairs were found in the victim and outside her vagina. Yet you also say there was no indication that she was raped?"

Ravek bobbed his head. "That's correct."

"You're quite sure about that?"

"There were no signs that the vagina had been traumatized as is often the case when someone is raped."

"But Ms. Turner did have sex with *someone*—isn't that right?"

"Yes. But based on the amount of semen found," explained Ravek, "I'd say the sexual relations occurred as many as twenty-four hours before she died."

Eldridge leaned over the witness. "Isn't it possible that the sexual relations actually took place much closer to the time Ms. Turner was killed?"

Ravek sighed. "Yes, I suppose so," he admitted, but added tautly, "That isn't very likely, though. There wasn't enough semen to—"

Eldridge cut him off. "What if the man Victoria Turner had sex with only partially ejaculated, or was wearing a condom that leaked?"

"I object to this line of questioning," Jordan spat angrily, rising. "These purely hypothetical questions call for conjecture."

"Your Honor," Eldridge said, "my client is on trial for his life. I know for a fact Graham Turner didn't have sex with his ex-wife the day she died. The evidence will prove that. But someone else did—quite possibly the man who killed her. If there is even the remotest chance that this someone should be sitting at that table instead of my client, I damn sure want it mentioned in this courtroom!"

Judge Grayson agreed, overruling the objection.

Ravek was forced to acknowledge that it was theoretically possible that Victoria Turner had sexual intercourse within hours preceding her death.

Jordan fumed. She knew the implications of Eldridge's strategy, even if it contradicted the hard evidence, and there was little she could do to stop him.

Later, Eldridge would call a criminalist to the stand to testify that the semen and hair samples found did not match Turner's DNA. If the jury believed that another man—a sexual intimate—could have been at the scene of the crime shortly before the murder occurred, then they could also believe he killed Victoria Turner.

For some reason, Jordan looked again at the spectator section, expecting to find Detective Harry Coleman. But he was gone.

CHAPTER THIRTY-SIX

When Jordan and Andrew left the courtroom, they found Harry Coleman waiting for them at the end of the hall.

He had watched the two attorneys carefully while they discussed their case. Now he intended to give them something else to chew on. Something that could put some serious holes in their attempt to have Graham Turner put to death.

Jordan stopped dead in her tracks when she saw Coleman approaching. He fixed her with fierce eyes as he said ominously, "I need to talk to you now, Ms. La Fontaine."

"I really don't think we have anything to talk about, Detective."

"I think we do," he insisted. "It's about Simon McNeil."

The name caused an uneasy reaction in Jordan, and in the process gave Coleman the instant respect that had previously been lacking from her.

Andrew gave Coleman a glance before he said to Jordan worriedly, "Is everything all right?"

"Yes," she said in a sullen voice, her gaze not leaving Coleman's face. "Everything's fine." Finally, she looked to Andrew and said, "I'll see you this afternoon."

He nodded, regarded Coleman suspiciously, and reluctantly walked away.

Jordan waited until Andrew was out of earshot before she glared at Coleman and said testily, "All right, you've got my attention. Now what's this all about, Detective?"

Coleman was not about to be dissuaded. "I was hoping we could talk somewhere more private. There's a deli not far from here that serves everything hot. I'll buy you lunch."

Jordan narrowed her eyes. "Listen, Detective Coleman, I'm not in the mood for your games—wherever you think they might get you. If there's something you have to say about Simon, I suggest you say it—right here and now."

Coleman knew this lady was every bit as tough as she was beautiful. He'd seen that in the courtroom. But she had met her match, at least in the toughness and determination department. He could see he had gotten to her by mentioning her lover and son's attorney. You ain't heard the half of it, darlin', he thought. But she'd have to wait a little while longer.

"I have evidence in the case against Graham Turner that I think you may find interesting," Coleman said with a glint in his eye. "Let me buy you lunch, Counselor. I guarantee I can make it worth your while."

He believed that curiosity and fear would get the better of Jordan La Fontaine. Now he had to take advantage of it.

The rain had begun to come down in buckets by the time they reached the delicatessen. Coleman had used his topcoat to shield them both, but some rain managed to get through, leaving him and the prosecutor with semi-dry clothing and wet hair.

Jordan did not seem fazed as she sat at the table. Her slickly groomed locks hung limply across her stiff shoulders. Without blinking an eye, she said sternly, "This had better be good, Detective Coleman."

Oh, it is. Good for me, maybe bad for you.

Coleman tasted his too hot coffee. He could see by the A.D.A.'s rigid facial muscles that McNeil meant far more to her than a romp or two in the hay. He wondered exactly how much Jordan La Fontaine knew about the man she was sleeping with. Or, more importantly, how much she didn't know about him?

"I understand Simon McNeil's defending your son." Coleman rested his arms on the table.

With a wariness mingled with the slightest optimism, Jordan asked, "Do you know something about the case . . . ?"

"I'm afraid this isn't about your son."

"Then why am I here, Detective? You mentioned evidence pertaining to the Graham Turner case."

"Yeah, in a manner of speaking." Coleman took a breath and, looking directly at Jordan, asked, "Are you aware of Simon McNeil's involvement with Victoria Turner?"

Coleman watched with satisfaction as Jordan cringed but tried to hide her shock.

"What the hell are you talking about?"

Was she really totally in the dark about this? Was she merely trying to protect her lover? Or save her son's neck?

It would be interesting to find out, Coleman thought.

"I have a witness who saw McNeil leave Club Diamonds with Victoria Turner on the night she was murdered." Coleman tasted more coffee and watched her stunned reaction.

"That's ludicrous!"

"Is it?" Coleman sighed. "I know about you and McNeil," he added. "The way I see it, your boyfriend was with Victoria that night, had sex with her, murdered her, and then framed Graham Turner for it."

Jordan's eyes were like slits as she leveled them at the detective. "How dare you? Whatever insane idea you have that you can smear a good man's name to try to get Turner off the hook, forget it. He killed his ex-wife and it'll be proven in the courtroom where it belongs."

"You think so, do you?" Coleman drummed his fingers on the table irritatingly.

"I *know* so." Jordan leaned forward. "Now you listen to me, Detective. I know all about your obsession in trying to save your partner from a murder rap. Well, it won't work. I strongly suggest, if you value whatever career you have left, that you give up this nonsense and stay out of my face. Otherwise, I'll have you brought up on charges of interfering with a prosecutor in the course of her work, or libel. The choice is yours."

Coleman gritted his teeth, fearing he had backed himself into a corner by approaching things this way.

Keeping his voice even, Coleman said, "I came to you, Ms. La Fontaine, because I wanted you to know what a snake Simon McNeil really is. Don't fool yourself into believing otherwise." He paused and held a hand up in the air. "All right, I admit I was also hoping we could work together to find the *real* killer of Victoria Turner, 'cause it ain't Graham Turner. To hell with what the evidence indicates."

What Coleman did not tell her was that he still didn't

have a hell of a lot to go on in investigating Simon Mc-
Neil. He'd found no apparent connection between Mc-
Neil and Turner that could lead to murder, aside from
the fact that McNeil might have been sexually involved
with the former Mrs. Graham Turner. But this still did
not prove in and of itself that he murdered her.

Since he felt there was virtually no chance that the Portland Police Bureau would reopen the investigation, he
had decided his best chance to stall the trial was the
woman sitting across from him. Coleman chose his next
words carefully. "Look, Ms. La Fontaine . . . my guess is
that you don't know everything about your boyfriend you
think you do. Or maybe you don't want to know . . . ?"

He tried to read the thoughts behind her sullen eyes.

"Simon is not a murderer," Jordan said curtly.

That remained to be seen, mused Coleman. *Anyone
is capable of murder if pushed hard enough, or desperate to the point of no return. Even Simon McNeil.*

"If McNeil has nothing to hide," suggested Coleman,
"then he shouldn't mind giving a DNA sample to see if it
matches the sample from Victoria Turner's body."

At the very least, Coleman thought, if there was a
match, it would create reasonable doubt that maybe
the wrong person was on trial. Or lead to a mistrial.
Even a conflict of interest on the part of the lead prosecutor was not out of the question.

Jordan faced Coleman with an implacable stare.
"Are you *insane*? I will not subject Simon to DNA tests
as a murder suspect in a case that's already gone to
trial."

"What are you afraid of, Counselor?" Coleman sensed
he had weakened her resolve and decided to keep the
pressure on. He peered at her. "Can you really afford to
turn your back on the possibility that McNeil might
have slept with Victoria Turner and killed her? Are you

willing to see an innocent man convicted of murder just so your son won't be?"

She did not respond, but the pain registering in Jordan's pensive eyes told Coleman he now had an ally.

At least temporarily.

CHAPTER THIRTY-SEVEN

The cheap motel was right around the corner from a topless bar and an adult video/bookstore in Northeast Portland's red-light district. Inside, a man sat on the couch watching Court TV. It was broadcasting live the trial of *The People v. Trevor La Fontaine*.

As far as he could tell, The People were winning hands down. Where the hell did La Fontaine get that attorney anyway? La Fontaine would have been a lot better off if he had Jerrod Wresler on his side. No such luck.

He put the bottle of malt liquor to his mouth and sucked down about half of it. At about the same time, he heard the lock of the door click. Instinctively, he grabbed the .25-caliber handgun sitting on the table and took aim. When the door opened, he saw that it was just his girlfriend. She jumped when she saw the gun pointed at her.

"You gonna shoot me or what?" She kicked the door shut. She was holding a bag of groceries cradled to her large breasts.

He put the gun back on the table. "I can't be too careful, baby," he said as his way of apology.

She walked up to him. There was a look of anger in her burnt-almond brown eyes, blended with trepidation. "Why can't you be?" she asked suspiciously. "What kinda trouble you got yourself in now?"

"No trouble." He put on his best innocent face, studying her. She was black with a butterscotch complexion, peppered with tiny moles but no wrinkles. Beneath a baggy sweater and tight jeans, her medium upper body rounded into wide hips and a big ass. He stood, and now her head only came up to his chest.

"I just didn't want the wrong person to come in here," he lied. "That's all, baby. Let's face it, this area is infested with whores, drug addicts, gang bangers, you name it." He peeked in the bag still in her arms. There was a frozen pizza, malt liquor, some frozen chicken, and a carton of cigarettes, which he now confiscated. Glancing at the gun on the table, he said, "If you ain't ready to get them first, they'll get you."

She brushed aside the thick bangs of the blond wig she was wearing, and said, "There you go talkin' crazy again."

She went into the kitchen to get away from him.

He followed. Once she put the bag down, he grabbed her from behind, turning her around in one swift motion. "Are you calling me crazy, bitch?" His bloodshot eyes pounced on her threateningly.

She choked back her fear. "No, baby," she pleaded. "I only meant that in a nice way. We're all a little crazy in this crazy world."

He smiled. "Yeah, I guess so." His momma used to call him crazy in the head. He didn't like that either. And he had made her pay for it.

He kissed his old lady, *old* being the operative word. She must have been forty-five, if a day. She was at least thirteen years his senior—and the only woman he knew who could outdrink him. At times he felt she smothered him, cramping his style. Do this, do that. Bitch and moan, bitch and moan. But she was great in the sack and could cook like his momma.

Now was not the time to bite the hand that fed him in different ways, he thought. Until he got back on his feet, she would have to do.

He kissed her again, lingering for a moment on her fleshy lips. She began to loosen up.

"What you watchin' on TV?"

"Nothing important." He put a hand on one of her huge breasts. *At least not anymore.* He put his other hand on her crotch. "I'm feeling kinda horny right now. How 'bout you, baby?"

She giggled coyly and hummed. "I'm always ready for you, sugar! Supper can wait."

At the bed, he pulled the sweater over her head and watched her big breasts flop out. He squeezed them while she made lustful sounds. They both got naked. While they stood by the bed, he fondled and stimulated her all over, becoming more and more aroused as she shook and moaned to his touch.

She went down on him and made him climax. Then he took her to bed, and fantasized that it was someone else he was with. Almost anyone would do.

When it was over, he smoked two cigarettes while she snoozed. He was starting to get that feeling again. It was far more powerful than the two orgasms he'd just had. Killing people had that type of effect on him.

CHAPTER THIRTY-EIGHT

Detective Carl Paris was in the witness box. The ten-year veteran sat poised while the prosecutor questioned him.

Wresler took a breath while studying the six-two, trim, bald detective. He made it a point to know everything about every witness he put on the stand. Aside from being an African-American who had managed to push his way past the glass ceiling to make detective rank, second grade, Paris was into his second marriage and had four children. He was also heavily in debt, due to a house he couldn't afford and overextended credit cards. Even working a second job as a security guard at a liquor store had done little to reduce his burden.

Wresler looked at him dispassionately, having already decided that Paris could not hurt the case against Trevor La Fontaine. "Can you tell us what you found when you arrived on the scene, Detective?" Wresler moved closer.

"Sure." Paris shifted a bit in the seat. "We found the victims shot to death . . . sprawled out in the backseat of the vehicle."

"The victims you're referring to are Nelson Neilson and Gail Marshall?"

Paris nodded. "Yeah."

Wresler left the witness to approach the jury. "Shot to death," he said almost to himself, but raised his voice when he asked, "Can you tell us where they were shot, Detective, and how many times?"

"Gail Marshall was shot once in the face and Nelson Neilson was shot three times—once in the face, back, and head," Paris responded matter-of-factly.

Wresler observed some of the jury members twisting their faces in anguish. Later, he would produce pictures that would guarantee they never forgot the faces—what was left of them—of Gail Marshall and Nelson Neilson. Or the man who murdered them.

"What else did you see when you and Detective O'Donnell arrived at the crime scene that night?" He faced Paris.

The detective considered the question. "There was broken glass all around the car from the windows being shattered."

Wresler sighed purposefully. "Were you subsequently able to determine what type of weapon the victims were shot with?"

Paris nodded. "They were shot with a .25-caliber handgun."

A gun that was still missing, Wresler knew, frustrated at the thought. Nevertheless, he fully intended to exploit the weapon and just what type of damage it was capable of inflicting. He hoped that, along with other physical and circumstantial evidence, would be enough to get a conviction.

Wresler put one hand in the pocket of his Ralph Lauren suit coat. Moving up to the detective, he asked, "Aside from the physical evidence collected inside the car, was there any evidence other than the broken glass found outside the car?"

Paris gave an agreeable jerk of his head. "There was blood," he began. "And a footprint."

Wresler peered at him. "What type of footprint?"

"It was from a man's boot."

"And what size was this footprint?"

"Size eleven."

Wresler gazed at the jurors without saying a word. He didn't want them to forget that size eleven. It happened to be the same shoe size of the defendant. And he happened to have boots that were a perfect match to the footprint left at the scene by the killer.

Wresler glanced briefly at the judge, and longer at Simon McNeil, before saying with satisfaction, "No further questions."

"How the hell does she manage to do it?" Amanda looked at Wresler dumbfounded as he drove to her apartment. "I think I'd go crazy if I had to try to take on a major trial and be one hundred percent supportive of my kid on trial for his life. Jordan must have nerves of steel."

Feeling his blood pressure rise, Wresler inadvertently pressed down on the accelerator, increasing their speed by twenty miles per hour. He slowed down while thinking, La Fontaine is definitely walking a fine line between being superwoman and a damned fool. He had underestimated her resilience and relentless determination. Having her show up at *his* trial regularly could somehow undermine his case.

What effect would all this have on La Fontaine's chances for the Bureau Chief spot? Wresler wondered. He had worked too damned hard and made too many sacrifices to let her ruin things for him. Whatever it took, he would do it—even if it meant seeing to it that La Fontaine's son was convicted of a double murder and put on death row.

Wresler looked at Amanda and gave her a fake smile. "Believe me, Jordan isn't doing anything you wouldn't do in the same circumstances."

"I suppose." Her body language suggested otherwise. "No matter what happens," she said sadly, "something tells me things will never be the same in the D.A.'s office again."

"Why the hell should things stay the same?" Wresler turned the corner at a sharp angle. "Life is about change and compromise." He blinked at her. "Don't go soft on me, Amanda. Not yet. I need to know I have your loyalty—in the courtroom and in bed."

She turned her mouth into a full smile. "Of course you do, Jerrod," she said. "If I made you feel otherwise, I didn't mean to."

Oh yes you did, he told himself. He had sensed from the very beginning Amanda's reluctance in her role as collaborator in putting Trevor La Fontaine on trial for his life. In a way, Wresler found her camaraderie with Jordan La Fontaine to be admirable. He had used this to his advantage in requesting Amanda to assist him in the case. He thought it was a masterful plan to secure his position and weaken La Fontaine's by using one of her few friends in the D.A.'s office to help him prosecute her son for murder. So far it was working like a charm, he thought. Not to mention the fringe benefits he was getting from it.

Wresler stroked Amanda's hair and said sweetly, "Why

don't we turn our attention to more important things?"

Amanda gave him an amorous look. "What did you have in mind, Counselor?"

He put his hand between her legs. "Figure it out."

CHAPTER THIRTY-NINE

Simon was cross-examining Detective Michael O'Donnell when Jordan entered the courtroom. Rather than take her normal seat behind Trevor, she elected to remain in the back. Somehow even in the midst of the cross-examination Simon seemed to spot her, offering a hint of a smile.

Jordan nodded at him, but her cordiality belied the uncertainty she felt inside. It had been two days since she had lunch with Detective Coleman. She had wanted with all her heart to reject his allegations as a preposterous last attempt to cast doubt on the case against Graham Turner—at least in *her* mind. Even stooping so low as to spy on her relationship with Simon.

But she knew that the crass detective had gotten her thinking about it, even when she tried hard not to. It would have been easy for Jordan to turn her back on Coleman's so-called witness and have the detective charged with falsifying evidence and perhaps illegal surveillance—had it not been for Coleman's mention of Club Diamonds.

Club Diamonds. The name had sounded vaguely familiar to Jordan. Then she remembered. She had found the book of matches on the floor in Simon's apartment on Christmas Eve. It was from Club Diamonds. She was sure the matches had fallen from Simon's pocket, indicating he could have been there that day. Or night.

Was it a coincidence? Or had Simon really been with Victoria Turner on the same night he had been with *her?*

Jordan recalled the blond hair she had seen in Simon's bathroom that night. They definitely belonged to a woman. And Victoria Turner just happened to have long blond hair. Was it her perfume that Jordan smelled in the bathroom that night?

Could Simon actually have murdered Victoria and framed Graham Turner for it?

The mere thought left a bitter taste in Jordan's mouth. Yet she found it hard to totally dismiss the possibility, though she desperately wanted to. For one thing, she had talked with Coleman's witness. Leona Kwon hardly seemed like the most credible witness. Nor was she prepared to give a positive identification in court that it was Victoria she saw, much less Simon. But the license plate, or the part that Leona remembered—LEO—was too much to ignore. It had to be Simon's car. Leona had described it perfectly.

Jordan believed that Simon *had been* at Club Diamonds on Christmas Eve, before he arrived at The Ranch. Was there time for him to have taken Victoria to his apartment, follow her home, violently murder her, change his clothes, and show up at The Ranch as if he'd been there all along?

Jordan considered this and the frightening implications as she looked up at Simon questioning the witness.

"Detective O'Donnell," Simon was saying, "isn't it possible that this lone size eleven footprint that was somehow found intact on an asphalt parking lot, where there was virtually no snow on the ground, could have come from someone *other* than the killer?"

"Not likely," O'Donnell said with a smirk, and turned his large body. "Everyone else at the scene was accounted for."

"Not *everyone*," Simon insisted adroitly. "The real killer definitely has not been accounted for."

O'Donnell curled a lip. "With all due respect, Counselor, I wouldn't expect you to say any different—considering your client faces lethal injection when he's convicted of killing those two kids."

"Strike that from the record," the judge ordered, and warned the witness against such future prejudicial comments.

Jordan's thoughts drifted in and out of the cross-examination. Her mind dwelled on the inferences—both personal and professional—that Simon could in any way be connected to Victoria Turner's death.

Simon circled the witness like a vulture, and said with a measured voice, "Isn't it true, Detective, that there is *no* murder weapon?"

"No, it isn't true, Counselor," O'Donnell said smugly. "There *is* a murder weapon. It just hasn't been found yet."

This drew some laughter from the courtroom that shut off just as quickly.

"But you did find a .25-caliber automatic at the defendant's house?" contended Simon. "Did you not?"

O'Donnell paused. "Yes, we found a gun."

"And it's already been established that the victims were both shot with the same .25-caliber gun. Is that right, Detective?"

O'Donnell gave a noisy sigh. "Yeah. I mean, yes."

"But *not* the gun you found in Mr. La Fontaine's home?"

O'Donnell lowered his head and said almost in a whisper, "No."

"Don't go quiet on us now." Simon glared at him. "Would you please answer the question again, Detective—only this time loud enough for the jury to hear? Is the gun you confiscated from the La Fontaine home the one used to kill Gail Marshall and Nelson Neilson?"

O'Donnell drew his brows together. "No," he said loudly. "It wasn't the same gun."

"You testified earlier, Detective O'Donnell, that the murder weapon had a gun barrel that had six lands and grooves and a right-hand twist. Is that correct?"

O'Donnell glanced in the direction of the prosecutor's table and back to Simon. "Yeah."

"And, if I'm not mistaken, the gun you took as evidence against Mr. La Fontaine had a gun barrel with *five* lands and grooves and a *left*-hand twist." Simon stood tall over him. "Is that correct, Detective?"

O'Donnell twisted his lips and barked, "Yes. That still doesn't mean—"

"I have no further questions for this witness." Simon dexterously cut off the detective and looked at the judge.

But I have questions for you, a voice inside Jordan's head screamed at him. Though she marveled at Simon's mastery in court, much to the benefit of Trevor's defense, Jordan was far from satisfied that he was getting the *best* defense—especially if his attorney was a murderer.

During afternoon recess, Simon took Jordan to lunch at the Café Renault, a stylish restaurant specializing in authentic African cuisine.

Jordan listened thoughtfully as Simon talked about Trevor's trial, the witnesses he intended to call, and the prosecution witnesses he planned to go after. All the while, she was picturing him having sex with Victoria

Turner. And stabbing her to death with the viciousness the killer obviously possessed.

Do I really know this man I've given my body and soul to? Jordan asked herself fearfully. This man I've fallen in love with?

Was that love gained under false pretenses?

Please tell me, Jordan moaned inside, that Simon McNeil is not this . . . monster that Harry Coleman says he is.

"Jordan—" She heard her name, as if coming from a tunnel. Her eyes turned to Simon's frowning face. "You seem like you've been miles away."

Jordan felt like she was looking at a stranger. "I'm sorry," she mumbled, trying to recall what he'd last said, even as she weighed her options. "It's just been hard to keep my focus with the prosecution's case against Graham Turner at a critical stage." Not to mention Trevor's ongoing trial, she thought, with Simon defending him. She wondered if the two murder trials were, in fact, interwoven—with Simon squarely in the middle.

Simon stuffed spiced broccoli and cauliflower salad in his mouth, and looked at Jordan tenderly. "I don't envy the position you're in. Not one iota." He chewed. "Look, maybe you should just put everything you've got into getting a conviction, baby, and let me worry about Trevor—"

"How can you say that?" she demanded in disbelief. "He's *my* son, dammit!" As though that was all this was about, she thought sickly.

"And he's my client, Jordan!" Simon snapped, wiping a corner of his mouth with a napkin. "You've put him in my hands and I'll get him an acquittal—if it's possible. . . ."

If it's possible? This was the first time Jordan had heard

Simon speak with uncertainty. Was he having doubts about an acquittal? Or doubts about Trevor's innocence?

Or was he slickly trying to shift the discussion away from The People v. Graham Turner?

Jordan sipped her Tanzanian peaberry coffee, then asked casually, "Did you know Victoria Turner?"

Simon lifted his brows as though caught off guard by the question. "The dead woman?" he asked.

"Yes."

"No," Simon said flatly. "Never had the pleasure." He waited a moment before saying, with a catch to his voice, "Why do you ask?"

Jordan had observed Simon carefully when she asked the question. She was certain it had unnerved him, if only momentarily.

"Just wondering," she lied. "I heard she was a regular at police and attorney hangouts, like Club Diamonds. I thought you could have run into her there and might know what type of woman she was."

He sighed. "I'm afraid not. Never even heard of Club Diamonds."

Oh yes you have, Jordan thought. She had just caught him in a baldfaced lie. Why? What was he trying to hide? She didn't even want to imagine—but knew she had to.

"I've got a terrific idea, Jordan," Simon said, having already forgotten about—or pretended to—Victoria Turner. "Why don't we go up to my cabin in the mountains this weekend, while it's still *my* cabin."

Jordan knew that last part was in reference to the very real possibility that Frances would try to get the cabin as part of a divorce settlement. But that's not my problem at the moment, she told herself. It's his. But it may not be the only thing he needs to be concerned about . . .

"I can't," Jordan told him. Was he trying to seduce her into rejecting her suspicions about him? "I have way too much work to do."

"It's just for the weekend, Jordan, for crying out loud," he pressed, clearly disappointed. "You could use the break. I know I sure as hell could."

The last thing Jordan wanted right now was to spend time alone with Simon—something that she could not have imagined feeling just days ago. But she couldn't ignore the circumstantial evidence or the bad vibes she was getting. *If he had actually killed Victoria and framed Graham Turner, what would stop him from killing me if he believed I was onto him?* Jordan wondered.

"I can't leave Kendre alone for that long," she said, averting Simon's gaze.

"We can bring her along," he suggested with determination. "There are plenty of things for her to do there to keep busy. If not, we'll invent some." When Jordan hesitated, Simon said entreatingly, "Kendre's not a little girl anymore, Jordan. I doubt she'll fall to pieces at the thought that we may be in the next room doing what people do who care about each other."

It's not Kendre I'm worried about, Jordan told herself. *It's you, Simon . . . and us . . . and Trevor . . . and Victoria Turner before the fact and,* she mused, *Graham Turner after the fact.*

Jordan closed her eyes for a moment, confusion and uncertainty giving her a headache. Why was spending time alone with her in his cabin so damned important to him? Was it really just to get away from it all?

Or was it to get her alone . . . for all the wrong reasons?

She opened her eyes to Simon's concerned look. She tried to picture him cutting up Victoria Turner the way the killer had. It was clearly the work of a man full of hatred with the propensity for the worst kind of violence.

No matter how much the possibility existed, Jordan could not believe that she could fall for such a man. Or that he would have been Eric's best friend and law partner without either of them suspecting such a dark side.

But still, Simon was definitely keeping something from her. Starting with Club Diamonds. Was there more?

"Jordan . . ." Simon clearly sensed that something was troubling her in a big way.

Jordan was hesitant but reassuring when she told him, "I'll have to think about the cabin, Simon."

"All right." He offered her a forced smile of acquiescence.

In her mind Jordan knew she didn't want to accuse Simon of being Victoria Turner's lover and possible killer. Not without hard proof.

CHAPTER FORTY

Coleman visited Graham Turner in his jail cell to brief him on the status of the investigation. He had briefed Turner's attorney previously. Now, for the first time, Coleman could see a ray of hope in Turner, hope that something good might finally be happening.

"So where do we go from here?" Turner asked optimistically, scratching his head.

"We get the case reopened," Coleman said, not hiding his own enthusiasm. "And that means a new police investigation into a *new* suspect."

Turner frowned. "You really think this lawyer, Simon McNeil, was seeing Victoria . . . and killed her?"

"I think it's a damned good chance. McNeil sure as hell didn't volunteer to come forward to say he was sleeping with her at the time she was killed." He leaned back in the chair. "Why not? In my book that makes him our prime suspect."

Turner stood and turned his back to Coleman. "Damn. I played ball with the son of a bitch. Now you're telling me he murdered my ex and framed me for it?"

"That's how it looks to me." Coleman knew that he didn't have all the pieces together to nail McNeil's ass, but that seemed to be a mere formality. Right now, he had to give Turner something to hold on to, until he could walk out of this hellhole . . . hopefully in one piece.

Graham Turner sounded like he needed this hope. "It's been a damned nightmare being in here, man. In fact," he grumbled, "it's been a thousand times worse than that. To tell you the truth, Harry, I'm not sure just how much longer I can take it. Especially when the asshole who sliced up Victoria is walking around a free man . . . trying to get that La Fontaine kid off the hook, so they can both dance on Victoria's grave."

Coleman regarded him compassionately. "That won't happen," he promised his partner. "Not if I can help it. With any luck, you won't have to take this crap much longer. If we can establish the strong possibility that you were set up, at the very least you should be able to get bail." He narrowed his eyes. "In the meantime, don't even think about doing anything stupid, Turner."

Turner gave Coleman a half-hearted smile. "I owe you, man. Whatever happens, I owe you a hell of a lot."

Coleman was genuinely moved, but shrugged it off. "You don't owe me nothin'," he insisted. "You would've done the same for me."

Turner flopped onto his unmade cot, which seemed too small for his tall, well-developed body. "So how are things between you and Jobeth?"

A dour look crossed Coleman's face at the thought. They had certainly seen better days. Right now they just seemed to be tolerating one another the way stepmothers tolerated stepchildren. He had no idea what the hell their future held. Save for the kids, they probably already would have joined the ranks of the divorced long ago. But that was between him and Jobeth.

"We're hanging in there," he said simply.

Turner slanted his head. "I know this . . . what you're doing for me, putting your career on the line . . . has to be hard on Jobeth."

Coleman saw no sense in denying it. "She has her problems with it," he conceded. "But deep down, Jobeth knows that right is right. Besides, our problems go back a long way. We'll work them out one at a time."

He wasn't sure he really believed that, but he was not about to give up on her yet.

Turner's eyes lit up. "Victoria always liked Jobeth. You know they should have been closer. If only . . ."

Coleman agreed. But if he had a quarter for every thing that should have happened, he would be rich, retired, and fishing every day off the coast of Florida without a worry in the world.

Unfortunately, things didn't work that way in the real world. At least not for people like him and Turner. Even so, he held out hope that at least justice would be served in Victoria's murder.

And that Simon McNeil would get what was coming to him.

Harry Coleman took his wife out to dinner that evening. He couldn't remember the last time just the two of them had gone out anywhere. Maybe that was part of the problem.

Jobeth was wearing a beaded silk silver dress he had bought her two years earlier to celebrate their sixteenth anniversary. Now, Coleman reflected sadly, she was probably ten pounds heavier and the dress looked as if it were smothering her.

He was in his one and only suit—a Haggar charcoal-black three-piece—that he'd had for years and wore only for special occasions. Or on nonspecial ones like this, when he was trying to kiss and make up with the wife.

They ate in silence for a long time before Jobeth said, "Why are we here, Harry? What aren't you telling me?"

She gave him an anxious, uneasy look. He sucked in a breath and said calmly, "I've been reinstated. Thought we'd celebrate."

Jobeth eyed him with skepticism. "When?"

"Today." Coleman pressed his lips together. "They realized they had no real grounds to suspend me. What I did on my own time was my business." What he didn't tell her was that he was still treading on thin ice. So thin that it could break through at any time. Captain Fisher did not like his authority challenged, even if there was clear justification.

And in Coleman's mind there damned sure was. He had given the department a viable new suspect in the Victoria Turner murder. Fisher had assigned a couple of other detectives to follow up on it discreetly, while refusing to make waves in the State's case against Graham Turner.

Coleman was given his job back on the condition that he keep his nose out of the Turner case from this point on. He had agreed, only because he had no other choice. At least not officially. But so long as Turner was kept caged like an animal for something he swore he didn't do, Coleman was committed to seeing this thing through come hell or high water.

"Just seemed like a good idea for us to spend some time away from the kids," Coleman told Jobeth, forking a piece of filet mignon.

She seemed pleased that he still cared enough to want to be alone with her in public. To Coleman, it was never a question of shame or displeasure, but rather staying focused on what was really important—even if he wasn't quite sure what that was anymore.

"What's happened to us, Harry?" Jobeth asked sadly while she stirred her vegetable soup. "Why can't things go back to the way they used to be?"

"We've gotten older, Jobeth. We're not the same people anymore. Hell, I'm not even sure we're on the same page as far as what we want out of life."

His expression betrayed the resentment he felt that she was no longer the same woman he had married. Never mind the fact that he wasn't the same man she'd married.

Jobeth blinked back tears, and Coleman hated himself at that moment for making her cry. He'd never been very tactful about anything, and he regretted it. They had married for better or worse, and he owed her as much respect and understanding as he expected from her.

He took her hand, steadying its shaking. "I'm sorry, baby. You know I don't mean to hurt you. I really want to make things work between us again." He locked eyes with her and felt the beat of his own heart. "Whatever it takes—you, me, and the kids are in this together for the long run."

Coleman wiped away the tears sending mascara down Jobeth's reddened cheeks. The two of them had reached a stage in their relationship where something had to give. He firmly believed that "something" was the wall that had been forming between them for some time, threatening all they had come to rely on from one another.

They made love that night for the first time in weeks. It was short and sweet but satisfying. Something to build on, Coleman told himself. Once Jobeth had drifted off to sleep, he turned his thoughts to Jordan La Fontaine and Simon McNeil. He wondered if they were in bed together at that very moment. More importantly, he wondered about the prosecutor's plan for going after the man who was defending her son. The man who may have killed the ex-wife of Graham Turner, and who La Fontaine was prosecuting for that very crime. The irony of the circumstances was as fascinating to Coleman as it was important to Turner.

After a while, Coleman drifted into sleep, still thinking about Jordan La Fontaine.

CHAPTER FORTY-ONE

"So do you plan to marry Simon, or what?" Trevor asked Jordan.

Jordan was not sure if it was a question or an accusation. They had been talking about his case and Simon's defense of him, when Trevor mumbled the question out of the corner of his mouth.

"How do you feel about it either way?" Jordan responded timidly. She had told him only that she was seeing Simon and liked him a lot—receiving a "tell me something I don't know" response. As far as Jordan could tell, Trevor had seemed fine with it. Now she wasn't sure how she herself felt, considering the fact that Simon might not be all Jordan thought he was. And perhaps far worse.

But this wasn't something to talk to Trevor about, she told herself. Certainly not while his future was in Simon's perhaps less than honest hands.

"I think you should go for it," Trevor said without hesitation. "I know that Dad's a hard act to follow. But if you and Simon love each other and want to make a life together, I'm not gonna stand in your way. Kendre feels the same. Simon's good stuff."

"How do you know he's good stuff?" Jordan asked pointedly, painfully aware that Simon was keeping secrets that could jeopardize not only their relationship, but Trevor's defense.

Trevor looked puzzled by the question, and drew on a cigarette. He had taken up smoking in recent weeks, to Jordan's disappointment. She hoped it was just a temporary thing while he was confined and unable to explore more healthy habits.

"He was Dad's partner, wasn't he?" Trevor said, almost as if to remind Jordan. "And the brother's crazy about you. He told me so himself." Another drag on the cigarette. "If that's not enough, the man's probably all that's standing between me and death row. If I can't believe Simon is good stuff, I may as well get used to the idea of spending the rest of my life in here . . . till they're ready to take it away."

Jordan felt the erratic beat of her heart as she thought of the lethal injection administered to Oregon inmates sentenced to death. The very notion of her son being subjected to that was almost unbearable. Whether she liked it or not, Simon was quite possibly Trevor's best hope in avoiding that fate. At this stage of the trial, it would be akin to legal suicide to replace Simon.

It was a chance Jordan was not willing to take in looking out for her son's best interests. Even if her own interests concerning Simon may well have hung in the balance.

Jordan left the question of marriage alone for now. There were still more disturbing unanswered questions about the man she wanted to love and possibly spend the rest of her life with.

* * *

After giving it much consideration, Jordan decided to take Simon up on his offer of spending the weekend at his cabin. Aside from her conflicting feelings, it seemed like the only way to confirm or refute that it was his sperm and hair found in and on Victoria Turner's body, without formally drawing Simon into the case or prematurely jeopardizing the case against Graham Turner.

Kendre was staying with Lenora over the weekend.

During the drive up Highway 26, Jordan let Simon do most of the talking. She wondered if she was doing the right thing in using their intimate relationship to get possible evidence that could be used against him. What if there was no DNA match? Could he ever forgive her? Could she ever forgive herself?

On the other hand, what if it was a positive DNA match? For one, Jordan knew it would mean that Simon had slept with Victoria Turner, probably on the day she was killed. Meaning that he could be the one who killed her, in spite of the strong evidence pointing directly at Graham Turner.

Most importantly, what would implicating Simon in Victoria Turner's murder do to Trevor's chances for an acquittal?

"If I'm boring you just say so." Simon's voice caused Jordan to jump.

"I'm sorry," Jordan said tremulously. "I was thinking about Trevor."

Simon frowned playfully. "No thinking about Trevor allowed, remember? Or, for that matter, anything else that can dampen our sprits this weekend."

Simon seemed to glow with self-confidence and anticipation. Not at all like a man who had something to hide—like murder. Am I going on a wild goose chase? Jordan asked herself. Maybe all her suspicions could be easily explained away—including the blond hair in his bathroom and the matches from Club Diamonds.

Maybe jumping on Detective Harry Coleman's bandwagon was playing right into the hands of Graham Turner, at Simon's expense. And her own.

Or maybe Coleman was on to something that couldn't easily be dismissed, Jordan thought, studying Simon's handsome profile behind the wheel. One thing she knew for certain: Victoria Turner had sex with someone other than Graham Turner the day she died. That person, whoever he was, could hold the key to her murder in either burying Turner that much deeper, or exonerating him.

Willing her mouth to curve into a convincing smile, Jordan answered sweetly, "Yes, I remember, baby. I promise, from this point on, I'll keep my thoughts on you and me."

She watched as Simon broke into a pleased grin. "That's a promise I intend to hold you to, sweetheart."

Jordan was still wrestling with the word "sweetheart," and wondering how many other women he had called that—maybe Victoria Turner—when they arrived at the cabin. It was nestled in the Cascade Mountains at the base of a waterfall. Simon and Frances had bought the two-bedroom pine cabin five years ago. Jordan and Eric had spent one weekend there two summers back. They had talked about borrowing the cabin for future getaways, but had never found the time to follow through.

Jordan regretted it now, as she and Simon unloaded their bags. It was as if seeing the cabin again reminded her of just how much she and Eric had intended to do and how short and unpredictable life was.

"I'll go out and get some firewood," said Simon, his breath indicating the chill in the air.

"And I'll unpack," Jordan volunteered.

She hung up clothes, put food in the refrigerator

and cabinets, and found herself dusting away the cobwebs. Anything to keep busy—to somehow get through this pretense and deception, not sure what was real anymore.

I guess I'll find out soon enough, she thought uneasily.

Later, by the fire, Jordan lay atop a brown leather couch in Simon's arms while they drank Chardonnay and he serenaded her with a surprisingly deep and velvety voice. Though wanting to resist Simon's charms, Jordan felt herself falling for them more than ever. Right now she wanted only to go with the flow, forgetting for the moment all the doubts.

"How beautiful you are, my darling," Simon whispered in her ear, tickling her earlobe at the same time. "Let me count the ways . . ." And he began counting with well-placed torrid kisses. "One . . . two . . . three . . ." He went from Jordan's face to her neck to her cleavage. "Four . . . five . . . six . . ."

Jordan tingled all over as his kisses burned to her very soul. Simon undressed her, slowly and deliberately. She did the same to him. They lay on a bearskin rug in front of the fireplace, where Simon resumed his counting as he kissed the skin all over Jordan's body.

"Twelve . . . thirteen . . . fourteen . . ."

Jordan bit into her tongue when he put his mouth between her legs and began to kiss her there. She tried to push him away. This wasn't what she wanted. Not now. She didn't want to enjoy him and have him enjoy her. But she hadn't counted on her body having a mind of its own. It yielded to Simon's touch in a way she could not have prevented.

A cry erupted from deep within Jordan, as Simon's tongue stimulated her clitoris relentlessly until she shuddered violently. She grasped his head, and held it tightly to her.

Simon slowly but surely worked his way back up Jordan's body, planting kisses along the way. Once their bodies were aligned, Jordan opened up to him and he drove himself in without preamble.

She winced slightly, and it turned into a lingering moan as she felt Simon deep inside her. She wrapped her legs around his hard back. All other things seemed lost to the moment. She wanted only to experience the breathless pleasure he gave her, while returning it in full force.

Simon screamed and cursed, his body trembling uncontrollably as he began to climax. Simultaneously, Jordan was basking in her own orgasm, feeling lightheaded and stimulated, her body responding to every contour of his. A final surge left both charged and grasping for the waning moments of sheer delight.

When it was over, Jordan lay beside Simon, her head on his chest, their bodies glistening with sweat and the sweetness of sex. Neither said a word, actions having spoken for them loud and clear. Jordan felt ashamed that she had given in to desire—to him—so completely and without compunction. Damn, she thought, you are so wonderful in so many ways. Please don't let this whole thing be nothing more than a front—while another side of you is capable of murder.

Even if a part of her wished she could simply ignore those doubts and fears, Jordan knew she had to put them to rest one way or the other. It was the only way she could even think about a future with this man. She needed to get what she came here for.

"I'd better go freshen up," she said.

"Hurry back, baby. I can't stand to be apart from you for even a second."

She kissed him and smiled warmly. "I won't be long."

Jordan left the bedroom and headed down the hallway toward the bathroom. On the way, she grabbed her purse from a chair. She entered the bathroom, closing the door behind her.

She glanced at her naked body in the full-length mirror. On her upper thigh she could see a small amount of ejaculation that had oozed out of her or never made it in. After contemplating further, she knew what must be done.

Reaching into her purse, Jordan took out a small plastic bag. She removed a cotton swab and dabbed it in the wetness till it disappeared. After placing the swab back in the bag, she sealed it, and put it inside a cosmetic case in the middle section of her purse.

Then Jordan sat on the toilet lid, where it was all she could do to keep from crying. She knew she was doing the right thing in making sure Simon had not done the wrong thing. But it was still tearing her up—for more reasons than one.

After a moment or two, Jordan got up and washed her face, knowing she had to go back out there and pretend everything was all right. Inside, she felt it couldn't possibly be okay . . . not until she knew if Simon McNeil was the man she wanted him to be.

CHAPTER FORTY-TWO

Willie Armstrong had been mixed up in drugs since being turned out by his mother when he was five years old. First it had been with his uncle. Then his aunt. Then other relatives and their friends.

By the time he was twenty-five, Willie had become a small-time drug dealer and gone from street hustling to pimping. His three girls sold roofies—the little white pills from South America—and their bodies. Some believed he was affiliated with the Bloods gang. Others took him to be a member of the Crips. The truth was, he operated alone. And for good reason. Why the hell should this brother share whatever he could earn, when it could all go in his pocket or up his nose?

When Willie Armstrong paid a visit to the cheap motel called North Hollywood, he came dressed to kill, figuratively speaking, in a three-piece Diamanti gabardine suit, black maxi leather coat, and Versace shoes. He liked wearing flashy, expensive clothes on his lean six-two frame. They were not only the trappings of success, but also a way to earn respect from his girls—and anyone who wanted to mess with him. His insurance policy was a .357 magnum and, like his American Express card, he never left home without it.

In the dingy room, Willie collected the evening's earnings from Tricia. She was a red-haired, chalky-skinned, tight-assed nineteen-year-old from Minnesota. A crack addict, she'd been turning tricks for him for two years. As a businessman, he knew she was damaged goods that could only go so far. But as long as she could still spread her legs, give blow jobs, and sell dope, he intended to milk her for everything her white ass was worth.

"This all you got for me?" Willie gave Tricia an angry, suspicious look.

Her face turned red. "I only did two tricks tonight," she stammered meekly.

He grabbed her roughly. "Bitch, you lyin'. Don't hold out on me!"

"I ain't, Willie." Her voice grew desperate. "I swear!"

He backhanded her, sending the high and frightened young woman flying across the room, collapsing to the floor with a thud. She struggled to her feet, wiping blood from the corner of her mouth and one nostril.

"Please, Willie," she wept, "don't hit me again."

But Willie came after her, prepared to do whatever he had to do to get what he believed she was hiding from him. "I ain't even gotten started with you yet. C'mere, bitch!"

With a quickness that caught Willie off guard, Tricia lunged toward the door. She managed to get it halfway open before Willie grabbed her by the strawlike hair that hung limply across her shoulders, and yanked her backward. He never imagined or expected that a man would be standing outside the door.

He was white, thin, and looked to be in his early thirties. In fact, unbeknownst to Willie, the man had been

Tricia's last john. He had a .25-caliber gun in his hand, and it was pointed at Willie.

Knowing his own .357 was tucked inside a pocket in his leather coat on the bed, Willie instinctively raised his hands, deciding against trying to wrestle this dude for the gun. He figured the man was probably at the wrong door, looking for his cheating old lady or something.

Willie Armstrong couldn't have been further from the truth. For the man with the gun had found *exactly* who he was looking for.

"Thought you could use some company, *bro*," he said, forcing his way inside with the gun pointed at Willie's face. He closed the door behind him, while keeping a watchful eye on Willie Armstrong. Not to mention his whore, who looked slightly relieved and concerned at the same time.

For his part, Willie was itching to go for his gun. But the white dude had crazy eyes and kept his finger too damned close to the trigger of his gun for Willie's comfort.

"Whatchoo want, man?" Willie felt himself perspiring, his hands still raised, and getting tired.

"Her." The man pointed at Tricia, who flashed him a smile of familiarity, and seemed to grow comfortable with the prospect of being rescued from her brutal pimp. "Come to think of it," he said with a chuckle, "I already had her. And she was good." He licked his lips lasciviously.

Tricia took an involuntary step backward, and a light-bulb suddenly flashed inside Willie Armstrong's head. The stupid bitch had probably stolen the man's wallet, he guessed, which she was prone to do with mild encouragement from Willie.

He turned to the white dude with the crazy eyes and gun, still aimed in his direction. Giving his best smile, Willie said, "Look, man, you can have your money back if that's what this is about."

The man smiled back at him. "Wrong again, bro," he said. "This ain't about money. It's about justice and power."

A look of trepidation flashed across Tricia's face as she began to sense that this man wasn't there to help her.

Willie got the same feeling and decided it was now or never to do something about it. He went for his piece, hoping the man was a bad aim. Or better yet, just bluffing.

But the man with the gun had anticipated this and fired without hesitation, striking Willie in the side of his face, shattering it. The black pimp went down as if sucker punched. A second, lethal bullet was pumped into his head, putting Willie Armstrong out for the count.

The gun was turned on Tricia. A bullet struck her in the chest as she made a feeble effort to avert it. Lying in her own blood, she tried to crawl away, begging her assailant for mercy. But, like the pimp, she got none. He shot her once more, this time in the back of the head, silencing her permanently.

The man took only a moment to savor the release his handiwork brought, before walking over the dead bodies and to the door, placing the DO NOT DISTURB sign on the knob.

He lit a cigarette calmly, laughed, and went on his way.

When the police arrived an hour later, they assumed it was a gang, drug-related, or sexually motivated double homicide. They could not have suspected that the killing had a lot in common with the murder of Gail Marshall, Nelson Neilson, Veronica Sanchez, and at least two others, including Constance Larchman and Nevada State Trooper George Bentley. And they never realized that the killer was currently living at the motel.

Detective Carl Paris went through the motions in the door-to-door questioning at the North Hollywood Motel, lending a hand in what was normally the grunt work in a police investigation. He expected little, if any, cooperation from the people who lived in the rundown rent-by-the-day, -week, or -month dump. He also knew that those who were only visiting had no desire to draw attention to that fact. People in this part of town tended to mind their own business. Not that he could blame them. Why tempt fate by incurring the wrath of the wrong people at the worst possible time: drug dealers, addicts, gangs caught in turf wars . . . even the run-of-the-mill rapists and killers? Especially when the authorities rarely came running, except when it was too late for some poor soul. Or in this case, the detective thought soberly, two poor souls.

Not a damn day went by in which someone wasn't the victim of a shooting, beating, or some other form of violence in Northeast Portland. This latest case of a pimp and hooker gunned down was just another example of urban violence run amok. There was little doubt in Paris's mind that these two had been shot execution-style by someone they had associated with—pusher, gang banger, rival pimp, or vengeful prostitute who'd had enough of a violent pimp or sadistic johns. He wouldn't even be surprised if the perpetrator was some insanely jealous husband, boyfriend, or former intimate.

Even though he recognized the bullet wounds as probably coming from a .25-caliber handgun, rather than one of the more powerful guns out on the streets these days, Paris still believed this was a case of occupational or acquaintance homicide rather than a random act of violence. Nevertheless, he hoped against hope that someone might have seen something that she or he was willing to speak about.

Paris knocked on the door three doors down from

the room in which the murders occurred. Maybe I'll get lucky, he thought, not really believing it. In his mind, there was no such thing as luck . . . other than the bad kind.

A rather frumpy looking white man in his late twenties to early thirties opened the door lazily. He looked as if he had been sleeping, though he was fully clothed in jeans, a flannel shirt, and scuffed boots.

"I'm investigating a double homicide that took place at this motel tonight," Paris said to him, and flashed his I.D.

The man stared at him, dumbfounded. "Don't know nothin' about it. Sorry."

Paris noticed he was fidgeting, but thought nothing of it in particular. Most people went into a panic when talking to the police, even if they had no reason to. "The two people were shot to death three doors down from you," he told the man. "You must have at least heard the shots?"

The man shook his head. "I was sleepin'. Takes a lot to wake me up."

Paris studied him curiously. "What's your name?"

"Joshua Morgan."

"You live here, Joshua Morgan?"

He nodded, yawning.

Yeah, right, Paris mused. And I'm about to be promoted to Chief of the Portland Police Bureau. Fat chance.

"Is there anyone else in there?" Paris noted that the door was open only enough to see Morgan.

"Just my old lady," he replied evenly. "She's in bed."

I'll bet she is. No use in wasting further time with this one. Prostitution—which was obviously what was taking place in there—wasn't his gig. If Morgan knew something, he wasn't talking.

"Go back to sleep," Paris said coarsely, and moved to the next door.

Joshua Morgan went back into his room. He peeked out the curtain at the black detective walking away. If only he knew the truth, thought Morgan, laughing. But most cops were so dumb they couldn't find a gun if it was shoved up their ass.

He lifted the .25-caliber gun from his side. He had been prepared to use it if push had come to shove, just like he had with the state trooper. Asshole. Once again, he had dodged a bullet. Just the way he had planned. Just be yourself, he thought, and everything will fall into place.

He removed his clothes and joined his big assed, black bitch in bed. She was out like a light after he had purposely gotten her drunk. When she woke up in the morning, she would never know how exciting the night had been. Her loss. He would sleep like a baby, then tend to his business as usual—which included keeping track of the latest happenings on Court TV and the very intriguing trial of Trevor La Fontaine.

CHAPTER FORTY-THREE

Simon dropped Jordan off at home half a day earlier than scheduled. She had made up an excuse to cut the trip short because of a motion that had to be prepared for Monday morning. Simon had been surprisingly agreeable, suggesting he too had work to catch up on.

Jordan held on tightly to her purse with the potentially damning evidence inside. She walked up to the house, thinking, Keep an open mind, girl, till the facts present themselves one way or the other. If Simon is guilty of anything it'll come out sooner than later.

Even that logic couldn't still Jordan's fears.

There was a red Camaro in the driveway, that Jordan didn't recognize. Must be a friend of Kendre's, she thought. What was Kendre doing home when she was supposed to be at Lenora's?

Jordan went in. One of the CDs she got Kendre for Christmas was blasting away on the stereo in the living room, but there was no sign of Kendre. In the kitchen, Jordan found a couple of empty malt liquor bottles and what was left of a still smoldering cigarette, using a glass as an ashtray.

What the hell . . . ?

Mild alarm gripped Jordan as she went upstairs. Had someone been in her house while they were away? She came to Kendre's room. The door was closed. She listened and heard muffled sounds of giggling and guffawing . . . and movement . . .

Holding her breath, Jordan clamped her hand around the doorknob and slowly turned it, opening the door.

Her eyes widened in disbelief. Kendre was on the bed, fully clothed, kissing a man. Or, it seemed, he was kissing *her*. His shirt was unbuttoned halfway down, revealing a hairy chest, and his hands were all over Kendre, who was obviously enjoying it.

Jordan felt a rage she rarely had before. To her, this was the ultimate betrayal. Her baby girl was having sex in her own bed when she was supposed to be at Lenora's house!

Jordan pushed the door open so hard that it slammed into the wall. This caused the two on the bed to jerk up and look toward her.

"Mom!" Kendre's face froze.

Jordan ignored her. Instead, she trained her eyes on the one Kendre was in bed with. He looked to be eighteen or nineteen, tall, well developed, with thick, dark box braids, and close-set, sable eyes.

Nkaki. The thought did nothing to curtail her anger.

"Get the hell out of my house!" Jordan shrieked at him. "Get out! My daughter is only fourteen years old. Having sex with a minor is statutory rape in this state, mister!"

He rushed to his feet, fastening his shirt along the way. "Ms. La Fontaine," he tried to say, "this isn't what it looks—"

"Like hell it isn't!" she snapped as he skirted past her and into the hall. "If I ever catch you in this house again, I'll have you brought up on charges. Do you hear me?"

"Yeah, I hear you!" He shot Jordan a spiteful look, then scrambled down the stairs and out the front door.

Jordan turned to Kendre, who was shaking on the bed. Yet Jordan could only see her own anger and disappointment. "How could you, Kendre? I trusted you."

"Nothing happened," Kendre said tearfully. "We were just—"

"You call that nothing!" Jordan's eyes were like slits. "I'm not blind, Kendre. I know what I saw. I go away for one weekend and you bring a man into this house to have sex—"

"We weren't gonna have sex," Kendre insisted, standing up on weak legs. "Nkaki and I were just making out. Everybody does—"

"Not you, young lady! Not at fourteen. You're not ready for this—even if you think you are!"

"How would *you* know what I'm ready for?" Kendre's tone was becoming increasingly bitter. "You never bothered to ask me."

Jordan got in her face. "Don't you *ever* talk to me like that again!" She felt her blood pressure rise. "I am your mother and you will respect me!"

Kendre backed off, rolling her eyes. "Does that mean I have no say in my own life?"

"Not when it involves doing things that can hurt you in more ways than you can imagine."

Kendre wiped tears from her eyes. "You can't get AIDS or pregnant from kissing, Mom. That's *all* we were doing."

"We'll talk about it later," Jordan said, still seething. "You're grounded."

Kendre stomped her foot defiantly. "You can't do that!"

"Oh, yes I can. I just did. Now if you know what's good for you, you'll quit while you're ahead." She stormed out of the room, and heard Kendre fall on the bed bawling.

In her bedroom, Jordan sat on the bed and caught her breath. She was shaking, her mind racing. It took her a few moments before she realized that she had probably overreacted with Kendre. She had taken out all her frustrations regarding Simon and Trevor on her daughter.

Jordan knew deep down that Kendre did not deserve the kind of treatment she had received, no matter what she had done or might have done if Jordan hadn't shown up. With things concerning Simon at a standstill, and Trevor's future still very much up in the air, Jordan could not afford to risk losing her daughter as well.

I won't let that happen, she told herself resolutely.

Jordan went back to Kendre's room. She was still on the bed, lying facedown. Her sobs had turned into a low whimper. Sitting beside her, Jordan rubbed Kendre's back and whispered, "I'm sorry I blew up at you, honey. I shouldn't have come down on you so hard. But I have to know that I can trust you and that you'll respect me as your mother."

Kendre did not look up but was now quiet.

Jordan felt her heart go out to her daughter. "Things are a bit crazy for me right now," she admitted, "and you were an easy scapegoat. But I won't apologize for loving you so much that I don't want to see you get hurt—even if I misjudged what you and Nkaki were doing when you were supposed to be at Lenora's."

Slowly Kendre turned around. Her eyes were teary. "I'm sorry too, Mom," she said genuinely. "We were at Lenora's house. But when she wanted to hang out at her boyfriend's, we just came back here. Nkaki respects me and he wasn't gonna try anything I didn't want to do."

She paused. "And I'm sorry for disrespecting you."

Jordan leaned over and hugged her. She realized in that instant, whether she liked it or not, her little girl had become a young woman practically overnight and she'd have to deal with that.

"I love you, honey," Jordan said. "Don't ever forget that—even if your mom can sometimes be a bit smothering."

"I love you, too." Kendre wept on her shoulder. After a moment or two, she looked up and asked, "Why did Dad have to die?"

It was a question Jordan had asked herself a thousand times. And the answer was always the same: "I don't really know, baby. I believe that his time on earth was far too short, but he did what he was supposed to and the Lord was ready for him to come home."

Kendre's voice cracked as warm tears went from her cheek to Jordan's. "I miss him so much, Mom," she cried.

Now Jordan was crying, for the same reason. "So do I," she told her. Maybe more now than ever.

CHAPTER FORTY-FOUR

Jordan was pouring herself a cup of coffee in the employee lounge when Jerrod Wresler came in. It was one of the few times they had been alone since he was assigned the case against her son. He had a smug grin on his face as he walked up to Jordan.

"You actually drink that stuff?"

She tried to ignore him while stirring in cream.

Wresler filled a cup with hot water. "Look, Jordan, I know you probably hate my guts right now, but I'm not doing anything you wouldn't do if the situation was reversed."

Jordan glared at the pompous son of a bitch, noting that he looked a bit less confident than usual. This gave her some satisfaction and hope that perhaps he was finally beginning to feel the heat in the trial—suggesting his case against Trevor may be crumbling . . . or, at least, not as open and shut as he'd insisted.

The fact that Simon was defending Trevor while she and the Portland Police Bureau were investigating him troubled Jordan deeply. But this, in and of itself, would not stop Wresler from doing what he felt he had to do. Deep down she knew there was some merit to what he'd just said. It was all about opportunity in this business. If Wresler had refused the assignment, it would have gone to someone else. And with it any chance he had for promotion.

Jordan's real problem with the brash A.D.A. was the enjoyment he seemed to derive from prosecuting her son, which had the effect of putting her on trial.

"I don't think we have anything to talk about," she told him.

Wresler dragged his hand through his hair, where the unusual gray thatch in the center seemed more prominent than ever, and said, "What do you say we call a truce, La Fontaine? When this is all over, I hope we can still be friends."

Jordan felt a spasm of anger shoot through her like lightning. "We were *never* friends, Wresler," she said in no uncertain terms. "Now if you'll excuse me . . ."

She sidestepped him and headed out of the lounge, half expecting Wresler to follow to plead his case. Instead he remained behind, probably gloating, Jordan suspected. She was fully aware that somewhere down the line the two of them would probably be paired together on a case. But that didn't mean she had to like it—or him.

In the hall, Jordan nearly collided with Amanda Clinksdale, who was heading for the lounge.

"Hi, Jordan," she said awkwardly, her thin arms pressed against her sides.

"Amanda." Jordan kept her voice perfectly even and emotionless.

Neither said a word for a moment or two, before Amanda said, "I hear you're almost ready to wrap up the prosecution's case against Graham Turner?"

Jordan pondered that, then said, "We're getting there, slowly but not always surely."

There was more awkward silence.

Amanda moved closer to Jordan, and confided in a low voice, "I want you to know, Jordan, that I hope Simon can prove Trevor really didn't kill those college sweethearts."

Jordan read the sincerity in her jade eyes and knew that she meant it. In turn, she felt a bit foolish for doubting Amanda's friendship when she had been put in an impossible position.

"Thank you," Jordan told her, and smiled.

Amanda smiled back, gently squeezing Jordan's arm in support, and went into the lounge to join her co-counsel and lover.

Jordan sucked in a deep breath and walked to her office.

She phoned the crime lab, where she had taken the sample of Simon's seminal fluid for analysis and comparison with that found in Victoria Turner's body. They told Jordan the results would be available this afternoon. It seemed like an eternity to her.

Meanwhile, it was business as usual.

Andrew was questioning Officer Gretchen Fitzgerald on the stand. The thirty-five-year-old wife of a fellow officer and mother of two sat poised as she swept reddish-brown hair from her face.

"What did you see when you first came into the room, Officer Fitzgerald?"

She considered the question, then answered, "Ms. Turner was lying naked, spread-eagle on the bed."

"Did you get any indication that something was wrong with her?" asked Andrew, deliberately leading the witness.

Gretchen choked as she thought about it. "Yes. I knew something was very wrong by her lewd pose. Also there was blood all over the bed. And the body had been badly mutilated."

"Can you be more specific?"

She sighed. "Ms. Turner's throat had been severely cut and one of her breasts had been removed. The nipple had been cut off the other breast." Gretchen gulped. "There were a number of other cuts and bruises . . . including to the area around the victim's vagina."

Jordan grimaced as though she was just hearing this for the first time. Occasionally she glanced at the defendant. He looked guilty, she thought. Or as much as anyone could. All the evidence they had said Graham Turner was guilty. But was he really guilty? Or had someone else carved up Victoria Turner like a turkey and served her on a silver platter—along with her ex husband?

"When did you first see the defendant?" Andrew asked the witness.

"When I looked to the side of the bed," Gretchen responded.

"And what was he doing?"

"He appeared to be hiding."

"Objection," called the defense attorney angrily. "Calls for speculation."

Judge Grayson looked at Gretchen, and said in a stern voice, "Officer Fitzgerald, please confine your answers to only what you actually saw."

Gretchen swallowed shakily. "Mr. Turner was crouched down on the floor."

"Did he have anything on his person clearly visible to you?" Andrew asked carefully.

"Yes." Gretchen looked toward the defendant, sighing. "He had a knife in his hands."

"Hands . . . ?" Andrew cocked a brow.

"His left hand."

Andrew lifted the murder weapon from the evidence

table and held it up to Gretchen. "Does this look like the knife you saw, Officer Fitzgerald?"

She took a breath and nodded. "Yes . . . exactly."

Graham Turner shook his head in angry denial. Jordan watched this, but remained unconvinced. For the moment.

Later it was Jordan's turn to call a DNA expert to the stand. Doctor Emerson Chang was one of the country's foremost authorities on DNA. The forty-nine-year-old Chinese criminologist had large midnight eyes and fine, gray-black hair. He sat erect in a tight russet-colored suit while Jordan questioned him in detail on his background and the foundation of DNA evidence.

"DNA, or deoxyribonucleic acid, is a substance involved in the genetic transmission of characteristics from generation to generation," explained Chang. "All DNA molecules consist of a linked series of units known as nucleotides. Depending on the type of DNA-causing organism, most DNA is found in a single chromosome or in several chromosomes. . . ."

Jordan could tell by the glazed look on the faces of the jurors that he was losing them, so she moved on to the aspects of DNA more pertinent to this case.

"I understand, Doctor Chang, that through DNA analysis of blood, hair, semen, and other human tissue, anyone's genetic code can be determined. Is that correct?"

He nodded. "DNA has two specific functions. One is to provide for protein synthesis in each of us, or the growth and development of organisms. The other is to supply all descendants of a species with protein-synthesizing information by duplicating itself and passing this on to offspring. This information, referred to as the genetic code, can be found in the sequence of bases of DNA, which specifies the sequence of amino acids present in a protein." He paused for a moment while leaning forward, then said in an expert tone of voice, "To answer your question, yes, sufficient samples of body tissues can be used to establish anyone's genetic code."

Jordan stepped to the witness's side so the jury could see his face as she asked, "How can you be certain that the genetic code established does indeed belong to that person instead of someone else—such as a relative?"

Chang licked his lips eagerly as he was now in his element. "Each person's genetic code or blueprint differs," he explained, "with the exception of identical twins. DNA profiling or fingerprinting can match a crime suspect or victim's genetic markers with DNA in human tissues such as blood and hair to a 99.9 percent accuracy."

The criminologist then went into a lengthy account of the singular relationship between a person and his or her genetic makeup, and the statistically minute chance that two people would have the same genetic code. He finished with, "DNA analysis can provide a virtually positive match of genetic markers to a particular individual."

Jordan stepped to her table for a quick glance at her notes. She then returned to the witness and asked, "Doctor Chang, did you analyze blood samples taken from a knife owned by the defendant, a knife that has already been introduced into evidence, and the clothes he and the victim were wearing the night Victoria Turner was killed?"

Chang nodded. "Yes, I did."

"I understand that there are two primary types of methods for testing DNA evidence." Jordan looked deliberately at the jury and back to the witness.

"Yes, there are," said Chang.

"Will you be so kind as to explain how these differ?"

"No problem. One is called Polymerase Chain Reaction, or PCR. This one requires only a minute amount of body tissue—like a blood sample the size of a pinhead or a single strand of hair—to establish a mathematically conclusive genetic match." He sighed, and his voice rose. "The more precise test is called Restriction Fragment Length Polymorphism, or RFLP. It requires a larger, higher quality DNA sample and takes longer to complete the test than a PCR, but is much more accurate."

"So the chances of a false positive with the RFLP method are highly unlikely?" asked Jordan.

Chang gave her a straight look. "When a match is made using the proper techniques of RFLP in criminal DNA testing, the results are unarguably precise."

Jordan gave him a practiced smile. "For the record, Doctor Chang, can you tell us which test you used to analyze the DNA evidence in this case?"

"The RFLP," he said, as expected.

Jordan glanced at the defendant with mixed emotions. It was hard to argue with DNA evidence, she thought. Her mind wandered to Simon and the DNA results to come. What if there was a positive match? How should she proceed then?

Would one match necessarily negate the other?

Jordan gathered herself and asked, "Doctor, what were the results of the analysis of the blood found on the knife?"

Chang paused, then said coolly, "The blood samples came from the victim, Victoria Turner."

There was some stirring and mumbling in the courtroom.

Jordan ignored it and followed the answer with, "Tell us, Doctor Chang, what type of genetic evidence, if any, was found from examining the defendant's clothing?"

"More blood was found that was a genetic match to the victim."

Jordan sucked in a breath. "Did the DNA tests performed on Ms. Turner's clothing the night she died reveal anything relevant to this case?"

Chang looked in the direction of the defendant, and eyed Jordan wearily. "In addition to more of Ms. Turner's own blood, several hairs were found on her clothing that have the same genetic makeup as Mr. Turner's."

Jordan allowed the jury to ponder the significance of Emerson Chang's damaging testimony against Graham Turner, and considered it herself. She couldn't help but wonder if, in this instance, the evidence showed only what it was supposed to, rather than what it should have.

"Can I buy you lunch?" Andrew asked Jordan on the way out of the courtroom.

Jordan frowned. "I'll have to take a rain check on that," she said, adding what was only a partial lie. "I have an appointment at one to see a doctor."

Andrew gave her a concerned look. "Something wrong?"

She sighed thoughtfully. "I'm not sure. I guess it all depends on what he has to say."

Twenty minutes later, Jordan was at a crime lab in downtown Portland. Hakeem Azikwe, a Nigerian-born Professor of Forensic Science at Portland State University, was also an independent criminalist that the D.A.'s office often used to support or refute findings. At forty-two, Hakeem was a tall man, slight in build with a walnut complexion and brown dreadlocks. He wore thin-rimmed silver glasses.

"I've compared the samples of semen," Hakeem told Jordan, his distinguished face not giving away the results. "As you know, semen and blood break down into the same components, allowing us to mathematically eliminate a match if the samples came from different blood types." He touched his glasses while Jordan stood on edge, her heart beating wildly. "The preliminary results show that the semen could have come from the same man."

Jordan felt herself become lightheaded. Using careful handling procedures, she had borrowed a sample of semen taken from Victoria Turner, labeling it A, while labeling the sample from Simon B.

"Sample B tested positive with sample A," Hakeem said unaffectedly. "This means the semen samples belong to members of the same male population—eighteen percent to be exact—whose blood type matches. Of course, a more detailed DNA analysis would be needed to get a more precise match."

But that could take up to two months, Jordan thought dejectedly, hoping to have excluded Simon from the genetic markers found in the semen inside Victoria Turner. Damn. The trial would likely end in two to three weeks. She could file a motion for a continuance, but the judge would never agree to it—not unless she had a valid reason why the State would want to delay the prosecution of Graham Turner. Any such reason could result in a mistrial. Anything less could result in the conviction of an innocent man.

"What about the hair samples?" Jordan asked, not expecting a different result. She had taken tiny hair clippings from Simon's razor after he shaved, just for effect, knowing that the DNA was the same as for his bodily fluids.

Hakeem removed his glasses with a frown. "Unfortunately, those results are inconclusive. Let me show you—"

He led Jordan to a microscope and had her look at the slide. Hakeem explained: "On the right are the hairs from sample A, on the left from sample B. You can see that the texture is the same, but the diameter and coloring are not a perfect match."

Jordan tried to see what he saw through the microscope. To her, there was very little difference, except perhaps the opposite way in which the hair on each side seemed to curl at one end.

Did this suggest these hairs belonged to two different men? Looking up at Hakeem, she asked, "But they *could* have come from the same man?"

"Yes, I think so," he said, adding strongly, "but quite possibly two different men."

In Jordan's mind, if not her heart, the circumstantial *and* physical evidence seemed to indicate that the semen and hairs belonged to one man. A man who had sex with Victoria Turner and may have murdered her—Simon McNeil.

CHAPTER FORTY-FIVE

When Simon walked into her office, Jordan did not stand up to greet him. Instead she waited unsteadily as he walked toward her, his dark olive suit looking as if it had come straight from his tailor.

"Your call sounded urgent," he said, leaning over to kiss her.

Jordan turned her head at the last possible moment. "Don't!" Her voice was terse. "You bastard!"

Simon wrinkled his brow, baffled. "Where did that come from?" When she did not respond, he sat in a chair and stared at her. "What's going on, Jordan?" he asked. "Has Trevor accused me of misrepresenting him or something?"

Jordan barely knew where to begin. This whole thing had suddenly turned into a bad nightmare, and seemed to be getting worse with each passing day. She closed her eyes and sucked in a deep breath. Raising her eyes, she gazed across her desk at Simon and said, "This isn't about Trevor. It's about you and Victoria Turner."

Simon's nostrils grew wide. "Me and Victoria Turner? What the hell are you talking about?"

Another deep breath did little to calm Jordan's trembling body, much less her anguished mind. "You were with her at Club Diamonds that night, weren't you?" Jordan's voice was more than just accusatory.

"What night?"

"Christmas Eve."

"I was with you that night," he said calmly.

"And *her*, dammit!" Jordan leaned into her desk so hard it hurt her ribs. "I saw the Club Diamonds matchbook on the floor in your bedroom that night, Simon. It must have fallen out of your pocket. And I saw the blond hair in your bathroom sink. Now you tell me, what am I supposed to think?"

Simon shifted unsteadily. "So what the hell does any of that prove?"

"It proves that you lied to me about having never met Victoria Turner and you lied about Club Diamonds. A witness saw you leaving there with her . . . in your Mercedes." Her voice grated with the betrayal she felt as a woman and lover. "You had sex with Victoria in your apartment that night, didn't you?" The question was actually more of a statement. "Did you kill her too?"

"Stop it, Jordan!" Simon's composure disappeared completely, replaced by a look of acrimony. "Have you lost your damned mind? Who's been feeding you this load of crap?"

Jordan hesitated, knowing what she said next would in many ways make her as guilty of deceit as him, and quite possibly forever change the nature of their relationship. She convinced herself there was no other way. It had to be done to get to the truth.

With a knot in her throat, Jordan said, "Your semen matched the semen found inside Victoria Turner." She left out the chin hairs of his she took from his razor, since her case was not as strong with them.

Simon glared. "How the hell would you know that?" he said. "I don't remember volunteering any semen to be tested."

Their eyes connected. In that moment Simon's face grew darker, and Jordan knew it was registering just how she had gained her intimate knowledge. She would give anything to have done it a different way.

"The cabin," muttered Simon thoughtfully. "You agreed to go there and make love, just so you could use my sperm to test your damned theory of sex, lies, and murder?"

Jordan wanted to say it wasn't true, but no words would come out of her mouth to contradict what her eyes were telling him.

Simon's head snapped back. "Why the hell didn't you just ask me straight out if I'd been sleeping with Victoria Turner?"

"Why would I, when you told me you'd never even met her?"

He bristled. "How could you be so damned selfish, Jordan, to use what we have—had—to try and get me for what . . . murder? Or being with someone else before you and I hooked up?"

Jordan hated to be in the position of defending herself, but she knew she had to. "I'm sorry, Simon," she said truthfully. "I never meant for this to happen—"

"The hell you didn't," he snorted angrily. "You could have been straight with me about your suspicions, instead of playing Nancy Drew and going behind my back."

Jordan inhaled, feeling as though she were suffocating. "I didn't know how to—"

Simon cut her off. "Did you think I would drop Trevor's case on a dime if you'd leveled with me?"

"I'm not really sure what I thought," she admitted, hating that it had come down to this.

As much as it hurt, Jordan knew she had come too far to backpedal now. There was more at stake here than Trevor being on trial. Or, for that matter, their personal relationship, as much as it meant to her—or had.

She gathered herself and said flatly, "Simon, I asked you here to come clean. If you did sleep with Victoria that day or night, we need to talk about it." Jordan hesitated, then said, "If you killed her, I think we need to talk about that, too."

Simon's rage and despair suddenly gave way to mirthless laughter. When he stopped laughing, his face became serious again, and he stated bluntly, "No, I did not sleep with Victoria Turner . . . and I certainly didn't kill her! Like I told you before, I never even met the woman, much less know her intimately. I'm afraid your damned test of my sperm is dead wrong."

Jordan looked at him, befuddled. "Are you saying you weren't at Club Diamonds the night Victoria was murdered?"

Simon gave a long pause. "Yes, I was there that night," he said uneasily. "But I never saw her there—if, in fact, she was there."

Jordan sensed he was holding back something. Something important. What was it? She thought, If you have information relevant to this case you might as well tell me, for your own sake.

"And the blond hair in your sink . . . ?" Jordan asked. All she could see was Victoria Turner in his arms and bed . . . before she was viciously murdered.

After a long moment, Simon answered with his head lowered, "They were Frances's."

Frances. His wife. Jordan was stunned. Too stunned to speak. When she did, it was with skepticism. "Those blond hairs did not belong to your *black* wife, Simon! Unless she turned white and her tight, short, street black hair became long and yellow overnight—you'll have to do better than that!"

Simon pursed his lips. "I'd say you need to brush up on your detective skills, Jordan," he said snidely. "And certainly on the latest in black hairstyles. The hair you saw in the sink was not Frances's real hair. As part of her 'new and sexy' look, she decided that long blond natural hair extensions somehow suited her. Who was I to argue since she left me for another man who apparently agreed with her?"

Jordan was once again speechless. Could those blond strands have really belonged to Frances? Admittedly Jordan was no expert on hair, having never worn a wig or extension. She had simply presumed with little more than a cursory glance that the hair she saw belonged to a white woman.

But he had lied about having never been to Club Diamonds, Jordan told herself, trying to find some justification for what may have been the biggest mistake of her life.

Simon seemed to read her thoughts as he said unapologetically, "I met Frances at Club Diamonds that night. She said she wanted to talk. I thought that maybe she'd had a change of heart. We went to my apartment. Turned out all she wanted was to try and lay a guilt trip on me for her own decision to walk out on the marriage. I told her to go to hell and that was that."

He cast a venomous gaze at Jordan as if to further humiliate her. "Then I called a cab and sent her home to her lover. The matches you saw belonged to Frances. She must have dropped them when she tried to lay on the couch after having had too much to drink." He sighed. "I denied having gone to Club Diamonds when you asked because I didn't want to admit to being with

Frances and making a damned fool out of myself—especially when things seemed to be going so well between you and me."

"I assume Frances will back up your story?" Jordan asked weakly, feeling as if she had just lost her best friend and lover with one wrong move.

"Why wouldn't she? It's the truth," Simon replied curtly. "Frances and I may have a history, but I doubt that she'll lie for me just to save my ass. It's not her style."

Jordan felt the color rush into her cheeks. She wasn't quite sure what, if anything, to say. If his story did check out—which seemed likely—what could she possibly do or say to make things right? Especially after she'd found a way to make them so wrong.

"If you're through with me," said Simon, lifting abruptly to his feet, "I'll be on my way."

Jordan's voice trembled as she said ruefully: "I know this probably won't make any difference now, Simon, but I'm really sorry I handled things the way I did."

"You damned well should be. I thought you knew me better than to think I could be capable of murder. And I certainly thought I knew you better. I really believed we had something special . . . with a real future. Turns out you used sex like some people use drugs—the performance was first rate, but the aftereffects stink all to hell!"

Simon headed for the door, then swiveled around and said in a cold voice, "By the way, I have no intention of abandoning Trevor the way you abandoned me. I owe it to Eric, if not you, to see this through."

On that note, he stormed out and Jordan was left with nothing but regrets for things she knew she couldn't take back, no matter how much she wanted to.

The following morning, Frances McNeil showed up at the office. Jordan had forgotten just how beautiful she was, petite with a streamlined figure and an enviable fudge-sundae skin tone. Her long, incredibly blond hair extensions hung neatly across the jacket of her burgundy pantsuit. She had bold café au lait eyes, pronounced cheeks, and full lips on a perfectly proportioned face. High-heeled sandals made her seem taller than she was.

Jordan felt her heart skip a beat as she stood face to face with the woman still married to Simon, but in name only. It was incredible to Jordan that this women actually had given up Simon for another. Whereas, she'd lost him because of a stupid mistake in a misguided attempt to do the right thing as an officer of the legal system. She supposed that made them both idiots in their own ways.

Fashioning her lips into a welcoming smile, Jordan said, "Hello, Frances. Nice to see you."

"I have to admit, Jordan," Frances began, with something resembling a smirk on her face, "I never thought we'd meet again, especially under *these* circumstances."

"That makes two of us." Jordan felt her mouth go dry. "Why don't you have a seat," she said, trying to sound in control, though feeling anything but.

After Frances sat down, Jordan smoothed the skirt of her camel suit and sat in the chair beside her.

"Isn't it rather ironic," Frances said, "that I should be Simon's alibi for a night he spent in bed with *you*?"

Jordan's temperature threatened to boil over. Apparently Simon had told her everything about them. "I didn't leave him, girlfriend," she answered testily. "You did."

"My mistake," Frances freely admitted. "But it sure didn't take you long to go after my man the moment the coast was clear."

"Listen," Jordan said with a sigh, "first of all, he went

after me. Second, what happened between us was never planned—not by me." This sounded lame even to Jordan.

"I thought I wanted something more than what we had," Frances said tonelessly. "I was tired of the constant bickering, the long hours Simon put in at work, and the routine we had let our relationship fall into."

"You don't have to explain it to me," Jordan made herself say. Maybe you should have talked about it with Simon when you still had him, she thought.

"Oh, but I do," Frances insisted. "On Christmas Eve, I got Simon to agree to meet me at Club Diamonds. He didn't want to, but I told him it was important." She gave an exaggerated sigh. "I didn't want to lose him—not the way things had ended between us. Basically, I got Simon back to his apartment with the hopes of seducing him. But things got out of hand and instead we ended up at each other's throat—pretty much ending any thoughts I had about getting back together."

Frances pulled a cigarette out of her purse, planted it between her lips, and was about to light it with a Club Diamonds match when Jordan stopped her. "Don't," she said stiffly. "No smoking allowed in this building." Certainly not in this office, she thought.

Frances frowned, removed the cigarette, and put it and the matches back in her purse without comment.

How could I have been so stupid? Jordan asked herself. She should have guessed that Frances would not go away easily, simply because she had moved on to another man. That was her fake hair in the bathroom sink. Her matches from Club Diamonds.

Damn you, Coleman. Jordan knew she had allowed herself to be manipulated by the detective, to the detriment of her relationship with Simon . . . with possibly no chance of repairing the damage.

Frances flipped her long, blond extensions across her shoulders. "Anyway, there you have it," she said. "Simon couldn't possibly have killed that poor woman any more than you or I could have."

"I know that now," said Jordan sullenly. I always knew it deep down inside, she thought. "I'm sorry you had to come down here, Frances."

"Don't be. I was only too happy to show Simon that I'm not so impossible after all. While I may not be a hotshot lawyer for the District Attorney's office, I'm smart enough to be able to figure out the good guys from the bad without having to trick a man into giving up his sperm." There was a wicked sense of self-satisfaction in Frances's voice.

Nothing I can do about that, thought Jordan, other than cling to the hope that things could still turn out as they were supposed to at the end of the day.

In the meantime, it was clear to Jordan that though Leona Kwon may have seen Simon's Mercedes at Club Diamonds the night Victoria Turner was murdered, she did not see Victoria leave with Simon, if Leona saw Victoria at the club at all.

Which meant that the mystery of whom Victoria Turner had sex with that day or night was still just that: a mystery.

As far as Jordan was concerned, they had the right man on trial for Victoria Turner's murder after all.

Jordan went to Detective Harry Coleman's office unannounced. He was on the phone. From the sound of it, he was talking to his wife. He cut the conversation short upon seeing Jordan standing in the doorway.

Not reading the anger in Jordan's eyes, Coleman said anxiously, "What's the word on McNeil?"

"There is *no* word!" Jordan was vehement as she

moved closer to him. "Your so-called witness's recollections of the night Victoria Turner was murdered were way off. Simon *was* at Club Diamonds that night . . . but with his *blond wife*—who doesn't look anything like Victoria Turner." Saying the word "wife" made it all the more painful for Jordan, yet she knew it was most apt in this instance.

In spite of the awkwardness they both felt, Coleman persisted with a grimace: "Are you telling me that—"

Jordan interrupted, glaring at him. "I'm telling you that Simon was not with Victoria Turner that night—and he certainly didn't kill her! Guess that puts you back to square one, Detective, in your search to find what's been staring you right in the face from the get go," she spat. "And I'm sure you know just where to look!"

Jordan took a deep breath, wanting to tell Coleman exactly what she thought of him for quite possibly destroying whatever had existed between her and Simon. However, judging by the grave disappointment that knitted the detective's brows, she suspected that Coleman already had enough of his own demons to deal with.

Jordan took the rest of the day off. It happened to be a day in which the trial had been postponed due to an emergency in Judge Sylvia Grayson's family. Her daughter was said to be giving birth to twin girls, and there were some complications.

At home, Jordan helped Kendre with her homework and then did some homework of her own. She scrubbed floors, washed walls, and dusted shelves—anything to take her mind off Simon, Frances, Coleman, Turner, and even the ordeal Trevor was going through. She knew this was only a temporary tonic to some hard questions she must face with answers that frightened her.

In bed that night, Jordan tossed and turned as she dreamed about Graham Turner killing Victoria Turner, and then trying to kill her. Simon came to her rescue—her knight in shining armor. But then he looked at her, his eyes filled with hatred, and walked away, leaving her alone.

Jordan awoke in a cold sweat and could hear herself pleading to Simon, "No, please don't go . . ."

The thought of Simon's abandonment had terrified her more than being attacked by Graham Turner. It was only a dream, she told herself, even if it seemed so very real and painful.

Jordan sat up. She realized that no matter what, Simon was not the enemy. But could he ever be her friend again?

She had no answer. But Jordan refused to give up on Simon, which, in many ways, would mean giving up on herself.

Her thoughts switched to Trevor. Simon had promised to stick with his defense no matter what. But could their broken relationship inadvertently affect Simon's ability to win Trevor an acquittal?

CHAPTER FORTY-SIX

Tracy Venus sat tremulously on the witness stand as Jerrod Wresler circled her like a vulture eyeing his prey before the attack. He studied the nineteen-year-old with the long brown hair tied in a ponytail and light freckles dotting her cheeks. She reminded him of a girl he knew in college. In fact, she was the first girl he'd ever had sex with. The experience was forgettable, but the girl was not. Briefly he wondered what had become of Eleanor Parker.

When Tracy Venus caught his unwavering eye and winced, Wresler smiled at her, letting her know he was on her side. After all, he thought, you're not a hostile witness—are you?

"Ms. Venus," he said for the jury, "you testified earlier that you saw a white Ford Explorer leaving Devil's Edge on Christmas Eve at approximately 10:15 P.M. Is that correct?"

"Yes," she answered nervously.

"And this was while you were a passenger in another car. Correct?"

She nodded. "Yes."

"And the car was driven by . . . ?"

"Jessie Thaxton."

"And who is Jessie Thaxton?" Wresler knew Thaxton was his next witness.

"My boyfriend." Her face turned florid as if she were embarrassed to admit this.

"How close was the car you and Mr. Thaxton were in to the Explorer you passed by at the scene of the crime?"

"We were right next to it," Tracy said. "Close enough that he nearly hit us."

Simon McNeil objected to the word "he," prompting Wresler to rephrase the question.

The answer was still the same.

"Did you see who was in the Explorer?" asked Wresler. Tracy looked up. "Yes."

"Did you recognize the person?"

"Yes."

Wresler took a couple of steps toward the jury box. "Is that person in this courtroom?"

Tracy fidgeted. "Yes."

The prosecutor moved back up to the witness. "Can you point the person out, please?"

Tracy took a deep breath and raised her hand, pointing a delicate finger and saying definitely, "It was Trevor—Trevor La Fontaine."

As murmurs whispered throughout the courtroom, Wresler allowed the words to hang in the air like pollution for a long moment, before pressing the witness for his audience: "Are you sure?" Before she could answer, he fixed her face and, playing the devil's advocate, added, "The defense will probably argue that it was too dark for you to have been able to see very much that night, let alone recognize anyone's face in particular."

"I saw him!" Tracy was emphatic. "The car lights must have shone on his face. I know it was him—Trevor."

That was good enough for Wresler. He was convinced it would also be good enough for the jury. "This wasn't the first time you saw Trevor La Fontaine," he asked skillfully, "was it?"

Tracy looked toward the defendant. "No. He used to date my sister, Rhonda."

Used to being the operative words, thought Wresler. If he had his way, Trevor La Fontaine's dating days were over for good. At least in the outside world.

"Was it the first time you saw Trevor La Fontaine that day?" Wresler stepped to the other side of the witness.

"N-No," she stammered.

"When did you see him prior to that?"

"At a party that night."

Wresler waited a moment then asked, "What do you remember about Mr. La Fontaine at the party that night?"

Tracy paused, and seemed reluctant but said, "He was at the party with my sister."

"Do you recall anything else?"

Tracy looked at the judge and back to Wresler. "Gail and Nelson were at the party, too."

"You mean Gail Marshall and Nelson Neilson?" clarified Wresler.

"Yes."

"Did you see Trevor La Fontaine, Nelson Neilson, and Gail Marshall together?" Wresler asked, knowing the answer.

Tracy blinked. "Yes."

"And what were the circumstances?"

She swallowed hard. "Trevor and Nelson got into a fight."

"A fight?" Wresler looked over at the jury. "Do you know what started this fight?"

Tracy shook her head, then said, "I think it had to do with something Nelson said about Rhonda."

Enough with the preliminaries, thought Wresler. Let's get to the meat of this brawl. "Do you recall what happened after the fight, Ms. Venus?"

Tracy hesitated a moment or two, glancing at the defendant, before stating sharply, "Trevor told Nelson that he was *dead!*"

Wresler peered at the witness. "Dead as in 'I'm going to kill you'?"

Simon vehemently objected.

Wresler withdrew the question. It had served its purpose. "No further questions," he announced, feeling triumphant.

Trevor La Fontaine was that much closer to being convicted of two murders. And, Wresler thought, he was that much closer to becoming the next Chief of the D.A.'s Homicide Division.

That evening Wresler celebrated his impending promotion by getting high on cocaine. He had been doing coke recreationally ever since college. The buzz it gave him made him feel more confident and in command. It also made him horny.

Sex was definitely on his mind as he watched Amanda sniff some of the white powder up her left nostril. She sneezed violently, turning red.

"Thought you said this stuff was diluted?" she whined.

"It is." He bent over and sniffed some more coke through a straw. The effect was instantaneous, and he took a moment to relish the high. A smile crossed his lips. "See—I'm fine." He licked some powder off her nose. "Just takes some getting used to."

"Thanks but no thanks. I'm not about to get used to it. Among other things, this stuff's illegal."

Wresler frowned. "So is double parking, but people

do it all the time. Believe me, it's no big deal. Even Wilson Bombeck isn't above taking a hit every now and then. We've partied together in this very room," Wresler lied. In truth, the D.A. had never set foot in his house, much less shared cocaine with him. But Amanda didn't have to know that. And she sure as hell was not going to confirm it with Bombeck.

Wresler inhaled more of the fine white powder, and then coaxed Amanda into sniffing some. She was looking particularly inviting in the leopard-print teddy he had bought her. He began kissing her chest, moving up to her neck, then her waiting mouth.

Amanda hungrily attacked his lips, as though desperate to have them on her own. Wresler felt her body begin to shake, which he attributed to a combination of the cocaine and flat out lust. He too was having trouble containing his desire, enhanced by the drug's effects. When he could stand it no more, Wresler scooped Amanda up in his arms and took her to the bedroom.

There he made love to Amanda Clinksdale with the same fire and passion that he once had with *her*. As much as he tried to forget her, Jerrod Wresler could not. She was constantly gnawing at his psyche, forcing him to remember. But he would not let her control his thoughts . . . his body . . . his very soul. Not anymore. As far as he was concerned, Victoria Turner was better off dead.

CHAPTER FORTY-SEVEN

Nearly a week had passed since Jordan had spoken to Simon. Or since he had spoken to her. She wondered if he would ever speak to her again. She could hardly blame him for hating her after what she had done to him.

Worse, Jordan knew, she had played right into Frances's hands. Frances had made her intentions perfectly clear: She wanted Simon back. And Jordan had made her quest considerably easier by humiliating Simon and questioning his integrity—not to mention his innocence—on two fronts.

In spite of his reassurances, Jordan half expected Simon to drop Trevor's defense in retaliation. Or, at the very least, turn the case over to one of his less experienced associates. But so far, to her delight, Trevor had told her that Simon was still on the job and seemed committed to seeing it through, no matter what.

Jordan had wanted desperately to call Simon to thank him. And to explain why she had done what she did. But she was afraid she would make more of a fool out of herself than she already had. She couldn't bear that on top of everything else.

Instead, Jordan did what she always did in times of stress: She focused intently on her work. It was the one thing of which she still seemed to be in control. She would tackle the issue of Simon and whether or not they still had something worth fighting for later. Right now there was an ongoing trial to deal with.

Sitting at her desk, Jordan went over the list of the State's final witnesses against Graham Turner when her secretary, Olivia, buzzed.

"There's a Mr. and Mrs. Earl Sanderson here to see you."

Who . . . ? Jordan glanced at her calendar. They were not on her appointment list. "What do they want?" she asked impatiently, her mind already looking beyond the unwanted guests.

A few seconds passed before Olivia said, with a catch to her voice, "They said it has to do with the Victoria Turner murder."

Jordan cocked a brow, her curiosity piqued. The Sandersons definitely knew how to get her attention. "Send them in."

Jordan watched as an African-American couple in their late sixties entered the office. The man—dark, short, and husky, with a horseshoe-shaped grayish hairline and gold-rimmed glasses—was dressed in blue-collar work clothes. The woman wore what almost looked like a homemade ankle-length pink dress that fit snugly over large breasts and wide hips. She had thin, curly white hair, a sagging light-skinned face, and big brown eyes.

The woman looked strangely familiar to Jordan as she shook her trembling hand. "I'm Jordan La Fontaine," she stated and listened as they introduced themselves. "Won't you have a seat?"

"Thank you," Earl Sanderson said in a strong baritone voice.

Jordan sat on the corner of her desk closest to them and asked in a friendly, though intrigued, tone, "I understand you have something to tell me concerning the Victoria Turner murder . . . ?"

"Yeah, we do," answered Earl. He looked at his wife. "Go ahead, honey."

"It's all right," Jordan gently coaxed her. "We're only here to help you." Her curiosity was threatening to explode, even as she tried to place the woman's face. Then it hit her. Of course! This was the elderly woman who lived directly across the courtyard from Victoria Turner. She had Alzheimer's disease. Judging by the alertness in her eyes, though, Althea Sanderson seemed to be perfectly aware of the current circumstances surrounding her. Perhaps this was a good day for her.

"What is it, Mrs. Sanderson?" Jordan's tone was more commanding, less patient. "Did you see something . . . someone that night . . . ?"

After a moment or two, Althea Sanderson looked directly at Jordan, and said in a surprisingly steady voice, "I seen a man run from Ms. Turner's house the night she was killed."

Jordan's heart skipped a beat. "Go on."

"I was walkin' my dog, Sparky. I always take her for a walk 'round eight-thirty every night. Just when we came near Ms. Turner's house, a man came runnin' out the front door so fast, you'd think his pants was on fire. Nearly ran me over. I seen blood on his hands."

Her voice choked, and Jordan leaned forward, wondering if this was another dead end, or if an unexpected turn of events had suddenly dropped a serious revelation on her lap. She said with a gasp, "Are you telling me you saw a man—other than the man accused of killing Victoria Turner—coming from her house around the time of her death?" Jordan assumed it was public knowledge by now, surely in that neighborhood, that Graham Turner was on trial for the aggravated murder of his ex-wife.

Althea looked at her husband, and back to Jordan, then responded confidently, "He was as close to me as you are now. It surely *wasn't* the man on trial, Ms. Turner's ex-husband, Graham."

Jordan got up and took a seat at her desk. She grabbed her case file and riffled through it until she came to the earlier statement from Earl Sanderson that his wife had Alzheimer's disease. Did she? Jordan looked at her now. Was this sudden clear memory simply a figment of her deteriorating imagination? Could anything she said be considered credible?

Peering at the woman, Jordan asked straightforwardly, "Do you have Alzheimer's disease, Mrs. Sanderson?"

Althea gave a hint of a smile at her grim-faced husband. It left her when she responded tautly, "There ain't nothin' wrong with my mind, Ms. La Fontaine. Nothin' at all. It was Earl's idea to say I had Alzheimer's. He figured if the police thought I'd lost my mind—or most of it—they wouldn't bother me none 'bout that night."

Jordan regarded Earl Sanderson and tried to understand his rationale better, even as she thought with some amusement, That's definitely a new one. Using Alzheimer's disease to avoid being called as an eyewitness to a crime. She was disappointed that the police had not followed up on this apparently bogus claim.

"Ms. La Fontaine, we just two old black people mindin' our own business," Earl said resentfully. "Not like you with the D.A.'s office and a number of good years still ahead of you."

Jordan thought that neither seemed quite ready for the grave just yet. Maybe not for a long time. But that still didn't explain the charade.

To Earl, Jordan said, "I'm not sure I quite understand where you're—"

"The police ain't never done nothin' for us," he answered bitterly. "Why should the missus do their job for 'em if they can't do it themselves?"

"Because she has an obligation to come forward if she knows something about a crime."

Earl lowered his thick brows. "Don't tell me 'bout obligation," he grunted. "When my son was killed fifteen years ago in broad damned daylight in front of his own house, not one witness came forward, even though everybody said they knew 'bout it. The police just looked at it as 'nother black-on-black crime. They had more important things to do than find my son's killer."

Meeting Jordan's eyes, Earl said, "You know just what I'm talkin' about—what with your own son on the other side of the fence fightin' for his life."

Jordan could feel his hostility, and maybe it was with good reason. She definitely could relate. Especially when she was dealing with Trevor being accused of murder while the killer remained on the loose. And the authorities seemingly had no interest to go after the real killer.

But even with that Jordan still saw herself as an advocate of the law. "I can't comment on your son's death," she told them, "because I'm not familiar with the case. What I do know is that a man is on trial for his life for the murder of Victoria Turner. Obviously by your being here, you want to do the right thing for the victim."

Althea gave a slight smile, while Earl Sanderson nodded his head.

Going back through the file, Jordan noted that the call to the police station on Christmas Eve night reporting the crime had come in at eight-forty, shortly after the estimated time of death. The caller had been an unidentified woman. Althea Sanderson had never seriously been considered that woman, given her alleged state of mind. Now suddenly some of the missing pieces were beginning to fall into place.

"You reported the murder." Jordan eyed Althea. "Didn't you?"

Althea nodded as though a great weight had been removed from her shoulders.

"What I don't understand," admitted Jordan, "is why you decided to come forward now."

Althea paused a moment, after which she said with trepidation, "I seen him again . . . that's why." She flashed her husband a look. He took her hand for support.

"Where?" asked Jordan anxiously.

"At a restaurant," Althea said soberly. "He and his lady friend was sitting two tables 'cross from us. I recognized him as soon as I seen his face."

The tension in the office was as thick as fog. Jordan found her hand trembling as she grabbed her notepad. "Can you describe him?"

As if it were embedded in her mind, Althea said, "White, 'bout forty or maybe late thirties . . . tall . . ."

Jordan heard a generic description of about three-quarters of the men in Portland. That would hardly be enough to conduct a full-scale investigation.

"But what I remember most 'bout him was his hair." Althea looked as if she'd seen a ghost.

"What about his hair?" Jordan asked.

"It's full and nighttime black, 'cept for a funny-looking gray streak that runs right in the middle, at the top of his head. You know, like a skunk."

A tremor involuntarily swept through Jordan like a cyclone. There was only one man who immediately came to mind whose hair fit that description. Even then, the notion seemed so preposterous that Jordan hesitated to even consider the possibility.

Jerrod Wresler and Victoria Turner?

Could Wresler have been Victoria's secret lover?
The implications were frightening.

"What happened when this man ran past you?" Jordan asked.

"He got into a dark blue car and drove off."

"Do you know what type of car it was?"

Althea thought. "An expensive one," she said. "You know, like a BMW, or somethin' like that."

Jordan took notes, her mind going around in circles. "Anything else you remember?" She looked across the desk at the elderly woman.

Althea seemed to be saving the best—or worst—for last. She shifted in the chair, took a deep breath, and said, "At the restaurant, I heard his lady friend say that he was 'bout to become the next Homicide Chief in the D.A.'s office."

CHAPTER FORTY-EIGHT

The last person Harry Coleman expected to hear from again was Jordan La Fontaine. When she called to tell him she needed his help, he was curious as hell, considering the last time he had tried to help someone it blew up in his face.

Coleman sensed he had in all likelihood done irreparable harm to whatever La Fontaine and McNeil had going for them, whether the wife was still in the picture or not. Worse, was that he had failed Graham Turner. Like La Fontaine, the police follow-up on Simon McNeil had turned up zilch—nothing to warrant further investigation.

Coleman knew Turner was only a step or two away from a conviction for Victoria Turner's murder. Which, if it came to pass, was a one-way ticket to death row.

And now Coleman was being pressured to take an early retirement, which he was strongly considering—especially if he could somehow prove Turner's innocence as a farewell present to the department.

Then Jordan La Fontaine phoned to say she had a

new lead into a possible suspect in Victoria Turner's murder, giving Coleman new hope that maybe this thing wasn't over just yet.

"Jerrod Wresler?" Coleman's eyes popped wide. They were sitting in uncomfortable chairs at Starbucks, drinking cappuccino. "Isn't he . . . ?"

She didn't force him to say it. Instead, Jordan did. "Yes, Wresler's the Assistant D.A.," she said a little stiffly, "who is currently prosecuting my son."

Coleman sipped the cappuccino, wishing he had something stronger. His first thought was that Wresler was a bit too convenient a suspect, under the circumstances. But that was before Jordan told him more.

"A witness has come forward who saw a man very much fitting his description—right down to an unusual white streak in otherwise black hair—coming from the house around the time of the murder," she said, "and leaving in a car that exactly fits the description of Wresler's topaz blue BMW."

Coleman studied her earnestly. "I hope the person's more credible than the can't miss witness I thought I'd produced."

"I think she is," said Jordan convincingly. "Althea Sanderson's the one who reported the crime."

It was getting interesting, Coleman had to admit. Could this be the break Turner needed to prove his innocence? "Do you think Wresler was sleeping with Victoria Turner?" he asked pointblank.

Jordan pondered. "It makes sense," she answered noncommittally.

Even if that were true, and he didn't doubt the possibility, Coleman knew they were still a long ways from pinning a murder on Wresler. "Assuming Wresler's our man, does this witness have anything that can tie him directly to the murder?"

"The time she saw him leave the house was around

the time the murder occurred," Jordan said over the rim of her cup. "She also saw blood on the man's hands."

Coleman gave a wry chuckle. "You've gotta admit, if Wresler was involved in Victoria's death, it sure could make things a hell of a lot easier for your son."

"And *your* partner, Detective." Jordan hit him where he felt it.

Coleman drank more cappuccino. "What can I do to help bring down this son of a bitch?" he asked openly.

"I need more before I can take this to the D.A. But I can't do it alone."

They went to Desiree Bryar's place. Coleman felt if anyone could place Victoria in the company of Jerrod Wresler, it was her best friend.

"Yes, I know Jerrod," Desiree said wistfully, her legs folded beneath her on a loveseat. "I dated him for three months."

Jordan and Coleman glanced at each other on the sofa.

"What about Victoria?" asked Coleman. "Did she date him, too?"

Desiree frowned. "We never dated the same men. It wasn't worth losing our friendship over."

Jordan detected a note of jealousy there. Or was it competitiveness? "But Victoria did know Jerrod Wresler?"

Desiree hesitated. "Yes, she knew him. We actually met him at the same time at Club Diamonds. But once I set my sights on him," she emphasized, "Victoria never showed any interest in Jerrod."

At least not that you know of, thought Jordan. Or are willing to admit to yourself.

"Did you and Wresler ever do drugs together?" Coleman asked.

Desiree unfolded her legs from beneath her. "Give me

some credit for having a brain," she said. "Do you really expect me to say I did drugs with an assistant D.A.?"

Coleman told her, "Could be in *your* best interests . . ."

Desiree was not intimidated. "I don't think so. No, I have *never* done drugs with Jerrod Wresler."

Liar, Jordan thought. She decided to take a different approach. "Just out of curiosity, why did you stop seeing Jerrod?" she asked, adding intentionally, "I mean, although I only work with him, he seems like the type of man any sister would want to hold on to."

Desiree sighed. "Dream on, girl. If you wanna know the truth, the man was insatiable. Way too much for one woman to handle—if you know what I mean? Believe me, I was much better off without him."

Perhaps far more than you realize, thought Jordan. She wondered just how far Wresler was willing to go to satisfy his sexual appetite. Had he met his match in Victoria Turner? Could she have been too much woman for one man?

Maybe Jerrod Wresler had decided he and the rest of the world were better off with Victoria dead.

CHAPTER FORTY-NINE

Coleman sat at the table with Graham Turner and his attorney, Lester Eldridge. Turner asked, "What the hell does Jerrod have to do with this?"

That's just what I want to know, thought Coleman. He asked his partner, "How long have you known Wresler?"

"A few years. I'd hardly call the man my best friend. We hung out every now and then and even went hunting together a couple of times."

Hunting? The irony was not lost on Coleman.

Nor on Eldridge, who asked Turner, "When was the last time you and Wresler went hunting together?"

Turner scratched his head. "Probably last fall," he said. "Went after some black-tailed deer."

"Do you remember if you had your hunting knife with you then?" the attorney asked, putting a hand to his glasses.

Turner sat back, thinking. "Yeah, I had it. So what?"

Coleman took the lead. "Do you remember if you had the knife *after* that hunting trip, Graham?" he asked.

Turner seemed to strain himself trying to remember.

Finally, he said, "I don't know, man. It could've been in my gear, or . . ." He checked himself, frowning. "Look, whatever you two are thinking, Jerrod Wresler didn't steal the knife and use it to kill Victoria. The dude may not be ready for sainthood, but he ain't a killer either."

"You got a better idea?" Eldridge yanked off his glasses dramatically. "Let's get serious here, Graham. This is your life we're talking about, man. Either you had the knife after that trip or you didn't. Which is it?"

Coleman watched as Turner's bald head sank deeper between his broad shoulders. He said unsteadily, "All right, I don't remember seeing the knife again after coming home. That still doesn't prove Jerrod—a damned prosecutor, for crying out loud—had anything to do with Victoria's death."

From where Coleman sat, it indicated he might have had everything to do with her death. "Wresler was seen leaving Victoria's place that night, his hands covered with blood," Coleman told his partner flatly. "Did you see him there?"

Turner's lips became a thin line. "The only person I saw was my *wife*."

Coleman connected with Eldridge's eyes in a moment of silent sorrow. They would let Turner's error in calling his ex-wife his wife slide. They recognized the strain he was obviously under.

Coleman kept his voice level while asking Turner, "How well did Victoria know Wresler? According to Desiree Bryar, not well at all."

"He knew she was my wife," said Turner. "Jerrod never went after her, if that's what you're asking."

"Someone sure as hell did!" Eldridge put his glasses back on. "Victoria—your ex—had semen and pubic hair in her that didn't belong to you. Chances are, we find the man she was sleeping with, we find her killer."

Persuasive Evidence

Coleman moved into Turner's face and said sternly, "I'd say we've already found him. And you, buddy, along with the good-looking prosecuting attorney Jordan La Fontaine are gonna help us nail his ass!"

CHAPTER FIFTY

Amanda Clinksdale conferred with Jerrod Wresler for an extra moment or two of strategy as the witness took the stand. They had reached a critical stage of the trial where DNA evidence was to be introduced that could either win Trevor La Fontaine an acquittal or propel him to a death sentence.

"This is your time to shine, Amanda," Wresler whispered in her ear. "Don't blow it."

Amanda took that almost to be a threat more than a friendly pat on the ass. Yet she flashed him her girlish smile, and said, "I don't intend to."

His eyes crinkled. "Your place tonight, or mine?"

She stalled. "We'll see. Right now, I'd say there are more important things we need to concern ourselves with."

Amanda knew he could hardly argue the point, as she left the table. She was well aware of what his priorities were. And her own, for that matter. She walked in short steps to the witness box.

Amanda thought briefly about her and Jerrod

Wresler. Though they were good in bed together—all right, great—she sensed their relationship was going nowhere. Wresler wanted a girl to have fun, sex, and cocaine with, and not necessarily in that order. She wanted a man who would be committed to her in body and soul.

In Amanda's mind, Jerrod Wresler was definitely not that man.

She smiled now at the prosecution's star witness, or at the very least their co-star. Jacquelyn Oppenheimer was a forensic scientist, specializing in DNA evidence. At forty-six and in great shape, she looked as though she could easily be in her mid-thirties. Her strawberry-blond hair was stylishly cut just above the shoulders, and her oval face was tautly defined. Focused aquamarine eyes stared back at Amanda, ready and waiting.

After whizzing through the witness's qualifications, Amanda wasted no time in getting to the root of her testimony. "Ms. Oppenheimer," she said in a tone as smooth as silk, "you performed DNA tests on blood samples found on clothing and in a Ford Explorer belonging to the defendant. Is that correct?"

Oppenheimer nodded, sitting stiffly in a black pin-stripe pantsuit. "Yes, it is."

"Can you tell us what type of DNA test was used to reach the conclusions?"

"We analyzed the blood samples using the PCR test." She paused a moment and added for clarification, "That's Polymerase Chain Reaction test."

Amanda wet her lips, then asked as she had rehearsed, "Is it true that this test can be done using as little as a pinhead amount of blood?"

"That is correct."

"And from this you can accurately determine who that blood belongs to?"

"Yes we can," Oppenheimer responded. "Unlike some

other criminal DNA testing methods, PCR-based DNA typing requires only a few cells of DNA to establish a highly probable genetic match. Furthermore, if I might add, PCR analysis can also be successfully performed on degraded DNA samples; and even specimens collected years after the crime was committed, with the same degree of accuracy."

Amanda glanced at Wresler, who winked at her. She ignored him, and instead focused on the defendant. Trevor La Fontaine looked tired and restless. Maybe even indignant. He did not look guilty, she thought. But that wasn't her call. She had to go with the evidence, even if she hated having to go against her own instincts. And against her friend, Jordan.

Amanda turned back to Jacquelyn Oppenheimer and asked in a level voice, "Can you tell us, Ms. Oppenheimer, what the test of the blood samples found on and in Mr. La Fontaine's Explorer revealed?"

After clearing her throat, the witness responded confidently, "The tests conducted show that the blood belonged to Gail Marshall."

Some groans erupted in the courtroom, forcing the judge to demand order with one swift smash of the gavel.

Knowing the momentum was on her side, Amanda went to the evidence table and lifted plastic bags containing trousers and a shirt that belonged to the defendant. Earlier testimony had established that they fit the description of clothes he wore the night Gail Marshall and Nelson Neilson were killed. Amanda held the clothes up in front of the witness.

"Are these the clothes that you lifted blood specimens from?"

Oppenheimer pretended to study the clothes. "Yes, they are."

"And were you able to determine who the blood belonged to?"

"Yes, we were."

"Can you tell us whose blood was found on the clothes belonging to Trevor La Fontaine?"

"Yes," Oppenheimer said with a tilt of her head. "The blood came from Nelson Neilson and Gail Marshall."

More reaction and murmurs, some coming from the jury box, told Amanda that she had done her job well. This, despite a sinking feeling that she was doing an injustice to the defendant.

Something equally troubling was on Amanda's mind. She had heard through the grapevine—Andrew Lombard—that an investigation was being conducted within the D.A.'s office that, as he put it, "Could blow the lid off both of its biggest trials in years." He wouldn't be specific, only advising her to distance herself from Jerrod Wresler before it was too late.

Amanda wondered if it already was.

CHAPTER FIFTY-ONE

Jordan sat in one chair, Andrew in another. Wilson Bombeck leaned toward them from his desk, shock spread all over his face like wrinkles, as Jordan laid out the facts she had on Jerrod Wresler.

"We have an eyewitness that saw him leaving Victoria Turner's townhouse at approximately the time she was murdered," Jordan said without remorse, "and saw his hands stained with blood. He then got into a dark blue BMW, just like the one Wresler drives. According to Andrew and Fred Edmond, Wresler didn't show up at The Ranch until nearly nine-thirty, giving him ample time to have cleaned up and driven there. Two other witnesses will testify that Wresler knew the victim."

Jordan sucked in a deep breath and tried to calm her nerves. "Jerrod also knows the defendant," she pointed out, which was another surprise to her. Somehow she couldn't imagine Wresler and Turner being in the same social circles. "The two went hunting together. Detective Turner claims that his hunting knife—the one used to viciously slice up Victoria Turner—has been missing since he and Wresler went hunting last fall."

Bombeck looked as if he had aged ten years in a matter of minutes. He clasped his hands together tightly on the desk, as if asking for divine intervention. "This is incredible," he muttered, shaking his head. "Jerrod Wresler a murderer?"

"At the very least," conceded Jordan, unwilling to convict the arrogant A.D.A. of first-degree murder just yet, "Wresler was definitely at the victim's townhouse that night. Only he can tell us what actually happened there."

As much as she despised Jerrod Wresler, Jordan was hesitant to out-and-out accuse him of Victoria Turner's murder. Especially considering the overwhelming evidence that still pointed toward Graham Turner as his ex-wife's killer. Yet there was little doubt in Jordan's mind that Wresler was in this more deeply than any of them could have imagined.

Not even the obvious benefits she stood to gain from his downfall made Jordan feel any better about the situation. She glanced at Andrew. He had been quick to accept the new revelations, telling her, "If you ask me, I wouldn't put anything past Wresler. Not if it meant saving his own red neck. Not even murder."

Peering at Bombeck, Jordan said, "Wilson, I need your permission to go after Wresler." She had considered going behind his back, but decided against it. It would be far better if she had the D.A. fully behind her on this one.

"You've got it," Bombeck reluctantly agreed. He took off his glasses and wiped the sweat from his brow. "What do you have in mind?"

"First, I may need a court order to get a DNA sample from Wresler to compare it with the DNA from the semen found in Victoria Turner."

Bombeck put his glasses back on. "I'll give Judge Crawford a call this afternoon."

"Thanks, Wilson." One big hurdle down. The next one was to confront Jerrod Wresler . . . and let the chips fall where they may.

Narrowing his gaze, Bombeck warned, "I hope to hell you know what you're doing on this one, Jordan. If it turns out that Wresler isn't the man you seem to think he is, it'll be your ass on the line, not his."

Jordan got the message loud and clear. The stakes couldn't be higher for her and Wresler. But it was a chance she was willing to take. She had no other real choice. Even though being wrong could jeopardize the very career she'd worked so hard for.

Not to mention the fact that Jerrod Wresler continued to be a major player in Trevor's trial, with little room for error should this thing blow up in her face.

CHAPTER FIFTY-TWO

Wresler was ordered to go to Jordan La Fontaine's office for a meeting. He was more curious than anything else. Maybe La Fontaine was ready to throw herself on the mercy of the court and beg for her son's life. The thought somehow made Jerrod Wresler chuckle as he straightened his Roberto Cavalli rose-colored tie, knocked once on the door, and went in.

Jordan was sitting at her desk waiting for him. Andrew occupied one of the two chairs in front of the desk.

Wresler uneasily took the other chair, then said with irritation, "Okay, La Fontaine, you've got my full attention. What's this all about?"

Jordan eyed him sharply. "It's about you and Victoria Turner, Jerrod."

Wresler felt his heart pounding. He was caught off guard. But he quickly regained control. Now was not the time to panic. "I'm afraid you've lost me," he said in a measured voice. "I don't know anything about Victoria Turner."

Jordan hardened her expression. "I think you do," she said. "Someone saw you leaving her house the night she was killed. They saw you with blood on your hands."

That damned old black woman, Wresler thought angrily. He had left the house in such a hurry that he barely saw the bitch and her stupid dog until they had nearly collided. By then, all he wanted to do was get the hell out of there as fast as he could.

Now Wresler wondered if he could have—should have—done something differently that night.

Too late now. He had to think and think fast.

Denial was the way to go when all else failed. He would be damned if some old hag would destroy his life.

Sitting erect, Wresler told Jordan, "Your 'someone' obviously has me mixed up with somebody else."

Andrew said in a no-nonsense voice, "Give it up, Wresler. It won't work. I doubt there are two people anywhere in this city with that weird gray streak you've got in your hair who also match the rest of the description our witness gave. My advice to you is to cooperate, while you've got your chance."

It was all Wresler could do to keep his cool in the face of the heat he was getting from the two of them. But keep it he must. They were expecting him to break down and confess. Well, forget it, he thought. If you think I'll make this easy for you, then you're both bigger idiots than I thought.

"You were sleeping with Victoria Turner, weren't you, Jerrod?" asked Jordan, keeping the pressure on.

"This is absolutely absurd," insisted Wresler with a straight face. "If this is some sort of attempt to try and save your son's neck . . ."

"Did you kill her?" Jordan demanded.

Wresler felt as if his tie was suddenly choking him.

He made himself look at Andrew, and said in a friendly manner, "You know as well as I do that I was at The Ranch at the time Victoria Turner was killed. Will you tell—"

"Not quite." Andrew cut him off abruptly. "You didn't show up there until well after the time of her death, according to the medical examiner."

The noose was getting tighter, and Wresler loosened his tie. It didn't help. He still felt like he was choking. "So what the hell does that prove?" He gritted his teeth.

"It proves you don't have an airtight alibi to exclude you from murdering Victoria Turner," Jordan responded.

"Why should I?" Wresler became desperate. "This whole thing is ridiculous. You know as well as I do that you're already trying the man who killed Victoria Turner."

Jordan narrowed her eyes. "We may have the wrong man on trial," she suggested. "Why don't you tell us about the hunting knife that was used to cut up Victoria Turner?"

You're fishing, thought Wresler. Hoping he would take the bait. Not a chance. "I don't know anything about a hunting knife," he lied.

"Do you deny that you and Graham Turner went hunting together?"

"Maybe we did," Wresler conceded that much. "So I'm friends with the detective." Not really, he thought. More like acquaintances while I had the hots for his wife. "That doesn't mean I had a damned thing to do with the murder of his ex-wife."

"I want you to volunteer a sample of your DNA to be tested," Jordan told him firmly, "to see if it matches the semen and hairs taken from Victoria Turner's body."

Wresler had begun to perspire. His whole world suddenly seemed to be coming apart at the seams. And all because of the bitch sitting in front of him at her desk like a damned judge. He collected himself enough to say: "I think I'd like to call my lawyer."

CHAPTER FIFTY-THREE

Judge Alfonso Crawford, a close friend of Wilson Bombeck's, with thirty years on the bench, signed the court order that would force Wresler to give a DNA sample to be tested. Jordan had hoped it would not come to that, but Wresler had rejected voluntary submission.

It was four o'clock when Jordan left the Criminal Justice Center. She expected Wresler to be served with the court order that evening. Judge Grayson had granted a motion for a continuance after both Jordan and Eldridge requested it.

Jordan got into her Legacy, tossing her purse on the passenger seat. She had just started the car when a gloved hand suddenly reached out and covered her mouth, pressing her lips tightly to her teeth.

"Don't scream!" There was desperation in the voice.

It took Jordan only a moment or two to realize it was Jerrod Wresler's.

"I have a gun, Jordan," he said from the backseat. "And I'll use it if I have to. Now don't scream, if you know what's good for you!"

Wresler slowly removed his hand from her mouth, and Jordan was left with bruised lips and the bitter taste of leather. Her first instinct was to ram the horn to alert someone that she was being abducted in broad daylight by a killer—who also happened to be an assistant district attorney. But Jordan's greater instinct was for survival, not stupidity. She raised her eyes to the rearview mirror. Wresler sat there smugly staring back at her with vacant eyes. She could not see the gun in his hand.

"You're making one big mistake, Wresler," she told him as forcefully as she could without provoking him.

"No, bitch," he shot back, "you made one when you went digging where you shouldn't have."

Jordan was determined not to panic—yet. "What do you want, Jerrod?" She assumed that if he wanted to kill her, he would have already done so.

She could hear his choppy breathing as he spoke. "I want you to drive."

"Where?"

"Just drive, dammit!"

Jordan pulled out of the parking lot, onto the street. Normally she would have expected to see any number of people who recognized her and Wresler coming to or from the Criminal Justice Center. On this occasion, there was no one to vouch for their leaving.

"Killing me is not going to solve the deep hole you've dug for yourself, Wresler," Jordan said, if for no other reason than to try to get in his head. "The court order has already been issued. Andrew knows everything. And so does Wilson."

"Who said anything about killing you?" Through the rearview mirror, Jordan watched his dark eyes grow darker. "That would be too easy."

"Then what are you doing in my car with a gun?" Jordan inadvertently raised her voice more than she had intended to. "Kidnapping an Assistant D.A. is not very smart, Wresler—not even for you. In fact, it may be one of the dumbest things you've ever done."

"Shut the hell up! You wanted to know about my involvement with Victoria Turner, so I'm going to tell you, on my own terms."

They came to a red light. Cars were freely crossing the intersection. Jordan considered plunging ahead. If she hit another car, causing a possible chain reaction, at least it would bring attention to her plight. And Wresler would find it hard to do something so foolish as to shoot her in full view of others.

"I know what you're thinking," he told her. "Don't try it, Jordan. If I go down, you can be damn sure I'll take you with me—right here and now."

Jordan sucked in a deep breath, waited until the light turned green, and proceeded. Desperate people do desperate things, she told herself. I have to play this his way. For now.

"So you have my undivided attention, Wresler," Jordan said. "Let's hear what you want to get off your chest."

Wresler remained silent for a moment or two, then admitted, "I had an affair with Victoria." He sighed. "My mistake. She liked—make that loved—to tease men, make them drool all over themselves for her. Why? To punish Graham Turner for what he did to her."

What about what you did to her, Jordan mused, but asked, "Is that why you killed her—because she was a tease?"

Wresler groaned. "I didn't kill her. Turn here."

It was Forty-Third Street. Where the hell was he taking her? She obeyed his command, hoping to come out of this in one piece.

"If you didn't kill Victoria Turner," she asked, trying to keep him talking, "what on earth were you doing at her house that night of all nights?"

"I came to tell her I was through playing her damned games," Wresler said bitterly. "I couldn't take it anymore—loving Victoria more than I'd ever loved anyone, but knowing I could never have her. Not really." He paused. "The door was open when I got there. I saw Turner's car in front of the house and knew there was probably trouble."

He shifted in the seat while Jordan pondered his words and, more importantly, his actions—past and present.

"When I went into the bedroom, I saw Victoria lying on the bed," continued Wresler. "There was blood all over her. It was obvious from the looks of her cut up throat and body that she was dead." His voice dropped. "Graham Turner was standing over her, holding the knife. He wasn't moving. It was almost like he was in a trance or something. I don't think he ever saw me. All I could think of was that I was in the wrong place at the wrong time." He sniffled. "Fearing for my own life, I hit Turner. That must be how I got blood on my hand. He had a lot on him. Anyway, he fell down and I got the hell out of there."

"Why?" Jordan asked, glancing up at him in the rearview mirror. "If you were truly innocent, that is?"

"That's just it," Wresler said, "I would *never* have been innocent in the eyes of the public. The press would have had a field day with this. Ex-husband murders ex-wife. Assistant D.A. friend of the ex-husband and obsessed lover of victim discovers body." He sighed. "The whole thing had a nasty feel to it. My career would have been over," he moaned. "At least any chance to move up the ranks where I belong. You know as well as I do that public opinion means everything—and in this case Bombeck wouldn't have had the balls to look the other way. The asshole would've probably bounced me out on my ear. I couldn't risk that happening, losing what I'd paid my dues to achieve."

Jordan became aware that a car was following them, while doing a very good job at making it seem as if it wasn't. She quickly averted her eyes for fear Wresler would notice, too.

"Turn right here," he directed abruptly.

"Where are we going?" Jordan asked him in her strongest tone yet. "You don't have to do this, Jerrod. If what you've said is true, then you can still get out of this with little more than a few scrapes and bruises . . . maybe a reprimand—"

"It's too late for that," Wresler said dejectedly. "The most I can hope for now is to salvage some dignity, and maybe my job, if I'm lucky—which I don't particularly feel at the moment."

And where did that leave Jordan. *Is he going to do away with me to save his damned dignity and career?*

Did he really believe that would happen?

She noted the car was still trailing them. Through the rearview mirror, Jordan looked at the gun Wresler was holding. It was clear that he wanted her to see it now, as if an indication of what was to come.

"Pull in here," he told her. It was an abandoned site that had formerly been an industrial plant, shut down after it was discovered that they had been illegally dumping chemicals into the Columbia River for years.

Jordan drove in slowly, fearfully. She didn't trust who-ever was following them—assuming it was friend—to get there in time to prevent this lunatic from killing her. All Jordan could think of was her children losing both their parents in little more than a year.

"Don't do this, Jerrod," she said, trying to reason with him. "I'm *not* your enemy. We're colleagues. I can help you, if you'll let me."

309

He began to laugh. "Help me? I'll just bet you can, La Fontaine," he said caustically. "You'd see me in prison or at the very least out of the D.A.'s office before you helped me. Why miss the golden opportunity for the promotion we've both fought tooth and nail to get when you've got me right where you want me. Or is it the other way around? Stop here!"

Jordan stopped the car in an area beyond the main building. Weeds were overgrown and there was debris scattered about from the previous owners, almost as though they wanted to leave behind something to remember them by.

"Get out!" ordered Wresler, and Jordan could feel the cold steel of the gun barrel against her neck.

Jordan didn't dare peek at the rearview mirror for fear that she would tip him off that they had company. Right now her only interest was to somehow distract Wresler . . . delay whatever it was he had in mind, while praying that it never came to pass.

Once outside, Jordan got a better look at the gun Jerrod Wresler had aimed at her. It was a .25-caliber automatic. The same type of weapon she owned.

And, more importantly, the same type that had killed Gail Marshall and Nelson Neilson.

Wresler's eyes lit up at her interest in the gun. "It's yours," he said to Jordan's surprise. "You wouldn't believe how easy it is to get things out of police lockup. Then again, of course you would. A.D.A.s go in there all the time to collect or send back evidence. Why, I'm sure you must have done that a few times yourself, La Fontaine."

His eyes became devious little slits. Jordan was beginning to see things more clearly now. He planned to murder her . . . and make it look like—

"In fact," bragged Wresler, "*you* even managed to take

your own gun out from under the police department's nose, Jordan. Everybody knows how despondent you've been over your son's trial and the pressures you feel trying your own case. It all became just too much for you, so you committed suicide."

Jordan's knees were shaking so badly, she feared she'd fall. "No one will believe that," she told him. "Not for one minute. I'm not that weak!"

"We'll see about that," Wresler said, sounding like a man who had already made up his mind.

Only now did Jordan note the blue BMW parked at the back of the building. Wresler obviously had planned this walk.

"If you're not a murderer, Jerrod," Jordan pleaded with him, "don't become one. It doesn't have to be this way. We can keep this whole little incident between us."

He gave her a sideways glance. "I really wish I could believe that, Jordan."

She sensed the slightest hesitancy and thought she may have somehow reached him. "You can believe it, Jerrod," Jordan tried to sound convincing, even as she considered that help may have arrived by now. Unless, of course, it was entirely her imagination or wishful thinking that they were being followed.

When Wresler pointed the gun at Jordan with renewed purpose, all hope seemed lost.

"You'll go before she does, Wresler," a strong voice boomed.

Wresler and Jordan turned to see Detective Harry Coleman on one knee some fifteen feet away, his gun aimed squarely at Wresler.

Jordan felt a mixture of relief and continued anxiety. I'm still a lot closer to Wresler and his gun, she thought, unnerved, than Coleman is to either of us.

"Put the damned gun down, Wresler!" Coleman ordered. "Or, so help me, I'll drop you where you stand."

Wresler seemed to weigh his options, which at that point were virtually none. Yet he kept his gun trained on Jordan.

"It's over, Jerrod," Jordan said tensely, almost scolding him. "You can't kill me now and possibly hope to get away with it."

"You heard the lady," Coleman shouted. "Do it, Wresler! Now! Put the gun on the ground, slowly . . ."

Wresler gave Jordan a hard, defeated look, before muttering a curse. He lowered the gun to his side. Coleman came up to them with his gun still directed at Wresler, and removed the gun from Wresler's hand.

"You all right?" Coleman asked Jordan with a weary grimace. She sighed, smiling at the detective.

"Yes," Jordan said gratefully, "I think I am."

CHAPTER FIFTY-FOUR

After passing a lie detector test to support his claim of innocence, Jerrod Wresler agreed to testify against Graham Turner, whose guilt was no longer in question as far as Jordan was concerned. Meanwhile Wresler faced a number of charges himself, including kidnapping and attempted murder. Bombeck had asked for and received Wresler's resignation, effective immediately.

That left Jordan solidly in the driver's seat for the position of Bureau Chief of the Homicide Division. That appointment still hinged on her getting a conviction against Graham Turner, which seemed a near certainty at this point. Then there was the little matter of Jordan's son on trial for the killing of two students. Despite Jordan's attempts to tie the case against Trevor to Wresler's personal quest for power and apparent vendetta against her—no matter whose toes he had to step on—Bombeck refused to drop the charges. Amanda Clinksdale had become lead prosecutor in the case.

After wrapping up the prosecution's case against Turner, Jordan waited to see if Lester Eldridge would call anyone to the stand in defense of his client. As it turned out, he called only one witness. The defendant himself.

Graham Turner, wearing a single-breasted navy suit, moved slowly and calmly to the witness box. He glanced at Jordan but showed no emotion.

Eldridge, looking desperate and worn down now that Coleman's investigation had failed to produce another viable suspect, pressed his client through a series of questions to tell the truth and nothing but the truth. Finally, to drive the point home, Eldridge asked, "Did you kill Victoria Turner?"

Turner took a long pause, then responded levelly, "No, I did not."

Eldridge looked at Jordan. "Your witness."

Jordan nodded and stood. It was almost too much to believe that Turner was on the stand, proclaiming his innocence in the face of overwhelming evidence, including Jerrod Wresler's damaging testimony. Jordan wondered if somehow Graham Turner truly believed he was innocent. She doubted it. There was nothing in his psychological profile to indicate he was suffering from delusions or other mental illness.

Why don't you fess up, Turner, so we can all go home, Jordan said to herself. She approached the defendant cautiously, knowing she had to do this right so that it didn't backfire on her.

"Mr. Turner," Jordan began in an almost friendly manner, "is it true that you beat Victoria Turner during your marriage to her?"

Eldridge gave a weak objection, which the judge overruled after Jordan reminded her that the defendant's prior history of abusing his wife had already been introduced into evidence.

Turner glared at Jordan and answered, "I wouldn't

call it beating. Yeah, we fought sometimes just like all married people . . . then we kissed and made up."

Jordan bristled at the nonchalant denial. "Are you telling this court that you think it's normal behavior to batter your wife so that she's left with several cracked ribs, broken bones, and numerous trips to the emergency room?"

Turner blinked at Jordan in defiance. "I never meant to hurt her," he claimed. "We both had hot tempers. Sometimes it escalated into something neither of us could control. It didn't mean I didn't love her."

Jordan's mouth became a grim line as she said scathingly, "Is that why you killed her . . . because you loved her? Or is it because you couldn't stand that she was making a life apart from you, including sleeping with men you knew, like Jerrod Wresler?"

"You don't know what the hell you're talking about!" Turner's voice rose in anger.

"I'm talking about *you*, Mr. Turner!" Jordan bellowed. "You and your obsession with Victoria Turner. If you couldn't have her, you were going to make damned sure that no one had her—not even your hunting buddy, Jerrod Wresler! Isn't that right?"

Turner looked as if he was ready to explode, which was precisely what Jordan was hoping for. She kept the pressure on, while endeavoring to keep her own temper in check.

"Your hunting knife was never really stolen, was it?" she asked the defendant. "That was just a convenient excuse to try and cover your ass. You sliced and diced your ex-wife after you cut her throat. *Didn't you*, Mr. Turner?"

"No, dammit!" His voice was weak.

Judge Grayson warned Jordan to tone down her language and theatrics.

Leaning over Turner, her eyes ablaze, Jordan disregarded the judge's directive as she said, "You murdered her because you felt she was your private property, didn't you?"

"No," he said sullenly.

"She didn't deserve to live if it wasn't as your wife and lover. Isn't that correct?"

"No."

Breathing in for a final burst of adrenaline, Jordan argued vehemently, "You cut off one of her breasts. You damned near took off her head. You hated your ex-wife for having the audacity to leave you, and then flaunt her beauty and sexuality with other men. You wanted to take that away from her—even in death. Isn't that right, Mr. Turner?"

"Ms. La Fontaine!" Judge Grayson snapped at her.

Turner's face contorted with anguish. Fixing Jordan with a furious glare he shouted, "Yeah, I killed her!"

Jordan's mouth nearly hung open in shock at the confession as she stared at the defendant. She glanced at his equally stunned attorney, then found her eyes meeting those of Detective Harry Coleman, who had been ever present in support of his partner and friend.

It became deathly quiet in the courtroom, except for Graham Turner's voice.

"She left me no choice," he said. "I didn't hate Victoria. I loved her. . . ." His voice trailed off as the courtroom became abuzz. "I loved her too much to let her go. She was mine—*every* part of her. No one was going to take her from me. No one . . ."

"No one except *you*," Jordan reminded him. "You have no one to blame but yourself for your wife leaving you. And no one else is to blame for what you did to her." Jordan took a moment to gather herself. She looked at Judge Grayson, who appeared relieved, and declared exultantly, "I have nothing else to say to this man, Your Honor."

It took the jury less than an hour to find Graham Dylan Turner guilty of the first-degree murder of Victoria Turner. He had refused to change his guilty plea, arguing that he had every right to take his ex-wife's life because she was his to take.

During the penalty phase, the jury voted unanimously that Graham Turner be put to death by lethal injection.

Jordan had little time to gloat over her victory, for she still had one very big hurdle to climb. Make that two. Trevor needed her in his time of crisis, as his trial was winding down with the verdict very much in doubt. And whether Jordan realized it or not, she needed Simon, maybe more than ever.

CHAPTER FIFTY-FIVE

Lenora Pitambe never had an easy life. Not like her friend, Kendre. Lenora had always envied Kendre up until her brother Trevor was arrested and charged with murdering two people at Devil's Edge. Since then Kendre had become withdrawn, moody, and not much fun to be with.

Though Lenora felt badly that Kendre had also lost her father last year, at least she'd had a father to lose. The only parent Lenora had ever known was her mother, who played both roles about as well as Cinderella's stepmother had. Her real father was a two-time loser. The first loss was when he abandoned her mother after he found out she was pregnant and before they could marry. The second was when he was deported back to his native Zimbabwe after it was discovered that he was in this country illegally. There were rumors that he was also involved in drug smuggling. Lenora's mother never saw him again.

Since then Lenora had seen her mother go through a

string of boyfriends—or jerks, she would say—most of whom stuck around only as long as it took to find someone better with more money. Lenora and her mother lived in a trailer park, not like the big house Kendre lived in. When Lenora's mother worked at all, it was usually odd jobs with low pay. Most of Lenora's clothes were hand-me-downs, borrowed from Kendre or other friends, or the occasional chic outfit she shoplifted. Still, she wouldn't complain. It was always worse for someone else, though few of her friends fit into that category.

At fifteen-and-a-half, Lenora looked more like twenty-five, with a mature body and heavily made up face. Her ever changing hairstyle was presently a series of off-black curls with streaks of gold synthetic hair extensions. Befitting her image, Lenora pretended to be eighteen for her current boyfriend, Sidney, who was nineteen. The fact that Lenora was not a virgin—and hadn't been since she was twelve—made it easy for him to believe her. Along with the fact that her breasts were a womanly 36D.

On this muggy evening, Sidney talked Lenora into going to Devil's Edge for some hanky panky, and maybe more. She was a bit leery about it after the trouble Kendre's brother had gotten into there, but Sidney convinced Lenora that it was safe, pointing out there had not been a single incidence of violence at Devil's Edge since the murders of Gail Marshall and Nelson Neilson. Besides, Sidney promised, he would be there to protect her.

Lenora didn't doubt that, feeling safe in Sidney's big arms, surrounded by his even bigger body. She all but forgot her fears, as they began making out in the backseat of his parents' Buick Regal. He put his tongue in her mouth, and his hand down her blouse. She unfastened his jeans and put a hand down his underwear, grabbing hold of his erection. This was where it gets fun, she thought, feeling giddy all over.

The dark green van pulled slowly into the parking playground called Devil's Edge. There was only one car there, after another loaded with drunken kids had screeched away, leaving behind a cloud of exhaust. He brought the van to a stop across the lot from where the car was parked. A cigarette dangled from his mouth and he smoked it a bit longer while eyeing his prey. There were two of them in there. He could only imagine what they were doing in the backseat. Not for long, he thought, smiling.

He removed the gun from the seat beside him and left the van with the engine running.

Lenora felt as if Sidney's weight were going to crush her like a trash compactor. So she adjusted her body as much as she could to give herself the slightest breathing room. She opened her eyes to see Sidney's eyes squeezed shut while he grew near his climax.

A few moments earlier, Lenora had seen the dark van park across from them. She had thought to herself: Cool! And a lot roomier for its lucky occupants to have sex than in the backseat of a Buick Regal.

Now she noted that a man had gotten out of the van and was coming toward them. She wasn't sure if she felt more alarmed or embarrassed, given what they were doing.

"Sidney," Lenora whispered. "Someone's coming."

"Don't worry about it, baby," he responded, more or less ignoring her, caught up now in the throes of his orgasm.

Lenora pressed her lips into a pout. She had decided from the start that this would not be very satisfying for her, but she did it anyway for him. Now she began to question the wisdom of always living her life for men instead of herself, just as her mother did. She'd have to talk to Kendre about it, especially now that she was seeing Nkaki.

The man was getting closer. Too close for Lenora's comfort.

"Sidney!" she shrieked, her breasts half exposed and legs spread awkwardly on both sides of Sidney. "I told you there's a *weird* man coming over here. Get off me!"

"Not yet, baby," he cried, refusing to budge as his big body quivered violently.

Lenora saw that the man was carrying something at his side—a gun. Suddenly all she could think of was Gail Marshall and Nelson Neilson.

And Trevor La Fontaine. And Kendre.

Lenora let out a piercing scream. Unfortunately, Sidney misconstrued that for a cry of passion and began pumping himself into her even harder.

Lenora Pitambe watched helplessly as the man raised the gun and pointed it at them. He fired into the window, shattering it. Lenora saw a bullet go through Sidney and felt it move into her. Then another took a chunk of Sidney's head with it, glass splattering on top of them. She was not sure if Sidney was even aware of what had happened, and Lenora doubted he would ever have the chance; especially when another shot rang out, once more hitting both of them.

Though she had never before felt as much pain as she did now, Lenora remained perfectly still, forcing her eyes to stay closed, as if she was dead. She could sense that he was still out there, studying them, making sure there were no living witnesses left behind.

She must have remained that way—buried beneath Sidney's suddenly rigid, heavy, cold body—for minutes, certain that if the man didn't shoot her again she would die from the two bullets already lodged in her chest.

Then Lenora thought she heard the van driving away and felt renewed hope that she might come out of this alive, before she blacked out.

CHAPTER FIFTY-SIX

Jordan clasped Kendre's hand tightly as Trevor took the stand in his own defense. It was a calculated risk on Simon's part, but he believed that Trevor's testimony was crucial at this point. Earlier, Rhonda Venus—the young woman whose honor Trevor was defending when he got into the tussle with Nelson Neilson—testified that Trevor had shown remorse after the fight and gave no indication that he ever had any intention of doing Nelson bodily harm, much less killing him and Gail.

Jordan had been of the opinion that Rhonda—who was nineteen, pretty, and slender with dark blond corn rows—had come across as a credible witness. She had visited Trevor often in jail, and both seemed to have come to terms with what had happened and had become much closer as a result.

After taking the oath, Trevor sat in the witness box. Jordan couldn't help thinking how handsome he looked. Gone were the dreadlocks, replaced by slightly teased, closely cropped hair. The goatee was also gone, in favor of a clean-shaven look. It was as if he'd had to remake himself in order to save his sanity and his life.

Simon spent several minutes going over Trevor's background so the jury could see that there was nothing in his past to lay the groundwork for him to become a vengeful murderer.

"Do you remember telling Nelson Neilson, 'You're dead, man'?" asked Simon evenly.

"Yes," Trevor responded.

"Do you often say that to people who make you mad?"

"No," Trevor insisted. "It was a stupid thing to say."

"Then why say it?" his attorney asked.

Trevor shrugged uncomfortably. "I don't know. I was angry and I guess it was the first thing to come out of my mouth."

Simon moved in front of him. "Did you mean it—that Nelson Neilson was a dead man?"

"No, I didn't!" Trevor looked at Jordan and Kendre. "Sometimes people say things in the heat of the moment. I wish I could take it back."

Simon paused. "Why did you go to Devil's Edge, Trevor?"

"Just to be by myself for awhile."

"Do you often go there by yourself?"

Trevor swallowed. "Not often, but sometimes. It's a good place to hang out if you need time to think."

"And what were you thinking about?" asked Simon.

"School, my momma, Kendre, bills, Rhonda . . ."

"But not Nelson or Gail?" Simon faced the jurors.

Trevor's brows drew together. "No."

"Did you know they were going to Devil's Edge from the party?" Simon asked.

"No."

Jordan watched as Simon stepped away from the witness box and looked her way for a long moment, giving her no indication of how he felt about her or their relationship. He abruptly returned to the witness box.

"When did you first approach the Chevy that Nelson Neilson and Gail Marshall were in at Devil's Edge?" Simon asked his client.

"After I saw the broken glass around the car."

"Did you see anyone else?"

"No—not at that time."

Simon rested an arm on the railing. "What did you see when you looked inside the car?"

Trevor sighed. "Gail and Nelson." He gulped. "They were slumped over in the backseat. I could tell they were hurt badly."

"Did you touch them?"

"I felt them to see if they were dead."

"And were they?"

"Yes—I believe so." Trevor bent his head.

Simon took a moment, then asked, "What did you do then?"

"I left," Trevor muttered weakly.

"Why?"

Trevor drew in a deep breath. "To tell you the truth, I panicked," he said in a hoarse voice. "I was afraid that because of what happened at the party, I might be blamed for their deaths."

Simon narrowed his gaze. "Did you kill them, Trevor?"

He responded firmly, "No, I did not."

Jordan made eye contact with Amanda. She knew her rival A.D.A. would give it everything she had to contradict Trevor's story, and make him out to be the killer. Jordan also knew that Amanda had inherited her role and was obligated to prosecute her son, for better or worse.

Just as Simon said, "No further questions," and was

headed back to the defense table, Jordan saw out of the corner of her eye someone approaching her. It was Andrew Lombard. There was a dour look on his face. He handed Jordan a note.

She turned painfully to Kendre after reading it.

Lenora Pitambe had been shot. She was in the emergency room at Rose City General Hospital fighting for her life.

CHAPTER FIFTY-SEVEN

Jordan and Kendre arrived at the hospital at the same time as Georgette Hollister, Lenora's mother. Her puffy face was golden brown, and the area around her black-gray eyes was red from crying. She looked as if she had thrown on the first thing she could find—a pair of well-worn faded jeans and a Los Angeles Lakers jersey.

"What happened to my baby?" slurred Georgette in near hysteria, her hand absently brushing her half-pressed and half-frizzy, brownish-black hair.

Jordan hugged her, holding back tears. "We don't know yet, Georgette," she lied. In fact, Jordan had learned that Lenora and a young man she was with had been shot multiple times. But what most stuck to Jordan's mind was where the shooting had occurred—Devil's Edge. Could they have been shot by the same person who shot Nelson Neilson and Gail Marshall?

The person who should have been on trial for their murders instead of Trevor?

The doctor—a slender, young black man with gleaming

black jerry curls—approached them. "Ms. Hollister . . . ?" He looked at Jordan.

"I'm Ms. Hollister," said Georgette, wiping her eyes. "Is my daughter all right?"

He gave her a serious look. "I'm Dr. Moore," he said. "Your daughter was shot twice in the chest. We had to do emergency surgery. She's lost a lot of blood and she has some internal injuries."

Georgette looked like she was about to pass out, and Jordan winced, before Dr. Moore said, "But, remarkably, no major arteries were hit. With any luck and *lots* of prayers, we think your daughter can make a complete recovery."

"Thank you, Lord." Georgette looked upward and a big smile spread across her face. She then shamelessly hugged Jordan and Kendre. "What about Sidney?" Georgette asked the doctor abruptly, as if his condition had just dawned on her.

Dr. Moore's brow creased and he looked at Jordan. "Are you Mrs. Friedrickson?"

Before Jordan could respond, a well-dressed African-American couple in their late forties rushed up to them. The man said in a nervous voice, "We're Sidney's parents. We got here as fast as we could. Is he all right?"

A sinking feeling came over Jordan, and she held on to Kendre as the doctor told the Friedricksons, "I'm sorry, but Sidney didn't make it."

Detective Paris stood by the side of the bed as the victim lay there with tubes coming from her body this way and that, hooked up to machines and monitors like a damned machine herself. Bad, he thought, but a hell of a lot better than the guy she was doing the nasty with in the back of the car. Half his head had been blown away, the other half might just as well have been.

Yeah, the girl was lucky she was underneath all that fat on her lover's big body—slowing down the bullets meant for her, Paris considered. Even then, the doctor had said if either bullet that tore into her chest cavity had been a shade to the left or right she too would be in the morgue right now.

The attack had taken place at Devil's Edge and was to Carl Paris frighteningly similar to the one that had occurred last Christmas Eve. The one for which Trevor La Fontaine was on trial. Was it a coincidence? Or had they arrested the wrong man?

"Only a few minutes, Detective," insisted Dr. Moore. "She has to rest."

His notepad out, Paris leaned over the victim, who looked reasonably alert, and said, "Ms. Pitambe— Lenora—do you know what happened to you?"

Lenora wrinkled her nose and said with some difficulty, "I was shot."

"Did you see who did it?"

She gave a slow nod.

So far so good, thought Paris. "Can you describe the person . . . male, female . . . ?"

Lenora squeezed her eyes shut and reopened them. "A white man, slender, looked like he was in his early thirties . . ."

"Did you know him?"

Her head shook. "Never saw him before."

Too bad, the detective thought. That would have made it easier. "Can you describe what he was wearing?"

"Jeans and a green jacket is all I remember."

Better than nothing. Paris gave her a slight *you're doing fine* smile. "What about the car he was driving?"

Lenora swallowed laboriously and said: "He got out of a dark green van—"

"I think that's enough for now," Dr. Moore said.

Paris agreed, especially since the young lady had given him much more than he had bargained for.

Outside the room, he told Detective O'Donnell, "Let's get a sketch artist over here for a composite of this bastard. Also, I think we ought to put a twenty-four-hour guard on her. Since she's still alive, the killer might try to get at her again."

O'Donnell agreed and didn't try to pull rank. "So where you goin'?"

Paris was thoughtful. "I'm on my way to ballistics. There might be something . . ."

Jordan had dropped Kendre off at home and come back to the hospital. She approached Detective Paris, after he had separated from his partner in the Intensive Care Unit, outside Lenora's room.

"Ms. La Fontaine." He nodded politely but seemed to be in a hurry.

"Detective Paris, what can you tell me about the attack on Lenora?" asked Jordan, needing to know for more reasons than one.

Paris hedged, scratching his pate. "Not much at this point."

Jordan had the feeling he was holding something back from her. "You know the shooting happened at Devil's Edge?"

He lifted a brow. "Yeah. So?"

"So it looks awfully similar to the murders of Gail Marshall and Nelson Neilson," she said bluntly.

Paris looked uncomfortable. "I wouldn't go jumping to any conclusions," he warned. "This has nothing to do with that case. Your son—"

Jordan's voice rose acrimoniously. "Whether you choose to believe it or not, Detective, this could have *everything* to do with the charges my son faces. If you know anything at all, dammit . . . please, tell me."

Paris muttered an expletive under his breath before saying, "You wanna take a ride with me?"

Jordan did not hesitate. "Let's go."

"The bullets definitely came from a .25-caliber gun," concluded Bob Arness in the crime lab where the ballistics tests were done on the bullets taken from Lenora Pitambe and Sidney Friedrickson.

Paris looked uneasily at Jordan, and back to Arness. Bob Arness was a thirty-five-year-old, lanky criminologist, with receding dirty-blond hair, Fu Manchu mustache, and a perennial deep tan.

"What can you tell us about the markings on the bullets?" Paris asked.

"Well, let's see . . ." Arness grabbed his notes. "The bullets were fired through a gun barrel that had six lands and grooves and a right-hand twist."

Paris frowned. *Damn.* The markings were the same as the bullets that killed Nelson Neilson and Gail Marshall. He could tell by the look on Jordan La Fontaine's face that she too made the connection. It was beginning to look more and more like Trevor La Fontaine might be innocent after all of killing those two students, the detective thought bleakly.

Jordan read his mind. "Still believe the two cases are unrelated, Detective Paris?" she asked, the optimism in her voice dampened by the desperation Jordan felt in clearing her son's name.

Paris refused to give a yes or no answer, though he knew by saying nothing he'd in fact said everything. "We need to compare the bullets taken from the victims to know for sure whether they came from the same gun."

CHAPTER FIFTY-EIGHT

The jury had already begun deliberations in Trevor's trial at the same time the ballistics tests showed a positive match of the bullets taken from Gail Marshall and Nelson Neilson with those removed from Lenora Pitambe and Sidney Friedrickson. Since this alone was not enough to prove Trevor's innocence, it became a race against the clock to find a killer at large.

Using a composite of the suspect, an A.P.B. was issued for a slender man in his early thirties, with short, curly, dark hair, wearing jeans and a dark green parka. He was driving a late model green van and was to be considered armed and dangerous.

Ruthie Maxwell watched the TV screen as the suspect's composite stared back at her. It was a crude representation, but she recognized the man. It was Joshua Morgan, her boyfriend and lover. Wasn't it?

Yeah, she thought, it had to be him. Joshua drove a green van just like the one they were looking for. They said he was suspected of shooting to death a young man and seriously wounding his girlfriend at the make-out spot known as the Devil's Edge. They said Joshua might also be connected with some other murders in Portland.

Joshua, a murderer—maybe a serial killer? Ruthie pondered this nervously, brushing the hair from her blond wig out of her eyes. She didn't want to believe it. Not someone she'd been sleeping with and taking good care of in other ways too. But instinctively, she knew it was true—Joshua *was* the man they were looking for.

Ruthie had known from the beginning that Joshua Morgan was not all there upstairs. She could see it in his dark and frightening eyes. Sometimes he would disappear for days, or even weeks. Whenever she asked him about it, he would get very angry, or sweet-talk her into forgetting about it.

Yes, thought Ruthie dreamily, it was the sweet talk that won her over every time. And the sex, which was ten times more powerful than anything she'd ever gotten from her three ex-husbands. Joshua—a cute white boy, she liked to say—made her feel young, attractive, and wanted. At forty-seven, she was smart enough to realize not too many men were going to come knocking on her door.

Ruthie's eyes focused back on the TV and the picture that looked so much like Joshua. There was a number to call for anyone who had information. Joshua had told her he wouldn't be back until tonight. This gave Ruthie the courage to do what she knew was right. Even if it meant losing Joshua.

She dialed the number and a police sergeant answered with a deep and suspicious-sounding voice. Ruthie found herself shaking as she spoke. "I recognize the man they're showing on TV."

"Oh, yeah?" The sergeant perked up.

Ruthie took a deep breath, knowing there would be

no turning back from this point. "His name is Joshua Morgan. . . ."

Joshua came in the door. He heard Ruthie on the phone in the bedroom, talking low. He looked at the television and was surprised to see that they were talking about *him!* That bitch he'd shot was still alive! What's more, he saw in disbelief, she had given the police a description of him and his van.

Joshua's face contorted with rage. He moved slowly to the bedroom door and listened as Ruthie told the police his name and where to find him.

Bitch!

He should have known she was no different from the rest of them. Now she'd have to pay.

The line suddenly went dead. Ruthie's heart raced as she turned to see Joshua standing there. He had come back sooner than she had expected. The phone cord was in his hand, torn from the wall. His eyes were like demonic black marbles.

She stilled her trembling long enough to say to him sweetly, "Hey, Joshua, baby."

"That was a bad thing you did, Ruthie," he said caustically, not fooled by her futile attempt to stay on his good side. "Really bad."

Without giving her the chance to lie to him, he wrapped the cord around her neck.

Ruthie wet her pants as she felt herself being strangled. The blood in her head had been cut off from her body and began to spurt out of her mouth. She couldn't believe this was happening—not to her . . . and not by him. She squirmed and fought, trying to break free and stay alive. But he was too strong, too determined, and too angry.

Ruthie felt pain throughout her body and wanted only for it to go away at that point. Mercifully, she collapsed into Joshua's waiting arms, achieving both their objectives.

CHAPTER FIFTY-NINE

Paris studied the composite. He had seen this dude before. Then it hit him all of a sudden. Of course, he thought. What the hell was his name? Joshua Morgan. Yes, that was it.

He and O'Donnell were already on their way to the North Hollywood Motel when the dispatcher reported that a woman named Ruthie Maxwell had called in to report that she believed her boyfriend—Joshua Morgan—was the man with the green van they were looking for. She said they lived together at the motel.

Other units were also dispatched to the scene for what could be a tense situation. No one doubted that the suspect was armed, and it was extremely perilous for anyone who came into contact with him. That included Ruthie Maxwell.

Driving above the speed limit, Paris had all kinds of thoughts running through his head—none good. Well, maybe one. It looked as if Trevor La Fontaine had been dealt a bad hand on this one . . . and his fine mother, Jordan La Fontaine. But there was still time to make

336

things right. Glancing at his partner, Paris could see O'Donnell felt the same way.

Now they just had to get their man—before he killed someone else.

At the motel, there was no sign of the green van. Someone had reported they heard what sounded like screaming coming from Room 113. Which was the room number Ruthie Maxwell had given the police.

Fearing foul play, the word was finally given to go in. Ruthie Maxwell was found dead on the bed. The phone cord was still wrapped tightly around her neck. And there was no sign of the suspect.

The jury had gone into a second day of deliberations, and Trevor's fate was still up in the air like a dark storm cloud. Jordan had no desire to gamble on a not-guilty verdict. Not when there was so much riding on the jury's decision. And not when the true killer had been identified and was still on the loose.

It wasn't about having a possible guilty verdict overturned once the truth had been clearly established before the judge in a court of law. It was about avoiding the stigma that came with being convicted of such a heinous crime—no matter the eventual outcome. Trevor, who had already been put through the ringer, deserved much better, Jordan thought. And frankly, so did she, as a mother who knew her son could not be capable of murder, and as a prosecutor who wanted to continue to rise in her field without being subjected to innuendo about something that was beyond her control. But now the tide seemed to be turning.

Jordan pulled into the parking lot of the North Hollywood Motel, where she had been told the killer was living. She watched as an ambulance pulled away. She didn't know it but the ambulance was carrying the body of Ruthie Maxwell.

Paris had a grim look on his face as he approached Jordan inside the room. "We have a positive I.D. on the suspect," he said, "and it doesn't look good. Name's Joshua Morgan. He was working as a janitor at Portland State at the time Gail Marshall and Nelson Neilson were killed. He was fired after a student accused him of sexual harassment. No one knew what happened to Morgan—until now."

Jordan didn't know whether to laugh or cry. This man could exonerate Trevor, but only if they could find him and tie up all the loose ends. With the jury set to return a possible guilty verdict at any time, leaving a permanent mark on Trevor in the minds of some, Jordan felt every moment was crucial in preventing a further injustice.

"It gets worse," muttered Paris. "Turns out Morgan's been in and out of mental institutions all his life. He killed his own mother—shot her to death—then set the body on fire for good measure."

Jordan winced. "Right now," she admitted, "I only care about my son."

An officer came between them. "The van was just spotted on Brookdale Street," he told O'Donnell. "In Ashland Heights."

Ashland Heights! The words echoed inside Jordan's head. Suddenly an ominous, instinctive feeling came over her. She screamed desperately at Paris, "He's headed to my house!"

CHAPTER SIXTY

Jordan rode with Paris and O'Donnell as they raced to Ashland Heights, a twenty-minute drive from Portland. She tried reaching Kendre on the phone, but there was no answer. Panic threatened to overcome Jordan like in a bad dream. Please, God, don't let him be there, she silently prayed. Kendre can't become a victim to this lunatic.

"Don't let your imagination run away with itself," Paris told Jordan compassionately. "Chances are Joshua Morgan has no idea where you live."

Something told Jordan that he knew exactly where she lived.

Kendre was listening to her stereo in her room. She was terrified that the jury would find Trevor guilty and sentence him to death. She feared not even the new evidence and suspect that had surfaced would be able to save Trevor before the jury delivered its verdict. Not that she didn't have faith in Simon McNeil. He'd impressed her as a pretty good lawyer—almost as good as her daddy had been. But even Simon's skills could fall short against Amanda Clinksdale. The woman used to be her mother's friend. Just as Simon and her mother were once close and seemed possibly headed for marriage, but were now barely on speaking terms. Somehow everything had changed—and all because of Trevor being falsely accused of murder.

Life sucks, Kendre thought with a sneer. And death did, too. She tried to imagine life without her father and brother. Losing one was bad enough. Both would be unbearable, even though she and her mother would still have each other.

But would that be enough for either of them? Kendre asked herself, stretched across the bed in a sweater and jeans.

She brightened up a bit when she thought of Lenora and how she'd kicked death in the face against all odds. Something good had managed to come out of all this tragedy.

She turned down the stereo and went to call the hospital. The phone on Kendre's dresser had no dial tone. That's strange, she thought. She went to her mother's room and tried that phone. It was dead.

Kendre thought she heard a noise downstairs. "Mom," she called. "That you?"

There was no answer.

She went down to investigate. It never occurred to Kendre that someone else might be in the house. Certainly not Joshua Morgan . . . and that he was looking specifically for her.

He watched from the shadows as she came down the stairs. She was even prettier than her mother, he thought. He liked her micro braids and wide-eyed curiosity, if not innocence. Her budding body was even more interesting. Hard to believe this was the sister of the son of a bitch on trial for murdering those two at Devil's Edge. She was certainly much more like her mother in appearance, which suited him just fine.

He'd followed Jordan La Fontaine home one day from the Criminal Justice Center just for the hell of it. He had become fascinated with her from Court TV, where they showed her trial and her son's trial every day. The way she moved that sexy body and the way she attacked people on the stand really impressed him. Frankly, he wished it had been her beneath him in bed instead of Ruthie. Maybe he would still get his chance.

He also liked how the camera kept focusing on Jordan during Trevor La Fontaine's trial. Almost as if they cared less about him than how she reacted to everything and everyone in the courtroom.

If only she had known that it was he—Joshua Morgan—who had killed those two from the college, and not her precious son. But then, Joshua imagined, by now she did know. Thanks to that damned bitch in the hospital—and Ruthie.

That was exactly why he had decided to pay Jordan La Fontaine and her pretty daughter a little visit.

Kendre had decided she was simply being paranoid, that she hadn't really heard something. She supposed that everything that had happened lately had freaked her out a bit. Who wouldn't be if they had gone through what she had?

After sucking in a deep breath and letting down her guard, Kendre was about to go back upstairs when she saw someone rush toward her from seemingly out of nowhere. The man grabbed her.

"Be a good little girl, Kendre, and don't scream," he warned her. He held a gun in his hand.

Kendre froze. She had seen the white lanky man with the dark, curly hair before. She had passed him on the sidewalk once. *Right in front of our house.* He must have been scouting it for a break-in or something.

It was the "something" that scared Kendre.

"Don't hurt me, mister," she managed, knowing real fear for the first time in her life. The fear Lenora must have felt before she was attacked.

He gave her a crooked smile. "Wouldn't dream of it," he said, and touched her cheek with the gun's cold barrel. "So long as you don't do anything foolish."

It was just about time for the fireworks to begin, Joshua Morgan thought. And he'd make sure that little Miss Muffett was the first one in the line of fire.

When Jordan and the detectives arrived at her house, they saw Joshua Morgan's van parked in the driveway so blatantly as to leave no doubt that he was inside with Kendre.

And, as such, he would be calling the shots for the time being.

S.W.A.T. teams, Special Forces, and other police officers had already surrounded the house and evacuated the neighbors. Since this was now a hostage situation involving a man with a history of mental problems—a man who had already killed at least four people, and probably more—it was a combustible situation if there ever was one.

"I'm going in," insisted Jordan, not caring for her safety as much as her daughter's.

Paris physically restrained her. "No, you're not, Counselor," he snapped. "We don't need *two* hostages in there—especially an assistant district attorney. Joshua Morgan obviously picked your house for a reason. Let's wait and see what it is."

"He's right, Jordan," said Harry Coleman, one of the first to arrive at the scene, even though it was outside his jurisdiction. "As long as your daughter's in there,

Morgan knows he's got our attention. He won't harm her as long as he needs her."

He steadied Jordan with caring eyes. Since saving her life, Coleman had become an unlikely friend. It was something Jordan knew he needed as much as she did after being rocked with the truth about his ex-partner, Graham Turner.

Jordan took a deep breath, realizing it had been foolish to try to storm in. That could only have gotten Kendre killed, and probably her as well. "Whatever happens," she said flatly, her eyes aimed at the hostage negotiator in particular, "I won't have my daughter used as a bargaining chip for any negotiations with Joshua Morgan."

The hostage negotiator—a rotund, balding man in his early forties, wearing a cheap suit and too much cologne—said to Jordan, as if he didn't mean it, "I understand." He added forcefully, "Just let me do my job and stay out of the way, and I'm sure we can resolve this peacefully."

How often had Jordan heard that, only to find out that it ended in disaster? She didn't plan to allow that to happen in this instance. To hell with the hostage negotiator.

Jordan saw the familiar silver Mercedes drive up. Simon got out and worked his way through the police barricade. He was tense as he came up to Jordan.

"I heard about it on the news," he said worriedly. "I came right away."

"Thanks," Jordan said. She could not tell him how happy she was that he thought enough to come. Was it out of a sense of duty, or because of his feelings for her?

Looking into Simon's unreadable gray-brown eyes, she asked the obvious question: "Has the jury reached a verdict?" Her heart stopped in that moment.

Simon sighed. "No," he said, a note of optimism in his voice. "They've been sent home for the night."

That was the best news Jordan had received in a long time. It bought her needed time to focus on the situation at hand, and the man who now seemed to hold the key to both her children's lives.

CHAPTER SIXTY-ONE

"Let the girl go!" a voice boomed over a loud speaker. "She can't help you now, Joshua."

Oh yes she can, asshole, Joshua Morgan thought as he eyed his captive. She looked like a frightened puppy as she sat on the bed, her knees pressed tightly together. She was his ticket out of the corner he'd boxed himself in.

One way or the other.

He picked up the ringing phone, which he had reconnected, and barked belligerently, "I'm calling the shots—not you!" All the while he stayed close to Kendre and away from the windows, the .25-caliber gun at his side, ready to use if he had to.

"My name is Pete Thayer," a voice said calmly. "I'm a hostage negotiator."

"I want a car," Joshua demanded, "a million in cash, and a safe path to the airport—where I want a plane to take me as far away from this hellhole as possible. And I want it in one hour. You hear me?"

"We hear you," said Thayer. "I'll be honest with you,

there's no way we can get you everything you want, Joshua, as long as you have the girl. Do us both a favor and let her walk out."

Joshua Morgan lit a cigarette, glanced at the prosecutor's terrified daughter, and inhaled nicotine thoughtfully. "The girl stays," he said succinctly. "I got nothin' to lose at this point. When I go, she goes with me. That's the deal, short and sweet. Now get me what I asked for, or we'll both be dead before you ever get to us. You've got fifty-nine minutes and counting," he said, pleased with himself. "Tick, tock, tick, tock, Pete."

He hung up.

Pete Thayer relayed the grim message from Joshua Morgan.

"Personally and professionally, I think the man's mad as a hatter," Thayer surmised. "I'm not sure if I can talk any sense into him."

Jordan was horrified. "So what are you saying, that he'll kill my daughter if his demands aren't met?"

Thayer regarded her anxiously, and answered honestly, "I'm saying that unless I have more time to work with, your daughter's only chance for survival may be for us to go in and get her."

Jordan knew the decision would ultimately rest with her. To storm the house could cost Kendre her life. But the alternative was just as bad. She could think of only one logical choice. But would this madman go for it?

The phone rang and Joshua Morgan answered it.

"This is Jordan La Fontaine." Her voice was calm, almost reassuring. "I want to speak to my daughter. I need to know if she's okay."

What the hell, Joshua thought. *Give the lady a gift.* He

put the phone up to Kendre's ear, and ordered, "Say something nice about me, baby girl," and made sure she felt the gun poking her side.

"Mom . . ." Kendre's voice broke.

"Are you okay, honey?" Jordan asked, fighting her own emotions.

"Yes," she cried. "Tell them to do what he wants. Please! I don't want to die."

"You won't die," promised Jordan, her own eyes watery. "We'll get through this. I love you so much, Kendre." She wiped tears running down her cheek. "Put him back on the phone."

"Satisfied?" Joshua asked gloatingly. "I haven't hurt your precious little girl, Jordan. At least not yet."

"Why don't you take me in exchange for her?" Jordan offered. "You obviously broke into my house hoping to find me. Well, you can have me. Just let Kendre go."

Joshua had to admit that it was an intriguing offer. The assistant district attorney—with the long locks and red-hot body—and him on their way to an enchanted deserted island somewhere where they could never be found. Nice. But he wasn't *that* damned insane. Not by a long shot. If Jordan La Fontaine wanted to come in, it could only be a trap.

"Nice try, darlin'," he told her wryly. "Thanks but no thanks. I'm afraid I just can't trust you, Jordan. Not with the whole damned police force surrounding the place just waiting to take me out."

"Yes, you can trust me," Jordan pleaded. "This isn't a trick. No one will hurt you. I'm the only one who can guarantee you safe passage wherever you want to go. Let me come in and let her go."

Joshua felt the pressure. He needed time to think. "Let me get back to you," he said, and hung up.

* * *

347

Kendre watched Joshua Morgan as he talked to her mother. She knew he intended to kill her no matter what. Unless she did something about it.

He told her thoughtfully, "Looks like your mom wants to trade places with you. What do you think about that, Little Miss Muffett?"

No way, thought Kendre stubbornly. She would not let her mother sacrifice her life for hers. Too many people counted on her mother, including her. If there was a way out of this, Kendre told herself courageously, she would have to find it.

"Why are you doing this?" she asked him, trying to sound chummy. "What did we ever do to you?"

Joshua mused over the question, even as he kept the gun right where she could see it, in case she tried anything stupid. "I'll tell you," he said, glad he could get it off his chest to someone—even if she would never live to tell anyone else. "Your brother did a dumb-assed thing and got himself blamed for my handiwork," Joshua said bitterly. "You see, I killed those two at Devil's Edge because of Gail. I saw her at the college and the bitch teased and laughed at me. I hate it when people laugh at me."

He scowled. "It would have been so perfect. The case would *never* have been solved if it hadn't been for your brother finding their bodies and being charged with the crime." Joshua rolled his eyes with disdain. "But then I said, why the hell not? If they wanna make him their scapegoat, then that's his tough damned luck!"

Kendre glared at him, hatred building even more in her veins. He was the reason her family—especially Trevor—had suffered all these months. She controlled her feelings enough to ask what her instincts told her was true: "You shot Lenora too, didn't you?"

He smiled as if it was no big deal, thinking of the

bitch in the hospital that had miraculously survived his bullets. "Yeah, I did it—just for the hell of it," he bragged. "The *feeling* came over me . . . she and the big boy were there all over each other . . . and, as they say, the rest is history." Joshua's brow furrowed and he pointed the gun at Kendre. "My only regret is that I didn't kill her. . . ." Like I will you if they screw with me, he thought, adding in his mind, You're dead either way, bitch.

Kendre willed herself not to show the fear and anger she felt. Her best chance, she decided, was to remain calm and think. "I have to go the bathroom," she told him.

"Don't we all," he quipped. "Go ahead. Just remember, I'll be right outside the door."

In the bathroom, Kendre looked around for anything she could use as a weapon. It seemed useless. They didn't keep potential weapons in the bathroom just in case they needed to fight sickos and killers. Then she saw something she thought just might work. She flushed the toilet, then quietly opened the window. It was dark outside and she couldn't see a soul. She certainly could not fit through to jump. She didn't know if anyone could see her or not, but this was her chance. Maybe her only chance.

After sucking in a deep breath of preparation, Kendre let out her loudest scream. She knew if her courage faltered in the slightest, she had just committed suicide.

Joshua Morgan heard the scream. It was a trick! That little cunt! He turned the knob. The door was locked.

"Open the door, stupid bitch!"

He thought he heard her climbing out the window. Then he heard noise downstairs. Footsteps coming up the stairs. They intended to kill him.

Maybe, but not before he exacted some payback

here, Joshua thought. He shot the bathroom doorknob, knocking it off. Kicking the door open, he rushed in and saw the window raised. She must've climbed out, he assumed, too agitated to consider otherwise. He ran toward the window, determined to shoot her before he himself was shot.

What Joshua Morgan did not realize was that Kendre had flattened herself behind the door. Knowing it was now or never, she stepped out with the full can of foaming disinfectant. When he turned around to face her, he was clearly caught off guard. Kendre began spraying the foam as fast as possible into his wide eyes, nostrils, and mouth—effectively painting his face with the powerful white froth.

Joshua yowled loudly, dropping the gun and putting his hands up to his eyes, rubbing them vigorously. Kendre took the opportunity to ram her knee between his legs as hard as she could, watching him double over in pain. She ran out and into the arms of a burly man who pushed her down to the floor while other heavily armed men rushed into the bathroom.

Within moments a disheveled Joshua Morgan, still moaning in agony, was in police custody, and Kendre was reunited with her mother.

"I was afraid we'd never see each other again," sobbed Kendre.

"It's all over now," Jordan cried with her, holding her close. Or at least, almost over, she thought. There was still one more thing to accomplish.

CHAPTER SIXTY-TWO

That night Joshua Morgan confessed to the attempted murder of Lenora Pitambe, the murders of Ruthie Maxwell, Gail Marshall, Nelson Neilson, Sidney Friedrickson, Willie Armstrong, and State Trooper George Bentley, along with several other unsolved murders covering four states—including a teacher named Constance Larchmen, and a prostitute named Tricia.

Detective Harry Coleman thought this was the perfect time to take that early retirement the department had been dangling in his face. Frankly, he'd had it with playing cops and killers. There was nothing left for him in Portland, he'd decided. His partner had betrayed him in the worst way imaginable. Turner had lied to him and destroyed another human being for his own selfish, sick reasons.

What hurt particularly was the faith Coleman had placed in a man he thought he knew and trusted. It was time to move on, the detective told himself. He had served the Portland Police Bureau well for the better part of twenty years, and he could leave with his head held high.

He was glad to see that things were working out well for Jordan La Fontaine. She too had been duped by people she thought she knew, and proved she could rise above the ashes to see another day.

At home, Coleman told Jobeth the news. "I was thinking," he said, "that we might move down to San Antonio—help your mother work that small plot of land she has. The kids can see what it's like to live somewhere other than Portland, where you see more rain than sunshine. And, if it's all right with you," he added, "maybe I could do some part-time work with the sheriff's department down there, if they can use a damned good Northwest cop."

Jobeth could hardly contain her enthusiasm. She hugged him, practically squeezing the life out of him. "Even if they don't need a veteran detective in San Antonio, I can always use a damned good part-time cop. So long as I get a *full-time* husband in return."

Coleman kissed her on the mouth, determined to make this work for both of them. "I'm all yours, baby," he promised. "And I mean all yours."

CHAPTER SIXTY-THREE

The jury had been called back in before rendering a verdict, at the request of the prosecuting attorney. Amanda gathered herself, then said in an even voice, "Your Honor, in light of the confession of Joshua Morgan to the murders of Nelson Neilson and Gail Marshall, and the accompanying evidence, including the murder weapon—the State asks that the charges against Trevor La Fontaine be dropped."

The judge crinkled his eyes and, looking at the defendant flanked by his attorney, mother, and sister, said, "The court happily grants this motion. The charges against the defendant are hereby dismissed. You're free to go, Mr. La Fontaine . . . and I'm sorry you were put through this ordeal. Try not to hold it against us."

Trevor hugged Simon first in a man-to-man embrace, then his sister, saving Jordan for last. She embraced her son tightly while they both cried.

"Thank you, Momma," Trevor said jubilantly. "We both know I would never have made it through this without you."

Jordan kissed his cheek and wept. "We'd never have made it through this without each other."

Kendre hugged her mother for the longest time, before Jordan and Simon embraced warmly.

"Thanks, Simon," Jordan said gratefully. "We owe you a lot." More than he could possibly know.

Still holding her, Simon whispered in Jordan's ear, "Consider your debt paid in full."

They pulled away from each other and Jordan believed this was Simon's way of telling her that now the trial was over, so was their relationship and anything resembling it. Jordan wanted to tell him that was the last thing she wanted to hear. Instead, she withdrew, content with what they had shared, though saddened to be losing her best friend and so much more. But she would not stand in the way of his happiness, even if it was with Frances and not her.

Right now Jordan wanted only to rejoice in knowing that both her children had survived their ordeals, and could get on with their lives. But could she?

Amanda came over and gave Jordan a tentative hug. "I'm really happy it turned out the way it did, Jordan," she told her sincerely.

As Jordan began to count her blessings, including regaining a friend and colleague, she responded, "So am I, Amanda. So am I."

A week later, Jordan was promoted to Chief of the Homicide Division. They threw a party in her honor at The Ranch.

Andrew bowed to Jordan in teasing deference and joked, "Is it all right if I still call you Jordan? Or must I now refer to you as Your Highness?"

She laughed. "Jordan will do. Maybe someday you can call me Your Honor. Until then . . ."

"Judge La Fontaine," quipped Amanda. "I think I like the sound of that."

"Over my dead body!" Bombeck made a face. "Jordan's too damned good a prosecutor to let get away as long as I'm the D.A."

Jordan raised her glass and looked at everyone. "I think I'd like to make a toast"—she waited until all glasses were raised—"to friendship and the rewards of damned hard work."

Her words were echoed by all as they toasted and drank champagne.

Then Jordan looked across the room and saw a familiar face. He held a glass raised in toast. It was Simon. He was smiling.

"Looks like congratulations are in order again," he said, once he had Jordan to himself.

Jordan felt the familiar butterflies as she gazed into Simon's proud eyes, smelled his smell, and luxuriated in his overpowering presence. "Again . . . ?" she swallowed.

"Yes. It seems like it was only yesterday we were here toasting to your success . . . and beating the hell out of me in the courtroom." He sipped his drink. "That was Christmas Eve and I knew then what I know now . . ."

"And what's that?" Jordan was almost afraid to ask.

"That I'm in love with you," Simon said point-blank, taking her hand. "And I don't want to let you get away."

Jordan was nearly speechless. "I thought you and Frances were . . ."

"Nope. Frances and I were through a long time ago," he declared. "And nothing that happened between you and me could ever change that."

Jordan tried to still her racing pulse. "I'm so sorry, Simon," she murmured. "I was so wrong . . . so stupid—"

He put his finger to her lips. "So was I, baby. You were only trying to protect me, protect us . . . hell, protect the system we both work for." He held her gaze. "You did your job, Jordan, in the best way you knew how. I understand that now. All I want is to start over and give our relationship the chance it deserves."

Jordan could scarcely believe her ears. Even after what she had done, he still wanted her. And she definitely wanted him.

"I want that too, Simon," she said tearfully, "more than anything. I've never stopped loving you."

"That makes two of us," he said, and kissed her lingeringly. Jordan was unabashed as their mouths engaged, as though no one was present but the two of them.

Holding up his glass, Simon declared, "Now we really have something to toast."

Jordan hoisted her champagne ecstatically. "I'll drink to that!"

FOR THE DEFENDANT
E. G. SCHRADER

Janna Scott is a former Assistant State's Attorney with a brand new private practice. She's eager for cases, but perhaps her latest client is one she should have refused. He's a prominent and respected doctor accused of criminal sexual assault against one of his patients. It's a messy, sensational case, only made worse when the doctor vehemently refuses to take a plea and insists on fighting the ugly charges in court.

Meanwhile, a vicious serial killer who calls himself the Soldier of Death is terrorizing Chicago, and it falls to Janna's former colleague, Detective Jack Stone, to stop him. Body after body is found, each bearing the killer's gruesome trademark, yet evidence is scarce—until a potential victim escapes alive. . . .

- -

ABDUCTED

BRIAN PINKERTON

Just a second. That was all it took. In that second Anita Sherwood sees the face of the young boy in the window of the bus as it stops at the curb—and she knows it is her son. The son who had been kidnapped two years before. The son who had never been found and who had been declared legally dead.

But now her son is alive. Anita knows it in her heart. She is certain that the boy is her son, but how can she get anyone to believe her? She'd given the police leads before that ended up going nowhere, so they're not exactly eager to waste much time on another dead end on a dead case. It's going to be up to Anita, and she'll stop at nothing to get her son back.

THE MOON POOL
MAX McCOY

Time is running out for Jolene. She's trapped by a madman, held captive, naked, waiting only for her worst nightmares to become reality. Her captor will keep her alive for twenty-eight days, hidden in an underwater city 400 feet below the surface. Then she will die horribly—like the others....

Jolene's only hope is Richard Dahlgren, a private underwater crime scene investigator. He has until the next full moon before Jolene becomes just another hideous trophy in the killer's surreal underwater lair. But Dahlgren has never handled a case where the victim is still alive. And the killer has never allowed a victim to escape.
